And Then Everything Changed

by Alaina Isbouts

D1614278

For Dana, Nikki, Steve, Jimmy, and Justin—my real-life people who I wouldn't really be me without meeting.

But most of all, for Philip. My forever travel partner, my everything, the love of my life. Without you there would be no story to tell. More than all the smoke in a herna...

This is the first day of my life
Swear I was born right in the doorway
I went out in the rain, suddenly everything changed
They're spreading blankets on the beach
Yours was the first face that I saw
I think I was blind before I met you
I don't know where I am, I don't know where I've been
But I know where I want to go

from "First Day of My Life" by Bright Eyes

Table of Contents

And
Then
Everything
Changed

1

August, Prague.

Mostecká Street is thick with people. New and foreign sights of people and buildings, letters and symbols I don't yet understand surround me. Plump, graying Eastern European women returning from the market, pulling merry-widows overflowing with rich leafy greens and meat packaged fresh from the butcher, juices dripping down onto the cobblestones below, with babushkas tied over their hair. Young men that I smell before I can see, a combination of sweat and musk and cigarettes, with shaggy hair and tight-fitting embellished jeans. Locals impatiently push their way through the tourists outnumbering them, their faces largely expressionless. A handful of languages hang in the air, as people from all over the world take advantage of this flawless August day to walk over the Vltava River, over a most famous and idyllic footbridge, Karlův Most, the Charles Bridge.

 Today is the first day of my new life, I am certain of it. A life I am creating out of nothing. For today being such a momentous day, I am feeling decidedly indifferent. My stomach is flat, not flipping with anxiety or butterflies like I had imagined. Today is a day of new sights, new sounds, new smells; a new city. Quietly, I observe, taking it all in.

 Constantly, my nose is assaulted with the smell of meat, spicy grilled kielbasa, and a sour smell I cannot yet identify, reminding me briefly of the specific pungent reek of my brother's hockey equipment after a game. Hurried locals bump into me occasionally, followed immediately with the undeniable whiff of stale sweat and movement. But

1

when I'm not passing a food vendor, or walking into others, the sweet smell of water and cinnamon sugar and possibility waft past my nose. Together, this is the smell of opportunity.

Above me, the sky is a most brilliant shade of blue, with picturesque clouds slithering past. It reminds me that this is the sky of the whole world; this same sky is above my family back in New York and my friends home in Denver. It's hard to reconcile that this world exists here at all times, while in the life I left behind back home, people are doing ordinary things like taking out the trash or studying for exams. Today seems to be a day I could have dreamed up in my imagination, but here I am, feet planted firmly on the ground in Praha. Prag. Praga. Prague.

I step over each cobblestone in the street deliberately, unsure yet of how to manage these roads with the many pairs of heels I have brought me. The stones feel foreign under my feet. They are spoiled, used only on the smooth sidewalks and poured concrete common back in the States. As my feet slide over each uniquely shaped stone, I am secretly already swearing I will only wear flats. Up ahead, my father is walking ahead of my mother and brother, who are side by side directly ahead of me. I had been hoping in the month leading up to this day to be here on my own, without my parents. But here we all are, a bizarre and unexpected family vacation of sorts, before my parents and brother fly back home in a few days and leave me behind. I am nearly counting the minutes.

There was nothing I could imagine more liberating than arriving alone, making my way in the city for a few days until Bara is available to meet me. I wished for the exquisite loneliness that comes with arriving in a foreign place by oneself, exploring the city for one's own. I ached for those first steps of making something your own. Of slowly peeling back the layers of this city like an artichoke, pulling past the hard shell to the soft and tender meat inside that you only get after putting in the work. This is to be my journey, even the hard parts. In my life so far, I've never had the luxury of being truly alone and that, above all, was what I was craving. But my parents wouldn't hear of me traveling alone to Prague. So I hang back from the group a little. They aren't noticing at the moment, which I am relishing.

I know where we are heading, Dad having announced it over breakfast earlier in the day. He is carrying his guidebook, but refusing to consult it. Since he has been here before, for a friend's wedding three years ago, he apparently has memorized all the information that he wants to share with us throughout the week. My mother points directly ahead of her, and turns around to face me. She gives me a warm smile, winking.

I return her smile halfheartedly, unable, in my unimpressed mood, to return it with the emotion she shows me. I feel as if this is my first time alone with my new city and someone is watching us, seeing how we move together, getting to know one another. The intimacy you can only find when you are alone in a big city has been taken from me. We continue walking, and now Dad is hanging back to let Mom and James catch up with him. Directly ahead of us lies the Charles Bridge, and I get my first glimpse of the magnificent structure. While it isn't terribly tall or even impressive, like the Brooklyn Bridge or the Golden Gate, it is wider than I expected. I knew it was a footbridge, but I see now the bridge could easily accommodate two lanes of traffic, though no vehicle could seemingly fit through the gate at either end. The bricks making up the bridge seem to be older than the cobblestones on the streets, though they are the same worn gray color, faded with time, layers stripped away by the weather. This is what I am longing to see, the city revealing itself to me, the secrets only we will know. The marks of the passage of time and the personality it reveals under the once glossy layers.

On either side of the bridge are fifteen or so statues, each standing a few feet apart, spanning the length of the bridge. Saints, the Madonna, and the Savior himself have been immortalized in stone over the bridge, their heads occasionally adorned with a halo or stars. Between each statue is an iron lamppost, reaching as high as the statues. I stop and my breathing slows as I take in the beauty of the bridge.

How old must it be? How many people have crossed this bridge? I can imagine now, horses and carriages, knights and kings all crossing this very bridge which lies in the heart of my ancient city. My dad has apparently been wondering similar questions, for ahead of me I see him crack open his guidebook and start eagerly flipping through the pages.

Catching up to my family, we start over the bridge, heading from Malá Strana to Staré Město. As we approach the first statues, I notice that some are polished and looking brand new, while others are blackened with weather and bird droppings. Each state represents something different, a varying lesson, virtue, or tribute that the Czech people wish to immortalize.

Dad is now reciting a brief history of each statue we pass. At each statue we pause briefly, to let him share his guidebook's knowledge. Right now, he seems to be interested in Saint Francis of Assisi, reminding us all he is the patron saint of Italy. While Mom seems interested, I am having a hard time listening. Instead, my eyes wander around the bridge, the rushing river below, and the old city that lay on the other side. There were so many things that had brought me to this point, to this city where I knew no one. I don't know the language or much about their culture. I have run away. As we move along to the next statue, Saint John the Baptist, one thought continued to hang over me like a dark rain cloud over this perfect summer's day.

Am I doing the right thing?

I have left behind everything I know, all familiarities, to come to a country halfway around the world. Why am I here, and what would I experience before I am to return, months from now? Will I be able to return months from now?

As my mind dwells on this unavoidable point, we continue to cross the bridge. My dad's voice is blending in with the bubbling sound of the Vltava below, while all around us people laugh and snap photos. My brother asks if we can skip a few statues, and with them the history lessons, and Mom laughs. Dad leads the group forward, directly to the middle point of the bridge, and stops.

In front of us is a bronze statue much larger than the rest. Not taller, but wider, with three different panels depicting various scenes, and a man adorning the top of the middle panel. His head is cocked to the side, his mouth agape, his eyes seemingly searching out some lost truth far beyond the tourists on the bridge. A few inches above his crown is a halo adorned with stars, and heavy in his arms he holds a cross. The man looks as if he is exhausted from carrying the weight of the world about him, and I feel heavier the longer I stare at him. But despite the depressing nature of the statue, a group of people are gathered underneath it. About seven or eight Japanese tourists huddle around the statue, talking animatedly, showing one another the pages of their guidebook. Each is taking a turn rubbing the statue while someone photographs them.

As a middle-aged man finishes his turn rubbing the statue, I notice a place on the bronze panel that was much shinier than the rest. The spot sparkled bright gold, while the rest of the panel and the statue above was heavily tarnished and looked to be a dark bronze.

"Dad, what is that?" I ask, finally paying my father's guidebook some attention.

He looks at his book and begins reading. "The statue of St. John of Nepomuk is the oldest statue on the Charles Bridge, and perhaps the most famous. Built by Jan Brokoff in 1683, it is made of bronze, and upon completion was held as an obligatory iconographic model for many other statues of the Saint made in Bohemia and beyond. Saint John of Nepomuk was a parson who refused to betray a secret, confided to him by Queen Sophia, to King Wenceslas IV. On the

King's demand, he was tortured to give up the secret but held fast to his loyalty. After he was tortured, he was thrown into the Vltava from the Charles Bridge in 1393."

I wonder what it is about this statue that makes it deserving of more space and attention than the others. Dad looks at the statue.

"Killed for loyalty to the queen," he says softly, and throws a downward glance at Mom.

She playfully pushes him on the shoulder. It's strange to see them like this, flirting and kind, after their years of separation and animosity. It adds to my inflective mood, wondering what is next for them, much like what is next for me.

As the tourists rubbing the statue begin dissipating, Mom walks closer to the base of the statue. "Why is everyone touching it?" she asks.

Dad checks his book once more. "It says that if you touch the spot here"—he points to the right panel that depicts Saint John being thrown off the bridge—"you make a wish, and it will come true."

Of course. It does not surprise me in the least that in the middle of this city, where I have come with nothing but my hopes and dreams, lies a statue that promises to make them real.

Mom laughs and smiles. "That is so interesting! But what about this spot over here? It looks like it has been rubbed quite a bit, too." She moves to the panel on the left, where a soldier, assumedly Saint John, and his dog are shown.

Looking back at his book, he reads one more time. "Rub the panel on the left of Saint John and his dog to ensure your return to Prague." He looks at Mom. "Want to touch it?"

"Wait!" I exclaim. "I want to get a picture of you two doing this together. It's almost too much..." I say slyly. As I yell, James walks back over to us from the opposite side of the bridge.

Mom extends her arm to the right panel toward the scene of Saint John being thrown from the bridge, and my father reaches for the left panel toward the dog. As they make contact with the statue, they turn and face each other, rubbing the statue. As they go to switch panels, Mom and Dad reach out together, and Dad's hand slides over Mom's and guides her to the dog. James glances at me, eyebrows raised. I lift my digital camera and snap a picture, just as their fingers reach the point that so many hundreds... thousands... millions... have touched. Their hands pull away after ten seconds or so, and Mom looks up at Dad. Their eyes meet. In this moment, all seems silent around us. They move toward each other and hug, my Mom burying her face in my Dad's fleece jacket. James nudges me and smiles.

After a few moments, they pull apart, arms still around each other's back. My father looks at me.

"Well, I guess we will just have to come back to Prague now," he says.

Mom laughs. "I guess so." She smiles as Dad moves his arm around her waist, and turns to James and me.

"Okay, you and James go now," Dad says to us.

Awakened by the scene in front of us, James looks at me for permission, and is visibly confused by my blank stare. He moves toward the statue before I move a muscle. He reaches his right arm toward Saint John, leaving me, presumably, with the dog and a wish to return to Prague. James turns around and looks toward where I am standing, thinking our picture would be taken at any moment.

"Hey, what are you doing Adriana?" Both my parents are looking at me now, as I stand frozen, still a good four feet from the panel I am supposed to be rubbing.

"Don't you want to rub the dog? You know that means you will return to Prague someday," my mother says, looking at me and smiling her kind, beautiful smile once more.

But I can't smile. "I know."

"Well then what's the problem? Other people are waiting for their turn," my father says to me.

I look behind him, and see another group of tourists is starting to gather behind his thick frame. People are excitedly reading their guidebooks, and anxiously awaiting their turn to make a wish and seal their fate to return to this fairytale city once more.

My feet won't move. I feel the true emotion swelling up inside me now, though where it's coming from, I haven't the slightest clue. "I don't want to touch it now." I explain. "I'll be here for months, I know I'll do it at some point."

Not convinced by my explanation, Dad pushes me once more.

"We all did it already, come on, do it with us as a family." His emphasis on the word *family* is unmistakable, but still I cannot bring myself to make a wish. I make my point by picking up my feet and moving to the next statue. James walks alongside me, and after a few moments, our parents begrudgingly start walking away as well.

While it is true that I will have the opportunity to rub the statue at any point throughout the upcoming semester, I can't explain the force that compelled me to not rub Saint John or the dog. A force stronger than me is at work, holding my hand back from the statue. I do not know what lies ahead of me in these coming months, but something in my heart tells me to wait, and that I will be back here when the moment is right. I imagine late nights with friends, crossing this very bridge at four in the morning under the starlit sky, laughing and stopping by these statues when no one else was around. I imagine the city as our own personal playground, this city I do not yet know, and these friends I have not yet met.

I imagine unlocking the city's secrets and decide that throughout this semester, I need to determine what wish, what deepest desire is so urgent within me that I will take it up with Saint John. The simple truth for today, is that this experience is not something I want to share with my parents. If I am ever to return to Prague after this semester abroad, I don't want to remember back and have my parents here for the moment responsible for it all. I want it to be mine.

2

May, Colorado.

We had been at the car dealership for hours. The air wasn't quite warm yet. The beginning signs of spring were just starting to appear. Sprigs of green were found among every fistful of brown stale grass. Buds were popping up on the trees, though none had yet opened. Seven o'clock, and the sky was darkening above me. Along the horizon, pale pinks and oranges blended together as the sun finished its final bow of the day, dipping slowly behind the Rockies.

Mark had spotted the car he wanted about two hours before, but we were still there while he hammered out the details of his new car loan. Put off by talk of interest rates and warrantees, I stepped outside into the fresh, early spring breeze. Goose bumps instantly sprung up on my arms, past my short sleeves to my hands, and on the tops of my feet past my rolled up blue jeans. I pulled my green pashmina around me tighter and walked through the rows and rows of cars. Fresh paint jobs, sparkling windows, and shiny door handles were everywhere. Letting my scarf drop around my elbows, I spread my wrists apart to touch each car I passed by. Shiny Acuras, gleaming Hondas, polished BMWs, glossy Audis, all waiting to be taken home for the right price. Mark had crashed his car in January and we had been sharing my Escape as best we could for the last few months, but we had reached a point where we could no longer share. This was mostly due to the fact that seeing one another that often was putting a strain on our relationship. It worked best when we both could get up and leave at any point, a choice we made every few months.

It wasn't that there wasn't any consistency or sense of commitment. When we were together, we were committed. We were a couple. But with our constant battles and arguments, never knowing what was going to set us off, we had become unpredictable. The only thing people ever knew for certain about our relationship, was that it would end and begin over and over, year after year. This cycle was going on five years now.

Our fights had made us infamous in high school and among our friends, we were sort of the WWE of relationships, only no one was acting. Chair throws, threats of wrist cutting, police interventions, late night drives, an attempted hit and run, eavesdropping and password breaking, phone spying, and public declarations of both love and hatred. What had set us off was wildly erratic. A joke Mark had made about something I was interested in, a sarcastic comment I'd quip about him, a text he'd get from a girl who just wouldn't leave him alone. And one of us would storm out. A few days apart, missed phones calls and the occasional text, feeble "I'm sorrys" and "me toos," laughter and inside jokes, and we would be back together. Our friendship hadn't stayed broken, even after our relationship had been so far past the point of saving. Such is the curse of the relationship of firsts, the growing up together, the losing of virginities, the going off to college together. Your bond keeps you stuck to one another, past the point of leaving.

I'd loved him. He was the first person I had ever whispered those words to, over the phone one night from my best friend's basement. "Thank you," he'd said to me, before explaining that he couldn't say them back just yet, but he cared about me and wouldn't do anything to make me regret loving him. It had been enough for me until he said it back, a few weeks later. We had been inseparable. Most weekends and many school nights, I'd run off to Mark's grandparents' home, where he'd lived, and knock on the basement window to his bedroom. We'd made dinner together, watched movies, downloaded music, and just had lain on his bed talking.

When Mark and I weren't fighting, he made me feel safer than anyone else in the world. If I had his back, I knew he had mine.

On nights we had wanted to see each other past my curfew, he'd drive out to my house and wait a few blocks down with the lights off, texting me to know he was waiting. I'd sneak out the back door, or after I'd been caught doing that, out the doggy door, and ran down to meet him.

We had applied to colleges together, knowing full well that couples who didn't go to school together usually broke up. He'd thought we could outsmart it, and while I wanted him to apply to schools out east in New York and Boston, he'd insisted that I apply to his dream school, Colorado State. His uncles had all gone there and he wanted to follow. When I got in and he hadn't, I went anyway. He'd taken classes at the local community college, and on Fridays he'd drive up and spend the weekend in my dorm. In spite of our best efforts, our on-again-off-again status had never really changed, and our breakups became more frequent. Even in those times apart, when I'd needed reassuring, he was the first person I would call. And he'd always answered. After just one year, I had left Colorado State, an hour north of our childhood home, to attend school in Denver and be closer to him. The bitterness I'd felt at attending a school I'd never wanted to attend—for a boy who hadn't even been there with me—had left me feeling like I wasn't a part of the community there, despite my best attempts to take part in the stream of endless frat parties and drinking in dorms. I'd told myself I was ready for something more grown-up. I then rented an apartment in the city and had my credits transferred to the University of Colorado's Denver campus. The school had been a much better fit.

Now that we were just a fifteen-minute drive from one another at our own places, Mark and I had spent more time together than ever before. But despite all the time we'd been sharing, it was becoming obvious to me that we were different people headed in different directions. He had dropped out of school, made good money bartending downtown, and was content to see where that would take him. I was more devoted to my studies, but had begun feeling like something was missing. I had dreamed of attending a big city school on the East Coast and moving out of Colorado. Instead, I had moved to Denver, where I felt like I was still in high school, but with legal drinks and less parental interference. Occasionally I'd fantasized to Mark about us running away, buying plane tickets to another country and not looking back. I was young and full of hope, and I had wanted to see what the world had to offer. But each time I'd brought up the idea of us doing something adventurous, he wasn't interested. "What for? We've got everything we need right here." So I would shut up.

After Mark's car accident, the car sharing had slowly become a problem. The past weekend, we'd jumped in my Ford Escape to head to Tommy's Thai, our favorite Saturday afternoon lunch spot. I had almost always worked on Saturday mornings, but as soon as I was done, I'd zip over to Mark's and we'd go out to lunch. I'd stepped on the gas, rolled the sunroof down, and started toward the stoplight to make a right and head toward Colfax.

"Where the fuck are you going?" Mark questioned, lifting a lighter up to his cigarette.

"What? I'm heading to Colfax from here. I can make a right at the light."

Mark had moved into his rental house in January, and Five Points, though just seconds away from downtown, was not a part of Denver I was too familiar with.

"No, the street ends and you have to make a left three blocks up. We go to this restaurant every fucking weekend, are you for real? Do you actually not know where you are going?" Mark took a drag of his cigarette and looked at me, blowing the smoke in my direction.

"Okay! Fine! You drive then! I didn't know, I forgot, I don't know, I don't care, just let me pull over and you fucking drive. Why do you have to be such an asshole all the time?" I slammed on the brakes, the car abruptly stopping and Mark sliding forward and hitting his elbow loudly on the dashboard. Ash from his cigarette fell onto the carpet.

Incidents like these were becoming too common, and it was my honest hope that getting him a car would avoid useless fights. After I had touched every car in the lot, I went back inside. Mark was still sitting at the salesman's desk, now having moved on to signing paperwork. I took the seat next to him, and he gently placed his hand on my knee. Ten minutes later, we were done. We left, finally in separate cars, and we drove back to his place. After I parked, I slid into the passenger side next to him, and we took his new car out for a spin.

It was the perfect night for a drive. Mark opened up the sunroof, showing off a bit, the stars visible through the tree branches overhead. The new car smell was overwhelming. Black leather, candy-apple red exterior, a sound system already installed. Mark turned up the radio, and the Foo Fighters joined us on our drive around Curtis Park. I closed my eyes and imagined we were flying, speeding away from Denver. I wouldn't become one of those girls I judged, who moved from our suburb into Denver and acted like what they were doing was important. Staying and trying to make it work with the same boyfriend and hanging out with his same asshole friends. We were flying. Just as the lie was beginning to feel real, we stopped. The engine shuddered as it turned off, the soft beeping letting me know that Mark had opened his door. As my phone vibrated against my thigh, I opened my eyes.

"Hello, may I speak to Adriana?"

"Yes, this is she, who is this?"

"This is Mary Ann from EOO. I am calling to tell you we've accepted your application."

"What?" My heart stopped. I froze, one foot in the Jetta and the other on the pavement outside.

"Who are you on the phone with?" Mark called from the front lawn. I stared at him blankly.

"Educational Opportunities Overseas. You applied to our fall program in Prague. You're in." On the other end of the line, Mary Ann must have sensed my shock. "Congratulations! You'll be getting some mail from us welcoming you to the program and listing the next steps for you to prepare. Let me know if you have any questions."

I didn't smile. I didn't move. The world stopped turning for a moment, and I looked at Mark. I hung up the phone, knowing full well what was about to happen.

"Aren't you listening to me? Who was that?" Mark was becoming more agitated.

I took a deep breath, shakily, as my smile began to spread. I wanted to do it quick, like a Band-Aid. I knew what he was going to say, but I wasn't sure I was ready to hear it all. "I'm moving to Prague."

"What?" He laughed. I had told him a hundred times of how I wanted to travel, and he never took me seriously.

"I applied to a study abroad program for the fall semester and my application was accepted, that was them. I'm going to Prague."

"Where the fuck is Prague? Why wouldn't you tell me about this? Aren't we supposed to talk about these things? Why the hell would you want to go all the way over *there*? What am I supposed to do? What about us?" His voice raised with each question, in a mix of confusion and anger.

"I knew what you would say so I didn't tell you. I'm leaving."

Δ

There is a trajectory of life; a path you start out on and, for the most part, continue down. I could see where I was headed. All the boxes were checked. I'd attended a small-town high school. Had a high school boyfriend I'd spent five years with, mostly on but occasionally off, during heated, drama-filled arguments. We were the reality show of our school. Everyone knew what had happened the weekend before, why I'd called it off this time. And now, here at twenty years old, it was a different school but the same boyfriend, the same arguments, the same destructive pattern. It was just as my parents had been, and despite their volatility, they found themselves engaged while still in college, planning a wedding shortly after graduation. I could see that next step ahead of me on the ever-obvious path. It was what people did, the arrangement of life I was inheriting.

It did not sit well with me. Mark and I hadn't made it twelve consecutive months without a breakup. How would we ever sustain a marriage? It couldn't be. And yet I let myself be led down the path, doing nothing to break away, never doing more than acknowledging the nagging feeling in my gut that this was not for me. It wasn't marriage; it was this place, this time. It was Mark. It was the small town. None of it was how I had imagined my life turning out, and I could see the mistakes my parents had made, and constantly wondered if I was destined to repeat them.

My mother was trusting. She grew up in the same small town in Colorado she moved James and I to after her divorce from Dad. Her family was the picture of American normalcy: her parents started a small, family-owned business, and she had been raised by a stay-at-home mother along with her brother and sister. They attended Bible study and church picnics, and after high school my mother drove off to Kansas to attend the same small liberal arts college where her parents had met. It was there she met my father, a rough boy from Queens on a full-ride football scholarship, playing quarterback. She would often tell me about how they met while she was jogging in the park, the week before college began. As she bounced past two football players walking home from practice, one turned around and whistled at her.

"Hey baby, you want some fries with that shake?" called a voice. She ignored the catcall, but quickly heard footsteps behind her, trying to catch up.

She struggled to catch her breath as someone grabbed her shoulder to stop her jogging. She was a gorgeous woman, and being catcalled was nothing she wasn't used to. A man grabbing her was new, however. He went on to apologize for his friend, who had embarrassed him by calling out such a lame pickup line. She was dazzled by his John Travolta hair and charming smile. They immediately hit it off, and within a few weeks were exchanging class rings. His brash New York attitude complemented her Midwestern innocence.

Their relationship was tumultuous, but passionate. They either loved or hated one another, and there seemed to be no in-between. After a while, the anger slowly rubbed away at their love. Their fights kept James and me up at night, with James crawling into my bed with me during especially loud ones. We knew they would split up, we just didn't know when.

When the divorce inevitably came, it wasn't because Dad wanted to. Dad never really stopped loving Mom. After a divorce, most couples stop fighting at some point. The rage subsides and an awkwardness, a terseness will take its place. But not this time. Dad's love for Mom bubbled under the surface, and they never stopped fighting. They would meet in neutral locations to pick up and drop off my brother and I, Dad unwilling to step foot in our old house but also unable to invite Mom to his apartment. All communication, good or bad, was done through James and me. If Dad called the house, Mom would announce his name from the caller ID. "It's your father!" meant "You answer it, because I won't." It was a constant struggle of "Tell your father to be on time next time" and "Your mother needs to switch weekends," and each calling the other one a liar through us, badmouthing until we'd ask them to stop and plug our ears.

As angry as Dad stayed with Mom in the decade following their divorce, his side of the family softened. He forbade his entire family from speaking to, or of Mom. When she would call Nanny's house while we visited for holidays, or the villa when we were there for the summer, my aunts would sneak on one end of the line, taking the long phone cord up the stairs and into the bathroom. Nanny would grab the phone whenever she pleased, daring Dad to say a word to her.

Dad was bitter, hurt, and wishing they were still married. His true nature was as a family man, and there was nothing he enjoyed more than a weekend filled with family dinners and barbecues, pouring wine for cousins and aunts, and staying up late into the night reminiscing. The divorce had nearly broken him, and he never seemed to fully recover.

Mom remarried quickly, but within a few years the union quickly deteriorated. Al had started out as her knight in shining armor, swooping in to rescue her from her heartbreak, but after a few years she discovered he was having an affair. This shocking discovery led to one even more disturbing: Al was also using cocaine. Often. In our home. And with other women. A double life that couldn't be any further away from the traditional home he and my mother had built in the country, with kids and dogs and cats and a trampoline and church on Sundays. As I shipped off to college for my freshman year, Al shipped off to rehab, hidden away in the mountains.

My mother had made a vow, for better or for worse, and she was determined to weather the storm this time. We all learned together that drug addiction is a disease, he didn't have control over it, and Al *certainly* wasn't to blame. When other girls in my dorm would take the occasional trip home for the weekend, I would drive to the mountains, stay with my mother in a rented cabin, and visit Al in rehab for family weekends. We made affirmations and held hands, took counseling classes as groups. He was progressing well and would be returning home within a few months. Mom welcomed him with open arms but a stern warning: relapse or cheat again, and it's over. She did everything she could to make it work, and for another year, Al did his best.

When his relapse came, it wasn't a surprise to me, but it crippled my mother. She wasn't ready for another divorce, but couldn't bring herself to continue down the path our family was headed on. A new rehab center in Texas, Burning Tree, was found for Al. Burning Tree specialized in people who had issues with continued relapse, and Al was headed there with a one-way ticket. The name "Burning Tree" scared me, and I hated that this was a place I was learning about. It shouldn't have been in my vocabulary. There were a lot of questions about what would happen with my mother and Al once he left, but I knew Mom would continue to support him.

He flew to Texas alone, a day before he was to be admitted. Mom called his hotel room to make sure he was up and leaving, and a woman answered the phone, telling her Al was in the shower.

"Can I take a message?" she asked.

Mom called me, hysterical. I knew it was over, but had to make sure Al knew it as well. As I ran out the door to be with my mom, I picked up my cell phone and called Al. After five or six rings, I got his voicemail. He must have still been in the shower.

"Never contact my mother or my family again. I swear to God, Al... never again." I said to his voicemail. I hung up, and sped toward my mom's house.

She was getting through the divorce, and knew she was doing the right thing. James and I made sure she knew, and were there to support her however she needed.

Δ

It was everything: the unexpected death, the dead-end relationship, the divorce, the drugs. They pushed me away. I wanted to save everyone. I wanted to save my mother from her hell of a second marriage. I wanted to save my father from his loneliness and grief. But I needed to save myself first, and everything that had happened the last few months slowed down my head and burdened my shoulders. Something was slowly breaking inside of me, and I was determined to fix it. Nothing was the way I wanted it to be. Life wasn't going as I had always imagined it would.

And then, it happened. The answer was so obvious. I stumbled on a website one day, bored at work. Educational Opportunities Overseas. It was so colorful. There were flags of countries I'd never seen across the page, faces of multiracial students smiling everywhere. An Asian girl next to an Irish flag. An African-American boy next to the Leaning Tower of Pisa. A Hispanic girl with a white boy holding hands in front of Machu Picchu. And at the top of the website, a large ad.

SPOTS STILL OPEN! NEW PROGRAM! STUDY IN PRAGUE 2006!

There were no pictures. I clicked. The deadline had passed, but they wanted more. I wanted more. Within the hour, I had sent in my application and the money. And nothing changed.

ALAINA ISBOUTS

3

August, Prague.

Our hotel was at the end of a small, dead-end street. Dad led us down the smooth, uneven cobblestones and toward the city's center. My feet navigated the surface, as unsure of each step on the outside as I was sure on the inside. We passed the American Embassy, situated right next to our hotel. Two flags hung straight out over the large, wooden arched entryway where two armed guards stood. An American flag and a Czech flag, both equally erect, both sporting the colors of blood, sweat, and tears. At the time, it seemed interesting to me that these flags could be so similar, yet so different. The same colors in different geometrical patterns, each representing something so different, hanging in harmony together.

We continued down the ancient drive. On the corner ahead stood an Irish pub with a patio, with half a dozen or so wrought iron tables flanking the doors. Between the tables, a set of stairs ran down into what looked like a small cave. As we got closer, I saw it was a bar hidden between the embassy and the pub. It seemed dark and foreboding, a place to drink and forget.

If it hadn't been for the harsh sounding Czech that was being muttered into cellphones and exchanged between passersby, I could have closed my eyes and imagined I was back in New York. Cars whisked by ahead of us on the busy avenue. The bell of a tram rang out,

21

waiting it's turn to cross the road ahead. A rectangular, blood-colored metal street sign nailed to the side of an old brick building on the corner told me that street was Tržiště. A man walked his dog past us, the dog yelping at everyone it dodged in front of. In front of the pub, a large delivery truck had pulled up; a young man was pulling a large wicker basket overflowing with freshly baked loaves of bread out of the back, yelling in Czech to his driver. The normal flow and sounds of a city, the same yet different.

Up ahead, Dad had his map completely unfolded and was turning it around, having lost which direction we should be heading. My mother and James were directly in front of me, Mom holding on to James tightly. For as distinguished and successful a woman she was, she had only been to Europe once—as a college graduation gift from her parents. They had taken her to Switzerland and Austria before she married my father, and she hadn't traveled outside of North America since then. While she was extremely intelligent, she seemed very awkward and out of place in Europe. Instead of embracing the foreignness of it all, it seemed to make her uneasy. She gripped James's arm with hers, as if any moment someone would come lift her off her feet and take her away.

While I had been worried about the cold weather, no one had warned me of the rain. On my last trip to New York, Nanny and my aunt had taken me to every department store in the city that had winter clothes in stock over the summer. With cashmere sweaters, peacoats, and new boots, I was ready for whatever Czech weather came my way. But during the summer, rather than warm weather and blue skies, down came the rain. I hadn't yet bought a blow dryer or straightening iron with me, and my hair was as big as Cher's in *Moonstruck*.

I lagged behind my family again. Mom and James were laughing about something, while Dad continued to pour over his map. The cobblestoned street came to an intersection and curved to the left. We followed the road, and about three hundred feet in front of us was the first tram stop we had come upon. They looked like the trolleys I had seen before in San Francisco, except these weren't meant to look vintage, rather, they just were. The faded paint was red with a thick white stripe across the center of the tram, the yellow paint on the front chipping a bit. Neon green letters scrolled across the top of the window, looking to me like a mess of letters. I struggled with the concept that I might someday actually know what words those letters formed, and use those trams to navigate my way across the city.

Past the tram stop was a McDonalds on the right-hand side of the street. I laughed to myself as I peeked inside—there were five different lines at the cashiers' stations inside. Souvenir shops littered either side of the road I now saw was leading us to the Charles Bridge. Money exchange stations. Cafés. Jewelry shops. Art galleries. Pizzerias. Glass blowing boutiques. I walked slower still, running my hand along the old, yellowed stones of the building beside me. I took a deep breath and steadied myself against the wall, pulling my right foot up to adjust the back of my sandal.

Half a block up, I saw Dad make a right turn instead of heading over the bridge, which led down a side street. Mom and James were close behind. I hurried up to the corner and glanced at the street name. Lázeňská. Immediately, the sounds of the city softened. Cars seemed further away, and the throngs of people we had shoved up against on the road to the bridge vanished. The old, stone-crafted buildings seemed taller on this narrow street, providing shade and cooling my already sticky face from the sun. I walked past a bar on the left side of the road with a large sign overhead. Zanzibar. Next to Zanzibar was another small restaurant, and more stairs that led to an underground bar called "The Cave."

Dad was standing in the widest part of the street head of me. "Skeeter, do you know what this is?"

I made my way over and met him in the middle of the vacant street. A path of cobblestones led up from the street to a grand entrance and a wall that stretched two stories high. An archway of carved wood was in the middle of the wall, with a door of the same wood design right in the center. A crest of red and white hung over the door, and wrought iron arched around the crest and topped the woodworked doorway.

"I have no idea," I replied, mildly irritated. How would I have any idea where we were? I stepped closer the doors to get a better look. A buzzer to the left of the door had three names listed, the first one of which was EOO. "Oh... is this my school?"

"Yep," Dad pointed to the map. "Can you believe this location? You can't get any better than this."

Mom let out a soft, "*Wooooow...*" as she looked up to the entrance. "I wonder what it looks like inside." She stepped up to the doors next to me, but there was no way to peer in. "We could ring the buzzer and see if someone could let us in," she offered, looking at me.

"No, it's okay." I took hold of her arm and walked away from the entrance toward Dad, who was still standing in the middle of the street. No cars or other pedestrians had passed. "Besides, we are meeting Bara at the end of the week, I'm sure she'll show us the university then."

"You guys want to eat? There's a pizza place down this way," James said, pointing further down Lázeňská, away from the bridge.

Mom and Dad agreed, and we walked away from the school. Before we rounded the corner, I turned back for one last look. It really was exquisitely beautiful. I wondered what was inside, and what it would be like to show up at that door every day during the week. It could not have been more different from school back home. It was exactly what I wanted.

Δ

The rest of the week dragged. Dad hired a private tour guide and we drove outside the city to see the antler collection of the

Konopiště Chateau, the drawbridges of the Karlštejn Castle, the bears of Český Krumlov, and the Gothic, Baroque, and Romantic architecture of Hluboká Castle. Each day I grew more and more impatient for my family to leave. I wasn't anxious to be alone, but I was filled with the nerves of meeting the other students in my program. The anticipation I felt was hard to explain; like waiting to hear of your own ancestry from a DNA test. I didn't know how at home I would feel in this strange and hauntingly beautiful city until my family had left and I had time alone with my new classmates. I felt constantly on edge and suspicious of everything I saw, wondering if everything would look the same once we were alone together. I felt as if I couldn't really begin my journey until it was just me and Prague.

There was something about the city that seemed perpetually dark. The sun shone every morning and it would rain a bit every afternoon, but to me Prague seemed like a city that was enticingly mysterious. Despite this, or perhaps because of it, the city was sickeningly beautiful. The sky-high towers and Gothic architecture made the castles and city buildings we saw look like Maleficent's castle in *Sleeping Beauty*. The statues on the Charles Bridge were dark, almost black; as if they had been there, weathered throughout the ages, since the beginning of time itself. The saints erected in squares throughout the city seemed to have been frozen, all looking as if they were cast in stone just as they were about to issue a stern warning or dark prophecy for future generations. I looked up at each of them and wondered what they would say to me now, if only I could pry the words out of their stoned mouths.

My parents and James, however, didn't seem as haunted by Prague's beauty as I was. To them it was a marvelous family vacation. My parents had grown visibly closer over the days, walking with their arms around one another and waking up early to have breakfast alone while James and I were showering up. Every night ended the same way: with a cocktail in the lobby of our hotel. Mom and I would toast with Kir Royales, Dad and James each with Grey Goose on the rocks. We'd talk about everything we'd seen that day and what it was like to be there, the four of us. The years we'd spent missing out on this was never mentioned.

At the end of the week, Bara and I arranged to meet outside of my new apartment. She agreed to bring the keys for me, so I could show my parents, and they could help me get situated. Both my parents really wanted to see the apartment, and I agreed to show them. Organizing was a specialty of Mom's, and I wanted to take full advantage of her help before she left. But the day we set off from Malá Strana to my new apartment, I was regretting the decision to show off the new apartment I hadn't even seen one picture of. I felt numb, completely and utterly numb. I wanted to walk inside by myself and not have to worry about anyone else judging the apartment before I could, or even judging my reaction to the apartment. I reasoned with myself. How bad could it be?

According to the address I'd been given, the apartment was in the fifth zone of Prague. Our hotel was in the first. We walked through the picturesque gardens of the hotel, complete with a bubbling fountain, and onto the cobblestoned street. Down the small hill to the main street at the Malostranské náměstí tram stop: Újezd. Right on Újezd. And straight. Straight, straight, straight. We made our way past cafés and beer halls, past Hellichova, and signs boasting Traditional Czech Food, and even one that touted "Probably the best food in Prague." Probably. Tens turned into hundreds, turned into thousands of cobblestones we must have walked over.

I examined, took in, learned. Thousands of cobblestones turned into millions. Who had laid these? Where had they come from? A fountain fizzed in front of us in three tiers; water spouted up from the top like a fire hydrant before it dripped down to the next layer in the middle, where it spilled over the sides and splashed on to the bottom. People sat around, reading, soaking up sunshine. *What a place to people watch*, I thought. I wondered if the water was on all the time, year-round. How cold did it really get here? Would I need all of those sweaters I brought? We walked and walked. Drops of sweat formed on the back of my neck and underneath my breasts.

As we turned a corner, we reached a square bustling with people. There were trams coming and going, stopping and starting, buzzing and ringing their bells. People jogging across the street in front of cars and trams. Restaurants and shops filled every window. An entrance to an indoor shopping center was just past the tram stop. I looked around. Another McDonalds, a KFC, and something large and obtrusive called Tesco, which had people filing in one after another. I felt more confused and further away from myself than ever before. We walked just farther, past the square and past a tram stop called Anděl to a large bus stop.

We passed people hidden from view elsewhere in the city: homeless begging for change, people letting their children pee in public right on the grass, grown men doing it themselves as if it was the most natural thing in the world. I noticed no English was spoken here, we had walked farther than English could reach. I hadn't noticed the border. There were signs for multiple busses. Dad had stopped in front of one with a schedule for the 137/501.

"Dad, are you sure you know where we are going?" I called over to him.

"It isn't much further, but it's easier to take the bus," he reasoned. Lugging up two suitcases and a computer bag, we boarded the bus. Expert that he was on local Czech transportation, Dad told us we wouldn't need tickets. The bus was big but just packed enough that we needed to stand in the middle. Huddling together near the center doors, we took off from the bus stop. Over the loud speaker crackled the most foreign-sounding announcement.

The bus shakily departed the station, apparently called Na Knízecí, and rounded a corner. We were on another busy street I hadn't noticed before, at the other end of the bustling square we had just left. Slowing down to stop at a light, I noticed an adorable little café on the left-hand side that said in bold letters CAFÉ ANDĚL with a picture of an angel next to it. Apparently *anděl* translated to *angel?* How did Anděl get its name? The first stop was Santoška, then a left up a hill and another stop at Václavka. It was a few more minutes and hills later before we passed an Albert, the local grocery store, on the right-hand side and stopped at Malvazinky. After a straight line and a mere forty-five more seconds on the bus, the female voice announced, "Urbanova." I was home.

The bus took off down the road, shuddering toward its next stop. We stood there in the silence, staring at the building. It was a quiet three miles from the city center. A large, chunky apartment building stood behind a row of thick, unruly bushes. I guessed it had been built by the Communists during the occupation, because it didn't look like anything else I had seen in the entire city. It wasn't dark, but it wasn't beautiful. It wasn't anything but a building.

Mom, forever viewing the world through rose-colored glasses, didn't say anything. I think it was too much for her to bear to know her only daughter would be staying here, in this foreboding building, across from a cemetery, in what looked to be the outskirts of a city, in a second-world country thousands of miles away from her. I walked slowly toward my new address, apprehensive but grateful that we were finally at our destination. We pushed past the overgrown bushes making their way on to the sidewalk. The door was a natural, bright wood with a silver doorknob and a key hole underneath the lever. There were eight or ten different mail slots on the left-hand side by the door, each with a different Czech name stuck above. Some of them overflowed with mail; newspapers, ads, and coupons littered the floor beneath the slots. Above me an old, motion-sensor light bulb dimly lit up. It was the only light I noticed on the entire property. Surrounding the bulb and light well was a thick, glimmering spider web with a spider the size of a quarter, keeping watch on anything that would dare to come near her. Directly above the keyhole, where you'd need to stand to activate the motion-sensor light. Strike one.

Bara was supposed to meet us outside of the building at about noon, but she was shuttling students to and from the airport all day. Everyone in the program was arriving. I sat outside with my family until she showed up, hopefully speaking English, with the keys. He had to speak English. She had to speak English. Was it a she? I wondered if Bara was considered a masculine or feminine name in Czech. He had to speak English. She had to speak English. I went back and forth. James made jokes, Dad played with his cellphone, Mom nosed around, peeking in windows, and I fought back tears. This was not the fabulous European apartment I had been picturing. In my daydreams, I never took the bus, let alone a bus and a tram just to get to school. These bushes would have to go—who knows how many crazy stalkers could hide in those bushes to prey on small American students? Why did I have to go to Prague? Why did I always have to try to be so different, I mean really, wasn't this the stupidest thing I could have done?

We sat in silence for half an hour before we heard someone down the path in front of the building. She was definitely not here for us. A woman trotted by, wearing walking shoes and what can only be described as pajama hot pants, high-waisted and maroon-gray plaid print on flannel. A loose, white thermal shirt hung off the woman's masculine frame, her brown hair streaked with gray hung wavy and plain around her round face. But her features were kind, and her blue eyes showed understanding even as they took in all of her surroundings completely. She walked toward us, shifting the weight of her backpack to her left shoulder as she veered toward the right and walked right up to me.

"Adriana?" she asked.

I started. "Yeah—uhh—" How the hell did you pronounce her name?

"*Bah*-ra, yes, that's me. Very nice to meet you. Here are the keys, please get rest and unpack, I must be off again to retrieve your roommates from the airport."

"Okay, well, thanks for dropping off the keys here," I said. I didn't know what else to say yet.

I fumbled for the keys as my parents introduced themselves to Bara before she rushed off again.

"I'm so glad we got to meet her," said my mom. "So she'll be like the go-to person if you need anything here, right?"

"Yeah, I guess so. I'm sure I'll find out more later," I replied. The truth was I didn't really know. I wasn't sure what was supposed to happen now. I felt disoriented, as if I was still trying to catch my breath and my feet weren't really firmly planted on the ground.

The door creaked open, and we walked up the open staircase to the third floor, Dad and James lugging my bags up the stairs. There were only two doors on the landing; mine was on the left-hand side. The door handle immediately confused me. It didn't turn. After fumbling with the lock for a minute, the door swung open forcefully.

A musty smell smacked me in the face as I pushed the door open in to the apartment. Strike two. The door fell closed with a slam behind us. It was much bigger than I expected, but sterile and unwelcoming.

There was a spacious living area with a secondhand (or thirdhand?) pink floral couch facing some built-in cabinets. The only notable detail about the living room was what it lacked—a television. This didn't worry me in the least; obviously, TV shows would be in Czech, and I intended to spend absolutely no time hanging around this hole of an apartment, watching TV. A vintage bar stood outside the living room in a sort of common area, little shot glasses picked from tourist shops flanked each side, each with *Praha* etched along the front. There was no art or anything on the walls save for one poster-sized map of the city, tacked up for our benefit by Bara, I was sure.

In the back of the apartment was a basic kitchen fitted with a small, round Formica table and four chairs around it. Off the kitchen was a bedroom with two twin beds with drawers underneath, an unmistakable purchase from Ikea, and a desk at the foot of each bed. Next to the kitchen was a no-frills bathroom, complete with a mini washing machine to the right of the sink. The black tile on the walls and the floor clashed alarmingly with the neon yellow plastic shower curtain, and showed every speck of dust. Next to the bathroom was the second bedroom. Again, two twin beds and two desks sat on either side of the room, but this bedroom also included two large wardrobes and its own door to the patio that spanned the length of the apartment.

"Okay Skeeter Bug, where should I take the bags?" my dad asked.

"Oh, definitely this one," Mom said as she walked into the second bedroom. "Look at these windows!" She pulled open the curtains, which obviously had come with the apartment.

I sat on the bed closest to the door, letting my backpack with my laptop rest by my feet. It was firm; the newness of the mattress was obvious through the sheets. I closed my eyes and exhaled deeply. *This would do just fine*, I thought. Nothing was upscale or even nice at all, but it was functional, it was clean, and it was far away from home. I opened my eyes to see Mom unzipping my suitcase.

"Let's get settled," I said.

4

July, Colorado.

I was ready to begin my last summer in Denver before Prague. Mark and I continued to spend our evenings together, usually at his place in Five Points, now that I had moved in with Mom. My lease was up at the end of May, and since I was leaving in August there was no use in signing a new one. We didn't talk much about Prague or what that would mean for us. Instead, we'd listen to music, drink beer in the backyard and play with our dog, or go out for drinks with friends. Weekends followed the same pattern, with Saturday afternoons still passing leisurely, eating Thai food, and nights spent at Mark's bar downtown.

The air had warmed up considerably, and the threat of a late spring snow no longer hung over our heads. Denver gave way to a wonderful dry heat, and nearly overnight, flowers bloomed and the green grass felt lush under my bare feet. Days would start at Mark's house with his roommates. My girlfriends would call to meet for dinner or drinks somewhere, and we'd eventually make our way to Mark's bar, where we didn't have to worry about a tab, or anything at all. Nights at the bar turned into 2 a.m. at our favorite diner, laughing and feeding each other scrambled eggs, tossing whipped cream from waffles across the table. It was my happiest time with Mark. Not once did we talk about what the end of August meant for us. Instead, we lived each day as it was.

It was a Sunday afternoon, and I was playing on Mark's computer, reading about Prague, while he watched a Rockies game, drifting in and out of sleep, half empty Corona bottle on the floor next to the couch. *The Czech Republic drinks more beer per capita than any other country in the world.* Tidbits like this stayed in my head, endlessly curious about the culture I was about to immerse myself in. I was about to close the laptop and wake him up when a new email popped up in my inbox. *Greetings from Prague!* the subject read. It was from a person by the name of Bara. The author introduced him or herself (was Bara a female name?) as the program director for the upcoming fall semester abroad in Prague through EOO. Bara explained that the email had been set up as a way for the participants of the program to contact one another before arriving in Prague.

My eyes widened. How many students were there? I had no idea. I had imagined that there would be at least fifty, but I had nothing to base this on. Where were they all from? My head filled with questions.

"Mark! Wake up!"

"I wasn't sleeping," he replied groggily.

I couldn't take my eyes off my email. "Come over here," I called. "I have an email from Prague."

He walked through the living room from the kitchen, grabbing his Corona off the hardwood floor. His feet shuffled into the sunroom, making their way over to the desk chair I sat in. "What's going on?" He leaned over my shoulder, setting his beer on the desk next to the keyboard.

"I got an email from the program director." I waited while he ran his eyes over it. In the background, I saw a new email pop up in my inbox. It was from the same email address that Bara had used. One of the students had come up with the idea to reply to everyone on the email and reach everyone at once. It worked. I gasped. "Mark! Look!"

The email was short, from a girl in Michigan. She introduced herself as Stephanie. She was a musician and had a boyfriend, and suggested everyone should reply and introduce themselves briefly.

Within minutes, emails started popping up from other students. As soon as I finished reading one, another few would be waiting in my inbox.

The second email that arrived was from a guy in Jersey, John. The message was riddled with spelling errors and the whole paragraph was one long sentence. I didn't quite know what to think of him. Before I had a further change to form an opinion, a third email arrived, from a girl named Noelle in Washington state. She was headed to Prague with three other girls and a guy from her college, none of whom wanted to go alone.

"So there are people going together?" Mark asked me.

"I don't know, I guess so." I hadn't even thought of the possibility of people studying abroad together in groups, and I wasn't sure how many other groups there would be. How many of these introduction emails would I be getting?

My email box lit up once more, with a fourth email in the chain. It was from another girl in Colorado, this one who also went to CSU. She seemed kind of straight laced, nice and polite, based off her message. She recommended that we all connect on Facebook or AIM so we could chat throughout the summer and get to know one another further. The fifth email was from a guy named Alex, also from Michigan. Alex said he had become too addicted to social media, so it was strictly email only for him. He said he was living in a co-op and was pretty "stoked" to head out to Europe.

"So what do you think?" Mark said. "They seem kind of lame so far," he said, answering his own question without waiting to hear what I thought. He walked out of the sunroom, and I heard him land back on the couch, clicking the volume on the game up.

My heart was beating faster than it should have been for reading emails. I couldn't stop thinking about these people—the plain girl from Michigan, John from Jersey, the group from Washington, Alex the social media addict, the nice girl up in Fort Collins. The people I had wondered about were becoming halfway real, with names and hometowns and interests.

A sixth email arrived.

What's up party people, my name's Nicholas and I'm living in LA going to UCLA. I've been spending my whole summer working like mad to make $ for traveling around. Dunno bout the rest of you but my schedule gives me a 4 day weekend! My friend just got back from the EOO summer program in Prague and he said he had an amazing time. He said the housing is actually pretty dope too. And everything's still cheap cause they're not on the Euro yet, especially beer! He had 50 krowns (or whatever their currency is) left so I traded it for $2, and he apparently still made a profit. Haha.

Are all of you from Colorado and Michigan? I dunno how life is over there but I'm ready to get the hell out of SoCal for a bit.

I've never been to Prague but my friends and I back-packed around western and mid-Europe after high school so there're some places I feel like going that you all should def tag along for. Any other places any of YOU know, let ME know! We have a huge break in Nov or something and big trips should be on the agenda. If anyone's down to taking an early quick trip down to the greek isles or italy before the autumn hits and the sun goes away, let me know! I know it sounds crazy but it'd be worth it I think. But then again I haven't researched it yet. Other than that I'll try to catch y'all on the AIM, or the 29th.

Alex, come on buddy. Set that account up, we're the only ones who have to know.

PS — anyone getting a Eurail pass?

Peace,
Nicholas

The thought of traveling around Europe before the semester started hadn't even occurred to me be. So concentrated in my mind was the thought of living in Prague, that I hadn't even considered things like fall break and what weekends would be like. Nicholas was the first one to say he was "down to travel" before the semester started, and that was when it hit me. I would be living in Europe. Weekends in Paris, fall break in Vienna, Thanksgiving in Rome, I could do it all. We could do it all. It was also the first time I considered that we could travel in groups. I'd been so consumed with the idea of getting away and being alone that I failed to realize I'd be meeting new people, forging relationships. New roommates, new classmates. Rather than email everyone back to the generic email address, I responded to just Nicholas.

I didn't have any experience backpacking through Europe like he seemed to, but what the hell? This was the time. I told Nicholas I'd be flying out on the twenty-fourth of August and that if he wanted to meet up before the program started, I'd love to. Sitting in Mark's sunroom, sending an email to a guy I didn't know, about traveling around Europe with him, my fingers felt weak. We still hadn't talked about the future of *us*. I had to press on the keys with concentration to get any letters to appear in my email.

I imagined myself in Italy, laughing with people I didn't yet know and boarding trains to cities I'd never visited. But mostly, I wondered about the authors of the emails flooding my inbox. How many of these students had been to Europe before? What were they studying? How did they come across EOO? But one question burned in my mind, more than anything else.

Why had they all chosen Prague? It wasn't Paris or London, it was a fairly obscure city. This was the first semester that the EOO had a fully operational program in Prague, other than the month-long summer program that just ended. Why would anyone choose Prague? Were they running away, as far as they possibly could, like I was?

By the end of the day, I had learned there were only seventeen of us, including myself. Everyone had taken their turn introducing themselves to the group, and several new Facebook friends and AIM buddies had been added to my lists. Seventeen. Nowhere near the fifty or so that I was expecting. They all had names now. Another email from Nicholas, the only one I was emailing one-on-one, popped up in my inbox.

Hey

I'm not arriving til day of, the 29th. Ur job is to get to know the town before I come in. I've been to Italy a few times... Venice, Florence, San Gimignano, Rome, and Brindisi, but never far south. I want to check that out. the Greek Isles are unbelievable. that's a place we'd have to visit when its still really warm tho...I had a friend spend a year in Barcelona and he said flying is the cheapest. I was talking to Stephanie, she said she also has a 4 day weekend, whats ur schedule like? I heard the program tries to not give you homework on the weekend because they emphasize travel, which would be dope. I put u on my AIM so try to get up on that.

Nicholas

I was fairly sure I had made one friend already. I closed my laptop and stretched out next to Mark on the couch, feeling confidently happy.

Δ

A few weeks later, a package arrived at my mom's for me. It was a large, padded envelope from EOO. Sitting down at the counter with Mom and two glasses of red wine, I eagerly ripped it open.

"What is that?" Mom asked, setting her glass of wine down on the granite counter top. Her many bracelets clinked against the green marble of the kitchen island as she looked at me.

Pieces of various colored paper slid out of the package in a folder. "Looks like orientation stuff for Prague," I replied. I thumbed through the pages, passing by packing lists, vaccination recommendations, and other technical information, until I saw a piece of bright yellow paper titled Housing Assignment.

"Roommate assignments!" I let the rest of the papers fall onto the counter and slid over closer to my mom. "Let's see... where am I? What do these titles mean?"

The sheet had a simple numbered list, with names under each section: U Apartment, Cozy House, Garden Apartment, and Bazaar Apartment. My name was listed under U Apartment, along with Emily, Jordana, and Alex.

"Do you know what those apartment names are?" my mother inquired.

"No, I don't know anything about them yet. This is the first I've heard of our housing at all," I replied honestly. "Wait... why is there a guy in my list?"

"What?" Mom looked confused.

"This one, Alex. We all got an email from him, he's a guy."

"Are you sure?" she laughed.

I wasn't sure. I quickly pulled out my laptop and searched for the names on my list. I already knew Alex was the dude who couldn't handle Facebook, but I couldn't remember Emily or Jordana. The email from Emily was short and sweet, though no real traces of her personality could be found. Jordana, on the other hand, seemed like she would get along well with Nicholas. Her email was mostly about finding places to drink in Prague and how ready she was to get out of Vegas (she was a junior at UNLV) and drink with new people. I wondered who, among this list of strangers, I would fit in with.

5

August, Prague.

My mom made organizing a sport. She knew just where to put everything, even finding little boxes and organizers for socks and underwear I would have shoved in the bottom of my closet. But once everything was in its right place, I had the feeling that I wished she knew where to put me. I still felt out of place in this apartment, wondering if I did the right thing or not. While Mom and I unpacked, Dad and James went to the mall back at Anděl and bought a cell phone for me and a few other things for the apartment. We decided we would meet them for dinner back at Anděl.

Mom and I opened the door to leave when we saw a girl about my height pulling a large roller bag up the last few stairs onto the landing in front of the apartment.

"'Oh, hello," she said to me. "Are you with EOO?"

She had pixie-cropped hair and no visible makeup. The only jewelry she wore was a nose ring, a little green stud on the side of her nostril. Her brown corduroy pants were faded at the knees, and her green hoodie was unzipped to reveal a plain white tee underneath, and a very obvious lack of bra.

"Yeah, hi, I'm Adriana. I guess we're roommates?"

She stumbled forward with her luggage and moved to shake my hand. "I'm Alex."

I stole a glance at Mom. Alex was a girl, of course. *Of course*, Mom mouthed to me. I smiled.

Alex came in and inspected the rooms. She chose the bedroom off of the kitchen, and for some reason I felt relieved. The roommate choosing would be up to Emily and Jordana, whenever they arrived. It was strange having my Mom there, and Alex and I couldn't really talk and get to know each other. It was tense and awkward, and I just wanted to leave. Mom invited Alex to go with us, and she said that she would love to ride the bus down with us, but wanted to explore the area on her own. We walked outside, and to the bus stop I learned was called Urbanova, the place where we would be picking up the bus every day. As we reached the corner where the bus had dropped us off a few hours before, a boy walked out of a filthy old phone booth.

"Adriana?" he asked.

I turned around, completely baffled. "Yeah?"

I definitely didn't know this guy. He wasn't much taller than me, just a few inches, and was very skinny. His tan skin went perfectly with his short, dark brown curls and his dark brown eyes. He was handsome in a deep sort of way, if a bit too skinny for my taste.

"It's Charlie. I'm with EOO too, I hope I didn't scare you, I recognized you from your Facebook picture."

Fucking Facebook.

"Oh, yeah, hi!" I said.

Charlie and I had chatted online a few times, but not for very long, and I hadn't really gotten to know him. But here he was, standing on the corner in front of me, already recognizing me. Meeting someone else gave me the feeling of picking up momentum, like a snowball that was just starting to take shape. I had seen some of Prague, my apartment, a roommate of mine, and now met Charlie, too. The semester was beginning to take shape.

He joined Mom, Alex, and me on the bus down the hill to Anděl, where we all parted ways. Alex and Charlie headed down the right side of the street, while Mom and I walked on the left side, toward the mall where Dad and James would meet us for dinner. It was going to be the last dinner with my parents and James before they went back home.

"They seemed nice," Mom offered.

"Yeah I guess so. Alex had kind of a strange smell." I made a face, and my mom laughed and pushed me. I knew I had to be nice to them, and of course I wanted to be nice to them, but I hoped that the rest of the kids weren't like Alex. I had imagined meeting people I had more in common with, even if just on the surface. It could potentially be a very long semester.

We settled on a pizza place at Anděl, inappropriately named Godfather Pizza. I pushed the food around on my plate, not knowing how to feel. I still felt isolated around my family but was eager for them to leave. I couldn't make sense of it to myself, but I just knew that once they left I would feel more comfortable. I sipped my mineral water and anxiously waited for our good-byes. I was going to stay the night at my apartment tonight, while they went back to the hotel before flying home early tomorrow morning. The end couldn't have come soon enough, but now that it had, I realized how much I would miss them all. Especially Mom. But more than anything, I knew how much I would worry about her.

We stood outside the restaurant, ready to part ways. Dad hugged me first.

"I'm so proud of you, Skeeter," he said to me. "Have as much fun as you can." Good-byes with Dad were easy at this point; we were both so used to them, since he had moved to Boston.

"Thanks Dad. I love you." He stepped back and let James have his turn. James and I had gotten very close in the last five years, ever since Mom had started having trouble with Al. I knew I would miss him so much. I was worried that he would be the only one taking care of

Mom while I was gone. "Be good while I am gone." I pointed my finger in his face, only half kidding.

"I will, you know I will," he said, letting me hug him. "Have a great time Addie. Really."

"Take care of her," I whispered to James, nodding toward Mom. She was standing behind him, tears already filling her eyes. He stepped back, and Mom immediately rushed forward.

"Oh, Addie. I love you so much." Her voice cracked, and she hugged me tight.

"I love you too, Mom. It's going to be fine, don't worry about me." I was determined not to cry. I chose this, I reminded myself. I could handle it. It wasn't being away from my family that was unnerving, but rather the situations they were going back home to that left me worried. I felt as if I was the parent letting my children go.

Mom turned around and I noticed Dad grab her hand, and they stood together next to James. I took a mental picture of my parents holding hands, and James smiling at me and waving. It was time for me to go. I walked away down the dark street, as if I remembered exactly where to go. Rain began to fall gently, prompting me to start jogging to hurry out of the nightly rain I had come to expect, but had not prepared for, toward what I hoped was the bus stop. I knew the bus number was 137, so I waited for one to pull up. I wasn't sure if I needed a ticket, but I didn't have one and had no idea where to get one. A bus flashing 137 pulled up. I hoped they all went the same places and made the same stops this time of night. I got aboard, sat in the back, and counted four stops. I had counted the first time I was on the bus, because the Czech names over the loudspeaker still meant nothing to me. They all sounded the same: alien.

I jumped off the bus and walked toward my communal apartment building as the rain picked up. I saw the stars above me and the cemetery across the street, but didn't stop to absorb it all. I quickly made my way past the bushes that invaded the sidewalk. I saw the spider above the doorway and made sure I knew which key to use before I dared to stand beneath the spider to slide the key in. It was impossible to find in the dark, but in order to turn on the motion sensor light I'd have to stand right under the web. I stuck my leg in front of the door and kicked until it triggered the sensor. I found the slender silver key and slid it into the lock slowly, turning it to the right until the door clicked open. The musty smell was the only thing I could discern in the darkness. I walked a few feet ahead in the darkness and waited for the motion sensor to turn on. Nothing. Cautiously, I felt my way to the staircase, my heart pounding. I didn't remember the steps well enough to find my way in the dark. All I could remember was the third landing and the door on the left. I moved slowly, praying no one would walk into the hallway and see me feeling around in the dark for my apartment door. What a fool I felt like. What a fool.

After a few tries with various keys, the door gave way. Finally, a light switch. I pressed the button for the light to come on in my living room, shook the rain off of myself, wrung out my hair, and wandered out onto the covered patio. There weren't any chairs out there, so I just stood right outside my door and looked as far as I could. It wasn't much of a view; Prague and the city center were the opposite way. I was looking out, far away from Prague. I wondered if I was looking toward the States and everyone I knew, or if this was even further away from them. I still felt unsure of my decision to move my life here for the next few months, but it was done. As the rain pounded on the concrete, I slid back inside and shut the glass door, pulling the curtains closed behind me.

I walked into my bedroom. There were a few bags out that I didn't recognize and makeup that wasn't mine on the desk on the other side of the room. At least one of my other roommates had showed up while I was at dinner. She clearly had been in a hurry; other than drugstore makeup scattered around, her bags were still zipped up. I walked into the kitchen, habitually heading for the fridge to get something to drink or eat. To my surprise, there were things in there.

45

Some milk, some strange looking jars and a few bottles of beer. Apparently someone had gone shopping already. What else had I missed that afternoon? I saw a note in the kitchen table.

"*Met up with the boys down the street for dinner. See you later.*" It was signed from Alex and Emily. I peeked inside Alex's room to see if there were any sign of Jordana's bags, but only saw Alex's suitcase parked next to the bed where she had left it. I wondered when they wrote that and how soon they would be home. I wasn't excited about being in the apartment by myself so soon.

To keep myself occupied, I figured there were still some things that could use some organizing. I rearranged some drawers, and got out my pajamas and toiletries for the bathroom. I washed my new city off my face. After brushing my teeth, I pulled my pajamas on and climbed in to bed. I tried to write in my journal, but still felt nothing. I couldn't force it. Feeling lonely, I missed Mark for the first time. *He would know what to say to make me feel better,* I thought. I grabbed my phone and called the States. It rang and rang, and finally on the third ring, he answered.

"Hey." He sounded so nonchalant. Didn't he even care that I was calling him?

"What do you mean 'hey.' I'm calling you from my Prague phone. You can't be more excited to hear form me?" I retorted.

"What's your fucking problem?"

"I don't know. I just don't know what I'm doing here." Tears were forming behind my eyes. I forced them back down.

"Well then why did you go? I don't know what you're doing there either."

"I just thought, I don't know, that I needed to travel and be away for a while. I just don't feel right. My apartment is weird, there's a door that goes outside that's right in my bedroom, and the one of my roommates I met is strange, and it's just weird here." Even I wasn't sure what I meant by *weird,* or what I wanted Mark to say.

"Everything is the same here. I made two hundred dollars last night, and some guy tipped me fifty bucks just to park his car up front. We went to Red Square after work and Zach threw up in the back of my car."

Not what I was looking for. "What is wrong with you? Why can't you be supportive of me, or just try to act like you care about what is going on out here? I don't know why you aren't—"

The phone cut off and some woman said something in Czech on the line. I didn't know what was happening. What was I going to say to him? Why wasn't he what? More understanding or more kind? Why wasn't Mark more like me? I had known it from the beginning that we were two very different people. I had never felt like I had a type, necessarily, or that there was one specific guy I was waiting my entire life to meet. I just had this feeling once in a while that Mark wasn't the one for me.

A few months earlier, we'd been walking downtown on our way to the movies. We had passed a homeless man, one of many on that block. He'd had no shoes, a cardboard sign, and a prosthetic leg.

I stopped and dug in my coin purse for some change.

"I don't fucking get how someone can be homeless. I mean, just get a job. Sweep some floors or something, you know?" Mark said, right in front of the homeless man.

Feeling guilty, I emptied my entire change purse into his hat.

It was just one comment, but I hated Mark for it. *The man I want to be with would never say something like that*, I had thought to myself. I had those thoughts all the time.

Two hours had passed, and still no sign of my roommates. I rinsed off in the shower, warmed up from the rain that had chilled me to the bone. The bathroom heated up quickly, filling the room with humidity and steam. Carefully, I stepped out of the shower and on to the cold, unfamiliar black tile, and over to the sink. Behind the condensation on the mirror was a blurry version of my face. I wiped the moisture off, studying my reflection. The skin of a twenty-one-year-old was a beautiful thing, olive and tanned, pulled snugly across my high cheekbones, still taught around my eyes. They were green today. Some days they were blue, but today the flecks of green around my pupils stood out more than the blue around the edges. My brows were beginning to look a bit overgrown, dark hairs straying too high above and below the usually impeccably plucked arches. It was the curse of being an Italian woman. Thick hair, yes, but it grows everywhere. Unruly brows were always too noticeable. I combed my dark, wet waves and pulled it into a braid for bed.

I pulled on some sweatpants and a T-shirt, and pulled the covers up over me. After a few minutes, it became obvious I wasn't going to be able to fall asleep. I climbed out of bed and found my portable DVD player. I picked out my favorite *Friends* DVD and put it on the corner of my desk, right by my bed. I lay in bed and tried my hardest not to cry. I stared out the door in my bedroom. What if someone came in? Who would I call? It dawned on me that I didn't even know the number for an emergency in Prague, that I didn't know who to call in case someone broke in or I choked or I fell down the stairs and broke my legs. And even if I did know who to call, would they even speak English? What if no one could understand me? Where were my roommates? I had been home for probably two hours, it was late, maybe 2 a.m. How long could it take to get dinner? What if something happened to them? I wouldn't know what to do or where to go in the morning, and who I would call for help, or how I would use the internet to email Bara and tell her what happened. I didn't know how to get ahold of my parents or exactly how to get back to their hotel if something happened. I didn't know what the hell had happened to my phone or how I could fix it.

The longer I lay there worrying, the more and more I questioned myself. What was I doing here? Why had I left everything behind to come here? For the first time, I regretted my decision. Why did I have to do this to myself? I always wanted everything to be so much more complicated than it needed to be, I couldn't have just stayed at UCD like the rest of the CU kids, I had to come here to do this. And now I didn't want to be here.

Ross and Rachel were having a fight on my portable DVD player. I closed my eyes and tried to think about *Friends* and not about everything that was wrong with my decision. As the tears started to leak out of the corners of my eyes, I huddled under the blanket and tried to remember the reasons why I'd left.

I awoke with a start, gasping for air. Someone was banging on the apartment door. Really hard. I woke up and sat straight up in bed, my heart already pounding out of my chest. *Shit, shit, shit, shit. This is exactly what I was worried about. There is someone trying to break in and I don't know who the fuck to call.* BANG, BANG, BANG. *Oh my God, oh my God, I'm going to be in the American papers, the study abroad girl who was stabbed to death in her bed. Fuck, fuck, fuck. What do I do? Answer the door? Hide out on the balcony?* I decided to get out of bed. I walked toward the door slowly, and with each step, my foot would stick a little bit to the dirty hardwood floor. BANG, BANG, BANG, BANG, BANG. *Why isn't there a peephole on this stupid fucking Czech door?!?!?!? What kind of apartment is this? What kind of neighborhood is this?* My mind was racing. I was running out of options and I had to make a decision, quick. Just as I had decided to go to the kitchen and find a knife, I heard giggling on the other side of the door.

"What is her name again?" a girl whispered loudly.

"I think it's Adrienne. Keep it down! You're too fucking loud!"

"ADRIENNE! ADRIENNE!" More giggling.

"I can't understand these keys. Where is the goddamned light switch?" I thought it was Alex's voice, but I hadn't heard it enough to know for sure. I decided to open the door anyway, feeling confident these had to be my roommates. I stepped toward the front door, opened the lock and pulled it open.

Alex was standing there in another faded sweatshirt, this one lime green, and an orange scarf wrapped around her neck. Next to her stood a pretty blonde girl, who shoved her way past me and into the apartment.

"What the fuck took you so long? We couldn't get the DOOR open!!" The blonde collapsed into laughter onto the couch. Obviously, they had found a bar.

I breathed a sigh of relief. "Oh, my God. I'm so sorry you guys, I didn't know it was you, and I didn't know if I should open the door or not."

"Well who else would it be?" Alex asked. Looking back, I realized she had a point.

I followed my roommates into the kitchen. Alex found the light switch and we each found a chair around the table. In the light, I finally got my first glimpse of Emily. She had solid, athletic build and was a few inches taller than me. It was obvious she wasn't wearing makeup and didn't need to; her skin had a perfect bronze glow with a few freckles dotting her cheeks. Her brown eyes were sparkling with fun and what I could only assume was Czech beer. I got the sense she was an athlete, the vibe of someone always up for a good time. I immediately liked her, and was glad she chose my room. She was ransacking the fridge.

"I'm so fucking hungry. We got LOST! Can you believe it? We got in this cab, and he tried to fucking rip us off. He drove us around in circles, and we were with the guys from down the street. Ohmygod that guy Mason is *sooo* hot. And we tried to get to Urbanova but I guess there is also Erbanova..." Emily was laughing and talking at the same time, picking up containers from the fridge, smelling them, putting them back.

Alex got up too. "I'll make scrambled eggs," she announced loudly. "Yeah, okay, so Charlie kept telling the guy '*Eeeeerrrrrrrrrbanova*' but the driver kept saying something to us in Czech, only we didn't know what the fuck he was saying..."

As my roommates broke out the frying pan and eggs, boiled gnocchi, and opened canned sweet tomato sauce at 4 a.m., we laughed together for the first time. My knot in my stomach dissipated. The lights blurred and the music of their conversation dulled, and I knew, in my heart and soul, that everything was going to be all right. For the first time in my life, I truly was where I was supposed to be, all nagging doubts of a few hours ago gone. All of the decisions I had ever made in my life had led me to this point. It was perfect.

August, Prague.

The next morning was the first day of official EOO events. Classes didn't start until Monday, but it there were mandatory EOO events before school began. We were supposed to meet the rest of the kids in our program for an orientation, along with some sort of get-to-know-Prague scavenger hunt, followed by an inclusive EOO "welcome dinner" that evening. Since the only people I had met in my program were my two roommates and Charlie, I was anxious to see what everyone else was like, and was determined to make the best first impression possible. I had learned from Emily and Alex the night before that there were three boys living in a house down the street from us, the Cozy House, just on the other side of the bus stop. We were the only ones living in this neighborhood as far as we could tell—but then again, no one had met anyone else.

   We hadn't really determined the bathroom situation with three girls living in the apartment (our fourth roommate had yet to show up), and the first morning was a bit awkward, sharing everything with roommates that were still strangers. I made a makeshift vanity out of my desk and a small mirror I found while I chatted with Emily. I found out she was from the D.C. area and had left a boyfriend behind. This was her last year of school as a business major from a big state school in Virginia. I had been right to assume she played sports—she had been playing lacrosse for years. I still hadn't learned too much about Alex, but with Emily and I sharing a room, it was much easier for us to talk.

While Emily told me all about her boyfriend at home, I carefully plotted what to wear. I chose my favorite pair of jeans, black tank top, and olive green cashmere sweater I'd bought on sale, then pulled on a pair of boots. I was ready to rock and geared up to meet the students I'd be spending the next four months with. Once the girls and I were dressed, we just sort of sat around wondering out loud what the day would be like until Bara arrived.

After nearly half an hour of waiting, our buzzer rang. We would learn that time is a much more fluid concept in the Czech Republic than it was to us Americans—a notion we quickly picked up on that morning. We grabbed our bags—Alex a tie-dyed messenger bag, Emily a backpack, me a vintage leather cross-body purse—and headed out the door. As we walked past the dangerously overgrown bushes, we saw Bara standing with the three boys from Cozy. I only recognized Charlie and gave a small wave of recognition.

The boy standing next to Charlie wasn't much taller than me, maybe even a bit shorter than Charlie. He was wearing a snug, faded blue T-shirt and a great hoodie zipped open enough to make out the word AMSTERDAM written in red letters with the city's crest in white below. He had on jeans that I didn't see many guys wear in Colorado; obviously he wasn't the guy from Denver. They were tight around the hips but somewhat low-cut, faded, and slightly ripped. He looked smart but gave off a sarcastic vibe that made me nervous to talk to him. It was the white Lacoste sneakers that threw me off; I'd never seen a guy wear them before. His dirty blond hair was cut short and spiked a bit in the front, and I could tell from my Facebook investigating (yes, I did it too, even though I had judged Charlie for doing the same thing) that this was Nicholas. He looked thinner and less fun than his profile picture let on. He didn't seem very happy or excited to meet anyone else, and I immediately dismissed him as stuck-up. He was from LA after all, I knew.

The third roommate was standing farther away from everyone else, nearly on the corner by the bus stop. I also knew from my Facebook habits that this had to be Mason. He was much taller than the other two (which wasn't saying too much) and had his straight black hair spiked up enough to give him two or three more full inches of height. He had on the twenty-year-old wardrobe: jeans with a studded black leather belt, a black tee with an artsy design printed on the front, and a black hoodie hanging open. His black Sketchers didn't have laces or buckles; he was working on bringing back the slip-on look. Mason didn't smile when he saw us either.

I was unimpressed and a bit intimidated.

The bus ride down to Anděl was fairly quiet. Bara questioned us about our first night in Prague, and I didn't dare open my mouth to tell everyone that I had nearly regretted my choice and mistook my roommates to be murderers. I just listened to the nervous laughter and chatter about the night before. Apparently, Emily and Alex met all of the Cozy boys for drinks, thanks to Alex grabbing dinner with Charlie, and Emily had already tried to make out with Mason. She seemed pretty unfazed by everyone laughing at her attempts to hook up with someone on the first night—even though she had already told everyone about her boyfriend.

Rather than going straight to the school for orientation, Bara decided that we would stop and get our first monthly pass for the public transportation system. It was a long and boring process. Bara was the only one of us who could speak Czech, and while she filled out papers, we stood around and got to know one another. I still felt shy and was kicking myself for having dinner with my parents the night before. If I had gone with Alex, I would at least have something to say right now rather than being the quiet librarian in the corner, listening to everyone's stories rather than taking part in the conversation at all.

"Oh, Adriana and Emily and Alex, I have to tell you," Bara called over to us from the window. "It will just be the three of you in your flat."

"What happened to Jordana?" asked Mason.

"She will not be joining us this semester," Bara replied.

Emily turned to Mason. "What do you think that's about?"

Charlie shrugged. "Who knows. Maybe she got cold feet at the airport?"

I thought about how nervous I had been, and the idea seemed almost understandable. I wondered what circumstances would be to have actually decided not to go.

"So which one of you ladies gets your own room?" Nicholas asked. His raised his eyebrows to Emily, Alex, and me. I noticed his sunglasses hanging off the front of his shirt, and the name *Marc Jacobs* printed on the sides.

"That would be Alex," I said, nudging her in the side. "Good choice on the bedroom."

Alex smiled. "Yeah, that will be kind of nice, to have my own room. I don't even have my own room back home."

"We all have our own rooms at Cozy House," Mason bragged.

"Yeah, Adriana, you should see it. It's a pretty cool house," Alex said.

I glanced at Charlie, Mason, and Nicholas. "Maybe I'll get an invitation sometime."

Over an hour later, we all finally had our passes. Bara led us back to the tram to get to school, four stops away. When our tram pulled up to Malostranské náměstí, I was able to make out our group immediately, standing on the corner by an outdoor café. They were all different: one tall, very masculine-looking guy; a girl with very long, straight brown hair and big, rosy cheeks; a beautiful blonde girl laughing with a few other students gathered around her; a tall, sullen-looking girl with pale skin and dark hair; a small-framed guy with lots of dark, curly hair; and a plain-looking girl with long dark hair who wasn't talking to anyone else. Seventeen of us, all together. How different could we all look on the outside—the list of superficial differences was endless. As was the list of ways we were different inside.

But how different could we really be? Sure, there are plenty of students who study abroad, millions a year, probably. But where do they go? Rome, Paris, London, Madrid, maybe Australia. What kind of student goes to Prague? Seventeen of us, that was it. When I had first signed up for this adventure, I thought maybe there would be hundreds of us. I knew EOO was a big company, who knew how many students had the opportunity to sign up for this? But I had learned, when we all started emailing each other through the generic email address, that this was EOO's first semester in Prague. We were the guinea pigs, the test babies. Seventeen. How different could we possibly be to all end up in Prague at the same moment in time?

There was something inside of me that made me choose Prague. Most other students went to those western European cities—different enough from home, but familiar enough to not be foreign. A rush, an adventure, a thrill without having to give up those American conveniences. Eastern Europe was the only place that seemed uncharted, yet close enough to forge connections. I had to be different. I'd inconvenienced myself and built my life around that fact—and obviously, so did these sixteen other students standing with me outside in the chilly Prague morning that August day.

Δ

The orientation breezed by. We were given a tour of our building: classroom here, computer lab there, library here, coffee machine there, bathroom here, don't smoke there. The university was steps from the Charles Bridge, and in one of the oldest buildings in all of Prague (which was saying something, since the city itself was widely untouched by bombings during WWII, as well as during the Russian occupation). I was surprised to learn that the entire university was two buildings. The first building was behind the grand entrance Dad had found the week before. The rounded wood door opened to a courtyard the size of a backyard, with nothing but cobblestones on the round. As quiet as the street was, the courtyard was dead silent. Nothing but the occasional echo of laughter—always by an American student—or footsteps on the stones could be heard.

Bara showed us to a small office she was renting as the EOO home base. It was right off the courtyard, the only other door accessible from the courtyard besides the one that led inside to the small classrooms. It was a two-roomed office. The first room housed a large table that served as a desk for her, with two chairs set out in front. Past Bara's desk was another larger, draftier room, with a large table and six chairs around it. Two desktop computers on small desks were pushed up against the other side of the room. She set it up to use as a study hall or a computer lab for students who hadn't brought laptops from home. The office had also been equipped with Wi-Fi, since none of our flats had it. It was to be open during all school hours, and any other hours Bara felt like it.

The university building was only three stories, with a few small classrooms scattered on each floor. There were no lecture halls with empty seats for hundreds, like in American universities, these classrooms were the size of high school classrooms. Some held desks with attached chairs, some had tables arranged throughout the room. Chalkboards hung in the center of each room, and no fancy computers, smartboards, or overhead projectors were around. On each floor was a coffee machine, small photos of warmed beverages and their names in Czech above each button. The second building was down the street, and consisted only of a room of computers that were available for students for schoolwork only.

After our tour, Bara brought us into an empty classroom and asked us to fill out schedules with our class preferences. I had been wondering how our classes were picked, but it seemed awfully last minute to pick classes on the Wednesday before they were to start on Monday. I sat next to Emily and peeked over at her schedule, comparing the classes I had checked to hers. The classes I wanted to take were at pretty good hours; the business and marketing classes that I luckily had no need for were mostly held in the evenings. Bad news for study abroad business students.

I checked the boxes for Gender and Culture, Social Anthropology, Religions of the World, and of course, Czech. Four was plenty of classes. I'd declared my major for my time in Prague as Eastern European Language, Literature, and Culture. My advisor back at CU had told me that would complement my creative writing major well. Emily and Alex had also picked the Czech language course, which was the earliest class, beginning at 9 a.m two days a week. The rest of the classes were held only once a week, but for four hours. I stretched my arms overhead and yawned, imagining the prospect of four-hour-long lectures.

Once we finished selecting our classes, we made our way back to the EOO office. We sat on the floor in the larger back room and had an informal question and answer session with Bara. She told us, right off the bat, that everything we did would be informal.

"Do not be shy," Bara said. It came out as more of a warning than an invitation. "I know you all have questions, and I am here to help and answer. And if I don't know the answer, I'll find it out for you. Better than you can." She smiled.

It was quiet. I knew everyone had questions—I knew I did—but I didn't even know where to start.

"Yes, John, is it?" Bara pointed to a guy sitting in the back. He was big, not fat but sizable and sturdy, like a football player. His face was boyish, and the well-worn New Jersey Devils hat on his head made him look like the quintessential American college student. His khakis were wrinkled and his blue button-up shirt had the sleeves pushed up.

"Uhhh, what's for dinner?"

Everyone laughed, the tension breaking around us.

"Tonight we have our welcome dinner," Bara explained. "It will be at a traditional Czech restaurant and it is already paid for. Come ready to make friends."

We met back up a few hours later in front of the large entrance to the courtyard. I hung back and walked alone, not knowing where I fit in. It hadn't clicked yet for me; that moment of clarity, where I knew what I was doing and why I was there, still hadn't happened. It was still new, but when would it come? Most of the other kids seemed to already know who they would be spending the semester with. I, on the other hand, was still waiting.

As I decided to hurry up and catch up to Emily, a girl grabbed my shoulder. "Hi! You're the other girl from Colorado, right?" Her chestnut waves hung just at her shoulder blades, and her brown eyes sparkled with kindness. I took to her instantly.

"Yeah, I'm from Denver. Sorry, what's your name? I've met so many people and I can't seem to—"

"Oh no, don't worry, me too!" She cut me off and giggled a genuine, girlish laugh. "I can't remember anyone's name yet except my roommates'. I'm Celeste, from CSU. You go to CSU, right?"

"No," I replied. "I went there my freshman year and then transferred to University of Colorado. I'm at the Denver campus now, but I miss Fort Collins sometimes."

For the rest of the walk, we swapped names of people we might and might not know. Turns out we had no mutual acquaintances, but as the only two girls from Colorado, we had something in common. After a few stops on the tram, we disembarked at Národni třida. We had crossed the river, and I didn't recognize anything around us. Bara led the way through small and winding streets, cobblestoned like the rest of the city. Locals on their way out to dinner hurried passed us, some stopping to stare at the group of American students making their way through this part of the city. Clearly, Bara had picked one of the least-touristy places she could think of. I appreciated this, though realized we looked out of place.

Inside, the host led us through the smoky restaurant to a private nook, where there were three empty tables waiting for us. Two were quite large, and the last one was set for only four people. Instantly all the boys (save for one I hadn't yet met) took one table, and everyone else sat at the other large one. Celeste grabbed my hand and pulled me to the smaller table.

"Come on, we'll be able to talk better here," she said, smiling.

I followed her. "Hey, Lexie! Come sit here. There's another spot!" I looked over at the direction that Celeste was waving and saw a beautiful and faintly muscular girl with long, blonde hair and shining blue eyes coming toward us.

"Lex is my roommate. She's from Washington, you'll love her!"

Lexie sat down across from me, and we quickly got the introductions out of the way. I learned both Lexie and Celeste were single, one of the first questions they asked of me. I tiptoed around the subject. "Not really. I have a boyfriend I've been on and off with for, wow, five years now... but we said our good-byes when I came out here."

"So did you break up?" Lexie asked.

"Well not officially, but I know it's over. It's one of those things where it works because we see each other all the time. Now that I'm out here, I just think it's a good way for us to end things." It sounded terrible, but it was true.

"I'm going through a breakup too," Celeste confided. "We were together for a year. He went abroad to Italy for six weeks last summer, and when he came home he just dumped me."

"Wow." I looked at her. "So you guys broke up a year ago?" I didn't want to push her, but it seemed like a long time to still be hurt over a guy.

"Yeah. I haven't totally gotten over it yet."

Lexie nodded. "I totally get that. I broke up with my boyfriend in the spring but he won't leave me alone. Now that I'm out here I'm hoping it will die out."

So I wasn't the only one running away from something. "I just don't want to deal with Mark, my boyfriend. I came out here for me," I added.

"Yes. Absolutely!" Celeste fervently agreed. I looked at Lexie, who was nodding her head too.

"I just want to find someone I have a connection with. And if after this semester I only have a connection with myself, that's okay." I smiled at my new friends as they raised their glasses to toast to what I'd said. Celeste and Lexie both laughed easily, something I quickly came to enjoy about their company. The rest of the welcome dinner was spent laughing and swapping stories, many of which were strikingly similar to one another.

I hadn't yet noticed these two girls before, and hadn't spoken to them at all during the meeting with Bara earlier. But the more we talked, the more I realized how strange it was that out of everyone here, the three of us together were alone at this table getting to know one another. We had the strangest things in common, and with each passing moment I started to feel as if these two were my guardian angels. Someone must have sent them to Prague just for me, for me to love and learn from, to bring out the best in me.

After our baked apples, apparently a traditional Czech dessert, were finished, everyone headed home. Bara gave each group of roommates pointed directions on which direction to walk back for their tram. I found myself walking back toward the river with my two roommates, and the boys from Cozy. Everyone was quickly becoming identified by their apartments while we all learned each other's names. All the other flats were on the opposite side of the river from us, and we were the only two groups so close to one another.

"Who wants to hit a bar?" Emily skipped forward, slinging her arm through Mason's. She'd pulled her shoulder length hair back into a loose ponytail that kept getting stuck on the straps of her black spaghetti-strapped tank top.

"Definitely," Charlie agreed. He brought a pack of Newports out of his pocket and drew one out, fitting in with the rest of the smokers on the uneven streets.

ALAINA ISBOUTS

7

August, Prague.

It was the darkest part of the night when we finally made it back to the U Apartment from the welcome dinner. We quickly discovered our neighborhood had no streetlights. I shut my eyes tight and opened them again, waiting to see if I could tell the difference between the night sky and nothing at all. My roommates and I, along with our new friends from Cozy, made our way to our flat.

Charlie hung back to light another Newport. Emily had jumped on Mason's back, and Mason didn't look like he appreciated the gesture.

I moved toward the lock, dodging underneath the spiders.

"Those are fucking disgusting," Nicholas said, looking up at the web above us.

I looked over my shoulder at him. "I know," I agreed as I shoved my key in the lock. "I can't stand under them and open the door at the same time!" My blood pressure started to rise, and I couldn't get the door to unlatch.

"You're fucking out of control," Mason said to Emily behind us, laughing. "What's your deal?"

"Whooooooo! I'm in Prague, motherfuckers!" she called out.

Alex shushed her. "You're going to wake people up!"

Nicholas's hand grabbed the keys from me as my hands shook. "Hurry the fuck up," he said to me with a smile. Grateful, I flashed him a smile and stepped back, letting him open the door for me.

Finally the door creaked open, and I ran inside first to avoid the spiders. "You guys, *where* is the light switch around here?"

"It's over here somewhere," Alex said, fumbling along the right side of the hall. "Ahh, there." The lights above us clicked on, and Mason jogged up the stairs. The rest of us followed behind.

"Do we need to turn them off?" I asked Alex.

"No, they are on a timer I think."

I didn't know how she had figured this out, but I didn't care. I had to pee and wasn't going to run up those stairs again in the dark after having to go back down and turn off the lights. She twisted the key in the lock of our apartment door, and it popped right open.

I ran in ahead of everyone else and straight to the bathroom. I was sure that everyone could hear me peeing with these deep European toilets, but after a second they were all laughing so loudly, I knew they couldn't hear me. By the time I finished, washed my hands, and made my way into the kitchen, Emily had opened a bottle of red wine and was emptying it generously into glasses.

"Where did you get that?" I exclaimed.

"I picked it up this afternoon. You guys, it was soooo cheap," she bragged. "Like, only a few dollars, I think."

One taste quickly told us why. The room temperature wine had a sour smell, and tasted the same way, as if someone had left it open in a hot room. I looked around as everyone else made the same face.

"Oh well, it's all we have now." Charlie laughed.

Emily got up and brought her laptop into the kitchen, pulling up some music. I took another sip of wine, deciding it wasn't terrible. If I had been sober I'd never been able to drink it, but the *pivo*, what the Czechs called beer, at the pub had dulled my taste buds. Emily started dancing in the kitchen as everyone grabbed empty seats around the table.

"So what's your story?" Nicholas said to me. I grabbed the empty chair next to him and sat down, laughing.

"My story? Like my life story?"

He took a swig of his wine. "God, this shit is awful."

"Well, I'm originally from New York. And I'm kind of drunk."

Nicholas laughed. "Me too."

"Which, the being-from-New-York part or the drunk part?"

"Both, actually." He smiled at me for the first time.

"I thought you were from LA?" I asked. I remembered the emails, he'd mentioned he went to UCLA. "Or do you just go to school there?"

"I've lived in LA for years now, but I was born in New York. My family moved to Pennsylvania when I was in elementary school, then out to the west coast."

I set my wine on the table a little too forcefully and wine slopped over the side, splashing onto the wood. "Get out. Me too! I mean, I was born in New York, and then my parents moved us to Pittsburgh when I was in middle school, and then out to Colorado."

Nicholas looked at me. "That's fucking weird."

On the other side of the table, Mason and Charlie were in a discussion about the song that was playing.

"This shit is fucking awful," Mason said to Emily. "What is this?"

She got up, knocking over the chair behind her. "Flaming Lips, I think," she said, turning the volume up. "It's soooo good. My ex took me to this show last year." She put her arms up, wine glass still in hand, and began to dance. Little drops of red spilled out of her glass, onto her shoulders and the kitchen floor.

"You're a fucking mess," Mason said to her, laughing. I got the feeling that Mason was definitely not shy about his feelings. He was calling it like it was with Emily, but she didn't seem to mind, or didn't notice. Alex had scooted her chair over closer to Mason and was asking him about bands he liked.

"I need another smoke," announced Charlie, pushing his chair back from the table. He left the kitchen and passed through my bedroom, opening the balcony door and stepping outside.

I turned my attention back to Nicholas. "So what classes are you taking? And is it Nicholas? Or Nick?"

"It's either one. My family calls me Nicholas, but my buddies call me Nick. And, I've got a Women's Studies course, Social Anthro, and a marketing class on Thursday nights. That one is going to fucking suck."

"Hey, I'm in all those except the marketing class," I said. I was happy to have one new friend in my classes. I'd learned at dinner that neither of my new friends shared a class with me.

"Yeah, I think everyone is taking the Czech language class. We're all gonna need it. What are you studying?"

"Well, I'm a creative writing major." I didn't know what else to say. "I really want to be a writer."

"I'm into creative writing, too. You know, essays, poetry."

"Wow, poetry, really? I could never... I mean, I've had to for classes before, but they're just awful. I do love writing essays though." I looked at him closer. *Poetry? Really?* We'd said a few words to each other at the bar in passing, but this was my first actual conversation with Nicholas. For some reason, I felt happy to have him to myself, as my roommates jockeyed for Mason's attention.

"Yeah, they just kind of come to me sometimes." He took another long drink from his glass. "The essays are mostly political." I was taken aback, again. Politics? Poetry? I looked him up and down again, and he noticed. "What?"

"Nothing. I just—you don't seem like the political or poetic type." This type of honesty gave me a reputation for being a bitch back at home, but here, I didn't care.

He smiled at me again, and for the first time I noticed his bright blue eyes. They were a deep, radiant blue, the color of oceans I'd only

68

ever seen in photos. My favorite color. The opposite blue of Mark's cool, icy blues. They were warm, inviting. He broke the silence. "You're into politics?"

"Yeah. I'm a pretty staunch Democrat."

"Me too. Kerry was never going to win."

Alex sloshed some more wine into my glass without me asking, and I picked it up again. "I really hoped he would. Bush—ugh. I took my brother to vote because I knew he was voting for Kerry."

"How many siblings do you have?"

"Just one younger brother. James. How about you?"

"Three sisters and a single mom. An older sister, a younger sister, and a twin."

"That's a lot of women to grow up with."

"Fuck yes it is. I'm the only guy my age who knows all the NSYNC lyrics, *Sex and the City* lines, and way too much about periods."

I laughed. "So are you admitting you're a big NSYNC fan?"

"Fuck no. But I bet you are. You look like a boy band kind of girl."

I shook my head furiously. "No, definitely not. My cousin Kimberly was huge into the Backstreet Boys, but I never really got into the boy bands. Unless you count U2 a boy band." I took another drink of wine. "And I *better* not look like a boy band kind of girl."

"No shit? I went to one of their shows a couple years back. The *Elevation* tour. Amazing show. Amazing." He took another long swig.

I had never met another U2 fan my age. Usually I raved about their music with Dad, and I had dragged Mark to a show that I had bought two tickets for just a few months earlier. Who *was* this guy?

"Oh, my God, I just went to the *Vertigo* tour in April! It was the best concert of my life." I said and gave Nicholas another look. I was surprised at how much we had in common, especially since I had written him off at first glance. He seemed so... *LA* at first. And now, well... now

69

I wanted to drink terrible wine and talk to him all night. I found myself smoothing my hair and pressing my lips together.

Emily, Mason, and Alex were all dancing in the kitchen now. Mason had put on some songs of Emily's he deemed "much better," when Charlie reentered the kitchen. He grabbed my hand and pulled me up to dance. I threw my hands up and closed my eyes, moving my head in rhythm with the unfamiliar song. This was what I had left for. I was dancing in my apartment in the middle of the night with five strangers, and it was the best time I'd had so far.

By the time the Cozy boys left our apartment to walk to their house, the sun was peeking into our bedroom. Emily yanked the thick curtains closed before collapsing onto her bed.

"I hope you don't care if I sleep naked," she said, wiggling out of her shirt and tossing it on top of her already-discarded underwear.

I flopped down on my bed, my head spinning. "Not in the least." I kicked my feet under the covers, pulling the blanket up to my chin and settling into the twin mattress. I closed my eyes and smiled, running the night over and over in my mind. I had made quite a few new friends. My mind buzzed with words from my conversations with Lexie and Celeste, and with Nicholas.

I didn't even hear my phone vibrate from Mark's phone call, over and over, as I fell asleep.

Δ

Tap, tap, tap, tap, tap, tap. My heels clicked against the cobblestones. The warm August breeze blew past us and we walked with it, moving like the wind, unsure of where it was taking us. The streets in Staré Město turned and twisted like snakes; maps were no match for the archaic avenues that sprawled throughout Old Town Square. It was a Thursday night and the same group that had gone out after the welcome dinner the night before, had met up again to explore bars in another part of the city.

Celeste, Lexie, and I were with all three of the boys from Cozy House, plus John. I was walking with Celeste and Lexie who were talking about their Thursday night rituals back home. Celeste was recalling evenings with her ex, while Lexie talked about getting drinks after ice skating practice. I thought of what I would be doing if I was home right now instead of nine time zones away. Thursday nights were always girls' night for Eliza—one of my best friends—and me. I'd park my car at the restaurant where Mark worked, and she and I would spend the night bar hopping. Neither of us had classes on Fridays or serious jobs where we couldn't show up hung over. I had a small pang of homesickness before I realized that I was doing almost the exact same thing here. Friends and bars and Thursday nights. A universal constant.

Nicholas and John were leading the pack, map spread out between them. Every few minutes they stopped and adjusted the huge piece of paper, folding and unfolding, twisting and turning. I wasn't sure where we were heading, but I was excited to be going there. The night felt full of possibilities. There was a certain energy that accompanied nights like these: out with people I didn't yet know too well, to a place I'd never been, in a city that was big and foreign and mysterious. I felt as if anything could happen.

We'd been walking for twenty minutes or so and had just turned onto a street we had definitely already walked down before. The same Bohemia Bagel café with its shuttered doors, the same hookah bar, dimly lit, windows thick with fog and smoke. Our group slowed to a stop again.

"You guys having some trouble?" I called to John and Nicholas.

John put his hand up. "We got it. We can handle this," he stared at the map intently. Lexie walked over to them and gently took the map out of John's hands. Nicholas gave up and walked over to Celeste and me.

"I'm pretty sure we've been walking in a circle." I laughed.

Nicholas frowned at me, looking thoroughly confused. "The streets out here are impossible!" He shook his head.

"That's why I'm not helping," Celeste said. John and Lexie were now huddled over the map together.

"Let's just find a bar. Any bar," yelled Mason. He held out his hand to Charlie, who pulled out his pack of Newports to share with him. "Ugh, I forgot you smoked menthols." Mason gagged.

"Where are we?" I stepped off the sidewalk and into the middle of the street, searching for a sign. The red signs with white borders were usually mounted on the side of buildings near corners, and always included the section of the city.

"Here. Masná," Celeste called out.

"Yeah, I saw that sign before too, Masná. I think this road curves. We've definitely been making a circle," Lexie agreed.

"Let's just walk down this way," I said, starting down the road. "I think there's a more main road here."

We headed against the flow of traffic, seldom passing a car. It was strange to me to see cars driving in Old Town. It was hard to process seeing vehicles on these timeworn cobblestoned roads, that were hardly wide enough to fit a car. We reached a wider road and paused again to regroup.

"Let's head this way!" Lexie said, making a right and leading the group away from Old Town Square.

"You smoke menthols?" Celeste asked Charlie, who had just caught up with us and Nick.

"Yeah, smoked 'em for years. Newports," he said. "You can't get them out here though."

"Did you bring some with you?" I asked.

"Yeah, multiple cartons. But when they're gone..." Charlie took a long drag of his cigarette. "You smoke?" he asked us.

Celeste shook her head vigorously. "No. Never."

"Once in a while," Nicholas revealed.

"Me too," I agreed. "A social smoker, I guess?"

Nick looked at me. "Same here. What do you smoke?"

"Marlboro Lights," I admitted.

He raised his eyebrows. "How very Carrie Bradshaw of you," he said sarcastically.

"Ha ha," I said back to him in the same tone. "My girlfriend Eliza smokes them so I always just shared with her." I thought of Eliza, wondering what she'd be doing for her first Thursday night without me.

And just as if he'd read my thoughts, Nicholas asked, "So if you were back at home, what would you be doing tonight?"

"I was just thinking about that," I said incredulously. "I'd be out with Eliza. We have girls' nights on Thursdays. How about you?"

"Me? I'd be working," Nicholas said.

"Where did you work?" I asked.

"A hotel in Santa Monica. I was a bellman. Great tips," he added, raising his eyebrows. "We'd get off at eleven and a bunch of us would go out after."

"I have a friend who does that, kind of. He's a valet." I was careful not to use the word *boyfriend*, but I was unsure of why.

Nicholas nodded. "The money's good."

We continued along. Next to me, Charlie and Celeste had gotten into a debate about smoking. Celeste was talking about her father's business—he was a mortician—and some of the awful things she'd seen from smokers. Nick slowed his pace down a little, and I slowed down too.

"Ooooookay." Nick dramatically dragged the word out, shaking his head toward Charlie and Celeste.

"Yeah," I snickered.

"So if you were out tonight, back at home, smoking your Marlboro Lights, what would you be drinking?" Nick asked.

Ahead, John and Lexie made a left turn, and we followed suit.

I thought for a second. "A gimlet. Gin, not vodka."

"What's that?"

"Gin and lime juice. That's it."

"Interesting. I'm not a gin person."

I looked over to him. "So what's your drink?"

"On a night like tonight? Vodka Red Bull."

I shook my head. "Ew." *Okay, maybe he is an LA douchebag*, I thought to myself.

We had stopped walking. In front of us was a bar, all lit up and crowded. Black awnings outside read Tretter's New York Bar. John was already pulling the door open and Lexie was walking inside.

Celeste turned around to me. "Is this what we were looking for?"

I shrugged.

Mason came up behind us. "Who cares, it's a bar, isn't it?" He walked inside, and the rest of us followed.

The bar spread over the left side of the room, with small round tables littering the right side. Thirties' jazz music bounced off the maroon walls and wooden bistro chairs, filling the air with tinge of nostalgia. The bar was busy but not yet packed. We pushed our way past the first few full tables, heading toward the middle of the bar.

"Why don't you girls grab a table, and we'll grab the first round," John called over the music to us.

We silently agreed, and Celeste, Lexie, and I snagged the first three round, high-top tables we could find together. I sat at the far end of the three tables, Celeste in the middle, and Lexie at the other end.

"This isn't what I was expecting to find," Lexie yelled over the music. The bar was trying for an upscale vibe, very different from the downtrodden pubs with slot machines in them that we'd passed along the way. There was a Prohibition-era style to the bar: maroon painted walls, vintage bar stools, and bartenders wearing white tops with black bowties.

Art deco pieces hung on the walls, along with black and white photographs.

Celeste eagerly nodded across the table.

"Me neither, but I love it," I yelled back. I looked over to the bar, where Charlie, John, Mason, and Nicholas were waiting for their drinks.

"It's perfect," Celeste said. "You guys, how lucky are we to be here?" She looked around.

I was quickly learning that Celeste was the eternal optimist, always making sunny statements and sharing her gratefulness for people or her surroundings. It was lovely to be around.

"Can we just do this all the time, and forget the whole school thing?" Lexie laughed, dancing in her seat to the music.

"I have a feeling this is what we will be doing a lot of the time," I said.

"All right, here we go," Charlie leaned between two stools, setting down four beers on the table. "They're all the same."

Nick was right behind him with three more beers and one cocktail glass, garnished with a lime. He set the half-liter glasses down in the middle of the table, then slid the cocktail glass across the table to me.

"What's this?" I said, raising my eyebrows to him and grabbing my bag off the empty chair next to me. I was hoping he'd sit in it.

He took the chair. "Gimlet. Gin, not vodka." He smiled at me.

"Wow." I raised the glass to my lips and took a sip. "It's perfect." I was surprised by his gesture. Was he being friendly? Flirting with me? I wasn't sure.

"Okay, let's have a toast," Nick called out to the table. Everyone raised their glasses.

"Wait. Where's John?" Lexie asked.

I looked over to the bar, where John was still waiting.

"Yo, John! We're having a toast here, come on!" Charlie hollered across the bar.

"One sec!" John bellowed. Moments later, the bartender set a large bucket on the counter and a tray filled with glasses. John balanced the tray in one hand, wrapped his other arm around the bucket, and made his way across the walkway to our table. He dropped the bucket onto the table, chunks of ice jumping out.

"What is this?" Celeste said.

"I figured we needed to kick this semester off right." John started handing out wide-mouthed champagne glasses to everyone at the table off the tray he had been carrying. "A champagne toast."

Lexie was delighted. "Oh, my gosh, you shouldn't have!"

He flashed her a smile. "It was nothing. The bottles were like twenty bucks." The table burst out laughing. Most of us had discovered the night before that Czech wine was nothing to spend money on, and I was sure the champagne would be the same.

John popped open one bottle, and I cheered, a habit I hadn't realized was strange until that moment. My mom always cheered and clapped when someone opened a bottle. Usually champagne was used to celebrate something, so she'd celebrate when a bottle was opened. I chalked it up to enthusiasm. He walked around the table, pouring a small glass for everyone. When the last glass was filled, he took the last empty seat next to Lexie and raised his glass.

"To an incredible semester filled with good times and good people," he declared in his low, booming voice. We all raised our glasses and toasted, edges clinking against one another. I turned to Nick and smiled as we each took a sip. Within minutes, we'd fallen into conversation on where we wanted to go this semester and what we imagined it would be like.

After the second champagne bottle was empty, Nick excused himself from the seat next to me to join the other guys at the bar to get a round of shots. I watched him walk over to the bar. John, Mason, Nick, and Charlie were standing huddled together. Each had a shot glass in one hand and their other was in the middle, hands stacking on top of each other. Nick looked in my direction and our eyes locked as the boys pulled their hands away and took their shots. Charlie elbowed Nick and his gaze darted away as he emptied his shot glass.

I turned toward the girls and jumped in their conversation as the night disintegrated into bottles of champagne and more rounds of pivo. We sat at our high tops for hours, getting to know each other and laughing into the night.

8

March, New York.

They weren't really hiring interns. After the lockout, people weren't paying as much attention to the sport. Die-hard hockey fans—kids who grew up in Bruins and Flyers jerseys playing street hockey, moving the battered plastic goal posts when cars rolled by—instead grabbed Red Sox hats and Phillies tees. Barry Melrose's slicked back hair ceased to cause hockey fans everywhere to lovingly grimace at the sight of him. The air time usually slotted with the day's best hits and saves and odd-man rushes, was now filled with Nascar and Texas Hold'em tournaments.

It never for one second mattered to me that no one else was watching the National Hockey League anymore. It was going to come back stronger than ever, I was sure, so I applied for their summer internship program. I spent hours on my resume, making sure that it was the perfect blend of professionalism and creativity. Knowing the internship would bring me back to the east coast, my father volunteered to make some calls to people he might know who could help me out. That was my dad's thing, he knew people. No matter what it was you needed, Jack Sorrentino had a list of people he could call to cash in any number of favors he was owed, or would be happy to owe in the future for someone willing to help out a friend of his. He was the kind of guy who instantly gave off the impression that he *mattered*; his frame, somewhere between a middle-aged Robert DeNiro, and Alec Baldwin during his early *30 Rock* days, was commanding; and his handshake firm. His laughter was a contagious, howling, belly-shaking ordeal that showed me, as child, that even when you were a grown-up, some things were still just *that* funny. It was off-putting to people who were unfamiliar with him, but to me, the sound of his laughter instantly transported me to my childhood. My cousins and I would sneak to the open window in the hallway of our summer house, the villa, and hide behind the white linen curtains as the summer breeze blew in. We'd listen to our fathers and uncles outside as the sweet, biting scent of their cigars made its way through the open window, the men laughing and quoting *The Pope of Greenwich Village, The Honeymooners, Seinfeld, The Godfather.* They had their own language in movie one-liners.

I desperately wanted to be back in the city, back in Manhattan. After my parents' divorce, I had joined my mother in her move back to Colorado to be with her family. My father stayed behind in New York, where our seemingly endless network of family was rooted. I left behind aunts, uncles, grandparents. But most importantly to me, I left behind my cousins. Charlotte, Kimberly, and I were raised as sisters. Our lives were an endless parade of summers spent at our summer house, the beach, Thanksgivings and Christmas Eves at our great-grandmother's house, Easter egg hunts in the backyard, and spring break trips together. We were separated by my parent's divorce, the path of my life suddenly turning down a very different road. I was thrilled for the opportunity to get back on what I imagined to be the right track, with Charlotte and Kim, living in the city.

Back when people were still Christmas shopping, Charlotte had secured a summer internship on 53rd Street, a block over from the NHL headquarters. That was her Type A personality. She was incessantly put together. Charlotte planned everything, but managed to make it look effortless. Her fusilli-like curls bounced around her olive complexion and clear skin, save for a few ideally placed freckles. Charlotte was always a step ahead of everyone else, ahead of me, ahead of Kimberly. She knew she was going to be a lawyer since middle school, found the perfect all-American dreamboat boyfriend as soon as she got into college, and continued on with blinders. Despite the many differences from my own manic and spontaneously lived life, we were sisters in every sense of the word—except the biological one. We had already fantasized about our daily lunch dates, happy hours, and our new grown-up lives together. We would walk the same walk every morning, up Ditmars, past the pizza places and nail salons, the only Starbucks in a sea of Greek delis and Italian bakeries, Rose & Joe's, and the shady electronics shop. We would ride the N train into the city and start our careers as lowly interns, she with Fox News and me with the NHL. We'd get coffee for executives who would let it sit cold, rings forming on the solid oak desk underneath, spilling it on proposals and memos and newspapers. It would be the start of the rest of our lives.

My dad came through and called a friend of a friend, an advertising executive for the NHL. He had a few people working under him, but his department was one of many downsized after the complete failure that was the 2004-2005 season. Thanks to Dad's persistence, or some small miracle, this friend of a friend advertisement executive wanted to meet me and requested that I come to his office for an interview. I quickly contacted him to arrange the meeting, and he suggested I come meet the (now only) two members of his marketing team between Christmas and New Year's. Surely just one of them would need my help. Three men, living in the city and working for one of the four major sports leagues in America... it just wouldn't be complete without the female college intern.

I wanted it too much. The league didn't even run an intern program any longer; but the friend of a friend was clearly going out of his way to be nice, and maybe get some free help out of it by way of an intern. And I deserved it. I was convinced I was the only twenty-year-old female who knew who Mike Bossy was, to appreciate and respect Bobby Hull and Gordie Howe, despite my utter loathing of the Red Wings, who knew every team Jeremy Roenick had played for and how much he had been fined for drinking a fan's Slurpee while in the penalty box, who had cried when Patrick Roy retired. Between my passion and my knowledge, I genuinely believed the internship would happen, and it was only a matter of time before Gary Bettman himself shook my hand and said, "Why didn't we hire you years ago?"

When the rejection email inevitably arrived in March, it hit me much harder than it should have. I'd been looking for a way to escape, and my plan hadn't worked. I felt stuck. The idea of a summer in the city had been my way of changing my circumstances. I needed space from Mark. I needed to clear my head. I needed, most of all, to move the direction of my life, but nothing seemed to be working. I knew, unequivocally, that I could not stay in Denver; that if I did, I'd end up moving in with Mark, getting engaged, and it would be too late to get out. It needed to be now. It was a hole I was desperately trying to dig myself out of.

It was time for a bigger shovel.

August, Prague.

It didn't feel like August. It was as if the world around us was perfectly room-temperature. Not a breeze stirred my hair, straightened and hanging around my face. My back, bare from the backless tank top I picked for the night, was without a single shiver.

Despite the lovely evening outside, I was getting anxious. We were standing outside our university, trying to figure out where to go for our first Friday night out. But we didn't really know where to go. Alex and Mason had run inside a pizza joint to grab a slice to eat on the way to the bar. Emily, Celeste, Lexie, and I stood in a circle. Charlie was standing in the middle of the street, smoking a Newport. John and Nicholas had a giant street map unfolded in front of them, charting out our route yet again.

"Uh, so we need to know where we are going first," Nicholas called over to the group of us.

"I have no idea where we should go," Celeste said.

I pursed my lips. "Well, where were we last night? There were some bars over in that area," I called over to Nick and John.

"Yeah, that sounds good," Lexie agreed.

Emily chimed in. "I heard there's a five-story dance club around here, just across the bridge."

I cringed. A five-story dance club? That wasn't exactly the kind of place I wanted to spend my night. Celeste and Lexie exchanged glances.

"I'm up for whatever," Lexie finally offered.

"Me too," said Celeste.

John looked up from the map. "Okay. Five-story dance club it is. Do you know where this place is?"

Emily was now leading the way. Alex and Mason ran up behind us, a slice of greasy pizza with green olives bouncing in Alex's hand. Emily's heels clicked on the cobblestones. After every few steps, she'd tip to one side, her arms straightening out to balance herself. Alex and Mason couldn't stop laughing, Alex's laughter more innocent than Mason's.

Just up ahead was the Charles Bridge. I hadn't yet seen it in the evening. In the light of the day, street lamps were camouflaged by statues, swarms of people and artists trying to make a buck. But at night, the soft, inviting, yet somehow ominous glow of the street lamps that stood between each statue were the real attractions. During the day, street performers and tour guides littered the bridge. Tourists walked through slowly, clutching purses and fanny packs tightly in front of them. Locals pushed their way through the crowds of people, walking right in the middle of the bridge with a sense of ownership. Music played and cameras flashed. But with the sun hidden far behind the castle, the bridge was quiet, like any other road in the city. The Vltava rushed below us, and unlike any other time, the bubbling was audible. A man was walking quickly toward us, his quick pace contrasted by long, slow drags of his cigarette. A couple sat huddled together near the statue of Saint Augustine, their hands entwined. The statues were more beautiful at night, the grime and imperfections hidden. The streetlights were kind to the statues and cast a soft, warm glow to each one.

"Oh, my gosh. It's so, so beautiful," Celeste said next to me, her tone hushed.

"Yeah. I've not been here at night," I agreed.

"I can't believe we're here. Just a week ago I was having dinner with my family at Austin's in Old Town. How am I in Prague right now?" She giggled.

I looked at her. There was something so genuine about Celeste. Her laugh, her observations. She wore her heart on her sleeve, and it was endearing. I put my arm around her and shrugged. "It's pretty amazing."

Behind her, Lexie let out a shriek of laughter. I spun my head around to see her and John walking twenty feet behind us. He was telling a story, animatedly, his arms spread out and his eyes wide. Lexie clapped her hands and threw her head back, her blonde curls falling down her back.

Celeste leaned in close to me. "I think there's something there," she whispered.

"Really?" It was just four days into the semester, and classes had yet to start for us. Were people already coupling off? With only sixteen of us, there were bound to be some romantic entanglements. My mind buzzed back to Mark. I hadn't spoken to him since my first night in the apartment, when I'd second-guessed my choice to come to Prague. Phone calls were going to be few and far between. Even texts to the States wouldn't happen often. International rates were astronomical with my prepaid phone, I'd learned the hard way. Already, I'd resorted to email. I had sent him a brief one yesterday from the EOO office, with a short summary of what had happened so far. I didn't miss him and found myself often forgetting about him, going hours at a time without thinking of him once. I couldn't tell if I was surprised by this or not. I was enjoying my space, my distance. It was nice to not hear Mark's voice, to not constantly check in. It was nice to be lost, and for someone to not know where I was every moment of every day, to ask someone's permission to go out with friends.

We'd made it halfway across the bridge when Alex started pointing to something in the distance off the south side of the bridge.

Mason and Emily were a few feet in front of her standing and looking over the water. Nick and Charlie were just ahead of us. Since the couple near Malá Strana, we hadn't passed another person. It was deserted.

"What is Nick doing?" Celeste wondered out loud.

Up ahead, Nick stopped in front of a big pile of something on the ground. He kneeled for a moment, and then continued on his way.

"What is that?" I asked.

In a few feet, I found the answer. A man was kneeling on the bridge, his forehead pressed against the cobblestones. His arms were stretched out in front of him, hands cupped together. There was no cardboard sign. No hat or cup collecting change. He wore a thick wool coat, warn thin into holes in patches. The smell of him wafted up toward Celeste and me. A single coin, twenty krowns, was in his hands.

We kept walking. When enough distance was between us and the beggar, Celeste sighed loudly. "Wow."

"Yeah," I breathed. I wished I had stopped, but I was too taken aback. I was used to cheeky signs: Why lie? I Need a Beer. Or travel routes, someone looking for a ride or money for a bus ticket. Never before had I seen someone literally begging. Down on his knees, too ashamed to lift his head. That was what it looked like to have nothing, to ask for charity, humbled as a human could be. Nicholas had obviously stopped to put the coin in the man's hand.

I looked ahead at him. "That was a kind thing to do."

Celeste smiled. "I think he's a kind guy."

"Yeah. He's not how I imagined he would be," I admitted.

"How so?"

"I don't know. We emailed, just once or twice, about meeting up to travel before. It didn't happen. But he seemed so jokey. I pictured him being more how John is, the class clown type of guy."

"We found it!" Emily's voice screamed. She and Alex hugged, jumping up and down. Mason and Nicholas were laughing about something.

"Let's goooooo!" Mason bellowed down the bridge to us.

Celeste and I picked up the pace, John and Lexie right behind us. At the end of the bridge we made a right, walking south along the water. The street sign nailed into the building above said Křižovnická. Staré Město was peaceful. No other twenty-somethings were on their way to the bar. In Denver on Thursday through Saturday nights, you couldn't walk down Market Street without touching another person. Bar after bar after bar had their doors and windows open to the street, music thumping, bouncers walking the line between inviting people in and pushing them away. I imagined something similar, a five-story club along a strip of other bars. Instead, Emily led us up to a building that looked like any other in Staré Město. It looked to be a few hundred years old and was painted the color of cream that had been sitting out for a few days. No windows open. No music could be heard. In neon lights, the name Karlovy Lázně shone over the windows.

Emily pulled open the doors and walked in, not waiting for anyone behind her. Mason and Alex followed. Nick stopped outside, waiting for the rest of our crew to catch up.

Charlie lit another Newport. "Man, smoking inside bars here. It's fucking awesome," he said to no one in particular, cigarette between his lips as he walked over the threshold. Celeste and I walked over to Nick.

"Where are John and Lexie?" he asked.

"They're just behind us," I replied. As if on cue, they rounded the corner, Lexie still laughing.

"You guys ready for some Eastern European dancing?" John called across the sidewalk to us.

"Yeah," Lexie said with faux seriousness. "Let's do this." She walked one foot in front of the other, sashaying her hips like she was on a catwalk to the front doors. She pulled one open, jutting out her hip and tossing her hair behind her. She turned around. "Come on in," she half-whispered, her voice jokingly sexy.

Nicholas walked in, John, Celeste, and me right behind. The walls were painted bright red, like a traffic signal glaring into the room. An oversized, black-lacquered chandelier, unlit, hung low in the center of the small room. To the right was an oversized bar, also black, lined with people holding glasses and bartenders mixing cocktails. Just beyond the bar was a packed dance floor, with a DJ in the back corner, dressed in black mesh from head to toe. His head bobbed up and down to the beat of the song he'd picked, an orange beanie pulled down over his forehead, eyes closed tightly, hands moving across the sound board he clearly had memorized. Lights flashed across the room, green and red and blue and purple. I looked up, mesmerized. There were four balconies above, each looking down to the central dance floor in front of me.

"So this is a five-story club!" Celeste shouted back to me.

I shrugged. "I guess so!"

Lexie appeared through the sea of people, grabbing Celeste's shoulder. "You guys, each floor has a different music theme! Where do you guys want to go?"

"To the bar!" I yelled over the deep bass music.

Celeste laughed and Lexie grabbed my hand. I reached back and grabbed Celeste's, and we pushed our way through the people. We had already lost the rest of our group. A cocktail of cigarette smoke, body odor, and skunked beer made its way through my nostrils. The music pounded inside of me. People moved over each other on the dance floor. I looked back and squeezed Celeste's hand. She grinned, ear to ear, and squeezed mine back. Lexie was still pulling my arm ahead, pushing her way through to the bar.

Minutes later we stopped. Immediately two Czech guys homed in on Lexie, drawn to her blonde hair. Three shot glasses were dropped on the bar in front of us, clear liquor spilling and splashing into the glasses and onto the counter around them. One guy, hair spiked and bleached, winked at Lexie and held up a glass to toast. The three of us took the shots, toasting the traditional Czech way. First clinking the rim of the glass, then the bottom, then pounding the glass on the bar, then bottoms up. We hadn't been here long, but it was one of the first things we learned—along with the Czech translation for beer.

"Wheeeeew!" Lexie screamed. Celeste puckered her lips and squeezed her eyes closed.

"Another round!" Celeste yelled.

I screamed with laughter, and our glasses were filled again.

Two more rounds and we left our shot glasses empty on the bar, cold glasses of Budvar accompanying us onto the dance floor.

There three of us danced together, beers in hand, purses slung across our bodies. It wasn't too long before Charlie found us on the dance floor. I grabbed his hand, claiming him as my dance partner. John and Nicholas showed up minutes later, and partnered up with the other girls, John with Celeste and Nicholas with Lexie. Minutes faded away and time was measured in songs and drinks; three drinks ago, I went outside; during the last song, she danced with him. We ignored the unfamiliar, senseless lyrics and paid attention to the parts of songs that spoke a language we all understood, and moved to the rhythm together.

"Need another pivo?" Charlie called to me as the music quieted. I shook my head no. "How about you?" he yelled to Celeste. She nodded, and the two of them made their way back to the bar.

Next to me, John and Lexie had found one another and were dancing, their hands woven together. He had his hands around her lower back, her hands up above his neck. They smiled flirtatiously at each other. There chemistry was obvious, as was their attraction and interest in one another.

The shots I'd taken with Lexie and Celeste made their way through my bloodstream. I finished my beer and put my hands over my head, closing my eyes and moving my hips to the Nelly Furtado song that had just started blaring over the speakers. It felt so good to move. The feeling of being lost in a crowd, alone, was not a feeling that scared me. I let the music fill me up and move me, alone. This was what I wanted. To feel unseen, one in a crowd, no eyes watching me. Just as I made my way past John and Lexie to the rest of the crowded dance floor, I felt hands on my side. Strong hands gripped my hips from behind, fingers wrapping around my stomach toward my belly button. I didn't move them, but flipped my head over my shoulder to see who was touching me. Nick smiled and moved with me, pulling me in closer to him, running his hands up my sides and grabbing my wrists. Our hands found one another's. I could feel his chest behind me, and I leaned into him. Lexie spotted us and raised her eyebrows at me, never breaking rhythm with John. I shrugged at her and kept dancing. I didn't want to think. The alcohol was making my mind a little fuzzy. I liked it.

When the song was over, I spun around to face Nick. "You're a good dancer," I said.

"Thanks. I've been dancing for years." He flashed me that smile I was starting to recognize: mischievous, kind, and sexy all at once.

I was taken aback. "Really?"

He laughed. "Yeah. Really."

The next song started, volume escalating. Nick's arms wrapped around me, his hands over the back pockets of my jeans. I raised my eyebrows at him, surprised at his forwardness. He let out a shy laugh but never broke my gaze. *Surely he was just having fun... right?* I played along, putting my hand behind his neck, running them up through the back of his head, through his sandy hair. We moved our feet together. Nick's face moved closer to mine, our foreheads nearly touching. My heart was pounding, my body temperature rising. I told myself it was just the music. Before long, I needed some air.

"I could use another drink," I said, breaking the tension. As much as my body wanted to be closer to his, I needed a break.

"Let's go," he said.

I instantly cooled off as Nick moved away from me, walking over toward the bar. I followed close behind him, not wanting to get separated. I no longer knew where anyone else in our group was.

"Where is everyone?" I shouted above the music once we stopped at the bar.

"Mason, Emily, and Alex were on the hunt for... something." He stopped short.

"What?" I inquired.

A bartender appeared. "*Dva pivos*," Nick called over to him. He turned his back to us, off to retrieve our drinks from a cooler.

"Coke, I think."

My stomach flipped. Drugs were not my thing. Mark had tried cocaine once, in high school at a house party. The night had ended with him holding a knife to his wrist, threatening to cut, me daring him to. I was hoping Nicholas wasn't into the drug scene. I knew Lexie and Celeste weren't into them, and knew my friendship with Nick would immediately cool down if that was his thing, too.

"That's really not my thing," I said nervously. "I mean, I'm really not into drugs. Especially coke."

He shook his head. "Me neither. Never tried it. Never will."

I breathed a deep sigh of relief, and a rush of affection flooded my body. What kind of guy was this? He liked U2, creative writing, wasn't into drugs. He'd flipped some krowns to the homeless man on the bridge and had the same sarcastic personality I did. He danced in a way that I knew I shouldn't appreciate so much while I was in a relationship with someone else. He seemed to be the anti-Mark.

The bartender came back, sliding two pilsners over to us. Nick pulled a few coins out of his pocket and set them down, handing me a beer. The icy glass felt refreshing in my hand, and I pressed it against my collarbone. I stared at Nick. A feeling I couldn't quite put my finger on was creeping over me. I couldn't take my eyes off him. His shirt stretched tight over his chest, and I could see his arms were solid as he lifted his beer bottle up. I had not been immediately attracted to him, but was finding myself undoubtedly drawn to him.

"Ready?" I asked him. I wanted to get back on the dance floor with him, wanted to see where the night would take us next.

"Let's go see if we can find Lexie and John," he said. I nodded my head and followed him through the crowd.

"I also haven't seen Celeste and Charlie in a while," I said into his ear, partially out of necessity and partially as an excuse to get closer to him. I looked across the dance floor. People filled every inch of the room, but I saw no familiar faces. We pushed through them, searching for our friends. A hand grabbed my shoulder.

"Hey!" Celeste appeared. "We've been looking for you guys!" Her hair had been thrown up into a ponytail, her face shiny, "Where have you been?"

"Dancing," I said. I tried to give her a look, but she threw me a confused stare, unable to figure out what I was telepathically telling her. "Just me and Nick. We don't know where John and Lexie are." I looked around. "Where's Charlie?"

Celeste giggled. "He was just right behind me," she said. "This place is *so* packed!"

I turned around to see Nick talking to John, Lexie dancing her way over to Celeste and me. "Let's goooooooooo," she sang, shaking her hips and putting her hands on Celeste's shoulders. "We haven't been to any other floors."

I grabbed Lexie's arm and pulled her closer to me and Celeste. "So Nick and I..." I stopped. We what? We danced? I couldn't tell if he was just having fun or if it was more than that. Surely no one could dance like that without some sort of intentions.

"Yeah, I saw you." Lexie looked at me, playfully hitting my arm and raising her eyebrows. "You guys were all over each other!"

Celeste gasped. "Adriana! Do you like him?"

I laughed. Was this eighth grade? "We were not *all over* each other, he just started dancing with me, and I went along with it. But..." My voice trailed off again.

"Go for it," Celeste said, raising her beer bottle. "I think he's into you."

"He was just dancing with me. But the way he was dancing..." I dropped my jaw to the girls.

"Yeah, that's what I thought too," Lexie giggled. John appeared behind her.

"Oh, my God, me too," he interjected, his voice high and girly. "I'm feeling a little parched. Headed back to the bar. Anyone else?"

"Yeah, I'll go with you," Lexie said. She playfully slapped me on the ass, then walked away behind John.

Celeste, Nick, and I started dancing, Nick showing off his moves with Celeste. I couldn't take my eyes off of him.

"You know, I think I'm going to run to the bathroom," Celeste said. She widened her eyes at me. "I'll find you guys in a little bit."

I knew she was giving us an excuse to be alone. I felt a knot in my stomach. Didn't I have a boyfriend at home? I hadn't even started classes yet and had already found something I was definitely not looking for. I shook my head, emptying the thoughts out.

"You okay?" Nick called to me. His hands found his way to my hips once more. I moved closer to him, my hands landing on his solid chest.

"Never been better." I looked up at him. He moved his face toward mine, his cheek to mine. I could feel his breath on my ear. A shiver went down my spine. I exhaled loudly as we once again found the music.

We fell into the same rhythm we'd had before, and things were heating up. His hands seemed confident, sure of their moves on my hips, my shoulders, my neck. I couldn't not think about what else his hands could do. I lost track of time, nothing else feeling relevant. My body was starting to tire, and I needed to take a breather. I stopped and turned around. Nick pulled his face back, no longer moving to the music. I stammered for something to say.

"I think I'll take a bathroom break," I said, shakily. My mind was cloudy. All I could think about were Nick's lips. This had escalated, quickly. I couldn't explain it, but I felt as if I needed him. I needed to feel his differences. "Do you know where it is?" It was beyond lame, but I thought it would get us somewhere quieter. I didn't know what I would do, what I wanted to happen. I just wanted him.

"I think it's down those stairs," he offered.

I stared at him blankly. He felt for my hand and laced his fingers between mine. We walked together toward the stairs and made our way down. The music was much quieter. No lights flashed on this lower level. A few round tables stood around the edges of the room, people sitting on plush benches mounted against the walls. I looked around. There was an empty spot in the far corner of the room, near a long and dark hallway where I guessed the bathrooms were. We walked in that direction. A line of people stood a few feet down the hallway.

I stopped in the empty corner, still holding Nick's hand. I made no move to start down the hallway into the line. The music thumped around us. We stared at each other, a foot or so of air between us. Nick dropped my hand.

"Are you going to go?" he asked.

I shook my head. I didn't know what to do now. I had just wanted to go somewhere quieter. Maybe talk to him. The booze was making a fool of me. I couldn't break his stare. He took a step closer to me, then stopped. I bit my lower lip, begging for what I was hoping would come next.

Within seconds, I felt my body push up against the wall behind me as Nick moved into me, his lips on mine impatiently. I put one arm around his back and the other in his hair, pulling him as closer to me, as hard as I could. He bit my bottom lip before kissing me again, harder.

I'd never had a kiss like it before. It was eager and feverish, more of a need than a want. He grabbed ahold of my hair at the base of my neck and pulled my head back just slightly.

"This is only for tonight," he said into my ear, his lips making their way down my neck.

I put my hand on his chest and pushed him, hard, away from me. "I'm not sleeping with you," I said, firmly.

He looked at me, confused. I softened.

"Tonight," I added, with a sly smile. He laughed. I grabbed the top of his jeans and pulled him close to me once more, my lips meeting his. I thought of nothing but how much I wanted to be exactly where I was, in a bar, in a strange city in Europe, making out with someone I hardly knew.

I don't know how long it was before we pulled away, searching for air. We made our way back to the main dance floor. I felt dizzy with passion and drink. At the top of the stairs, Celeste, John, Lexie, and Charlie were standing and talking. The dance floor had fizzled out, and only half the number of people were dancing now as when Nick and I had first disappeared. The girls looked at me, mouths dropping.

"Ohhh damn!" Charlie yelled.

I blushed and looked down. Nick walked over to Charlie and John, who immediately led him over to the bar, away from me.

"What did you do?" Celeste yelled to me through a grin.

"How can you tell?" I looked up. I could feel my face flush again.

Lexie tousled my hair. "Oh, please. Your hair. Also, Charlie said he saw you guys."

"It just... happened," I explained. "I don't know."

"I knew he was into you," Celeste shrieked.

I shook my head. "I need some water."

"I think we are all kind of ready to go," Lexie said. I nodded, and we started making our way outside. The quiet was startling after the noise of the club. My head was starting to pound and swirl.

"There's a Triple A cab right there," Celeste said, pointing across the street. "Let's just go now." She turned to Lexie, and the two girls trotted across the cobblestones.

"Niiiiight!" I yelled across the street. They each waved before jumping into the backseat of the cab.

I took a deep breath. After the crowd and the noise inside, it was lovely to be alone with the silence. The sidewalk by the dance club looked down onto the river. I walked over to the railing and leaned over. The rushing water bubbled underneath. I wanted to stay there all night.

"Adriana!" I heard Charlie, but didn't move. His footsteps grew louder, closer. "You okay?" He put his hand in the middle of my back.

"Yeah, I'm fine." I turned around. "I love the water."

He reached for his pack of Newports in his pocket, and flipped the top open, offering me one. I shook my head.

"Ready to go?" he asked.

"Yeah. Where are John and Nicholas?"

He lit his cigarette, took a long drag. "Just calling a cab," he said on his exhale, blowing the smoke away from me. He looked me in the eye. "Be careful."

I looked at him, puzzled. "What are you talking about?"

He put the cigarette to his lips again. "With Nick. Just be careful."

"What is it?" Did he know something I didn't?

"Nothing," he said, inhaling deeply.

From the corner, I heard Nick's voice. "Cab's here!" he called over.

Charlie flicked his cigarette onto the cobblestones below, stepping on it as he walked over to me. "Let's go," he said, linking his arm through mine.

Nick slid into the front seat next to the cab driver while I crammed in the back, sandwiched between John and Charlie. John's apartment was in a part of the city not near anyone else, so he was heading back with us to crash. The cab sputtered and sped through the dark, winding streets toward Prague Five, where the Cozy House and U Apartment were. We were the farthest out of the city, but the only two apartments that were very close to one another. Paris Hilton's voice cracked through the radio—for some reason her single was everywhere, inescapable—John singing along for comedic effect.

I stared straight ahead into the darkness. The streets ahead were sporadically lit by streetlights, some much darker than others. We passed trams once in a while, running on an infrequent nightly schedule. At stoplights, late night drinkers could be seen through the windows of *herna non-stops*—bars that had a slot machine or two and were open twenty-four hours. Our driver cracked his window, lighting up a cigarette as we paused at a red light.

It was after 3 a.m. by the time we finally pulled up outside the U Apartment. I dug into my bag for my keys as the guys horsed around behind me on the sidewalk. Inside, we found our way to the staircase in the dark. I still couldn't find the light switch, especially not in my current state. I counted the platforms until we arrived at the third landing, and made my way to the apartment door I knew was somewhere straight ahead of me. I grappled with the keys, struggling to get the key in the lock, when I heard a shriek inside my apartment. Confused, I whirled around to look at the guys.

"I guess everyone made it back here," Charlie said. *Of course*, I thought. *It was Emily and Mason and Alex.*

"Okay, Addie, I think you're cut off now." Nick moved past Charlie and took the keys from my fingers. He snapped the key into the lock on the first try and pushed the door open.

Music spilled into the hallway. Emily was dancing, mostly jumping, in the living room, while Mason sat on the couch.

"Is that how you dance?" he yelled, cackling. He was shoveling popcorn into his mouth, occasionally chucking handfuls at her. How had the neighbors not come upstairs yet?

"Hey guys." Alex greeted us as she walked into the living room, gripping the necks of three beer bottles between her fingers. "You made it back!"

John slapped Mason a high five and plopped down on the couch next to him. Nick walked over to Emily and started dancing with her. Emily didn't even notice.

I threw my bag down on the couch and took the beer Alex offered me. "When did you get back?"

"I guess an hour ago or so? I don't know. We're all pretty wasted." She seemed to have her wits about her, despite her statement suggesting otherwise. "Where's Charlie?"

I looked behind me, but he was gone. I shrugged. I took a swig of my beer. "Ugh," I nearly gagged. "I *so* don't want this." I held it out to Alex. "You take it. I'm going to bed."

Mason was continuing his judgment of Emily, who was still dancing solo. Nick was heading toward the sliding glass door that led to the patio, where I saw Charlie out smoking a cigarette. I got up and started toward my bedroom.

"Night," Alex called after me.

I walked into my room, closing the door behind me. I slung my purse over my desk chair and sat down on the edge of my bed, kicking my shoes off. What a night. I knew I was playing with fire with Nick, but I didn't care. It had been *fun.* I stood up and unbuttoned my jeans, sliding them off, when I heard the patio door open on the other side of Emily's bed. "Hey Em," I said, assuming it was her, not turning around.

"Whoa," a male voice said softly.

I whipped around to see Nick standing next to Emily's bed. The patio door he had come from clicked softly behind him. I quickly snatched the comforter off my bed and held it in front of me.

"What are you doing here?" I demanded.

Nick seemed frozen to the spot. His voice was quiet. "I, uh... I was outside on the phone... Emily said I should just crash in here... she's not..." he stammered. He had clearly been caught off guard by the view of my ass he'd just had full on.

I stood nervously at the foot of my bed. "You're sleeping in here?" I asked again.

He started toward me, silently, his steps not making a sound on the thick carpet. He stopped right in front of me. "Unless you want me to go," he said, his eyes searching my face.

I gripped the comforter tighter. "No," I whispered. I couldn't break his gaze. He inched closer to me, his breath on my face. Suddenly, I was very aware I wasn't wearing any pants. I cleared my throat. "Um, just let me get my pajamas..."

Nick stepped back. "Oh right, yeah," he said. He sat on Emily's bed, facing the windows to the patio. "I'm not looking," he announced, bending down to untie his shoes.

I dropped the comforter back onto my twin bed and slid some pajama pants on from my wardrobe. Underneath my shirt, I unhooked my bra and pulled it out of my sleeve. "Okay, you can turn around now." I climbed into bed. "So where's Emily sleeping?"

He stretched out onto her bed. "I think she's sleeping in Alex's room," he said.

I was confused by the nonsensical sleeping arrangements, but I was too tired to care. I lay on my left side to face him in Emily's bed. He rolled on his side to face me.

"I'm so tired," I yawned.

"Me too," he agreed. "Are you a night person?"

"Yeah. I'm definitely not a morning person."

"I'm the same way."

We lay in our separate beds, falling into conversation about our usual routines back at home, things we liked and disliked. Before long, the sun started to peek in through the curtains of the windows. As the rest of the apartment fell quiet, I drifted off to the sound of Nick's voice talking about soccer teams.

10

February, Colorado.

As most Italian grandmothers are, my Nanny was famous for her red sauce, or gravy, as people in the neighborhood called it. No one could make it but her, and anyone who tasted it swore it was the best. I was trying my hardest to duplicate it, but my last lesson had left minor details such as specific ingredients and measurements to the imagination.

"Okay Nanny, so how much olive oil do I put in?"

"Well dawling, use about this much." She poured in a dollop of olive oil, and instantly the kitchen smelled of robust and ripe olives, as if they were crushed just under my feet.

"Ummm, okay, was that a quarter cup? And how much of the wine do I use?"

"Well love, I use about this much." Nanny picked up an open bottle of Merlot and drizzled the deep crimson wine into the pot, the green of the olive oil and the red wine making a new color below. She splashed a little into her glass and handed it to me, letting the bitter and stale wine wash into my underage mouth. She'd been drinking wine since her teens, and having a glass of wine was nothing anyone needed to be of a certain age for, as far as my Italian family was concerned.

"But that's not an amount. I'm looking for, you know, half a cup of this, three tablespoons of that, a recipe." I looked at her face, framed with dark waves of dyed black cherry hair, styled and set each week at her beauty salon up the block. Her eyes were tired but her spirit was always alert, present, kind.

"My love, you cannot recreate years of tradition. How about I make a batch and send it home with you?" Then came a full hug, her frail bones squeezing me tighter than you would think a woman of sixty-nine would be able to squeeze, followed by a kiss on the cheek and a pinch from her long red nails. I could feel her thick lipstick sitting high on my cheekbones. She had a way of lingering in a room after she'd left it. Her lipstick, her smell of garlic and cigarettes, her voice. Always leaving something behind.

I had browned the pork sausage and ground beef, sautéed the garlic and omitted the onions (my hatred of onions had only gotten worse over the years). I was attempting to do my best at recreating her masterpiece, but without her direction I knew it wouldn't be half as good. We had poured in the canned tomato puree and the only clear instruction I had gotten from Nanny: the day-old red wine. The wine was mostly being passed around, and after I splashed some into each glass I'd dash a bit more in the sauce, darkening the color. The back door to the house was open to the yard, but the kitchen still smelled of garlic and wine. Mark and I were in the kitchen doing the cooking. We were having a good day together. Not every day was a good day, but today was. Laughter hung in the air with the garlic.

"Everyone is going to love my sauce tonight," he said, a grin spread over his unshaven face, his morning-sky blue eyes twinkling. "It really is the best."

"You aren't doing anything!" I yelled, unable to give the credit to anyone but me, or perhaps Nanny, but especially not a German boy whose only kitchen talents were stirring and antagonizing the chef.

"Hey, I'm stirring!" he yelled, shoving a piece of crusty Italian bread in his mouth.

I laughed and grabbed the bread from him. "We're supposed to be saving that for dinner," I chided, picking up the rest of the loaf and hitting him with it. Crumbs showered onto the kitchen tile. Over in the living room, I could hear my phone ringing. I ran over to it and saw my dad's phone number flash on the front, and ignored the call.

Ever since my father and I had most of the United States separating us, about seven years before, he called me a few times a week to chat. He was my wake-up call in high school, calling my phone line every morning at seven. Once I got into college, I had to wean him off of the early morning wake-up calls to my dorm room, because he'd either wake up my roommate or call on a morning I hadn't made it back to my dorm. But complain as I did, part of me looked forward to his phone calls. Not too many fathers talked to their daughters as often as mine did.

I walked back into the kitchen, taking the wooden spoon out of Mark's hands and dipping it into the deep red of the pot. I heard my phone ring again in the living room. Out of the corner of my eye, I saw Mark reach for the bread again.

"Stop snacking! You won't even be hungry for dinner by the time it's ready," I said.

"I'm just sampling." He smiled at me, and dipped yet another piece of thick bread into the pot.

Over my annoyed laughter at Mark, I heard my name from the living room.

"Adriana! It's your dad again. It's like the third time," Mark's roommate, Jason, shouted over the television. I went back into the living room to answer the phone, annoyed at my father's persistence.

"*Buon giorno!*" Mark called from the kitchen, truly in the Italian spirit. I hoped my dad didn't hear. He wasn't the biggest fan of Mark.

"Hello, hey Dad." I laughed, trying to ignore Mark's jokes.

"Hi, Skeeter. You should sit down. I have something to tell you." My dad had been calling me Skeeter or Skeeter Bug for as long as I could remember. His voice cracked on the other end, and I sat on the couch Mark and his roommates had picked up from a garage sale. As the Volkswagen commercial on the big screen TV blared, I heard my father's faraway voice. "Pop had a heart attack."

It was if I'd started falling through a hole, the voices in the living room and on the television were far above me, growing quieter each moment as I sank further and further away.

"What?" It didn't make sense. Pop had diabetes, not a heart problem. Heart attacks weren't a complication of diabetes. This was clearly a mistake.

"He was in the garage, he'd been shoveling snow, and—" My father's voice stopped. He tried to hide his sobs, but they came through the speaker of my phone as gasps for breath.

Tears silently slid down my cheeks before I even realized I was crying. I couldn't hear anything my Dad was saying anymore, the phone having slid out of my hand and landed on the hardwood floor. I stood up and started walking upstairs to Mark's room, closing the door quietly behind me. Downstairs, the I could hear the referee's whistle from the Broncos' game on television, Mark and his friends screaming about a call. The sun was shining brightly into the bedroom where no curtains hung on the front-facing window. I hadn't had a chance to buy curtains yet, and knew Mark would never do it himself. I walked over to the bed in the middle of the room, and sunk into the mattress. The plaid duvet cover over Mark's down comforter puffed up around me. I grabbed fistfuls of the soft feathers and pulled them into my body, sobbing.

Pop and I had been close. Not confide-in-each-other close, but James and I had been the light of his life, and we knew it. The only man I was used to seeing cry was Pop, when my father would drive us to LaGuardia so we could fly back to Colorado from our visits. We'd look out the back window of the car and wave, while my father would load the trunk up with our bags. Pop would hold up one hand and sniff, wiping away tears that fell from his eyes like a reflex. Even as kids we had known how hard it was for him to see us leave. Pop had struggled with diabetes and had lost a few toes, and eventually half of his leg, in the past seven years. It had been hard to see him reduced to a wheelchair, after watching him spend hours gardening at the Villa and in his own yard in Astoria. His roses on the corner had been the envy of his block, and he took pride in his garden the way Nanny had taken pride in her cooking. We always knew that he wasn't very healthy, but never expected a heart attack. Does anyone ever expect a heart attack?

I didn't hear the stairs of the old house creaking as Mark ran up them, or his door opening and closing again behind him. He was just there, laying on the bed beside me, holding me as I sobbed.

We had rented *When Harry Met Sally* to watch after our family dinner. Mark put it on in for me in his room as the sun set slowly, and the rest of our makeshift family started dinner downstairs. Some sort of food had been delivered after I'd given up on the sauce. I didn't leave the room for the rest of the night. When the movie ended, it started over automatically. I didn't leave the bed for the next twenty hours. "It's amazing. You look like a normal person, but actually you are the angel of death," Sally said over and over.

On Tuesday, the morning of my twenty-first birthday, James and I caught a 5 a.m. flight to New York for the funeral. Though he would never admit it to me, I knew Dad was taking Pop's sudden death incredibly hard. My father never opened up to me about their relationship, but anyone with eyes and ears knew they had argued a lot, and Pop had disagreed with some of Dad's choices ever since his divorce with Mom years ago. By the time my father had arrived in the city to see Pop after the heart attack, machines were keeping him alive. There had been no chance for a good-bye.

Even Mom was worried about Dad, and she was nearly driving me crazy asking about him every day. They had been divorced over a decade and still never spoke. She had been at a conference when Pop passed away, and quickly, silently, caught a flight up to New York for the services. She and Pop had butted heads often, but there was no one who loved my mother more than he did. They'd bickered about milkshakes over milk, when we did and didn't need to wear winter coats, and Pop's tendency to take us places without asking. But there had been no more devoted grandparent than he, which my mom knew and loved about him. She stayed in the back at his funeral, saying nothing to anyone and heading straight to the airport from the church. I didn't even know she was there until we walked out to *Ave Maria*, playing from behind the casket. I saw her in the last pew, gripping a tissue tightly, her head bowed in prayer and grief.

Δ

How do you pack for five months—or for a trip you might not return from? What do you leave behind, what do you bring? What is replaceable? Pictures stayed. No friends or family, no pets or vacation memories. Memories are replaceable, collectible. Tees, wool sweaters, boots, socks came. No curling iron or blow dryers—I'd purchase the European equivalent when I arrived. Books, maps, and empty journals with pages waiting to be filled took up space in my suitcase. While I had told my parents I'd return to the States in December, in my heart, that didn't feel right. I already had the idea of staying longer, much longer, planted.

One afternoon, as I sorted through *coming* and *staying*, Dad called to tell me he'd decided he would fly over with me. He had been to Prague for a wedding once, and was going to show me all around the city. I was secretly relieved, not knowing what I would have done if I had to land alone in a foreign country. I bounced down the stairs to tell Mom. She sat at her desk, glasses pushed down her nose, as she read intently from her desktop.

"So Dad says he is going to fly to Prague with me, and he wants to bring James also. But do you think it would be better if I went by myself?"

The unmistakable look of disappointment fell over her face. She looked up from her computer and whipped off her reading glasses. "Your father is going?"

"Well he hasn't booked the tickets, but he wants to go."

"Oh. I wanted to go. I wanted to take you and James out a week before your classes started."

"I didn't know that. You haven't been to Europe in twenty years."

"I know, so what better time to go back? I'll email your father and tell him I want to go."

Not wanting to be there for the argument, I turned around and retreated up to my room. I lost days in my room. I made piles, give and take, throw out and save, replace and remind, now and forever. Mom came upstairs and announced we would all be going, as a family, her, my father, James, and me. We hadn't done anything as a family since before the divorce. My parents had been having the same argument for ten years, and because of one semester abroad, they were ready to put it all behind them. We were all moving in the same direction. Away.

I spent the day before my flight with Mark. We didn't speak of what was ahead of us. Instead, we ordered Thai and drank beer. We played with the dog and made love. I had a feeling it was over with us, that when I said good-bye to him it was for a much longer absence than we admitted to each other. It was the unspoken truth between us. And it was much easier to walk away than I thought it would be. I was certain he felt the same.

And just like every day before it, the sun rose on the day I was to leave. I felt like it was any old trip out east. I made my bed and took one last look around my room.

Despite leaving the house just after five in the morning, the sun was already peeking over the horizon, and I was wide awake. The air was full of honeysuckle that Mom had planted in abundance around her front door. Though I didn't have any real emotional attachment to the house she had bought just four months prior, it was starting to feel more like a home to me. As my brother snored in the backseat, Mom ran through the checklist, the way mothers do. I knew I had packed everything I would need, and what I needed most of all couldn't be packed alongside socks and snow boots.

"Underwear?"

"Yes."

"Electrical adaptors?"

"Yes."

"Winter coat?"

"Yes."

"Toothbrush?"

"Yes."

My father, an expert traveler due to his work demands, had made all of the flight arrangements for us. Mom, James, and I would fly to Philadelphia, where we would meet him. From there we would fly to Frankfurt, then board the plane for the last leg of the trip to Prague.

As I settled in to my window seat, my eyelids began to feel heavy. Mom sat next to me, her hand on my knee, gently holding my leg so I knew she was there. My eyelids closed over my eyes with increasing frequency as we taxied to takeoff, and as I felt us finally leave the solid ground of Colorado, I fell asleep.

By the time I opened my eyes again, we had landed in Philadelphia. People were already beginning to stand up, stretching their legs and arms in the narrow aisle. We trudged through the airport, and to the newsstand where Dad had arranged to meet us. His flight from Boston landed half an hour after ours, with an additional hour after that before we would take off for Prague.

The terminal was slowly filling with people. Suits and well-traveled luggage told stories of mostly business travelers at lunchtime on a weekday. Some scrolled through emails on Blackberries, passing others standing in inconvenient places chatting on phones. I leaned against the window keeping my eyes open for Dad, occasionally yawning as I tried to recuperate from my nap. Mom busied herself shopping for trail mix to stash in her bag, while James thumbed through magazines. My mind was fuzzy with lack of sleep. I hadn't slept much the night before; frenzied unpacking and repacking of little things I'd worry about forgetting plagued my night. When I was lying in bed, all I could focus on was the knot in my gut. Excitement, anxiety, and uncertainly balled up together to create a cloud that hovered over me. I was unable to concentrate on any one thing, or keep my eyes closed for more than two minutes at a time. But now the travel had started, and I felt like a weight had been lifted. There was no turning back. All that was left to do was discover.

Mom snuck up next to me, slipping her arm around my back. "How are you feeling?"

I yawned again, my eyes watering. "Good, tired. Are you ready to see Dad?"

She waved her hand in front of my face. "Oh, we'll be fine. This trip is about you, not about us. Don't worry about us."

I knew she was right, and I didn't need to worry about them. But I couldn't help it. Their fights were brutal screaming matches you couldn't hide from. They spoke rarely, and saw one another maybe once a year, in passing.

I knew Mom was nervous. She was too kind to make a thing out of it, but as we watched Dad approach us from his gate, she fidgeted. She twisted her rings, moved her bangles and fluffed her hair. He waved at us as he got closer.

"Hey-y-y-y," he said across a few passing travelers.

"Hey!" I moved forward to greet him, but I missed the mark. Dad stepped right past me to Mom, pulling her into a tight hug. I stared as James walked up next to me. We made eyes at each other in disbelief.

Realizing they'd lingered a bit too long, Mom pulled back, smiling. "How was the flight?"

ALAINA ISBOUTS

Dad beamed and pulled James and I both into a quick hug. "Great, no problems. You guys hungry?"

"Yeah, I could eat," James replied. I agreed.

"There are a few restaurants up here, we can grab something before the next flight." He shifted his carry-on to his other shoulder, and pointed the way. "Let's go." He and Mom started walking away together, already in conversation. James and I followed.

We hurried through lunch and made it to our gate, just in time for boarding.

I moved toward the line for coach, checking my seat assignment. James was on the aisle next to me, and I was in the middle. I turned to Mom. "Where are you sitting?"

She blushed a little, and turned to Dad. "Well..."

"Actually..." Dad jumped in. "We are in first class."

James perked. "What? You two are in first class? Together? Alone?"

Dad smiled and looked in Mom's direction. "I just upgraded us. She's never flown first class, and it's a long flight."

I laughed in disbelief, shaking my head. Just a few months ago, I would have never imagined them smiling in the same room, let alone sipping champagne together in first class on a family vacation.

"But you can come visit us!" Mom squealed with delight. "We'll see you guys on the plane!" And they whisked away to the red carpet of their first-class line.

James was dumbfounded. "Can you believe him?" He shook his head. "What the hell is going on with them?"

"I don't know... but something. It's so bizarre to see them like this. Just wait. They'll be killing each other on the flight home." I elbowed James. "Have fun with that."

Our group was called to board, and we made our way back to our seats. As close as James and I were, I couldn't have been less excited to sit next to him for nine hours on a crowded plane. I had been hoping to sit next to Mom to have someone to talk to so my mind would be quiet, be still. But it wouldn't take long before James would slip on headphones, sleep, and snore.

We settled into our seats, and within minutes James was pulling out his gigantic headphones. I closed my eyes. *There's no turning back now*, I thought to myself as the plane gained speed and shook, pushing off from the runway. *There's no turning back now.*

It had been a long journey to the flight I was taking. I closed my eyes, thinking of everything that had happened since I first sent my deposit in to EOO. What had led me to that Web page? There had been a desperate need in me to not just get out of Denver, but to leave Colorado. But what exactly was I running away from? I turned to James, hoping we could watch something together to keep my mind occupied. But sure enough, his eyes started to hang. I suggested we watch a movie together, and he just asked for my pillow. I handed it over reluctantly and got out my new journal that I had bought, just for my semester abroad.

August 24ᵗʰ, 2006. Finally on my way to Prague! I don't know how I should be feeling right now, but I don't really feel anything. I guess it's just because

I put my pen down. Could I sound any more trite? It wasn't worth writing. I closed my journal and slid it into my bag. I clicked on my television and browsed through the movies. I wanted something mindless, something to make me laugh. I settled on *Last Holiday*. I watched Queen Latifah's character dream of going to the Czech Republic, and decided she would do it before her death. My interest piqued when her plane landed in Prague, and I watched intently as she traveled to Karlovy Vary and tried to speak Czech, and braved the snow and cold weather there.

By the time we landed in Frankfurt, it was Friday morning. We stopped for coffee and croissants before catching our final flight. I felt tired and hungry, and not much else. We boarded a much smaller plane after breakfast. It was only about an hour flight, and I made sure to get the window seat. My eyes were glued outside, eager for a glance at my new home country. I put my iPod on shuffle and waited. It wasn't until we started our descent, that I sat on the edge of my seat. It was fields as far as the eye could see, just green and brown, hills and a few trees. It was hard to wrap my mind around the fact that all if this had always been there, half a world away from me, despite seeing it for the first time. It was then, as we got closer to Ruzyne Airport, that my iPod spoke to me:

> Well it's a hustle, it's a hustle every day of life,
> And it's enough to keep your head above the water, see.
> It seems the older I get the more freedom I have,
> But everything is complicated to me
> Take a long drive, cause I'm still alive,
> And if the pressure didn't get me then, won't get me now.
> Stay high as the sky and bust the fuck out.
> Free.
> Free.
> Free.

11

September, Prague.

A chime reverberated throughout the flat. I walked over to the doorbell panel, still in my bra.

"Yeah?"

"It's Mason," a voice cracked through static.

"Come on up," I said, pressing the button to unlock the apartment's main door. I flipped the deadbolt so he could push the door open when he got to our floor, ran into my bedroom, and pulled on a tee that had been crumpled on my bed. The apartment was finally starting to feel comfortable, familiar. Light switches and the buttons on the washing machine all no longer felt like strangers. My feet found their way into my black patent flats I'd started wearing everywhere. My boots had already been abandoned, relegated to a back corner of the stand-alone wardrobe set up at the foot of my bed. My head had been pounding since that morning, but I was trying my hardest to clean myself up. I couldn't waste a day up in the apartment.

"Where's Emily?" I heard Mason's voice in the entryway.

I pulled my hair up into a topknot and rooted around for some Chap Stick in my desk drawer. "Uhh, I don't know... are you supposed to meet her?" I walked out of my room and found Mason sitting on the pink floral couch in our living room.

"Yeah. We were going to grab dinner." He wore what I was starting to realize was his standard uniform of skinny jeans, a studded belt, and a black tee, his black hair spiked as always. He was definitely an attractive guy, but not my type.

"Dinner?" I questioned. I knew I had slept in late, but I didn't think it was dinnertime yet.

He shook his head. "Yeah, it's like 5 p.m. Hungover?"

I nodded, laughing. "A little. I need some food."

He stood up. "Let's go then, fuck Emily."

We jumped on the bus, heading down the hill toward where the restaurants, shops, and bars nearest to us were. We walked around Anděl looking for a place to eat. The square was bustling with people. It was a Sunday, and people were clearly out doing their final weekend shopping before the work week began in the morning. Mason pointed out a restaurant with large Hoegaarden beer signs on the awnings.

"I heard this place serves three-liter beers. That's happening," he said, walking toward the door.

I followed him into a booth and slid across from him. I wasn't sure I was up for three liters of any kind of alcohol, but I was too out of it to argue. Within minutes, our first three-liter beer was plopped down in the middle of the table, two thick, neon green straws tipping out of the glass toward each of us.

I hadn't spent too much time with Mason, with the exception of an afternoon at an internet café a few days before. Everyone else had gone on a day trip to Český Krumlov and we had opted out. Though we had bonded early our mutual obsession with Blink-182 and other faux-punk bands in high school, I didn't yet know him too well. I knew he was from Long Beach, he didn't give a shit what anyone else thought about him, and he was always stirring up trouble within the group— gossiping, spilling secrets, and openly telling people how he felt about them, good or bad. Unlike everyone else, Mason was staying in Prague for the year, rather than a semester. It was an idea I had already kicked around a little bit, but wasn't really to pull the trigger on just yet.

"So what happened with you guys last night?" Mason inquired.

I shook my head. "Not much, just too much dancing and too much drinking at the five story, then Celeste and Lex—"

He cut me off, shaking his head. "No, no, you know what I'm talking about. With Nick. You two get down and dirty last night already?"

I took the straw from between my lips. "No." I was taken aback by his forwardness. "Nothing happened."

He scoffed. "You two were that drunk, slept in the same room last night, and nothing happened?"

"He slept in Emily's bed. Really. Nothing happened. When I woke up he was gone."

Mason took a long swig of Hoegaarden through his straw. "Good. You don't want to mess around with him. He wants Lexie."

My heart sunk. "Really?" He hadn't seemed like he was paying attention to her, did he? Would I even have noticed?

"Yeah, he was talking to Charlie about how hot she is the other day." Mason didn't seem to notice the shakiness in my voice, or that I hadn't taken my eyes off him since he said it.

So that's what Charlie meant, I thought to myself. I grabbed my straw back and took a few angry gulps of beer. "Well, nothing happened, so I really don't care." I looked down. "He's wasting his time if he's into Lexie though, she's into John. And I know John really likes her, too."

Mason laughed. "We haven't even known each other for a whole week yet."

I nodded. "Yeah. But there aren't that many of us, all living in close quarters, spending all our time together." I knew I was trying to justify my behavior. Most people in the program that I'd talked to already knew I had a serious boyfriend back home, and I really didn't want to get a reputation as *that* girl. I felt used, frustrated, lied to. I decided I was done with Nick. I wasn't here for this drama.

To my surprise, we easily made our way through our giant beer glass. It wasn't on purpose; the beer was literally cheaper than ordering a bottle of water or a soda. When we sat down at a restaurant, the cheapest and easiest thing to order was a pivo, just like any local would do. Mason ordered a plate of goulash. I really needed to eat something—I was already lightheaded from the beer—and ordered potato pancakes. I was glad my classes didn't start until Tuesday and I had the whole day tomorrow to recuperate.

Mason's phone vibrated on the table. "It's Charlie," he said, checking the message. "He says they are all at a bar over by John's. Wanna go?"

I didn't know who "they all" were, but I wasn't in the mood to make my way back to my apartment alone. I knew I'd sulk about Nick and feel guilty about Mark. "Yeah, let's go." I rooted around in my bag for some krowns to leave on the table.

I hadn't yet been over to John's part of the city, Prague Three. I'd discovered that the city was divided into sections, with Prague One being the city square and radiating out. The U Apartment and Cozy House were in Prague Five, but nearly everyone else was in Prague Two. Only John and his roommate were out in Prague Three, near what was known as the TV Tower. The TV tower was a big metal tower used for broadcasting, with a restaurant at the top. It looked like nothing I had ever seen before, a strangely modern structure seemingly out of place in this gorgeous Gothic city. It consisted of three massive silver poles that formed a small triangle, with cubes that had large windows in the middle. But the strangest part of the tower was the large metal baby statues that dotted the tower, looking as if giant robotic children were crawling around the structure. The tower was surrounded by a park, and John's apartment was just off the park. It wasn't a bad neighborhood—not purely residential, not just for business, either. Apartment buildings lined the much quieter streets, with bars and restaurants dotting the landscape.

Mason seemed to know where he was going, so I followed him into a bar on a corner across from the park. It was easy to spot our friends. They really were all there, huddled around one small table. My eyes immediately fell on Nicholas, who was talking loudly with Charlie, John, and Stephanie, beer in hand. I figured he'd be here, but had no interest in seeing him. Next to them were Celeste and Lexie, who were talking to Alex and Noelle. I was thankful to see them, and decided the best course of action for me was to ignore Nick. I didn't want to get involved with any drama. We'd kissed, and of course I'd felt something— but he was apparently interested in someone else, and I needed to deal with the Mark situation. *This was not why I came here,* I reminded myself firmly.

"Heyyyyyyy!" Celeste called out as I waked up to their table. Lexie reached out and put her arm around my waist. "Grab a chair," she said. I slid an empty chair out from a deserted table next to us and wedged myself between Lexie and Alex, down the table from Nick where he was out of my line of sight.

Alex turned to me. "Where were you two?"

"Mason came over, I guess he was meeting Emily for dinner, but she was gone, so we got three beers—I mean three liters of beer..." I couldn't keep my words straight, and my mind went fuzzy once I heard Nicholas laugh at the other end of the table.

Alex laughed. "Emily is here, somewhere, I think. Who knows with her, she's always just disappearing."

I looked down at Celeste and Lexie. "What have you guys been doing?"

"We've been here for over an hour," Lexie said. "Celeste, Noelle, and I went over to have dinner with John and then everyone sort of just met us after." She took a drink of her beer. As usual, everyone had a pint glass in front of them, sipping pilsner of one sort or another. "Come on, let's get you a drink."

I walked up to the bar with Lexie. "*Dva Staropramens, prosim,*" she called to the bartender. Clearly she hadn't had as much to drink as I had. "Are you okay?"

I nodded. "Yeah, I'm fine." She cocked her head to the side and widened her eyes. She wasn't buying it. "I just really regret what happened with Nick last night," I said finally.

"What happened with Nick...?"

"Oh nothing. After you guys left, I just, I wish we hadn't, you know... I don't want to complicate things out here."

She nodded. "Don't worry about it so much, it's no big deal." I knew she was right. It was only a big deal if I made it a big deal.

"Besides," I continued, "I hear he's into someone else." I knew I shouldn't be telling her, but the beer was pushing the words out of my mouth before my brain could stop. I raised my eyebrows at her.

"Oh, shut up, he is not," she said. "It would never happen." She looked over at the table in John's direction. He noticed and gave her a big smile, raising his glass to her. "He's so funny." The bartender set two beer glasses in front of us and walked away.

"Who, John?" I asked, reaching for a glass.

She nodded. "Yeah." She broke into a big smile. "He just makes me laugh."

We grabbed our beers and headed back to the table. Alex and Celeste were laughing loudly. Charlie had slid his chair down to our end of the table next to mine, and was entertaining the girls with a story. My eyes wanted so badly to dart in Nick's direction, and it took all of my willpower to keep my eyes in front of me. I fell quiet, letting Charlie tell his stories, the girls around me chiming in and laughing.

We drank more beer. We told more stories. Laughter resounded around us. After countless more rounds, I had drunk much more than I'd wanted to and still hadn't eaten anything but the soup, that had now been hours earlier. I mostly kept to myself, listening to everyone around me talk and trying not to pay attention to Nick, who had been up at the bar talking to a Czech girl for the better part of the last hour.

Alex leaned over to me. "Ready to head home? We're going to grab a cab with the Cozy guys," she said, meaning Nick, Mason, and Charlie.

The last thing I wanted was to get into a cab with Nick and hear about this girl he had been chatting up, also figuring we wouldn't all be able to squeeze into one cab. I paused for a minute, then looked across the table at John, who had been deep in conversation with Lexie for most of the night.

"Hey John, can I crash at your place?" I asked.

He frowned, clearly a little confused. "Uh, sure," he said.

I looked back at Alex. "I'm going to stay here."

She shrugged. "Suit yourself." She grabbed her sweater and started heading outside.

Lexie, Celeste, and their roommates, Stephanie and Noelle, waved good night to everyone, and also headed out to find a cab. Everyone was abandoning the table at once. I watched as Nick headed outside with the Czech girl, her blonde bob bouncing as she walked next to him. I felt sick. Was he taking her home with him? Why did I care so much? I felt relieved I wasn't getting in the cab with both of them. I simultaneously was aching to know and not wanting to find out.

Before long, it was just John and I at the bar. "You okay?" He put his arm around me and pulled me close, in an older-brother type of hug, as we stood up from the table.

"Yeah. I just really didn't want to get into a cab with Nick," I admitted.

John nodded. "Yeah, I get ya. Don't worry about that girl," he waved his hand, as if waving her out of our conversation.

"What's his deal?" I asked as we headed toward the doors. "He kissed me last night, he's talking to this girl tonight, and Mason told me he is into Lexie," I shook my head. "I don't need that."

John patted my back, seemingly unfazed by this Lexie revelation. "Don't worry about him." He opened the door and the cool evening air brush into us. "Let's go."

We started down the sidewalk, and before long, a familiar voice called after us. "John!"

John and I stopped, turning around to see Nick jogging up the sidewalk. "Hey man, what are you doing?" John yelled to him.

"I was just grabbing a cab for Denisa, and everyone left without me," he said, caching up to us. "I was going to jump into the cab with Mason, but I think they thought I was leaving with her." He looked at me. I looked at the sidewalk.

"We'll all just crash at my place," John said.

I threw him a look. The whole reason I hadn't gotten in the cab with Alex was to avoid spending time with Nick, and here we both were, crashing at John's together. This was not what I wanted.

I hung behind and let John and Nick walk together a few paces ahead of me. I don't know if Nick noticed that I was ignoring him, or if he didn't care, but either way he wasn't fazed. I could hear him talking to John about the girl from the bar. She was Czech and a couple years older than him, and he'd gotten her phone number for a date. I tried to block him out.

When we arrived at John's, he turned down his bed for me, insisting that he and Nick would take the couch and I could have his room. I was grateful he didn't turn Nick and I out to sleep on the couch together. I would rather have taken a cab back by myself.

I hugged John good night, and shut the door to his room. I kicked my shoes into a corner and sprawled out onto the bed, grateful for the quiet and privacy. Within minutes, I was asleep.

I woke up to my phone buzzing in my bag. I rolled over, rubbing my eyes. It took me a minute to remember where I was, and that John and Nick were sleeping on the couch outside. I laid on my back and stared at the ceiling. Before long my phone started buzzing again, and I reached down into my bag just in time to answer.

"Hello?" I half-whispered. I had no idea what time it was or who could be calling me, but I didn't want to wake anyone else up.

"I'm fucking lost in Boulder," Mark's voice was drunk and irritated on the other end of the line.

"What?" I replied groggily.

"I'm lost. In fucking Boulder," he yelled.

"Okay... what are you doing in Boulder?"

"Jason wanted to come up, there was some shitty band he wanted to see, but the show sucked so I left, and now I don't know where the fuck I am." He sounded exasperated.

"Okay, but Mark, what do you want me to do?" I was already annoyed he'd called me like this.

"Well you're my fucking girlfriend, I thought you'd care that I don't know where I am."

"Yeah, but I'm in Prague, you know, so I don't know what you want me to do," I whispered.

"Can you SPEAK THE FUCK UP!" he yelled into the phone.

"Don't yell at me, you woke me up to tell me you're lost on the other side of the world and there's nothing I can do for you, you know?" I was annoyed, still whispering, not wanting to wake up the boys. It was embarrassing, having a conversation like this.

"Jesus Adriana, you're always so fucking selfish," he called, starting a tirade.

I hung up. I was sure I'd pay for it later, but I didn't care. I wasn't about to get into it with him from John's bedroom while he was drunk and lost. This was one of the things I hated about Mark sometimes, his complete disregard for other people. My phone started buzzing again, Mark calling me once more. I clicked a button to ignore the call and then promptly switched it off. I couldn't deal with him right now. I could hear voices on the other side of the door. Mark and John were up.

I pushed off the covers and searched for my clothes. Once dressed, I opened the door carefully, slowly making my way into John's living room. He and Nick were standing up, already having made the couches back from being beds.

"Good morning!" John bellowed.

"Morning." I smiled at him, still avoiding Nick's gaze.

He stared at me square in the eyes. "You ready to go?"

It dawned on me that I would have to make my way back home with him. It was unavoidable at this point.

"Yep," I said, not ready to say more than one word to him. I slung my bag over my shoulder. John let us out of his building. We agreed we'd see each other at school the next morning.

Nick and I walked side by side down the sidewalk, making our way to the metro. It was a beautiful day outside, and birds sang around us as we started through the park. We'd take the metro to the other side of the river, then board our bus. I knew we couldn't not talk the whole way, but I was determined not to be the one to break the silence. It wasn't long before Nick started conversation.

"I feel really bad about last night," he started.

I looked over to him. Was he just jumping right into it? I decided to play dumb. "Why?"

He sighed. "Charlie was kind of into that girl I was talking to at the bar," he said. So he was completely oblivious then.

"Yeah? Why were you talking to her then?"

"I wasn't hitting on her, we were just having a conversation. You can talk to women without hitting on them," he explained.

I looked away and rolled my eyes.

"Well it looked like you guys were really hitting it off," I said. We started down the stairs do the metro station. "Charlie didn't seem upset to me, though."

"Well, I get the feeling Charlie isn't so open with his feelings."

"And you are?" I retorted, challenging him.

"I try to be, yeah."

We boarded the metro, grabbing seats next to each other by the door. I didn't know what he was talking about. Was some sort of honest moment coming between us? Should I start it off, say I was annoyed with him? Or was I hurt? Or angry? I was having a hard time pinpointing my feelings toward Nick. Or maybe that I knew how he felt about Lexie? We fell silent as the metro lurched forward, racing toward the next station. I was thinking too much about what to say, and ended up saying nothing. The doors opened and closed, we sped forward. Four stops later, we got off the metro at Můstek to switch to the yellow metro line.

"By the way, I owe you a thank you," Nick started.

My stomach turned over. "Why?" I asked.

We boarded the next metro, cramming between people and finding seats again down the car. "For not making things weird after the bar the other night."

I was confused. Things were definitely weird between us, though I did agree that I wasn't the one that made them weird—it was him. "Oh, yeah..." I stammered. I had no idea what to say.

"I mean, it's not like we came out here to hook up with people, and I know you have your boyfriend back home."

The doors on the metro closed once more, and a static voice came through the loudspeaker announcing the next stop. I kept quiet.

"I'm glad we can just laugh about it," he said.

I lifted my gaze from my feet up to him. "Well yeah, it wasn't big deal," I agreed. It hadn't been a big deal. And If I was going to move past whatever I thought I felt for him, I was going to start right now. "We were just drunk, you know? It was nothing. Don't worry about it." *Laugh about it?* I wasn't sure it was a joke.

He looked at me, smiled, and nodded. I smiled back. "Sometimes it's just nice to be close to someone, you know?" I did know what he meant. We were far away from everything familiar. It was nice to feel someone's touch. Lips on lips, hands on hands, feet bumping up next to one another on the metro.

"Yeah," I agreed. "So what about you and that girl from last night?"

Nick moved his arm off my shoulders. "I don't know. The other night, we made a pact not to go out with any American girls, so I just thought I'd give it a shot when she struck up a conversation with me."

"Wait, what?" I asked. "Who is *we*?"

Nick laughed. "John, Charlie, and me. At Tretter's. We all agreed we wouldn't date American girls but get to know Czech girls instead."

I frowned at him. *Maybe that was what Charlie meant when he told me to be careful?* The red flags were piling up.

"Do you know what a douche you sound like right now?" I said, taken aback.

He looked at me. "Yes, I know," he said. "But it's true. I'm just being honest."

His directness took me aback. "John doesn't seem to be paying attention to the pact," I said, sidestepping Nick's assertion of honesty.

"Yeah. He's definitely into Lexie."

I nodded. "Yeah, there's something there."

The metro lurched to a stop at Anděl and we stood up to disembark.

"Does that bother you?" I looked at the ground.

"Because he's ignoring the pact?" Nick asked, stepping off the bus.

"No, because you're into Lexie," I stated. *If he wants to be honest, let's be honest,* I thought. I didn't even know if it was true, but surely Mason hadn't just made it up.

He scowled at me. "What? No, I'm not. I mean, she's an attractive girl, but she's not my type." We started up the long escalator to street level. "I like a woman who challenges me. Someone who disagrees with me and shares her point of view, instead of agreeing with everything I say."

I took a step back from him on the escalator. His straightforwardness once again left me speechless. I didn't know how to respond to him.

"Besides," he continued. "Like you said, there's definitely something between her and John."

Sunshine broke in ahead of us as we reached the top of the escalator. We made our way to the bus stop to see the 137 waiting there, doors already opened. Nick held his arm out in front of the door to make sure I jumped on before they closed, then boarded right behind me. There was standing room only, and we stood uncomfortably close together.

"So what about you?" He gave my leg a playful tap with his foot.

"What about me?"

"Your boyfriend?" he asked.

I sighed. "Oh, yeah. I don't know. Honestly, it hasn't been working for a long time. I think this trip was kind of an excuse for me, really, to break it off." While Mark and I had been notorious around our friends for our very rocky, on-again-off-again relationship, things had been at their best before I'd left. We had reconciled and were making it work this time, we really were. At twenty, I was convinced I had learned lessons about love. That it takes effort. That you sometimes give much more than you receive. That sometimes you aren't really happy, but it ebbs and flows. That you fight hard and make up harder. I had told myself this was all normal, this was how love was in real life. It hadn't taken me more than a week out in Prague to doubt that theory.

Nick raised his eyebrows.

"I mean, we've been together for years, but I find myself constantly questioning my feelings for him." If Nick was going to be an open book, I thought, then I'd try to be, too. "I feel like if I'm doubting it all the time, then it can't be real. Besides, it was way too easy for me to... you know, the other night with you..."

He nodded. "Yeah, I understand." He fell quiet. I stared out the window, my thoughts fixed on Mark. It was time to address the situation.

Δ

When my parents broke up, my mom remarried quickly. Almost too quickly, which planted the seed in my head. It was fed here and there by the shitty things my father had said about my mother. He'd never come out and say what happened to them outright, and I'd never asked. I didn't want to know. It was easier to think of my parents not as real people, but as just that: parents. Mom and Dad. It was far too complicated to think of Jack and Janie, man and woman, one time husband and wife.

I knew it was going to drain my phone of pre-paid krowns, but I felt like I couldn't move forward with my life until I knew. It was time. I picked up my phone and dialed my mom.

"Hi, honey!" Her voice was bright on the other end. Always bright, always happy. My mom.

"Hi, Mom. I need to talk to you." I sat on the edge of my bed. Emily and Alex were gone, and I needed privacy for this talk.

"Everything okay?"

"Yeah, things are fine. I just don't want to use up all my phone credits and have to ask you something." I took a deep breath. My voice was shaky—not with emotion, but with the candid question I was about to ask. "Did you cheat on Dad?"

My question was met with an icy silence on the other end.

"I'm not mad," I hurriedly added. "I just... there are some things going on, and... I... I have to know." And with that, I launched in to a quick version of what had happened so far, all the while pacing around my bedroom. The inexplicable pull I felt to Nicholas, the distance I felt from Mark. I asked her all the rhetorical questions I'd been asking myself for years. Would I know if it was real? Would I want to be with someone else if I were really meant to be with Mark? What about the things he did that I hated, the things I found myself thinking that my love, my real true love, wouldn't do? Was Nicholas just a catalyst to get me to see what else was out in the world? Did it matter? "I don't know why, but I need to know about you and Dad to help me figure this out. It's okay. I just need to know." I finished up and sat back down on the bed. I'd never been so honest with her before.

"Yes, I did." Her voice was strong. She didn't sound upset, sad, or even remorseful. Just stating a fact.

For a second, I felt like I'd been stabbed in the heart. I felt pain for Dad, but no anger toward Mom. I tried to understand her as a complete person instead of just my mother. She continued on.

"I regret it, I absolutely do. But your father and I were broken long before it happened. That just made my mind up about what I needed to do, which was to file for divorce."

I didn't know what to say, and was thankful when she continued talking. In just the right way, she told me I wasn't married. That it was okay to be confused, that kisses happen sometime, and did I really think that Mark hadn't had a kiss here or there? It wasn't something I'd thought about before. But I was far too young to have this much on my mind, she said.

"Live," she said. "Just be. Take some time to figure out who you really are, to be where you are, and give this all a rest." She was right, the way mothers are.

This space between Mark and I, this actual geographical space, was a gift I should take advantage of. There was no way we could run into one another at a party, or feel lonely and show up at the other's place in the dead of night. I wasn't happy with Mark. And why did I think I deserved anything less than to feel complete, all-consuming happiness? I didn't know if Nick was a symbol the universe was dangling in front of me, of what could be—a reason for me to end things with Mark—or what he was meant to be for me. But I had heard what I needed to hear, and had unequivocally made up my mind.

Δ

I'd cleaned myself up and headed back down the hill to a cyber café at Anděl. How was I going to say what it was I really wanted to say? If we spoke, I knew I'd never find the words and we'd end up arguing.

Mark,

I wish I didn't have to do this over email, but I think it's best. Every time we talk it's yelling and arguing and I just don't have the stomach for it anymore. I feel like I'm always being cut off and I never really get the chance to say what I have to say. So all I can do is send this email and hope that you read it all.

I stopped typing, took a deep breath, and laid my forehead down on my keyboard. It was just too much. We hadn't spoken since he was lost in Boulder, but other than the phone call to my mom, I'd kept my phone off since leaving John's apartment. I had nothing to say to Mark. There wasn't any point in telling him what happened with Nick. It wouldn't change anything. It was a symptom of what was wrong with Mark, not the reason I wanted to end things. It was a sign that it was time to move on. I wasn't going to waste my time abroad arguing with him, being screamed at on international phone calls. I knew now what I should have realized much earlier: Mark was one of the reasons I left.

We'd tried to end it so many times, each time falling back into one another like an old habit. Just one cigarette after a stressful day. A quick nibble of your fingernail. A stolen French fry off someone's plate. It was a slippery slope.

It wasn't that I didn't love him. It was that at this point, the love was more habit, more comfort, more convenience than anything else. Loving Mark was easier than finding someone new. And even when I felt confident I could slip away, he'd pull me back in. He didn't deserve that, and neither did I. The break had to be now, with an ocean between us. Now, it would stick. There would be no bump-ins, no drunken text messages. Once I hit send, it would be over, and there would be no more discussions until I got back to the States. And knowing that, I let it all go.

I didn't feel angry, or sad, or bitter. It wasn't that Mark was an asshole, or that he'd done anything wrong at all. We were just clearly not compatible, not meant to be with each other. It was so clear now. I said everything I had never been able to say, fingers clicking away at keys, not knowing what I really wanted to say until I saw the words appear on the screen. That I felt like we were holding each other back. That we needed this time apart, this time to figure out who we both were independently before we really committed to one another, if that was the way we thought we should go. That I didn't think love should be this hard, and I didn't know what that meant. That I wanted to have this experience away and I wanted him to respect that, and not contact me. That we could reevaluate when I got home and see what we wanted to do then. And then it was gone, off into the cyber-universe. I hadn't even reread it.

I let my head fall forward into my hands, hair falling around my face. I closed my eyes. I did not like this person I had been the last few days. What a sad, college-girl cliché. Arguing with my long-distance boyfriend. Jealous about some boy I had only kissed once. I hadn't come out to Prague to find love, I had come out to challenge and to find myself. I decided, right there, to be done with it. I had already dismissed Mark for the remainder of my time in Prague.

I needed to let Nicholas go, too.

It wasn't like I had been falling for him. I'd had a little crush on him for a few days, we kissed, and that was it. This was not the time or the place to start a relationship. I was acting like someone I wasn't, and that needed to stop. I shook my head quickly, emptying thoughts of Nick out of my mind.

If only it was that easy.

12

September, Prague.

Tuesdays, Wednesdays, and Thursdays were my school days, and everyone else either shared this schedule or at least had a three-day weekend. It was a study-abroad student's dream schedule. It was clear that studies weren't the emphasis for anyone at EOO; the culture, the people, and Prague itself were our true subjects. Reading textbooks and taking exams weren't high on the priority list. Each class met only once a week, but each class was four hours long. Most decent professors offered a break in the middle of the stretch, when we'd huddle outside the one vending machine on the third floor. For twenty krowns, a plastic cup the size you'd see in a bathroom for mouthwash dropped down a chute and filled with a selection of sweet, steaming coffee drinks. Lattes, hot chocolates, and flavored coffees. The perfect pick-me-up, the only pick-me-up available in the drafty, old, brick university. If we were really desperate, we'd run down the block to a small convenience shop aimed at tourists crossing the Charles Bridge, but we knew prices were marked up to take advantage of those who didn't know any better.

Most of us in our group of friends—already we had naturally split off into groups—had classes at some point between nine and four. Nicholas had two of his classes with me, and the other two with Lexie. Despite what he'd told me on the bus, I couldn't tell if he was interested in her or not. He was spending more and more time with Lex, Celeste, and me. Besides Nick, Celeste, and Lexie, the other students in my classes were from all over the world. Students from Belarus, Italy, and South Africa studied alongside EOO students, some of whom I rarely saw outside of classes. Noelle, a girl Lexie went to school with in Seattle, and Stephanie, a Chicago-area native who came to Prague alone, leaving her longtime boyfriend behind, were both in classes of mine. Noelle wasn't a big drinker, choosing to stay in most nights all of us went out. She seemed very interested in her studies. The only thing that intrigued her about the Czech culture was the food. Noelle called herself a foodie, sampling different restaurants each night and becoming somewhat of a connoisseur of honey cake, a traditional Czech dessert. Stephanie spent all of her time either on the phone with her boyfriend back in Chicago, or with Mason. She and Mason were an odd match—him with his tattoos and jet-black hair, her with strict Christian values and penchant for folk songs she wrote and strummed on her guitar while perched on the bay window in her apartment. They had the same taste in nothing, it seemed, but were inseparable. It was obvious they had a connection, though none of us dared bring it up to either one. They were oftentimes joined by my roommate Emily, who obviously was into both Stephanie and Mason. It was an interesting threesome.

With our fourth roommate never showing up, there were only sixteen of us. We had all found our places. With such a small group, tensions and relationships were inescapable. Feelings cropped up, small, like weeds in a confined garden. There was nowhere else to grow, nowhere else for those urges, stolen glances, and flirtatious friendships to go. Now, everyone knew that Lexie and John were into each other, but that didn't seem to count for much. They were very casual and were taking things so slowly, that we weren't sure there was anything going on at all, really. But around the group, people knew. There were whisperings about Nick and me, but I dodged them as best I could, shaking my head if anyone ever asked anything. I was determined not to play into any drama.

The entrance to school was actually quite grand. Literally only steps from the Charles Bridge, it was situated on the first road on the west side of the Vltava River, in an area called Malá Strana. Going down that road, Lazanská, you would pass a small market where you could get snacks like bags of nuts and dried fruits; a nice-looking pub called Zanzibar that was filled with light, compared to the normal Czech dark and dreary beer halls; a small restaurant with windows that were always flung wide open, revealing comfy benches inside with pillows thrown about, and a chalkboard list of all the various teas and sandwiches they carried; and an antiquated building on the other side of the cobblestoned street, perpetually under construction. It was next to the small café that stood two extremely large, foreboding wooden doors with a small red crest above them. Our school.

What was once foreign was quickly commonplace. It was second nature to pass through the overbearing doors, pushing with all your weight after being buzzed in. The silence of the courtyard that once stopped me in my tracks, now was a welcome respite from the hustle of Malá Strana. Some days, fragments of lectures could be heard in the courtyard from classrooms surrounding the courtyard. Occasionally, a professor stuck his or her head out of an age-old window, to shush students in the courtyard that made too much noise then slam closed the large, wooden shutters that were usually open to the courtyard.

The EOO office inevitably became a hangout for all of the EOO students. It wasn't big, but it was enough. It became our student lounge, our meeting point. It was also the only place besides internet cafés that had wireless internet. People would show up to class hours early just to hang out in the office with the other students. Students would pop in on their break from the grueling four-hour lectures, stay after class to study or screw around on the internet, writing love letters to boyfriends at home or Skyping with parents. It was our home base.

Whatever was going on in her office, Bara was always at her desk. She was always hard at work on something: corresponding with prospective students, coordinating activities for the group of us, or putting together weekend or day trips for later in the semester. She arranged walking tours, soccer games, museum tours, and hosted movie nights. Mostly it was the Garden Girls, plus Gavin and Noelle, who attended. My friends and I spent most hours outside of class together, grabbing bagels at the shop near school, Bohemia Bagel, or drinking at the pub next door to school, Zanzibar. On weekends, we found new pubs to dry, preferring quieter beer halls where we could talk to the dance clubs Mason and Emily dragged Stephanie to.

Some of us had started thinking of traveling. Nick, John, and Charlie had taken a weekend trip to Amsterdam, and had come back refusing to speak of it. We didn't know what had happened and didn't press them for answers. Celeste, Lexie, and I had begun spending all of our time together, we threw a margarita night at my apartment while the boys were out of town, and even found a place to get pedicures over in Anděl. We started looking ahead to our fall break at the end of October, now just a little over a month away. The three of us girls decided we wanted to go to Italy, specifically to Venice and Rome. When Lexie mentioned it to John, he told her that he, Charlie, and Nick had been talking about doing Rome and Florence, so plans quickly formed for the six of us to travel through Italy together.

I'd grown accustomed to our routine at this point, no longer missing my family or friends back home. I felt comfortable in my surroundings and didn't think of Mark nearly as much as I had in the beginning. I wrote weekly emails to my parents and James, updating them on travel plans, things I'd seen, and day-to-day life in Prague. I looked forward to each day with an enthusiasm I'd never had before. Going to class wasn't dull when your classroom was inside one of the oldest buildings in a medieval city. The commute to school wasn't grating when it involved a creaking tram zigzagging through cobblestoned streets, with a front-row view to some of the most intricate architecture in Europe. I couldn't get enough. I craved the streets, the foreignness, the liberation that came with being alone in a strange and crowded city, the beer, the conversation with acquaintances rapidly becoming my best friends. I wanted to get lost in the city each day. I wanted to lose myself to my thoughts, ride the tram around and gaze out the window.

Things with Nick had cooled down, and we were able to maintain a friendship close to what I had with Charlie and John. I was still very attracted to him, and felt like there was a connection between us, but nothing more had happened and we had stopped acting flirty toward one another. It was easier this way, I knew, and didn't want to mess with the friendship we'd been building. We really did have a lot in common, and spent a significant amount of time together, between the classes we shared and time with our mutual group of friends. I pushed down the butterflies in my stomach every time he was around, forcing myself to act natural and keep things on an even keel. It worked well. Mostly.

Δ

Charlie walked over to the table, hugging four half-liters of golden pilsner to his chest, unlit cigarette hanging between his lips. "That's all the pivo I can carry," he said, sliding onto the bench opposite mine. He slid a beer across the table to me, one to Alex, one to Nick, and kept one for himself. "I think we're even on rounds now," Charlie made a point to say. He was always the accountant of the group, keeping tabs of who ordered what and how many rounds each person had paid for. Everyone paid their own way, and when Charlie was involved, he made sure of it.

We'd been at the bar for a couple hours, a local bar that Alex's new "friend" Richard, a Czech guy she'd been hooking up with, turned us on to. We affectionately nicknamed it "*Richard Bar.*" It was close to where we picked up the bus from Anděl and was incredibly cheap. It was a locals-only place that was always nearly empty, with foosball tables and sixteen-krown beers. Though we rarely were drunk, beer was constantly in our glasses. The Czechs drank beer, pivo to them, like water, and it was the cheapest and easiest beverage to access in any pub. Clubs weren't really our scene, so we'd spend most of our evenings in pubs over pints of pivo, talking, laughing, getting to know each other.

Emily and Mason had been betting shots at the foosball table for the last hour, each game and shot progressively louder than the one before. Alex's friend Richard and his friend Jan sat at the end of our table, deep in conversation with Alex, drinking their Braniks twice the pace of anyone else. Charlie, Nick, and I had been having our own conversation for over an hour, which had evolved into a loose game of King's Cup with the deck of cards Charlie carried everywhere. Oftentimes, nights that were spent at Anděl were without Celeste and Lexie, who had a hard time getting back across the Vltava this late at night.

Nick poured a splash of his fresh beer into the communal cup in the middle of the deck of cards. He had pulled the last king.

"Aren't you going to drink that?" I asked. Each one of us had drawn a king already, and the half-liter glass in the middle of the table was about a quarter full with a mixture of Budvar and Staropramen.

"Ughhhhhhhh. Was that the fourth king?" Nick groaned, slapping his hand on the table.

Charlie dug his lighter out of his pocket and flicked it, lighting the tip of his cigarette. "Bottom's up," he said.

Nick grabbed the glass and held it up. "*Na zdraví.*"

Charlie and I raised our glasses. "Na zdraví," we said together, touching the top of our beer glasses together, then the bottom, then tapping them on the table before we raised our glasses to our lips in unison, the three of us.

I set my beer on the table and checked my phone. It was 12:50 a.m. I had class in the morning. We had begun to differentiate between weeknights and weekends, though not by much. School nights we'd only stay out till 2 a.m. or so, with weekend nights stretching into the next morning, the sun rising over the top of our apartment building as we laughed up the sidewalk home. My head was feeling cloudy and my throat scratchy.

"I think this'll be my last round," I declared to Charlie and Nick. "I feel like I'm getting a cold and don't want to be totally wiped for class tomorrow. I think I'll catch the 1:08 bus."

Overnight, our bus slowed to once an hour. Other than walking the half hour uphill home, there was no other way to go. If we missed the bus, sometimes we'd head back to the bar—one of the shady bars at Anděl near Na Knízecí, with all-night gambling and locals that drank the night away alone.

Nick took the last swig from the communal cup. "Yeah, I want to head home too. I'll go with you."

I looked to Nick. "Are you feeling sick?"

"No. I just want to go home with you," Nick said.

Charlie set his glass down a little too loudly.

"I mean, early. I want to head out early too," Nick said, correcting himself.

I smiled. "All right."

"Hey, I've got winner!" Charlie called over to Emily and Mason.

"What do you think is going on over there?" Nick nodded toward Alex and her Czech friends, his voice low. "Threesome?"

"Ew!" I squealed. "I really don't want to think about that."

Nick raised his eyebrows. "I don't know... they've been huddled like that, the three of them, all night."

Charlie leaned in across the table closer to Nick and me. "Have you ever had a threesome?"

I picked up my beer and took an overly long drink to avoid answering. Both boys immediately looked in my direction. Nick raised his eyebrows. I kept drinking.

"Well, I haven't," said Charlie. "I'm still trying to figure out one woman at a time." He picked his cigarette up, taking a long drag.

I set my glass down, looking at Nick.

"Almost. But no," he said.

"Almost?" I inquired.

"Yes, almost. But no." He picked his glass up, eyes not leaving mine.

"I never... no. No. Not me," I stammered. I always felt so nervous around Nick when sex came up. I was not a shy person by nature. I didn't have anything to hide and never minded talking about taboo subjects or things that most people didn't want to discuss. But around Nick, I measured every word. "Well, whatever they do," I said, nodding in Alex's direction. "I just don't want to hear it in my apartment."

Charlie and Nick laughed. "Yeah, that's not something I'd want to hear either," Charlie agreed.

Just then, Emily slid next to me on the bench. She grabbed my glass from in front of me and downed the rest of my beer. "Mason's a fucking cheater," she slurred.

"What the fuck?" Mason laughed across the table from us, next to Charlie. "Em, you're ridiculous. Who cares?"

Emily looked down toward Alex. "How does she get so much ass?" She was a little too loud, had obviously drunk too much, and was a little jealous of the attention Alex was getting.

I laughed. "I don't know. But I'm heading home." I stood up and stepped over the bench, grabbing my bag. "Are you still coming?" I said to Nick.

"Yeah." He picked up his beer and finished it off. "Let's head out."

We said our good nights and made our way up the stairs and outside. A few men were huddled next to the entrance of the bar, smoking. We turned the corner and headed toward the bus station, walking in silence.

"So what's wrong with you?" Nick's voice broke the quiet between us.

"What?" I looked up at him, puzzled.

"You said you're getting sick. What's wrong?"

"Oh. I just have had a nagging headache and feel like my throat is getting scratchy." I cleared my throat. "It might just be all the cigarette smoke though," I justified.

"Yeah, but you don't want to take chances. I have some NyQuil at Cozy, I'll get it for you." He put his arm around my shoulder. It wasn't cold out, but my body immediately warmed up.

"Ugh, I *hate* NyQuil!" I complained. "It's the worst. Any medicine that isn't a pill makes me gag. My ex once tried to get me to take Chloraseptic spray for a sore throat—"

"Your ex?" Nick cut me off. His voice raised on that last word, along with his eyebrows.

I looked up at Nick as we crossed the street. "Yeah. Mark and I broke up." I wanted to make sure he heard me. I hadn't heard a word from Mark since I sent him the email, which had now been a few weeks ago. I didn't think I would, but I took his silence to mean he would give me space, or perhaps was just too angry to talk to me until I got home in December. *If* I went home in December.

Nick stopped walking. His arm fell off my shoulders as he turned to face me. "I'm sorry. Are you okay?"

"Yeah, I'm fine," I said.

"What happened?"

"I just... it wasn't working. I've known for a while but it's been too hard to cut the ties. I mean, I came out here, and then that thing with you... and it wasn't just that—I mean... there are just things he does..." My voice trailed off. I wasn't sure how to explain it, especially to Nick, but didn't want him to think that I ended things with Mark because of what had happened between us. I took a deep breath. "I found myself questioning our relationship, my feelings for him, way too often for them to be real. I think if it's real, you just know. You don't constantly ask yourself if it's real. You don't have to convince yourself that you are where you should be. You just know."

Nick sighed and shuffled his feet, looking at the ground.

"Besides," I continued, "I think when you're with the right person you don't want to be with someone else." I let the words lay out, almost visible in the space between us.

Nick looked up at me. "You want to be with someone else?"

I had said the words without realizing them, and now it was too late. "Not *want to be with*, I meant because we'd kissed. If I were with the right person, I wouldn't have wanted to kiss someone else."

He nodded, in understanding or in kindness, then looked back at the ground. "Come on. We don't want to miss the bus."

We walked toward Na Knízecí, arriving just as the bus was pulling up, and boarded silently. I settled into a seat by the window, Nick sliding right next to me. He started talking about our Gender and Culture class we had the next day and an assignment that was due. I listened, nodding periodically as the bus climbed the hill, but my mind wandered. I was trying not to analyze Nick's abrupt reaction to my breakup with Mark. He wasn't the reason we'd broken up, but I was still hoping for something a little more from Nick. I stared out the window, the bus leaning back and forth on the winding streets. Sometimes I was convinced the bus would tip over on those tighter turns.

"*Příští zastávka, Urbanova,*" the automated voice called out.

I reached my arm up and pulled the cord. Nick and I inched out of our row toward the doors, holding on to the dangling handles above. Moments later, the bus slowed to a halt. The accordion doors folded open and we were once again outside under the night stars.

"Well, see you in the morning," I called behind me to Nick, starting toward my apartment.

"Aren't you coming over?" Nick asked.

I turned around, puzzled. "What?"

"The NyQuil."

"Oh, right. Yeah." I had never taken NyQuil in my life, but I didn't want to miss out on some alone time with Nick.

We crossed Peroutkova and wandered down Xaveriova, parallel to the cemetery across the street from the small alleyways where Cozy House was sat. It was a still, quiet night, and we passed no one. We had left all the street lights behind on Peroutkova, and Xaveriova was nearly pitch-black. The normally colorful houses were all the same color now. Occasionally, I'd stumble over a cobblestone in the sidewalk.

"I never remember which turn it is," Nick said. "It's always further down than I think it is." He stopped and squinted at the house numbers on the side of the building.

I had only been to Cozy once before, and had never been further than the entryway. We turned off Xaveriova and walked up a small alley. The backs of the homes on Xaveriova all faced the street; to access the homes, you walked up an alleyway and turned onto what looked like a small and narrow park that was sectioned off into small front yards, each with its own waist-high gate. We walked until we saw number eighty-eight, where Nick pushed the gate open. I followed as he fished his keys out of his jeans pocket. When we got to the door, he stuck in his key, turned the lock, and pushed the door open forcefully with his hip.

He flicked a light switch inside. The light illuminated a narrow hallway about twenty feet long. Nick walked down the hallway as I shut the door behind me. At the end of a hall was a few hooks with miscellaneous coats hung, scarfs falling to the floor. A few pairs of shoes were scattered underneath the hooks. The hall turned to the right, and opened up to another hallway on the left, which led to the living room, a curved staircase directly in front of us—which I assumed led to the bedrooms—and a closed door immediately to our right. Nick turned to the closed door and opened it. He walked across the room in the dark and turned a switch on a lamp, illuminating what I saw to be a bedroom.

"Oh," I said, bewildered. "This is your room?"

Nick laughed, moving his backpack off the floor and into his desk chair. "Yeah. This place has a weird layout. My bedroom is on the first floor and the kitchen is in the basement."

I surveyed the room but didn't enter. A twin bed was in the corner to the left, and opposite the door to the room were two big windows that looked out to the front yard. There was a small desk next to the windows that looked just like the other desks I'd seen in everyone's flats. Nick had an actual closet in his room just a few feet from the door to the room, which I was instantly jealous of.

"You have a real closet!" I exclaimed.

"Yeah," he said, fumbling with papers and things on his desk. He looked up at me and noticed I was still standing in the hallway, peering inside the room. "You can come in, you know."

I walked in carefully, breaking an invisible barrier in our relationship. I was in Nick's bedroom. The sheets were pushed toward the foot of the unmade bed. A few shirts were scattered on top, including the blue shirt with "Amsterdam" on it that he had been stuck wearing the first few days, when his luggage was missing. Jeans were on the floor next to the bed. A few books had been kicked underneath, where I noticed his suitcase was stored.

"I have it here somewhere..." he mumbled to himself, opening his desk drawer.

On top of his desk sat a white Apple PowerBook. "Oh, you have a laptop here," I said in surprise. I had never seen him with it—never brought it to Bara's office, not at an internet café or in class—so I had assumed he didn't bring one.

"Yeah," he sighed. "I lent my power cord to Stephanie our first weekend here, because hers broke and we have the same laptop, and she broke it. And then my battery died. So I'm stuck with a laptop that won't work for the rest of the semester."

I shook my head. "That's awful," I said incredulously. "Won't she replace it?" "Yeah, I'm sure she will at some point... here it is!" He pulled a blue and green box out of his desk drawer and walked over to me. "Let's go."

"Where?"

"Back to your place," he answered, grabbing a crumpled hoodie off his bed.

"What?" I asked. I felt like there was something I was missing.

"I can't let you walk home in the middle of the night alone. I'll walk you back to your place, and you can keep the NyQuil till you're done with it. Or until you get me sick." He zipped his hoodie up and walked over to me. His hand met the small of my back as he gently led me out the door of his bedroom, turning the light off behind him. Down the hall we walked, toward the front door.

It had gotten colder outside in the few minutes we'd been inside Cozy House. I shivered as Nick pulled his front door closed once more, locking it behind him. We made our way toward the gate. As he paused to open it for me, I stopped.

"Nick?"

He turned around, already through the gate. "Yeah?"

"Why are you doing this for me?"

He frowned. "What do you mean?"

I shrugged. "The NyQuil, leaving the bar with me, walking me home. It's so... nice. Thoughtful."

He smiled. "I never really thought about it. You're important to me. You're getting sick. And it's just common sense not to let a girl walk home alone after midnight."

A knot rose in my throat. My eyes filled with tears, glossy, staring out at him. "Thank you. I guess I'm not used to being around such a nice guy." I walked over to him and put my hand on his arm, squeezing it. "You're a good one."

He put his arm around my shoulders again. "I know."

I laughed. We made our way through the silent streets once more, our voices disrupted the quiet around us. It was as if we were the only two people in the whole city. I hated the idea of being in my apartment alone, but I knew it was unlikely Alex or Emily would be back, unless they took a cab by themselves, without Charlie or Mason. I didn't want to invite Nick up. I wasn't ready to hear him say "no," but also wasn't ready to change the dynamic of our relationship. We'd finally gotten to a good place after our five-story night, after the mess of staying over at John's apartment. I let my mind wander to what might happen if he did come up... or if he asked to come up. And before I knew it, we were at my front door.

"Okay," Nick said. He stood in front of me and handed me the box of NyQuil.

"Thank you for this," I said, taking it from him. "And for walking me home. You did not need to do that." I shook my head and stepped forward, pulling him into a hug.

"It's nothing. I hope you feel better." Nick held me tight. I let my eyes close for a moment, savoring the feeling of his arms wrapped around me. My head rested, for a moment, on his shoulder. He broke away.

"See you tomorrow." He stuck his arm out and waved at me, walking slowly backward down the sidewalk.

I waved back. Once he was out of view, I pulled the door open and walked up to my apartment. It was pitch-black and silent. I closed my apartment door and sat down on the floor on the other side of the door. My mind, as usual, drifted to Nicholas.

He went out of his way for me. I'd never really had someone take care of me like this before, and all he did was lend me NyQuil. I looked at the bottle in my hands. Slowly, I turned the cap and lifted it up to my nose. It smelled disgusting. How had I lasted twenty-one years without ever taking NyQuil? There was no way I was going to start tonight.

Buzzzzzzzzzz.

I jumped and let out a startled yell. My doorbell had just rung. It had to be Nick. What did he want? To say something? To ask if he could come up? *I should have asked him to come up,* I thought. I stood up and pressed the talk button.

"Hello?"

Nick's voice was loud over the speaker. "You better actually take that NyQuil," he scolded.

A grin broke out over my face. "How did you know?"

"Ahhh, I'm getting to know you. Take the damn medicine."

I closed the lid on the NyQuil bottle and hugged it tightly to my chest. "Good night, Nicholas."

"Good night, Adriana."

I kept the button pressed down, until I heard his footsteps fade away over the speaker.

13

September, Budapest.

Part of Bara's job was to organize weekend trips. We wouldn't have been bored staying weekends in Prague; we were content to wander the cobblestoned streets and frequent our favorite pubs. But with Prague's central geographic location within Europe, it was incredibly easy to travel to other amazing destinations within rail distance. After a month in Prague, we were ready to get out for a weekend.

Bara planned a weekend in the countryside, first wine tasting in Moravia, and then two days in Budapest. It had been weeks since the boys had all gone away to Amsterdam, and this trip was going to be the first time we would all spend any "quality" time together, day and night. It was going to be a test, if nothing else.

Our train was scheduled to depart for Moravia at 8 a.m., so Emily, Alex, and I made a plan to leave our apartment by seven. It was a bus ride and a metro ride with a line change before we'd arrive at Hlavnii Nádraží, and Alex was insistent that we stop by Kava Kava Kava for coffee. We arrived at the train station, coffee in hand, with a few minutes to spare.

"Yes, hello, good morning," Bara greeted us. "Please get on the train now." Bara was earning a reputation for being good natured, but direct. It was endlessly amusing to watch a Czech woman force herself to exert the typical cheer Americans are accustomed to.

I shifted the weight of my backpack onto my other shoulder, its zipper hardly containing all of my supposed weekend essentials. I made my way up the clunky metal stairs and turned right into the long, narrow hallway of the train. I'd traveled enough to know that the trains in the Czech Republic were lacking. The western European trains I'd seen were shined on the outside, had a slanted nose for the sake of speed, and a knack for efficiency (for the most part). The train I'd just boarded looked like it would fall apart if I kicked the side hard enough. Just as that thought crossed my mind, I tripped over an empty Staropramen beer bottle. At 7:54 a.m.

"Morning!" was called out of the cabin we were passing. It was Noelle, who was seated along with the girls from the Garden Apartment. Alex ducked into the cabin, seeing her friends.

"Where's Stephanie?" Emily asked. Stephanie peeked her head out from behind one of the girls and waved, and Emily walked into the cabin behind Alex.

I wasn't stoked about the idea of sitting with the Garden Girls for five hours. I wondered if I should keep going, hoping I'd find my friends, or settle in. Right on cue, I heard Celeste's contagious laugh from farther down the hall. I kept walking, and two cabins down, I found my people and ducked into the cabin.

Mason was doing some horrendous impression of Bara to get Celeste to laugh. Next to Celeste was Lexie, looking unbelievably put together for such an early train, who was already in conversation with John. On the bench across from them, sitting next to Mason, was Charlie, shaking a pack of cigarettes, and Nick, wearing a tight-fitting Holland football club tee. He nodded in my direction.

"Hey. Ready to drink some wine?" He smiled.

"Yup, it's 8 a.m., so bring it on," I laughed.

Within moments, the train jerked out of the station. Before long, Prague was whizzing past us out the window. We all chatted excitedly as our host city faded into industrial buildings, then slowly into countryside.

Eight hours later, after a stop for lunch, another train ride, and then a bus ride to a river, we arrived. Bara had arranged a dinner cruise to a local vineyard, where we'd spend the evening sampling wines native to Moravia. The bus let us off at a rickety dock, boards sticking up in some places. It was not what one would picture when imagining a riverboat cocktail cruise. Ahead of us, a boxy riverboat floated at the end of the dock. White and orange paint was chipping off in most places, and an overweight captain stood outside it on the deck, smoking a cigarette.

"Yep, that seems about right," Nicholas said as he stepped off the bus. He walked over to where Celeste, Mason, and I were standing.

It was another few minutes until everyone, and their bags, were unloaded. Bara instructed us to wait for her before boarding the boat. She did a quick head count, exchanged words with our bus driver, and greeted the riverboat captain. We waited as they conversed in Czech, glancing between the boat and the group of twenty-somethings waiting to board and drink.

"Yes, okay, we can get in the boat," Bara said, walking back toward us. "Please go inside first for the meal."

Single file, we boarded the boat, which was just as disappointing inside as it was out. We ducked to enter the dining room set up in the cabin inside. Two narrow tables stood along either side of the boat, with one side looking out of small, round windows and the other side with people's backs against the windows. The tables and benches alongside them were bolted to the floor. A single life raft hung on the wall, a very obvious crack in one side. I grabbed a seat facing a window. Outside, the sun was already beginning to set, and above the tall grasses bordering the river, the sky was tinged with orange and pink. Celeste found a spot on the bench next to me, and John, Charlie, Mason, and Nick sat on the bench opposite us.

The "meal" that was promised was crusty rye bread, olives, and some indistinguishable cheese that quickly filled the boat with its smell. It didn't take long for us to push it aside in favor of the wine that had started to make its way around the room. Before long the first, second, and third bottles were empty at our table, while the food had remained largely untouched. Stomachs filled with nothing but wine, the rest of the night passed in a blur.

At some point, we disembarked the boat at a vineyard, and spent the rest of the evening in an underground tasting room resembling a cave. Our entire group, including Bara, was seated at the sort of long table you'd find in a beer hall, where we were served one variety of wine after another. I lost count of the types of red wine we tried, and when those bottles were empty, we moved on to white. Each of us had small, shot-like glasses that were filled repeatedly by our host, an old man with a long white beard and potbelly. When he wasn't pouring wine, he played accordion and serenaded us in Czech. We toasted before every round and made up ridiculous things to drink to. We linked arms and drank. We took photos of bottles and my camera was passed around to the group, everyone taking photos from their own uniquely blurry point of view.

Eventually, we somehow made it to the hotel Bara had arranged for us, where I found myself in a room with Celeste and Lexie. There was a twin bed in the corner that Nick helped me into. And then I remembered nothing more.

The sun was bright through the faded, yellowed curtains. From my bed, I could just make out that there had once been flowers printed on them, but the colors had long dulled from years of hanging in the sun. I pushed myself up and saw Lexie and Celeste, both already awake, in the queen-size bed in the middle of our room. The other twin bed that I'd been in was opposite their bed, pushed up against the wall, facing the window. I struggled to gain my bearings.

"Morning!" Celeste called cheerfully.

I moaned. "Oh, my God." I rubbed my head, which was already throbbing.

"I know," Lexie said. "Me too."

I eased myself out of bed and climbed into theirs, right in the middle. "What the hell did we do last night? Did they spike that wine with something?"

Celeste giggled. "You guys, I think we each took down at least two bottles."

"I only remember parts." I closed my eyes to recall. "We must have done that Borat-toasting thing like a hundred times." My mouth stretched into a smile, despite the hammer slowly beating my brain. "I don't even remember getting here. Somehow I put my pajamas on though, so that's impressive."

Celeste laughed louder. "Nick did that," she said.

I turned my face toward her. "There's no way that he was in here last night."

Lexie leaned over and grabbed my camera off her nightstand. "Let's see if this helps jog our memories." She flicked it on and handed it to me.

We looked back on the photos, laughing harder with each blurry frame. Someone laughing, someone drinking, someone kissing. It looked like it had been a fantastic time. Celeste hadn't drunk nearly as much has Lexie and I had, so she remembered far more than we did. Apparently, we'd crammed into the back of a taxi with John and Nick. Charlie and Nick had helped Lexie and me up into the room, and Nick pulled off my jeans and put on my pajama pants for me before putting me in bed. Charlie had seemed fine, Celeste said, and then through laughter recounted how he'd run into our bathroom and returned all the wine he'd drunk to the toilet.

It was slow moving that morning, and nearly another hour before we met the rest of our group downstairs for breakfast, where we learned that Emily, Nick, and Mason had actually gone downstairs to the bar of our hotel and continued drinking last night. There had been a local guy who Lexie had apparently invited to come to the hotel with us and hang out, and then we'd left him downstairs in the lobby.

We greedily tore open croissants, and gulped down coffee to chase the Advil Noelle passed around. Bara came around and reiterated the itinerary for the day. We were scheduled to continue on to Budapest in just half an hour, and meet for a walking tour before enjoying some much-needed downtime to explore the city.

Once every last crumb was gone from our plates, we went to gather our bags. When we got to the stairs, we saw Nick, Charlie, and John with their bags, heading down to check out. I shyly caught Nick's eye. I vaguely remembered sitting next to him at our long table, glasses clinking together time and time again, but that was about it. The photographic evidence on my camera showed us engrossed in conversation in the background of a few photos; in others we laughed, his arm around me as I leaned toward him. One photo in particular stuck out in my mind. Lexie, Celeste, and Charlie all looked at the camera smiling for what had apparently been an attempt at a posed photo. John and Nick had their glasses raised to toast, as I sat next to Nick and stared at him. In my eyes, caught on camera, were my feelings for Nick. It was obvious to me, and Celeste had remarked about it when she saw the photo. *He's going to catch you looking at him like that,* she'd said. I had blushed and moved on to the next photo.

"Hey hey, how you ladies feeling this morning?" John asked as he descended the last stair.

"I'm fine, but these two..." Celeste grimaced as she pointed to Lexie and me. I shifted my glance down to the floor as Nick looked at me.

"Noelle has Advil," Charlie said.

"Yeah, we got some," Lexie replied. "How are you guys feeling?"

Nick laughed and turned to John. "Well..."

"Someone puked in my bed," John said. "Not sure who that was. And someone walked into the wall in the middle of the night and then fell on the floor and slept there."

"Hey, it was actually more comfortable than my bed," Charlie interjected.

I laughed. It was good to know that Lexie and I weren't the only ones who had been in bad shape.

"Where are you headed?" Nick asked the three of us.

"Getting our bags," Celeste answered.

"Meet you outside." Charlie was already reaching for his cigarette pack.

I passed by Nick on the stairs, and bumped right into his backpack as I tried to avoid his gaze. I looked up to apologize, and he smiled warmly.

"Get it together, Adriana," he said.

I blushed, only managing to nod in return. I turned around and hurried up the stairs after Celeste and Lexie. What had I said to him last night? I said a silent prayer that it wasn't anything incriminating or humiliating. Celeste said he'd helped me take my jeans off. Knowing Nick as I'd come to, I was sure it was a gentlemanly act. Had I done anything desperate? Tried to come onto him? I had no idea, and decided I wouldn't ask.

Δ

It wasn't too hard to drag the pillowy down comforter off the bed and climb onto the roof, blanket trailing behind. The couch cushions were a little more challenging, but we made a chain from the couch to the roof, passing cushions out the window and up onto the rooftop. I stood at the bottom of the narrow ladder that was clumsily bolted to the side of the building outside our window, passing the cushions up the ladder to Nick, who tossed them up to John, who

153

handed them to Lexie, who was arranging a makeshift couch for us on the roof of our new hotel. It was Celeste's idea when she looked out our hotel room window and saw we had easy access to the roof, but she had opted to crash early. It was just John, Lexie, Nick, Charlie (who had collected money from everyone and went to pick up some beer), and me. After passing the last cushion up to Nick, I climbed up the ladder carefully.

Outside, the wind was bitter. The weather had been just right for our walking tour earlier in the day, and for our dinner alfresco just a few hours earlier. It had been a gorgeous day of sightseeing, and we'd spent the afternoon walking the Chain Bridge from Buda to Pest and getting lost. I zipped my hoodie up and continued up the ladder. John and Lexie were already sitting on a group of cushions, their back to the wind. There wasn't enough room on the makeshift couch for Nick, and he sat across from them huddled in the down comforter we'd tossed up onto the roof. He held his arm out, motioning for me to join him under the blanket. I wasn't going to turn that offer down for anything.

Lexie was mid-laugh, as usual. It was one of the things I loved most about her. John was animatedly telling a story that had Lexie and Nick laughing hysterically. John was a natural story teller, always knowing which words to hit and when to pause for laughs.

"So they ordered a bottle of sauvignon blanc," he said, emphasizing *sauvignon blanc*. "And they're shouting at the television in the bar, that the ref made a bad call on the quarterback, the whole time just pounding sauvignon blanc." He waited while his audience, captive, caught their breaths. "I mean, who goes to a sports bar and orders sauvignon blanc? Who watches football on a Sunday morning and just goes to town on bottles of sauvignon blanc?" They'd laugh more every time he said it. Sauvignon blanc.

Across the roof, footsteps headed toward us. We fell quiet as we wondered if it was hotel security, or an employee who'd been complained to of noise on the roof.

"So the only thing I could find, is a beer called Dreher," Charlie said.

I breathed a sigh of relief, happy to see it was just Charlie.

"I actually bought it from the guy at the front desk." He passed bottles around, then sat down between the makeshift couch John and Lexie were sharing and the blanket Nick and I had, forming a sort of circle.

"Budapest is so different from how I imagined," Lexie said, staring off into the distance. From our rooftop, we could see the Chain Bridge that connected Buda to Pest, and the Danube sparkling underneath.

"What did you imagine?" Nick asked, popping his bottle open.

"I don't know, not so nice I guess?" Lexie seemed like she wasn't sure. "I didn't think Prague would be so nice either, though."

I nodded. "I had no idea Prague would be like it is," I agreed. "I pictured something... so much more cold."

"I'd never even seen a picture of Prague before I got there," John said.

I scoffed. "Are you serious?"

He nodded. "Never been to Europe before. I went to San Fran once to visit my brother. That's about it. It's not really the same."

We started talking about the places we'd traveled. For both Lexie and John, their time abroad was this, their first time in Europe. For Nick, not so much. He told us about how his parents were both European and he'd traveled back quite a bit as a kid to visit them, his mother's family in Austria and his father's in Denmark. Turns out he had also backpacked with three of his best friends from high school the summer before they started college.

Before long we'd sectioned off again, Charlie deciding to go and find a bar, Lexie and John lying down, cuddling on their couch and whispering, leaving Nick and me alone yet again.

"So what's your favorite place you've traveled?" I asked him. We'd repositioned ourselves, lying the comforter out like a picnic blanket and lying on top of it, gazing at the stars.

"Hmm. Florence. We made a long trip there when I was younger and I just loved it all. My dad took us through all the museums and art galleries. It was so gorgeous."

"Yeah, I love Italy too," I said. I thought I sounded dumb, vague, so I propped myself up to take another swig of beer. "I think Rome is my favorite though."

"I'm not a big fan of Rome. My favorite European city is definitely London."

"London? Really? I thought it was kind of dull."

"I would love to go back someday. I was only there for twenty-four hours by myself, before I met up with friends."

"That's how I felt about Amsterdam. I'd love to go back someday. It's so gorgeous." I glanced over at Nick. "Probably not the way you went with Charlie and John though..." We laughed.

"Yeah, probably not. Definitely not. I'd worry about you."

I raised my eyebrows. "Please. I could handle it." I was flattered he'd worry about me, but wanted to make sure he knew I didn't need his worry.

Nick stretched his arms out and folded them behind his head, sighing heavily. "This makes me miss home."

"What, drinking on rooftops?" I lay back down next to him, but not too close. There was just room enough between us. Our sweatshirts touched, but our bodies didn't. Enough room for the Holy Ghost, my dad would have said.

"No, Orion."

I looked up at the stars. I wasn't familiar with constellations, other than the Big and Little Dipper, which we'd hunt for during summer trips to Lake Powell with my mom's side of the family. "Which one is that?"

Nick's arm extended into the sky. "See that especially bright star over there?"

The sky was full of stars, mostly indistinguishable from one another. Budapest wasn't bright enough to hide the sky's light.

"Which one? That one?" I pointed toward a star, hapless, hoping I'd pointed to the right one. I had no idea where I was supposed to be looking.

Nick's hand grabbed mine, and he pulled my hand over to where he was pointing. "There. Here's his torso, and his arm, holding the bow." He gently traced the constellation.

I didn't dare move and startle his hand out of mine. "Why does it make you homesick?" I asked.

Nick lowered his arm, my hand still in his. "It makes me think of my friends. We'd sit on the beach and drink, just hang out. And you'd always be able to see Orion."

I stayed quiet. I wanted him to keep talking, to open up. I wanted to know so much more about him. Everything.

"My group of friends is very close. We all started hanging out as misfits, guys who didn't really belong in any other group. But they're all really great guys."

I'd never heard a guy talk about his friends like that. It was endearing.

"I don't really miss them, though. My buddy studied abroad in Barcelona last year. He told me while I was gone, not to talk to anyone. Not an email, not a Facebook message, no phone calls or texts."

I turned to face him. "Why?"

Nick's eyes were still fixed on the stars. "So I would focus on where I am. Just be. Enjoy Prague, be present, and not worry about home."

"That's really good advice." I wasn't sure I could have done that myself, but I understood the appeal. "So have you done it? Have you talked to anyone from home?"

"Well yeah, my family. My dad is coming out to visit, and I've been emailing my mom. And my sisters, of course. But I can't not talk to my sisters."

"Why's that?"

"I have three sisters and a single mom. It's part of my job to make sure they're okay. I have to look out for them. I meet the boyfriends, I hear about drama with friends, make sure they're making the right moves with their jobs."

I wanted to squeeze his hand, but was afraid to call attention to the fact that they were still entwined, fingers laced together tightly. "That's really sweet," I said softly.

He turned his face toward mine. "It's just how I was brought up."

"So who looks after you?"

"I try not to make my sisters, my mom, worry about me. I don't bring girls home. I don't get into trouble. I do my own thing. I've never actually met a girl I've even wanted my family to meet. Never wanted to give anyone the wrong impression by bringing them home to meet the sisters." He sighed, looking toward Orion once more.

Pieces were starting to come together. He'd never really been in a relationship. He didn't like drama. Nick seemed to be effortless in his movements, his speech. It all just flowed, so sure of himself. But behind the scenes, I could see he considered each move in his life, like a big game of chess. He was responsible, deliberate, strong. I felt another surge of affection for him. I'd never met anyone like him in my life. And we lay on the rooftop, in Budapest, holding hands, gazing at the stars, the feelings I'd been fighting for him unequivocally growing.

Lexie and John had dragged their cushions over by us. They'd gotten another few bottles of beer from downstairs, and John popped a couple open and handed them to us. I'd been so engrossed in my conversation with Nick that I hadn't noticed they had left and returned. We sat in our circle once again, moving in close to form a barrier against the wind. Nick wrapped the comforter around us, his arm stretched around my back, pulling me close to him and leaving his arm around me. I looked out across the sky, at the shimmering lights of Budapest. I was doing just what I had come across the globe to do. We sat like that for hours, as we laughed and talked and dreamed, clinking beer bottles, until the sun was visible over the Danube, and the stars faded into a pale pink horizon.

"All right, guess we should head back to our room. It's only another hour until we have to meet downstairs for a tour of God knows what. All I know is that it better include breakfast," John said, standing up to stretch and motioning to Nick. "You comin'?"

"Right behind you," he said.

I knew the night had to end sometime, but I wasn't eager to leave the cocoon Nick and I had spent the last few hours in. He stood up, then turned around and offered his hand to help me up. I bent over to gather the comforter while the others worked on the empty beer bottles and couch cushions. We climbed back down the ladder one by one, through the window, and back into our hotel room. Inside, Celeste was sleeping in one of the two queen beds. Quietly, we tiptoed through the room and into the living area. John and Lexie hugged good night, and she made her way to the bathroom, and John down the hallway to his room.

The clock on the coffee table read 6:13 a.m. John was right, we were supposed to meet back in our hotel lobby at seven for yet another walking tour before our sleeper train home. I noticed Nick was lingering at the door.

"I can't believe we were up there all night," I said.

"It was a pretty fantastic night," he replied. He shuffled his feet, still postponing his exit. I thought I knew why, and hoped I was right.

"The most fun I've ever had in Budapest," I said with a smile.

He laughed, then shook his head. "Well..." He turned to start down the hall, then whipped back around. He took a step back toward my hotel room.

I was still standing inside my room, leaning against the hotel room door, ready to close it behind him just a moment earlier.

"Good night," he mostly whispered.

I froze. For half a second, he moved forward, leaning in as if he might kiss me. My breath caught in my throat, unable to say anything to respond. He lingered for a second, then broke off from my gaze, and turned to walk down the hall. I shut the door the rest of the way, resting my forehead on the inside of the door as it clicked shut. We were so close. I knew he'd felt it too.

For the first time in a long time, perhaps in my life, I was just living as me. Obeying each whim I felt inside me, weighing impulses as I felt like, moving my life in the direction I wanted to go in. I wasn't sure what that direction was right now, but I liked where I was headed. It felt honest, pure, and real. I did what I wanted. And right now, what I wanted was to kiss Nick.

The butterflies that always fluttered in my belly when Nick was around rose up higher into my chest at the thought. I'd had enough beer to think I could do it and enough moxie to not care either way. Without another thought, I flung the door open and ran down the hall to the staircase, thick blanket still wrapped around my shoulders. The hotel was ancient; there was no elevator to the top floor. When I got to the top of the stairs and still didn't see Nick, my feet carried me down the first flight, nearly slipping. As I got to the landing I saw him on the next flight of stairs.

"Nick!" I whisper-yelled.

His head whipped around. Seeing me stopped on the landing, out of breath, comforter wrapped around my shoulders, he started back up the stairs toward me.

"What are you doing?"

"I... uhh..." Nothing came out. I saw him there, in front of me, his own person. And I realized maybe he hadn't kissed me for a reason. Maybe he wasn't there yet. Maybe we were headed somewhere different. There was no denying we had a connection, and perhaps this was destined to be more of a friendship than a romantic relationship. I started thinking too much and my earlier impulsivity was gone. "Good night."

He smiled and shook his head softly, looking up at me from a few stairs down. And then he turned and walked away.

Δ

It was almost midnight by the time we boarded our train back to Prague. We'd spent the better part of the past hour sitting on the platform in our sweatpants, playing cards. Laughter echoed through the station, open on one side for trains to arrive and depart the city. Every few minutes, a booming voice on a fuzzy loudspeaker had made an unintelligible announcement and we'd look at Bara. Our train had been delayed for nearly two hours. Backpacks were being used as pillows by the overtired members of our group. Celeste and I leaned against each other. I was exhausted from being up on the rooftop the night before, and walking throughout what felt like the entire city of Budapest today on our tour. I was ready to lie down and sleep, even if it was basically on a yoga mat drilled into a bench on the side of a train wall.

When our train finally pulled up to the platform, we struggled to get up and gather our things. We were scheduled to arrive at six in the morning, a Monday. I knew some of the group had classes on Monday and I felt awful for them. I'd never been quite so thankful for my Tuesday through Thursday schedule as I was at that moment.

Bara had assigned us to cabins, six to each. She was adamant that boys and girls should not be in the same train cabin. The five guys loaded into one cabin, leaving one bed empty. The four garden girls, plus Alex and Bara, had one cabin. The last cabin was left to Emily, Stephanie, Celeste, Lexie, Noelle, and me.

Immediately, I threw my backpack onto a middle bunk and climbed on. As usual, I was sandwiched between Celeste and Lexie. We said our good nights and curtains were pulled shut. I rolled onto my side, trying to get as comfortable as possible. The bed was only slightly more comfortable than the cement train platform, but it was all we'd have for the next six hours. I closed my eyes, and immediately traveled back to the rooftop in Budapest, my hand in Nick's, Lexie's laughter echoing in my ears. It was a happy, safe place. I already ached to go back.

"Hey, Addie, are you up?"

I opened my eyes. Lexie's face was peering down from above, her blonde waves hanging down past my bunk.

"Come over to John's cabin with me."

"Why, what are they doing?"

"I don't know, but he wanted me to come hang out. I don't want to go by myself!"

I sighed. "Lex, I'm so tired from last night." *Nick would be in that cabin, too*, I thought to myself.

"*Pleeeeease?*" Lexie squealed. "I don't want anyone to think anything's going on with us."

I laughed halfheartedly, and pushed myself up to be seated, my head hitting Lexie's bunk. I shrunk back down and rubbed it.

"Fine," I agreed.

She jumped down off her bed quietly, and I followed. I couldn't find my shoes without turning on the cabin light, and I knew by the calm breathing that the other girls had already fallen asleep.

Lexie pulled the door of our cabin open and stuck her head out into the hallway. I was sure she was looking for Bara, who was strangely interested in keeping us apart from the guys. I wasn't sure what she was so worried about. What could we do on one night on a train that we couldn't do any other night? Apparently deciding the coast was clear,

Lexie crept into the hall. As soon as I walked out, I saw John already standing in the hall, door to his cabin open. He was looking at the window.

"Uh, excuse me, miss, I'm going to need you to get back to your bed," he joked, a little too loudly.

"*Shhhhhhh*!" Lexie giggled. She walked over toward him, and their eyes found one another. I had no idea what I was doing there, but it was immediately clear I wasn't needed, or wanted.

"Uh, Adriana, Nick's still up inside if you want to hang out. My bunk is free." I wasn't sure if he thought I had come to try and find Nick, or if he was just trying to get rid of me. I was too tired to care either way. Saying good night to them, I walked into the cabin where the boys were staying.

The lights were already out. Nick was lying in the middle bunk with his iPod, same spot where I'd been in my cabin, and the bunk directly below him was empty, which I assumed was John's.

Hearing me enter, Nick turned toward the door. "Hey, what are you doing here?" He pulled an earbud out of his ear. I could hear soft music through the little speaker.

I really had no idea what to say. "Lexie wanted me to come hang out, but she and John are going for a walk I think?"

Nick looked at me, puzzled. "Okay..."

I shook my head. "I don't know. I'm too tired to think after last night."

"Why don't you take John's bunk?"

I nodded. "Yeah, that's what I was going... yeah. Thanks." I muttered. I looked pretty stupid. I wished I could just walk out and go back to my bunk, but I knew I wouldn't do it.

I didn't know what I was expecting. I didn't think he'd abandon his bunk to come down to my sleeper bed and share with me. I didn't think that he would invite me up to share with him. But I didn't care. I knew I wouldn't be able to sleep in the cabin next to his, knowing that on the other side of the wall Nicholas was there sleeping, breathing. Would our breath match up through the wall? Was he thinking about me on the other side of the metal and plastic? Would we drift off to sleep to the sounds of the same songs?

The trouble was, I couldn't sleep *inside* his cabin either. Right above me was Nicholas. Above him on the top bunk was Charlie. Each bunk had curtains that could be pulled closed around it, allowing an illusion of privacy and providing shade from the lights in the hallway. Everyone had pulled their curtains closed except for me and Nicholas. I looked around at the curtains shifting back and forth as the train shifted. There was nothing to be heard but the hum of the engine, loud at first, but background noise at this point. There was nothing to feel but the gentle swaying of our train running smoothly on its track.

I lay on my back, head off to the side, dangling off the bed and peering at the bunk on top of mine. Above me, I saw Nicholas pressing buttons on his black iPod, untangling his earphones.

"You going to sleep?" he asked, maybe mildly uncomfortable and unsure of why I was there and why I was looking at him—I couldn't tell.

"Oh, um yeah, I'm going to just hang here in John's bed until he needs it back. I don't know if I'll fall asleep. I told Lexie I'd wait for her. I don't know what they're doing." I stared into his crisp blue eyes once again, looking for some sort of signal, any sort of sign, but I couldn't get anything. He could be unnerving like that.

"Okay, well I'll see you in the morning then." He pulled his curtains shut like everyone else in the cabin had.

I didn't move for a second, wanting him to peek his head back out. After a few seconds when I could hear him rustling around and getting himself situated for sleep, I drew my own curtains closed. I stared at the bottom of his bunk. I was about to put on my own headphones when I heard the musty curtains open above me. I waited, but didn't open my curtains.

"You know, it was kind of a great trip," Nicholas hoarsely whispered into the dark. I could tell by the closeness of his voice that he was peeking his head out of the curtains ever so slightly.

I smiled to myself. "Yeah, it was."

It was silent for a moment before he closed his curtains again. I knew our night was over. I rolled on to my stomach and plugged my headphones into my iPod, not knowing if sleep would come for me at all that night. My brain was too busy processing the developments of the weekend, my heart fluttering. I didn't know what to make of any of it. It was clear Nick didn't treat me like a friend, but he hadn't made any advance that was a clear green light. I wasn't used to being treated like this. He wasn't taking advantage of the fact that we had taken things too far our first weekend together; he was pretty much ignoring it. I wasn't sure if it was annoying me or if it was exactly how I wanted him to treat the situation.

Nick was unlike any other guy I had met. Our relationship was different. I treated him differently than I did Charlie or John, and he treated me differently than he did Celeste or Lexie. But there was also nothing tying us to one another. Our friendship was a new one for me. I had feelings for him I was fiercely trying to sort out, and I knew he had feelings for me too. What those feelings were, however, as well as what they meant, remained to be seen. As I had nothing else to do but dream, I imagined what it would have been like if he had kissed me, softly as I knew he could, up on the roof back in Budapest.

The lights were on, dimly, in the hallway outside our cabin. DeVotchKa softly piped through my headphones into my ear. I opened the window curtains that looked out into the hallway enough for one of my green eyes to peek out and see who was still up outside the cabin.

Lexie and John were standing in the hall, between the cabin I was in and the cabin I was supposed to be in. One of the hall windows was cracked a bit, and the breeze was blowing Lexie's soft waves behind her. She was smiling, a wide, toothy grin, but it was her eyes that caught my attention. John was leaning up against the window, facing Lexie, and her eyes were lit up—the eyes of someone completely enchanted. Her face was shining.

Time had stopped. The whole world had stopped. I could feel the train moving, could hear the music in my ears. I could feel the plastic cushion squeak against the metal bars underneath the sheet I had clumsily tucked over the seat. But my eyes... my eyes were seeing the invisible. It dawned on me, as Lexie laughed and John reached out to gently tough her forearm, that I was watching them fall in love. *So this is what it looks like*, I thought to myself. It isn't one glance that you know it's love. Maybe it's not the first kiss or the first conversation. But every two people have that moment, where something else makes itself present. Sometimes it's not known, sometimes it's not welcome, and a lot of the time it's inconvenient. But it's always true. There's always the moment. That moment where you recognize a piece of yourself in someone else, and they recognize it too. That tiny, sliver of a second where you feel like the words that person is saying is familiar to you, things you have thought before and never dared to say out loud.

There was a small part of me that felt guilty, as if I were spying on something more intimate than two people making love. This was creating love. This... this was something completely different. It was pure, it was innocent, it was real. And I could see what they couldn't.

I smiled, my eyes brimming with tears. I wanted that. I wanted that moment, that connection, that person. I pulled the window curtain closed and rolled onto my side, facing the train wall, and wondered when it would happen for me. I'd never felt that with Mark. When we'd been together, I listened to music he liked. I drank what he drank. I watched the movies he wanted. I always thought of it as trying new things, out of my comfort zone. But the truth was that I never really felt like my true self around him. I was so busy with who he thought I should be that I never found out who I really was. Whenever I exerted myself, stood up for what I really wanted, we'd yell and scream and breakup. In those brief weeks, or sometimes just days (once, a few months) that we'd spend apart, I was myself. I felt free. But eventually he'd always come back apologizing. And I would always forgive. It was our repetitive dynamic, like this, on and off for five years. It took me flying over five thousand miles away to unburden myself of our miserable relationship. But slowly, I was feeling my life take over permanently, rather than living it between breakups with Mark.

John never came in and woke me up. The next morning, as life was slowly brought back to the train, I learned Lexie and John had stayed up all night in that hallway, talking and laughing. They were both changed, forever.

14

October, Prague.

Fall had arrived in Prague while we had our weekend in Budapest, and the last degrees of warmth were gone from the air. I'd dug out my sweaters from my suitcase and made it a habit to throw a scarf on every morning before I left for classes. The leaves on the trees outside my apartment had turned vivid shades of orange and red. Some had already fell to the ground, crunching beneath me as I would run to catch the bus.

Prague no longer felt like a strange city I had been dropped off in. I had come to know her. I was used to the cobblestoned streets, the way my heeled boots sounded, and where to step to not twist my ankle. I knew our bus and tram schedule by heart. I knew the narrow alleys and streets, the shortcut to school from the tram stop. Czech no longer sounded foreign and I expected the smell of cigarettes everywhere we went. My group of friends had been solidified, and we had a usual bar and a usual bagel shop where we'd all casually bump into each other before, after, and between classes. It felt like home. It already felt as if I'd known Celeste and Lexie a lifetime. Lexie and John were now officially an item—the first and only, so far, in our EOO group. When John wasn't with Lexie, he spent his time with Nick and Charlie. The six of us were together in all our spare time. It was comfortable.

I jumped off the number twelve tram, backpack swinging off my shoulder, speed walking down Mostzecká, hoping I'd make it in time for anthropology. Past the tourist shops selling amber, past the McDonalds.

I made the quick right on Lázeňská, trotting past the café with the windows always flung open, classical music constantly pouring out of them and filling the otherwise quiet street. Mostzecká was always filled with tourists hurrying toward the Charles Bridge, but turning onto Lázeňská was like finding a hidden street known only to locals. It was quiet, calm, and usually nearly empty. I impatiently pressed the buzzer for Bara's office, waiting for her to let me into the courtyard.

She had the funniest accent, our anthropology professor. It was as if she had never properly learned English, and to make up for the fact that she had a limited vocabulary, she over-pronounced every English syllable. She was impossible to understand, and the class constantly had to ask her to "repeat that word, one more time please?" Words like "assimilation," "boundary maintenance," and "ethnocentricity" did not make for easy guessing.

Apart from getting to spend four hours seated next to Nick, I didn't know why I was taking the class. I was no longer an anthropology major (I had been for one semester), or minor (as I had been the semester after I had declared it my major). But there was something I liked about anthropology. The study of people in all times and places. What was just as interesting to me, was that there seemed to be something about anthropology that Nick liked too, though he also wasn't an anthro major (or minor). While I hated the class, and struggled due to our incomprehensible professor, I would never miss a class. Not as long as he was going to be there.

The class itself was dreadfully boring. Our professor was constantly drawing charts on the blackboard and rarely turned to face her students. Nick and I would pass the time by writing notes or playing hangman. Sometimes he would close his eyes, and I would watch him. I wondered what went on behind his eyes after I could no longer see them. I couldn't help myself. I wanted to know what he dreamed of. I wanted to learn if he snored or if he talked in his sleep, if he stole the covers or kicked. I'd count the freckles on his arms and hands, so I could be sure I knew everything about him.

She had just started her lecture when I pushed the door open, silently making my way to an empty seat. Nick was already there. He raised his eyebrows to me as a greeting as I slid into my chair and let my backpack fall onto the floor. He was doodling on a piece of graph paper, his left hand moving back and forth across his notebook. I'd already tuned out our professor as she droned on about the habits of Swedish mothers to masticate their children's food for them. I stared at Nick's arm and started counting freckles. I got to two hundred forty-one spotting his left arm and down the hand before class ended. Nick and I walked out of our first-floor classroom, him stretching from his nap and me trying to walk gracefully without tripping down the stairs to the courtyard.

"I'm starved." He yawned, rubbing his stomach with his hand over his white Lacoste polo. When he stretched and arched his back like that, I could see a sliver of stomach just between his jeans and shirt. I quickly blinked and looked away. Charlie walked out of the EOO office and right into us.

"Let's go get a beer at Zanzi," he offered immediately.

"I could go for a beer," Nick replied.

"I'm in," I nodded, not wanting my time with Nick to be cut short.

Charlie reached in his pocket for a Newport, putting an unlit cigarette in his mouth and rooting around in his pocket for his lighter. "Yo Adriana, I think Celeste was asking for you," he said, pointing inside the office.

"Okay. Give me just a sec," I said, turning to head into the office. "Celeste?" I called into the office. No answer. I turned to Bara. "Is Celeste here?"

"Yes, they are all in there at the computers," she replied. "Doing something quite funny I guess."

I continued into back room. Celeste, Emily, Mason, Lexie, and John were gathered around the two desktop computers. I tossed my backpack on to the table on the left by the window, peeking outside to see if Nick and Charlie had left without me. They were gone. I rolled my eyes. What was Charlie's rush?

At the computers, Celeste let out a giggle. "No, no, use this one!" she said. Lexie let out a burst of laughter.

"Oh, yeah, that one's perfect," Mason said. I walked over to see what was so funny. Someone's Facebook page was pulled up, and they were also going through my pictures. "Hey, did Charlie take Nick?" Mason asked me.

"Yeah, why... what are you guys looking for?" I asked.

On one computer, Emily had some photo editing software pulled up and about ten different photos of Nick were visible on the screen. Mason was in the process of saving a photo I had taken of Nick and John at a drinking game party we had at the U apartment a few weeks ago. Nick was wearing John's A's hat and a black sweatshirt, the hood pulled over his hat. A fake-serious look was in his eyes, his mouth open and cocked to the side. He was clearly goofing around for whoever was taking the photo (me).

"We're throwing a surprise party for Nick's birthday," Emily answered.

"Yes!" I immediately brightened at the thought of a surprise party. Was there any better kind?

"It's at Cozy on Friday," Mason explained. "It's a heaven-or-hell themed party, perfect for Friday the thirteenth."

"Heaven or hell?" I asked. "How are we going to do that?"

"You don't have to do anything. You're going to keep Nicholas distracted all day. We'll do the decorating," Mason explained further, pointing at himself, Emily, and Celeste. Celeste shot me a look and raised her eyebrows.

My heart did a backflip. How was I going to keep Nick occupied for the entire day? And how the hell would I get him back to Cozy at night, just the two of us? It would never happen. Well, maybe I could do it. But then again...

"Wait, what? *Me?* You really think I can keep this secret? You guys know I can't keep secrets and I'm a terrible liar," I admitted. "I just don't know."

"Yeah, you know, she's right, guys," Celeste recalled. "She couldn't even hide the cigarettes." Lexie immediately started laughing.

A few weeks before, we had gone out to a Mexican restaurant that has a thirty-page menu. Literally. It was all Mexican food, and it hadn't been bad either, considering we're pretty far from Mexico, but the reason we went was for the menu. It was right by John's apartment, and he had been there once and nearly dragged us back with him. The descriptions of the food were hilarious, elaborate, and nonsensical—with a poorly-translated paragraph dedicated to each dish they serve.

"*The Blue Mountain Steak is big enough for a bear to eat, but don't worry, because there are no bears here in Praha that will eat the steak. It will make you thirsty, but not so thirsty that a glass of pivo won't cure your thirstiness...*"

After dinner, we'd been splitting up the check and Charlie went out to have a cigarette. While he was outside, we had decided to hide the rest of his Newports to scare him. Somehow, it was decided the best place to hide them had been in my purse. We'd finished paying the check, Charlie came back, and when he'd tried to put his lighter back in his cigarette pack, he realized they weren't on the table where he'd left them. Naturally, he had started looking around, and asked if anyone had seen the Newports. Scattered murmurs of "no..." had made their way around the table—except for me. I had immediately begun to giggle, and in the most unconvincing way said, "No, I don't know *where* they could be..." Charlie had given me another look, and asked for his Newports. Seconds later, I'd pulled them out of my purse. Everyone had groaned and rolled their eyes at me. From then on, no one told me any secrets or let me in on any jokes.

"Addie, you won't tell Nick because you know everyone is working hard at this and we'll all be really fucking pissed off if you tell him. This can be your chance to redeem yourself," Mason said.

I didn't know if he actually believed I could keep the secret, or if he was baiting me. I decided that I was getting the short end of the stick, and even though I was a liability, I had to keep Nick distracted because no one else wanted the job.

"Fine," I said, looking at the rest of the pictures Emily had pulled up. A few minutes later, Mason printed out a flyer to hand out to the EOO kids and some of our other classmates.

The flyer read HEAVEN or HELL. Next to each word was a photo of Nicholas, looking innocent next to the word *Heaven,* and devious next to the word *Hell.* Mason gave each of us a few flyers to pass out in our classes, and I started plotting how I could keep Nick busy.

Δ

The rest of the week was a dream, like every week in our fairytale city. Nicholas, Charlie, John, Celeste, Lexie, and I were spending every evening together, meeting up at Bohemia after class for lunch and heading to Zanzi in the evenings. But the part of my day I looked forward to the most was the nightly bus and tram rides back to my apartment, after Lexie and Celeste would find a tram to Staré Město, and John would find the metro toward the TV Tower. Charlie, Nick, and I always had a long bus ride to look forward to.

I still wasn't used to Nick's touch, despite spending every day together. Each time he bumped into me on the 137, my hand or arm or leg or whatever he had touched would tingle, as if his touch left something behind. Sometimes, Nick and Charlie would get into a conversation that I wasn't a part of and I would catch myself staring at

Nick. Celeste was good at catching me. She always knew which leg was mine to kick under the table, or would say my name in just the right tone to snap me out of it. But on the bus, at night, no one was around to wake me up. Somehow, Nick never seemed to notice.

Despite how much time we were spending together the week before the party, I didn't know if Nick would go for an entire day alone with me. It might strike him as suspicious, because no matter how I played it in my mind, I couldn't ask him to hang out with me alone without it sounding like a date. I brought up the subject to Lexie and Celeste at Café Louvre, Celeste's favorite internet café, situated in Národni třida.

"Oh, sweetie, don't worry! Of course he'll want to spend the day with you!" Celeste was trying her hardest to make me feel better.

"Absolutely not. I'm not asking him out, and that's how it is going to come off. The only thing I can think of is telling him that we are all going to hang out, the six of us, but then the four of you will cancel. That's not too weird, right?" In the few days that had passed since I learned of my mission, this was the best plan I had come up with.

Lexie looked at me. "Why don't I just hang out with you and Nick, that way it will be easier. We can take him shopping for his birthday!" Lexie had a point.

"You know what, Lexie, I think that's perfect. I mean, he has three sisters and a single mom, I'm sure he likes to shop," I said. As much as part of me wanted to be alone with Nick, I knew that I would find a way to screw up the whole surprise if I were alone with him. Either that, or I'd blow some other secret I didn't want to tell him. "So you'll go with me then!"

Celeste told us where they were getting the decorations, and that Mason and John were trying and find a keg, which would be quite the accomplishment. Mason and Celeste had decided that the basement was going to be hell and the upstairs was going to be heaven. It was going to be a great party, if we could just pull it off. If *I* could just pull it off.

The night before the party, Lexie and I told Nick that we thought we should take him shopping the next day for his birthday. He needed to buy himself a birthday present, after all. Celeste, Charlie, and John all admitted they had some studying to do before midterms, which were the next week. Strangely, Nick didn't give them shit for studying.

"Actually, I could use a pair of shoes," he admitted. Before long, we were making plans to meet at Bohemia Bagel for breakfast before heading out.

My alarm went off a full hour before I had to leave. I took my time getting dressed, picking out my favorite black leather flats with the bows over the toes, and pulling on the jeans that I thought looked the best on me. The thought of spending a whole day with Nicholas, even if Lexie was around as well, had me feeling anxious in the best way. I grabbed my slouchy shoulder bag and headed out the door, my stomach beginning to rumble. Outside my apartment, the trees whispered secrets to one another and leaves played chase across my shoes. Before I even crossed the street, I had already grabbed my scarf out of my bag and pulled it around my neck. The sun was warm and reminiscent of summer, but the cool breeze of autumn reminded me it was October. I picked up the pace to cross the street when I saw the bus rumbling along from Farkáň, the stop after Urbanova. I slid into a seat by the window and glanced outside to see Nick jogging to the bus. The doors of the bus shuddered closed.

"Wait!" I exclaimed and stood up, raising my arm. The bus driver, clearly puzzled, turned around and muttered something in Czech to me, then begrudgingly pulled the lever for the doors to open once more as Nick banged on them outside.

He climbed up the steps, offering his breathless thanks to the bus driver, then shoved into the seat next to me.

"Hey." I could instantly smell his cologne, and felt my heartbeat quicken.

"Morning." I smiled at him. "Happy birthday."

"Today isn't my birthday." Nick shook his head at me. His leg touched mine as he settled into his seat. My face flushed. Already I was on the verge of screwing up the surprise.

"I know, but we are shopping for your birthday, so..." I let my voice trail off. "So what did you do last night?" I immediately changed the subject, determined to not blow the party so early.

"Uh, Mason and Charlie were watching *Always Sunny*, so I hung out with them..."

I was staring at Nick's lips moving as he spoke, and stopped paying attention to what words were coming out of them. I knew, if he had any inkling of what was going on tonight, he would ask me—and I would tell him anything he wanted to know. I willed the bus to move faster, antsy to get to the bagel shop.

I let Nick do all of the talking as we switched from the bus to the 22 tram toward Bohemia Bagel. I jumped off the tram as soon as the doors would allow, and rushed us toward the entrance. Inside, Lexie had already snagged a booth and was sipping her favorite foamy latte out of their signature yellow thick plastic mugs.

"Hiiiiii," she breathed, as always.

I slid into the booth next to her and Nick picked the side of the booth next to me. I widened my eyes at her, signaling for her to take over the conversation and that I was already in trouble. She took control, and I sat back into the booth, relaxing at last.

Lexie and I knew we had the whole day to kill, and we couldn't risk being finished too soon. After our leisurely breakfast, we decided it would be best to walk to Národni třida and then on to Václavské náměstí.

The day had warmed up a little outside, the breeze breaking to give the sunshine its moment. We left Újezd and wandered across the Vltava, the conversation drifting to birthdays. We talked about our best birthdays: the most outrageous parties, the best gifts we've ever been given, what our twenty-first birthdays were like. I recounted to Lexie and

Nick my horrible twenty-first, the wake and the funeral. They looked at me with more warmth than the sun could have offered. Nick put his arm around my back and pulled me close to him, telling me he'd also lost a grandfather on his birthday once. Yet again, I felt the pull to him grow stronger.

Lexie wandered into H&M, convincing him he needed clothes for Italy. Rows and rows of plaid shirts, destroyed jeans, metal-studded leather belts, cheaply made graphic tees, and buckets of scarves, hats, and gloves for the upcoming harsh winter. We went through them all, dressing Nick up like our own little doll, having more fun than I thought was possible while shopping under false pretenses. He tried on clothes for us, we told him no, more color, smaller sizes, different styles, making him come back again and again while we judged his outfits that we picked out. No matter what he was wearing, he looked the same to me. His blue eyes still stuck out so brightly, I wondered how anyone could notice anything else about him, he still had faint traces of freckles splattered across his nose and cheeks giving him more character than he knew of, his hair was still the perfect kind of messy. He didn't look at all like any of the guys I had been interested in before. I loved that about him.

After H&M, we tore off to find shoes. Only two and a half hours had passed.

"What are we going to do?" Lexie whispered as we ducked into a shoe store in Wenceslas Square. "We still have to kill at least another three hours!"

"Just keep bringing him shoes," I said, picking up a pair of black pumps and pretending to examine them. Nick was a few rows away, checking out some soccer shoes. "Let's just keep bringing him shoes to try on."

So we did. Lacoste and Adidas, Nikes and Pumas. We asked the sales clerk for more shoes than I knew they had stocked in his size, until finally Nick started to grow annoyed.

"Enough! God*damn*, you girls are crazy when it comes to shoes. It's one of these two pairs, so help me choose," Nick said, clearly almost exasperated. I gave Lexie a nervous look. She winked at me.

"Oh, Nick, you've *got* to go with the green striped ones. You have waaay too much blue already," she said, giving me a clear sign. Nick made a move toward the Adidas box that housed the white sneakers with green stripes.

"But Lexie, he has so much blue because it looks fantastic on him! I mean, the way it brings out his eyes..." I wavered, holding up a white Nike sneaker with a blue swish next to his eyes. Nick moved away from me, motioning toward the blue shoe.

"Adriana, come one. He's going to be wearing the blue shoe with jeans. It's too much blue. Won't work," Lexie explained knowingly, taking the green shoe out of Nick's hand. "You know you want the green ones."

We were right on track, confusing the hell out of him and killing time. "Oh Nick, don't listen to her. You have more blue already, so these will go with more things that you already own. What do you have that's green? I mean really?"

Nick looked at us both as if we were crazy, moving his head between Lexie on one side with the green shoe and me across from her with the blue. Then, he started laughing. "I can't handle this anymore. I know about the party," he blurted.

"WHAT?!" Lexie and I both said in unison. Lexie gave me the look.

"I didn't tell him, I swear!" I said, defending myself.

She looked at Nick.

"No, she didn't tell me, Lex. I just kind of overheard everyone talking about it," he explained. "You guys aren't nearly as sneaky as you think you are."

"Well, what do we do now?" I asked. "Should we just get the shoes and then go help with the party?"

"No. I'll give them a call and see how much longer we need to wait, but they don't have to know that Nick knows," Lexie said. She grabbed her phone and walked over to the window. "You know how pissed Mason will be."

"Oh, my gosh, Nick, I'm so sorry. I know I blew it somehow," I said, walking up to him, blue shoe still in hand. "I didn't do it on purpose. I was trying so hard!" To my surprise, I was genuinely disappointed; I had tried so hard to act nonchalant. For the last few hours, the truth was the party had completely slipped my mind while we were having so much fun shopping.

"It's okay. Seriously, it wasn't you. I heard the guys talking about it the other day. But I wanted to go shopping with you girls," he said with a smile, taking a step closer to me.

I looked over at Lexie, who was still on the phone, her loud laugh echoing near the window.

"Besides," Nick continued. "I still do need a pair of shoes." He half whispered this last sentence before bending closer to me and sliding the shoe out of my hand. I stared at him, blue eyes matching perfectly with the shoe, just like I had argued. He met my gaze, us catching one another's eyes. I didn't want there to be a party anymore, or shoes, or shopping, or Lexie. I wished it were just the two of us like this, not having to meet anyone else later. And the way he was looking at me, for that moment, I'd swear maybe he was thinking the same thing.

"Okay, good news and bad news," Lexie announced, her cheerful self having returned. Nick moved his eyes away first, to Lexie. I followed. "The good news is they have no idea that Nick knows, so we can just pretend like it's still a surprise. The bad news is that they are nowhere near done and are going to need at least another four hours."

"Four hours??" I exclaimed. What were we going to do for four more hours?

Nick just smiled again. Nothing was fazing him today. "Banditos?" he asked. He grabbed the box of blue shoes and walked to the register.

Lexie looked at me, a mischievous grin on her face. "He's buying the blue shoes?" she asked with a wink. We both watched him pay for the shoes, while Lexie gave me a playful nudge.

"Oh, shut the fuck up, they are just shoes," I said.

Lexie just laughed her loud, trademark laugh and headed toward the stairs.

Δ

Since we still had hours to kill, we walked to the Bazaar apartment building. Lexie went upstairs to get a change of clothes for the party, while Nick and I went inside to get a table and a few beers. The place wasn't too crowded, so we went to the first table by the door and ordered a round of Budvars.

"Honestly, I'm glad you know," I admitted. "I was so nervous I was going to blow the whole thing." I anxiously sipped my beer, not knowing what to say now that we had the privacy I always so desperately craved. It almost felt awkward.

"I figured you would have told me too," he said with a smile. I playfully hit him on the arm. "But honestly, I can't believe you kept it quiet as long as you did."

"I wasn't the one who blew it!" I reminded him.

There was some loud, awful eighties' music blasting on the speakers. Two Czech women walked into the restaurant and right up to the bar, lighting up cigarettes as soon as they sat a cheek on the barstool. After enough time in Prague, I'd learned to spot a Czech woman by her hair. I took another drink of Budvar.

"So do you know the theme?" I couldn't help it.

"Theme?" Nick set down his green beer bottle, now only half full. "There's a theme?"

I don't know why I'd said it, and immediately regretted it. However, it now appeared that once again I had a secret to keep. He didn't know there was a theme. Shit.

"Don't tell me, Adriana, please don't tell me," he pleaded, closing his eyes in anticipation. I didn't want to tell him.

"Okay," I said, smiling.

"You're going to tell me, aren't you? My God you *are* trouble," Nick joked. I didn't want to tell him.

Just then, we both heard Lexie give her breathy "Hiiiiiiiiiiiiii!" as she pulled out a chair at our table. "Sorry I took so long, you guys."

"Oh, no worries," I chimed. Just then, our waitress passed by. "*Jedna pivo, prosim*," I said to her. She came back a second later with another cold bottle of Budvar for Lexie. Lex had a small backpack with her. "What did you bring?"

"Oh, just a little outfit for the party," she replied.

"She's bursting at the seams. You have to help her. I didn't know it was a themed party and now she's dying to tell me what it is." Nick ratted me out, looking over the menu like it was nothing.

"Adriana! Don't tell him!" Lexie said incredulously.

We all looked over the menus, trying to find something for dinner, knowing how much we'll be drinking later. Nick kept throwing glances my way. I willed my mind back to dinner, wondering what I should order. But every time his eyes caught mine, I felt the secret bubble closer to the surface. *Why do I want to tell him so much?* I asked myself. *The only thing that will happen is that I'll ruin the only surprise that's left, that my friends and our roommates have worked so hard for.*

We ordered some appetizers and guacamole to share, and another round of beer. We were always in the habit of ordering another beer, always saying yes when asked if you want one. The service in restaurants was so slow, usually by the time your glass is empty, you're still waiting for the second drink. The one you ordered earlier.

Lexie and Nick kept looking at me off and on, as if I would blow the secret at any moment. Or was it my imagination? Maybe they'd moved on, sure the moment had passed and I'd keep my mouth closed. But of course, I knew I wouldn't. Just like I had to constantly fight down the urge to tell Nick how I felt about him. He wouldn't feel the same way, I felt sure. He'd mentioned his pact about not dating American girls, and if he was interested in me, he would have made a move. And even if he did have feelings for me, we wouldn't be living in the same country after December. It seemed as if all roads lead to heartbreak at some point—either when the secret came out, or when the semester inevitably ended. So what difference did it make? But inside, I knew that I'd tell him how I felt, just like I knew I'd tell him about heaven and hell. But which was heaven and which was hell?

I started to get upset with myself. Why couldn't I keep anything to myself? It was as if I was incapable of not sharing, things I didn't want to tell always making their way to my journal, begging to be found. I shook my head to empty the self-doubt, when I felt Nick's hand cover mine. It covered mine perfectly, his fingers wrapped around to the palm of my hand on the table below. What just happened? I looked up at him, but his gaze was on his hand, that was now lifting mine up toward his lips. His sweet, soft, pale pink lips grazed the top of my hand. I watched, dizzy, trying to keep my eyes from filling with tears I couldn't fully explain. He held his lips on my hand for a second. Not knowing what else to do, I broke the tension by looking at Lexie across the table, who was also staring at my hand.

"It's okay," Nick said softly. "Just stop thinking about it."

How did he know? Maybe he was supposed to know, maybe inside he knows I have something to say and wants to hear it, wants to hear it all. Was my anxiety, my complicated feelings for him reverberating around the table like some sort of invisible wave? He held my hand in both of his, as if trying to warm it up.

"It's a heaven and hell party," I whispered. There's nothing anyone could have done to stop it. I was in hell.

Δ

After the last plate had been cleared, Lexie called Celeste to see how much longer they needed. On the other end of the phone, I heard Celeste ask for another hour or two. Lexie nodded, motioning to me, and asked if there was anything else needed to do before heading over to Cozy.

"Okay," Lexie said while sliding her phone back into her bag, "Celeste said they need another two-ish hours, and more decorations. I guess they're moving furniture, and Mason and Charlie went to get a keg."

"Two hours?" I looked up at the ceiling. At this point, I wasn't sure I was actually looking forward to the party. The mandated alone time with Nick was just as much fun, and I almost wasn't looking forward to sharing him once again.

"How about I run over to Tesco and get the decorations, and Nick's costume, and you guys grab another drink?"

Nick finished the last of his beer. "Works for me."

"It's not like you can do any more harm, Addie," Lexie joked. She grabbed her jacket from the back of her chair and stood up, ready to go.

"We'll walk with you," Nick said. I looked outside and noticed for the first time that the evening sky was darkening. We'd been there for hours.

We walked to the tram and rode down two stops to Národni třida, where we split off, Lexie heading into Tesco.

"So where to now?" I asked. We had no computers to bring to an internet café, and Nebe was too far away for a drink.

"I don't know." Nick looked around. "Let's walk."

We started wandering down the street, alongside the trams. Street lights lit up around us, as the sun hung over the horizon somewhere. Because of the river and the castle and the buildings all around, it's impossible to tell where it was; we only saw its faint glow along the river. For the first time that day, Nick and I were quiet.

"What's this place?" Nick had stopped right next to the entrance for Celeste's favorite internet café, Café Louvre, and in front of a coffee shop that somehow, I'd never noticed.

"I have no idea," I replied honestly. I'd been to the Café Louvre dozens of times with Celeste and Lexie, but had never seen this coffee shop. The ceilings were high, like thirty feet, with decoratively placed wood beams across the top. A few mismatching tables and chairs, were scattered throughout the place, but it mostly was filled with overstuffed couches and chairs, oriental rugs, and low-hanging lanterns. I was instantly drawn to it. A four-piece band played in the corner. I couldn't hear them, but I knew I had to. I wasn't the only one feeling it.

"Let's check it out," Nick said, already opening the door. As he pulled it toward us, music blew across our faces like a sharp, hot breeze. It sounded like salsa music. At the moment, I couldn't have imagined anything more inviting. Nick found an empty table for two and pulled out a chair for me.

The musicians danced as they played, giving everyone else permission to dance in their seats. Feet tapped, hands clapped, heads bobbed. The music pulled us in immediately, and though we sat in silence at our table, we hardly even noticed a waitress walk up to our table, shouting above the music. Nick requested a cup of tea, and I got the same.

We sat across from one another, simply enjoying the music together. After our waitress came back with our tea, I sipped it with my eyes closed. *Maybe this is what it would be like if we were on a date?* I thought to myself. I imagined it was so. I imagined about if I'd told him my secret over dinner, him grabbing my hand and without another word pulling me out the door here to be alone. And we were there now, sipping hot tea, not speaking but connecting through the music.

Finally, as the band finished their set and the café broke out into applause, Nick turned to me. "I almost wish we didn't have a party to go to," he said, taking another long sip of his green tea.

"I know, right? This place is great!" I said, meaning every word.

"Well, we'll have to come back sometime," he said to me. I felt a buzz from my jeans pocket. Lexie was already done at Tesco.

We agreed to head to my flat since Lexie and I still had to change. She'd gotten me an angel costume at Tesco, and a devil one for herself. Mason had told Lexie that he'd already got a costume for Nick, but he went with us so we could change. We blasted music from my iPod, did a few shots and a bit of dancing, just the three of us for an hour before we finally got the message to head over to Cozy.

It was after ten o'clock by the time we got to Nick's place, and it was completely transformed. Candles were lit along the sidewalk in the front yard, illuminating the path to the front door. Nick pushed the door open, fully expecting what was to come.

"SURPRISE!" came from a dozen different voices, followed by laughing and yelling. As we moved past the entrance, we noticed the rest of the decorations. There were signs all over the first floor, labeling it *heaven.* Silver streamers hung down from the ceiling and glitter covered the floor. The only light came from candles everywhere, on every table and clustered in corners on the floor of each room. Music blasted from the living room, where a few party goers were already dancing. Behind the dance floor, signs directed us downstairs, where red streamers hung over the stairway entrance, light bulbs had been replaced with black lights, and strobe lights were flashing. More music, heavy meal, echoed downstairs, where a keg was kept on ice in the bath tub. Half our friends were wearing solid black robes and red-horned headbands; the other half were dressed as angels, white sheets tied around their necks like togas. Lexie had gotten me wings at and a wand, resulting in more of a fairy godmother look than an angel. Mason had bought Nick a floor-length black cape with red on the inside, as well as vampire teeth, his idea of a devil costume.

I lost sight of Nicholas quickly, as the night devolved into keg stands and drinking games. Up in heaven there was a makeshift karaoke going on to Beatles songs. In hell, shots of cheap Czech vodka at were passed around at midnight for the moment Nick turned twenty-two.

The party didn't die until about 3 a.m., when John was so sick he threw up in Mason's spare bed. Everyone decided it was time to go. There weren't nearly enough beds; people started doubling up on couches and cushions on the floor. The party was still going on in hell, where Mason, Nick, and a few others were still making their way through the keg. Lexie was going to sleep upstairs by John to take care of him, and told me that Nick told me I could have his bed.

I walked into Nick's room on the first floor, thankfully finding it empty. I had no idea if Nick was coming to bed at all, but the mixture of booze and exhaustion left me neither caring nor thinking straight. I could hear people still screaming downstairs, and a pounding noise above me. I kicked off my shoes, pulled my bra out from my shirtsleeve, tossed my wings and my skirt onto the floor, and climbed into Nick's bed. I closed my eyes, pretending there was no one else around and I was surrounded by peace and quiet.

The music was still beating downstairs and I could hear Nick yelling. The room was tilting, leaning ever so slightly to the left. I put my hand on the wall to steady myself and closed my eyes to the shouting downstairs. The down comforter Bara had bought for each bed from Ikea was around my hips; I pulled it up above my head. The world quieted down. The room stopped spinning as my eyes fell shut and I surrendered to sleep.

Δ

Footsteps startled me awake, but I wasn't ready to open my eyes. They were tiptoeing, around the bed, toward the foot of the bed by the windows, trying—and failing—to be silent. More footsteps told me someone else was entering the room.

"Ohhhhh, look how cute, he's the big spoon and she's the little spoon!" I heard a girl's voice whisper.

"Ohh how sweet... where the fuck are my shoes?" I heard Emily say groggily. Spoon? I thought. Huh?

Looking down, I saw arms lifelessly draped over my hips and felt the heat of a body behind mine. Nick must have found his way to bed last night and had his arms around me, his hands entwined with mine. I smiled, squeezing his hands gently and closing my eyes once again, drifting back toward blissful sleep.

When I opened my eyes again, it was silent. The sun was peeking through Nick's curtains, his face was right in front of mine. Our heads were only a few inches apart, facing each other, our hands at each other's waists. I wasn't sure how we had ended up this way, but I wasn't about to move. Just as I was wondering, Nick opened his eyes. I realized at once that I didn't know his looks well enough; I couldn't tell if he was happy, surprised, confused, or just hungover. I played it safe.

"Happy birthday," I said with a small smile.

"Thanks. Not a bad way to wake up on my birthday." He smiled back.

I laughed and looked down, realizing I wasn't wearing any pants. Though I was in his bed, I was surprised to be waking up next to him.

"When did you come to bed?" I asked.

He shifted his weight, the sun falling onto his hair. "The question is, when did *you* get into my bed?"

I pushed myself back a bit. "You told me to sleep here!" I said nervously. "Didn't you?" I rubbed my eyes. "Lexie told me to crash here, that it was your idea."

"Ahhhh," he said, knowingly. "I may have said that. Who knows." He covered his eyes with his palms. "It's all a blur. I just remember stumbling in here and pushing you over so I could have some room."

"Oh please, at least I wasn't snoring!" I playfully pushed his chest back.

The rest of the morning was as if I'd dreamed it, leisurely spent in Nick's bed together. He held my hands and we laughed about the night before, getting into a small pillow fight and pushing one another out of the bed. We told stories of what we could remember from the party, laughed at what a bad secret keeper I was, recalled the decorations Mason and Emily had put up, and grabbed my camera to go through all the pictures. We laughed at a picture of someone's breast, remembering that we ran in to the Garden Apartment girls in their devil/angel get-ups getting onto the same bus as us on our way to the party. Gradually, life was coming to the house around us as other people woke up, but we were unsure of who was still in the house. It didn't matter. For the first time ever, we had created our own little world in that bed, and neither of us were quite ready to leave it yet.

15

October, Prague.

Days and weeks were moving faster than ever before. October was rushing along as quickly as the leaves were falling off trees, littering the sidewalk and grassy patches across the city. Prague was revealing more of herself to us each day, as the tourists faded away and the weather grew cooler. The strong sunlight we had grown accustomed to during the day was found later each time it rose, and was melting away earlier each evening.

Though we had only been in Prague for just over seven weeks, I could feel myself changing. I had finally found a place where I felt at home, where I could truly be myself without any expectations. I wasn't sure how I knew, but I was certain that I wouldn't be ready to go home in December. I'd floated the idea to my parents, who were surprisingly supportive. After that, it was all too easy to mention to Bara that I was interested in staying through the spring to finish out the school year, and she couldn't have been happier. One deposit check later, and it was official. Prague would be my home until at least May. Mason and I were the only two staying the year, and though I knew I couldn't go home in December, I was anxious at the idea of my newfound friends leaving, and new people taking their place.

I knew the rest of the semester would pass into a series of mile markers. We started to more seriously plan the trip to Italy that Celeste, Lexie, and I were taking with Charlie, John, and Nick over fall break.

After our trip, which was rapidly approaching, it was Halloween, then a weekend in Poland, which would lead into Thanksgiving, then December. Our program officially ended on December fifteenth. It was only another eight or so weeks away.

While the end of our semester was drawing near, no matter how much or how little we thought it over, I enjoyed every moment of the middle. The middle was the best part. In the middle, we really hit our stride, made a routine for ourselves. There were now usual spots. I knew exactly when to walk into Bohemia Bagel or Zanzibar and find my best friends, munching on tomato basil bagels or sipping pivo. There were inside jokes, meet up spots, usual orders, standard commutes.

But nowhere was the middle more obvious than when I was around Celeste, Lexie, Charlie, John, and of course, Nicholas. These people, who only weeks ago were strangers to me, I now realized knew me better than most of my friends back in the States. They knew the real me that I was able to be in Prague. They knew my secrets and I knew theirs. There was no judgment. I loved them for it. We'd all made our way down different life paths until know, where they all converged in Prague. We had this all in common.

The two weeks following Nick's birthday was filled with Italy plans. In all our spare time, the six of us would meet in cafés to supposedly look at hostels and train schedules, museums and cathedrals. Instead, we mostly daydreamed about what our vacation would be like, all the things we would see, the wine we'd drink, and the foods we'd eat. Lexie and John were an official couple now, and increasingly often, Nick and I spent our time with them to make a foursome. Somehow it never seemed awkward hanging out with a couple, even though Nick and I were not one. We'd meet up for Italy planning sessions if Charlie was out drinking with Mason or Celeste was in class, usually rolling into dinner out, the four of us. John and Lexie would always walk together, her arm hooked in his, her laughing endlessly at his jokes. Nick and I got increasingly used to our nightly bus rides home together, lingering longer each evening as we said our good-byes.

One afternoon, the four of us planned to meet at Coffee and Cigars. It was a loud coffeehouse off Wenceslas Square that had Wi-Fi and served sweet coffee beverages and desserts. Flat screens adorned the walls around the big windows that opened to the street; pop music videos could be seen from anywhere in the café. Fergie and Lily Allen danced tantalizingly, making it impossible to study. But it was close to the Bazaar Apartment and was easy to access with the metro, for those of us on the other side of the river, which made it an ideal spot to meet for Italy planning.

Nicholas and I walked in the side door off Vodičkova, and it wasn't difficult to spot John and Lexie right away. They were sitting across from one another at a four-person table in the middle of the café, each in their own white leather high-backed chair. I laughed as we walked toward them and I noticed they were sharing an iced coffee of some sort, piled high with whipped cream. Lexie was always indulging in whipped cream, despite being lactose-intolerant.

I pulled out the chair next to Lexie as Nicholas sat down across from me.

"I brought my laptop," I said, pulling it out of my backpack. "Ready to plan?"

"Yes!" Lexie opened the laptop that had been sitting closed in front of her. "I'll search Rome."

I searched Florence, clicking my way through budget hostels and flipping through train schedules. On the other side of the table, John and Nick were making fun of a music video.

A waitress strode up to the table to take our order.

"Water, with gas," I requested. I'd learned early on that gas meant carbonation.

She made a note in her pad and turned her head to Nick.

"Nothing, *prosím*." He gave me a sideways look, then turned back to John.

"You don't want anything?" I pried.

Nick took hold of my laptop, slid it over to himself, and started typing something. "I'm not staying very long." He avoided my gaze.

Lexie frowned. "Where are you going? You have plans with people other than us?" I looked at her and smiled. She was right—we had been spending all our time together.

He cleared his throat. "I uhh—I have a date." He tried to sound nonchalant, but I thought I could detect nerves in his voice.

My stomach flipped, but I managed to keep my face stoic. He was going on a date? Was it someone from the program? From school? But what about the pact? She had to be Czech.

"Whoaa, a date," Lexie replied. "When did this happen?" I gazed at the music video on overhead, avoiding her eyes.

"I met her over a month ago, like when we first got here. But she just texted me the other day. We're meeting up for drinks."

Our waitress arrived with my sparkling mineral water, and I busied myself opening the bottle and filling my glass halfway.

"That girl you made out with? She's pretty hot, for a Czech girl," John chimed. I look up at him, but couldn't bring myself to say anything. When was he making out with girls in bars? My stomach dropped again.

"You made out with her? She's Czech?" Lexie demanded.

Nick froze and glared at John. Clearly, the kiss was not meant to be common knowledge. He opened his mouth to speak, and then closed it again.

"Yeah, it was at that bar by my place. After you girls left," John answered for him. Lexie glared at John. He half-shrugged to her and made a face, mouthing "What?" as Lexie gave him an exasperated look.

We had made plans to grab dinner after Coffee and Cigars. Now not only was Nick going on a date, but I was missing out on time I would have spent hanging out with him.

"So no dinner?" I asked. It was the first time I caught his eye.

Nick shook his head. "I always meet girls for drinks. If it goes well, you can roll it in to dinner. If not, no harm done. At least you got a drink out of it. But no, I probably won't meet up with you guys after."

I cocked my head to the side and rolled my eyes at him. I felt sick. "LA douchebag," I said, truly meaning it, and sliding my laptop back towards me. I couldn't focus on booking a hotel anymore, but I pretended to be searching away.

Nick smiled at me, but his eyes dug deeper. He stood up. "Actually, I should head out now."

I said nothing as John and Lexie wished him good luck, instead scrolling down the Web page with hotel listings Nick had pulled up. As he walked past me, he tousled my hair with his hand. Then he was out the door.

We got back to our planning, and I pretended I wasn't upset. I kept the act up all the way to dinner two hours later, after we'd left the café. As soon as I had a moment alone with Lexie while John was in the bathroom, I rounded on her.

"He has a date? What was that about?"

Lexie shrugged. "I'm sure it was nothing. He said it was just drinks."

"Yeah. It's just that... I don't know. I have no right to be upset, I know. But we've been so close, and waking up together on his birthday... this is just throwing me." I sighed and shook my head. "What a mess. I fucking hate it."

Lexie put her hand on my shoulder.

"I didn't come out here for this Lex, I came out here to get away from it. To get away from Mark, from everything else at home. I didn't want to fall for—you know what I mean, some guy out here. I thought I'd find myself... what a fucking cliché."

I was so frustrated, with Nick and with myself. I hated that I liked him so much, that I wasn't content with our friendship. I hated that he sent shivers up my spine every time he touched me. I didn't want to be *this girl*, the girl I was being.

"But you can't help how you feel, Addie. It's not your fault. You didn't look for this, it just happened." Lexie moved her hand to my back, and moved it up and down my spine. It helped, so much.

"Yeah, you're right. I know." I felt helpless. My brain had been overtaken by my heart. But more than my heart, it was my gut. My instincts were pushing me to Nick, more than any other person I had ever been around. It was never like this way with Mark, or any other guy I had dated for that matter. I felt compelled to be around him, to make up excuses to see him and talk to him, to accidentally bump into him. I hated myself for it, but it was true. I had come all this way to end up chasing a boy. An American boy, in Prague.

John reappeared at the table. "Who's ready for pasta?"

This was one of the things I loved most about John. He could make anyone smile at any time. His heart was so big and his sense of humor matched it. I grabbed the menu and pushed Nick out of my mind, reading the English description of dinner offerings, when I heard my cell phone chirp in my bag.

Where are you guys? It was a text from Nick.

The pasta place by Bazaar. You coming? I texted back. I had hoped his date was a bomb, and maybe my wish had come true.

Be there in 15. I couldn't help but smile.

We waited for him before we ordered, and he showed up twenty minutes later.

"No good with the Czech girl?" John asked.

Nick looked at me before answering. "No. She invited me to a yoga class. It was kind of weird." He didn't offer any further explanation, and I didn't ask. But under the table, I felt his foot feel for mine. Confused, I looked across the table at him. Nick was still looking at me, smiling. I smiled back, and his foot moved away back to his side of the table.

Δ

Nick wasn't at the bus stop at our usual time. I decided to let the 137 pass and wait for the next one, on the off chance that maybe he was running a little late. I was almost always late for class, so this was no big deal for me. But after seven more minutes, there was no sign of him. I boarded the bus, sure I'd see him in class.

When I climbed the two sets of stairs up to the classroom, I only saw Lexie sitting next to my seat. Nick's was empty. I slunk in quietly to not disturb the lecture, wondering where he was. Wednesdays were a pretty easy class day. After Gender and Culture, we'd usually head over to Bohemia Bagel and meet up with Charlie or John. The rest of the day was usually spent wandering through new parts of the city, finding pubs to stop into, or just walking to Old Town Square for the hundredth time. It never got old.

When class let out, Lexie and I walked downstairs together. Out of habit, I started walking toward the courtyard door. Lexie broke for the EOO office.

"No Bohemia?" I asked.

"I have to get this stupid market research project done," she said, shifting her backpack to the other shoulder. "Text you when I'm done."

I peered through the windows of Bara's office to see who was inside. No sign of Nick or Celeste. I grabbed my iPod out of my backpack and put my earbuds in.

The fall weather in Prague was absolutely perfect. Summer had been a bit too hot, filled with the stale air of body odor and overcrowded with tourists. Fall was much better. The days were cooler, the breeze was crisp, and leaves fell along the cobblestoned streets, crunching underneath our feet. It was more than picturesque. It was the sweet spot. I decided to walk over to Bohemia rather than take the tram.

I passed by Zanzibar, the Lennon Wall. Passed by the computer lab where Nick and I had once messaged each other from neighboring computers, right after our night at the five-story club. Passed by the café on the corner that always played classical music, passed the art gallery, passed the high stone walls of the Mandarin Oriental. It had been two months that I'd been in Prague. It now felt like home. The ancient streets no longer confused me; the tram and bus schedules came to me like second nature. I felt so comfortable.

I opened the door to Bohemia, scanning our usual booths for familiar faces. To my surprise, I didn't see one person I knew. Where was everyone today? Actually studying?

I walked up to the counter and ordered my usual—an Italian vegetarian sandwich on a tomato basil bagel. Deciding it would be rude to take up a booth for just myself, I wandered into the back room. I'd never sat back there before, but it was home to just six or so smaller tables. My backpack and I claimed an empty table. The place was pretty quiet today. There was only one other person there, in the same back room, seated in a chair facing me.

One thing I loved about Bohemia Bagel was that they didn't have internet. There was no fighting for outlets or people hunched over their laptops, headphones over their ears. Music played throughout the café, and people just sat and talked. It was remarkably normal. A waitress arrived with my sandwich.

"Prosim," I said politely.

She stared at me blankly.

I turned to my backpack and pulled the zipper open. I wasn't prepared to sit here by myself. There had to be something I could read in there. We didn't have a textbook for Gender and Culture, so other than a worn copy of *The Unbearable Lightness of Being* I felt like I should read, I had nothing to do. I took out the Kundera novel and opened it.

"Is that any good?"

I peered up from my book. I hadn't even read a sentence yet. Since there was no one else in the room, I assumed the voice was addressing me. I looked at the cover of the book, as if an answer would be written there.

"I don't really know," I answered. "I keep picking it up and not really reading. I haven't been able to get into it."

The guy nodded. "It seems very intellectual."

I frowned, unsure what he meant. "It's a pretty popular Czech book, so I figured I should read it." It wasn't until that moment that I realized he spoke perfect English. I looked him over. Cargo shorts and a fitted black T-shirt with a New York Yankees hat, dark curls sprouting out from underneath. He was definitely American.

"I'm Asa. Hi." He waved, but made no move from his table to come any closer.

"Hi. Adriana." I waved back. "You study here?"

"Yeah, NYU. We have a campus here." I'd heard that NYU had their own campus for study abroad programs, so they didn't actually attend any other universities. It almost seemed like it defeated the purpose to me.

"Are you a Yankees fan?" he asked me. I wasn't sure what it was I was doing that would lead him to believe that.

I shook my head. "I don't follow baseball," I admitted.

"Ahhh. I get it. Not into sports."

"What makes you say that?"

"You don't follow baseball, and that book you're reading." He was very matter-of-fact. It was strange.

"Okay," I said, and went back to my book.

He didn't seem like the guy I wanted to talk about hockey with, and I wasn't really in the mood to talk. Across the room, I heard a chair screech out from a table and footsteps. I looked up and saw him pulling another chair up to my table, right next to me. He was bigger than I'd judged him from across the room, the kind of build I'd put with a football player, not a baseball fan.

"So where are you from?" Asa asked.

It seemed a little bold and entitled of him to assume I still wanted to talk. I didn't answer, but instead stared at him with a look of disbelief.

"I'm from New York. Manhattan," he clarified.

"Me too," I half-lied. He was looking at me like I was less-than, and now I was feeling the determination to one up him. "Village."

"My dad works at Columbia. I get down to the Village sometimes though. You ever been to Little Owl?"

I nodded. "Yep." I wasn't sure what to think of Asa, and was mostly talking to him since no one else was here. I hadn't met any students outside of my classes, but I'd heard the NYU kids had a reputation for partying.

"Well, you don't seem really interested in talking, and I have to get to class anyway." He stood up and pushed his chair back to the table he had borrowed it from. "Maybe you'd rather talk to me tonight? Over dinner?"

I was surprised by his forwardness. We'd only talked for a minute. What made him think I'd have dinner with him? I immediately opened my mouth to say no, when a voice in my head piped up. *Why not? You're not dating anyone. It might be fun. Something different. What's the worst that could happen?*

"Maybe," I said coyly. I grabbed a napkin from underneath my sandwich and a pen from my backpack, jotting down my phone number. "Why don't you try your luck later?"

He took the napkin and smiled. "See you tonight."

Other than his overly-confident demeanor, I couldn't come up with a good reason not to have dinner with Asa. He grabbed his backpack and left, leaving me alone in the back room. I went back to my book and sandwich and put Asa—and Nick—out of my mind.

It wasn't until I had finished my lunch, a few chapters of *The Unbearable Lightness of Being,* and gotten back to my apartment that I got a text from Asa.

La Bodeguita. Old Town. Reservations at 7pm.

I had nothing else to do. *See you there,* I replied.

As soon as I hit send, my phone buzzed. It was Lexie.

"Hey," I answered.

"Hey, I finished up my project. We're going to have some drinks at Zanzibar. Meet us?"

"I just made plans, actually," I said.

"What? With who?" Lexie asked. It wasn't as if we had hundreds of people we knew. If I ever made plans, it was with her and Celeste, and if I had plans with Nick she'd know about it.

"I met a guy at Bohemia, and I'm going to dinner with him tonight. I've got to get cleaned up."

"Whaaaaaaaat?" She shrieked. "Details!"

"There isn't much to tell. We only talked for a little bit, but we're going to some Cuban place in Old Town. He made reservations."

"Ohhh, *fancy,*" she joked. "Well, Nick will be bummed you can't join I'm sure..."

"Nick's going?" I tried to keep my voice steady. "Well, if he can date, I'm sure he won't care if I do."

"Do you want me to tell him?" she asked.

"Sure, it's not a secret." *If anything*, I thought. *It might make him a bit jealous.*

We said our good-byes, with plans for her to text me after they finished at Zanzi's and let me know where they were headed.

Once I got back to my apartment, I threw on some music and turned the water on in the shower, letting it heat up. I tried to remember the last time I was on a date, a real date. There were more nights with Mark than I could actually recall, none of which were especially romantic or wonderful. It would be fun to go on a date, I reasoned. Even if he seemed like a bit of an ass, how bad could it be?

Out of the shower, I threw on a pair of jeans, a bold bra, and a sheer black top, and ditched my flats for a pair of high-heeled boots I'd brought. I quickly dried my hair and spritzed on perfume. It was a bus and metro ride to the restaurant Asa had chosen, just a few blocks off of Old Town Square. Walking through the square, carrying my clutch, the sound of my heels on the cobblestones felt surreal. Going out on an actual date gave me a spring in my step, though I had little hopes of a love connection at dinner. It didn't matter to me. After Nick's date the other night, it felt good to have some male attention.

It took me a few tries to find the right place, but once I found it, I was shocked I hadn't noticed it before. It was large by Czech standards, and had all the windows thrown open to the streets outside. Loud Latin music poured out the windows, along with laughter and the smell of seafood and garlic. I opened the door and immediately saw there was live music in the bar. *Not a bad place for a date*, I admitted to myself. I immediately realized I had only seen Asa in shorts and a baseball cap, and wasn't really sure what he looked like underneath. I scanned the bar, not sure if he was there or not. I decided to order myself a drink and take a lap.

I pushed my way to the bartender. "I'll have a gimlet," I called over the music. As he set off to mix my drink, I saw Asa walking toward me.

He hugged me and kissed me on the cheek. "You look incredible," he said.

I was glad I'd fancied myself up a bit, even if I was overdressed. "Thanks," I said.

As he leaned into me, I could smell his cologne, spicy and musky. It was then that I noticed he was actually quite attractive. Where the Yankees hat once sat was a mess of dark, curly hair. His eyes were a very warm brown, and his skin was olive-toned like mine. He wore jeans and a white button-up shirt, a gray blazer thrown open over it. He had a bigger build, but was not overweight. It was comforting.

"You clean up pretty nicely yourself."

"Yeah? Let's go to our table, it's ready."

"Oh, okay, well I just ordered a drink," I said.

"Don't worry about it, I put in an order for a pitcher of mojitos at the table." He grabbed my hand and pulled me away from the bar. Clearly it didn't matter if I liked mojitos or not, and we were apparently not waiting for my gimlet.

We walked back to the hostess stand, where a tall girl in a tight black dress grabbed some menus and led us down a flight of stairs to a quieter dining room. Sure enough, a tall pitcher filled with soda and mint was sitting on top of our table. I wasn't quite sure how he'd pulled that off.

As soon as we sat down, Asa poured two glasses. "Have you ever been to Cuba?"

I shook my head. "I don't think most Americans have been," I said.

"We stopped there on my grandpa's yacht once," he said, then launched into a story about Cuba and this yacht and how his mom's family made their money. He didn't stop talking about himself until our server finally, mercifully, arrived to take our order.

"I'll have the pork belly," he said, pointing to the menu. "And she will have the chicken supreme."

"Actually, I'll have the tuna steak," I interjected. No one had ever ordered for me before. Asa's confidence had officially crossed into cockiness, and I wasn't having it.

I mentally willed our food to come as soon as possible. He hadn't asked me one thing about myself, and I was done listening to his self-centered, upper-class bullshit. He was polite, sure, and seemed like a gentleman. But this was definitely not as much fun as I'd hoped.

I started talking about New York, and we chitchatted about school, the city, and our families. Before too long, our food had arrived. I was happy to see my fish arrived and not the chicken Asa had tried to order for me. Halfway into our meal, Asa's phone rang. He'd had it sitting on the table our whole date, which would have annoyed me if I'd cared. As he talked to someone on the other line about some sort of party happening, I grabbed my cell out of my clutch to see if Lexie had texted me. Instead, I had a missed call and two texts from Nick.

Movie night at Cozy. Get on it. And then. *Are you coming? I've got to make an extra bag of popcorn if you are. Let me know.*

I thought for a second. I didn't want to miss an opportunity to hang out with Nick, and this date was a complete bust. It didn't appear Lexie had told him about my date, or he wouldn't have invited me— unless he was just playing dumb. I sent Nick a quick text. *Be over when I can.*

Across the table, Asa was finishing up his call. "My roommate said there's a crazy party happening near Wenceslas Square. He met this Czech waitress and she invited him over to her place, and I guess it's nuts over there. We'll head over after dinner." Once again, he seemed to not care what I wanted to do.

"Actually, I just got a text from my roommate," I lied. "She's locked out, and I'm the only one with a key. I have to get back and let her in.

"Oh, uhh, okay, I'll get the check and go back with you." He held his hand up and motioned to our waiter.

"No, no, please, it's okay," I said, a little too forcefully. I wasn't sure I wanted Asa to know where my apartment was, and definitely didn't want to get caught in my lie. "I have to take a bus, I live a little ways out of the city center. It's kind of a trek. Thanks so much for this though." I stood up, and opened my purse to grab some money. I was embarrassed to see I only had a couple hundred krowns, certainly not enough for such a fancy dinner and the slew of cocktails he'd ordered for us. I grabbed some out, when Asa held up his hand.

"Please, don't insult me. It's my pleasure." He waved my money away and stood up, placing both his hands on my upper arms.

"Okay, well, thanks again, and—"

"I'll call you later tonight," he said.

I knew I wouldn't take the call, and immediately felt guilty. He leaned forward and I moved my face aside, giving him my cheek, then blushed and ducked away.

I hopped up the stairs and was outside in the cool, evening air moments later. I walked toward the nearest metro station at Můstek, and started the long trip to Cozy House. I decided I wouldn't go home and change first. I sent Lexie a text to see if she was over there with John. It wasn't like I had gone out with Asa just to make Nick jealous, but if that happened, I'd take it as a nice perk. The date wasn't all that great anyway. There had to be an upside.

But as soon as I walked into Cozy, I got my answer.

"So how was your date?" Nick asked, before anyone could even greet me with a hello.

"Oh, it was okay," I said, walking over to his couch. John and Lexie were lying on the floor together, and Charlie and Mason were on the other couch. I playfully hit his legs with my clutch. "Move so I can sit."

"I don't know, sounds like you might be taken. Your boy might not want you sitting next to someone else." He was joking, but was definitely still wanting to talk about my date.

From the floor, Lexie made eyes at me.

"Oh, please. It was just dinner. And drinks. I know *you* don't usually have dinner with girls, but…"

Nick moved his legs from the other side of the couch. "Only the special ones get dinner," he said.

Mason stood up. "Can I put the movie back on or what?" I looked at the TV and saw they'd paused it for me. "Shut up you two."

I tried to figure out what movie we were watching. A few minutes in, Nick leaned over to me.

"So did he make a move?" he whispered.

"No." I kept my eyes on the TV.

"You must not have been giving him the signs," he said, knowingly.

"Yo, can we watch the movie?" Charlie said, annoyed.

I turned my head to Nick. "What signs?" I hissed.

"You know. You have signs."

"Oh, you know my signs, do you?"

He raised his eyebrows and leaned back on the couch, putting his legs up over my lap. I shook my head at him and turned back to the TV.

16

October, Prague.

The week before Italy was also the week of midterms. John, Charlie, and
Nick were leaving on Thursday after their last exams, but Celeste, Lexie,
and I didn't fly out until Friday evening. We would be arriving hours
after the boys would. Our plans were for the six of us to rendezvous in
Venice somewhere. With midterms consuming our days and planning
for Italy consuming our evenings, I couldn't wait to get out of Prague and
onto the coast.

John had a friend from home—an ex-girlfriend—who was
studying in Florence and passing through the city for a night with a
friend. He had made plans to go out to a jazz club with her, along with
Lexie, of course. Not surprisingly, the prospect of spending an evening
with John and his ex didn't sit well with Lexie, and she'd begged me to
go along with her. I knew I should probably spend the evening studying
instead, but I'd lent my laptop to Nick so he could study. Besides, the
thought of taking my mind off counting the moments until Italy at a jazz
club sounding much more fun, and finishing one midterm already, most
likely the most difficult one, was worth celebrating.

Tuesday evening, I took my time getting ready. I wanted to
throw something on besides what had become my uniform of jeans, a T-
shirt, a scarf, and flats. I drew liner over my eyelids. I let my hair fall in
its natural waves and put cream on it to keep it polished. I fished a long-
sleeved red T-shirt dress out of my closet with an open back, cinched a

belt around my middle, and slipped on a pair of kitten heels. I pushed a few bracelets on my wrist and threw a chunky gold necklace over my head before waltzing out the door. It was a gorgeous evening, and I felt more at home than ever walking through my neighborhood to the bus stop. The sun was turning the sky over Peroutkova a deep orange and bright pink. I stared at it as I sat on the bench, waiting for the 137. I wondered how much time I had spent staring at that sky every day as I waited for the bus.

"Adriana?"

I flipped my head around to see Nick walking up the street to the bus stop. He was sharply dressed, wearing jeans, a deep green button-up shirt, and a black linen jacket over it. "What are you doing here?" I asked him. "I thought you were studying?"

He stopped directly in front of me. "Wow. You look... wow."

Warmth spread over my cheeks as I felt them flush. I smiled. "Thanks. You don't look so bad yourself. Where are you going?"

Nick settled next to me on the bench. "Oh, John guilted me into keeping him company with his ex tonight. He really didn't want to be alone with her and Lexie."

I laughed. "No fucking way. That's where I am going."

"What?"

"Yeah, Lex begged me to go."

"So neither of them want to go out with this girl, so they are dragging us along. Nice."

"Yeah, well at least it's a night out if nothing else," I commiserated.

We caught the next bus, then jumped on the metro to Old Town. The jazz club, Agharta, was not far from the Můstek stop off of Old Town Square. We took our time walking through the curved, cobblestoned streets of Staré Město. It was a perfect fall evening. Making my way over each stone on the ground, I was feeling that sense of belonging. Prague was no longer feeling like a strange place I was getting to know; I was no longer an imposter. I lived here, I belonged here. The sounds around me, the chatter of Czech and the smell of cigarettes had become familiar, comforting even. It was a welcome change, and the realization of it warmed my heart as I crossed the square with Nick.

It was a little harder than we'd hoped to find the jazz club. A small sign outside saying Jazz Club was the only hint we had; the club was down in the basement. We followed the steep steps down into a crowded bar in what felt like a cave. White stone walls and low ceilings gave the bar, already packed with people, a very cramped feeling. Nick started pushing his way through people, looking for John. I skimmed the bar, but didn't see any sign of him or Lexie.

Then, through all the noise, I heard John's loud voice. I turned around to see Nick pointing to Lexie's blonde hair, and we gently nudged people aside until we got to their table. John and Lexie and the ex were sitting at a small bar table.

"Hey," John boomed. "Look at you two."

"We have two extra seats we've been saving," Lexie said, dragging her chair off of an old, small barstool.

Nick motioned for me to take the first one. I sat, immediately noticing the legs were uneven.

"I've got the other seat here," the ex said to Nick. He made his way around the table to sit between her and John.

"Thanks," Nick said. "Umm—"

"Maura," she finished.

Lexie and I had referred to her as "the ex" since we'd found out about her coming. I hadn't heard her name until now.

"Maura," Nick finished. "Thanks, Maura."

"So does the band go on in here?" I asked, looking around. There wasn't a stage in sight.

"Turns out you need tickets. Who would have thought, right?" John joked. It took a lot more than that to get him upset. "But thankfully there's a bar here, so we are just hanging out, having a few drinks, catching up."

The server came by, and Nick and I each ordered a beer.

"So what brings you to Prague solo?" I asked.

"I'm studying in Florence this semester, and my roommate wanted to come for the weekend. So I'm here with her."

I looked around, and noticed she wasn't with anyone else.

Maura giggled. "She's out with some friends from college who study here."

I nodded. Our beers arrived, Lexie preemptively asking the waitress for a refill.

If Lexie was nervous, she wasn't letting it show. She let Maura and John reminisce, and let John tell his stories about their friends back home. She laughed when appropriate, was perfectly polite, and seemed genuinely interested in Maura—which I found hard to believe. John recounted story after story of their growing up in Jersey. We spent a couple hours laughing, ordering new rounds whenever our glasses were too light. After my third or fourth round—I'd stopped counting at some point—I felt my phone buzz. I reached down to grab it and saw it was past eleven. The last metro
left at midnight. The message was from Asa, and I didn't even bother reading it.

I made eyes at Lexie to let her know I'd have to go, and she nodded her approval. I kicked Nick under the table.

"Hey, it's after eleven. Want to head out soon?"

He picked up his glass and downed the rest of his pilsner in one drink. "Let's go. We have that Gender and Culture midterm tomorrow, too."

We said our good-byes and headed back up to the street. The square had emptied out considerably, the Jan Hus memorial that sat in the middle of the square was nearly deserted. A couple sat on one of the benches, kissing furiously. For a people that seemed so cold and distant, rarely smiling or offering pleasantries of any kind, they certainly had no problem with public displays of affection. It was uncomfortable, at times. Except for that couple, and a group of guys on the other side of the square, all was quiet. It was Nick who broke the silence first.

"That couldn't have been comfortable for Lexie," he said.

I nodded. "Yeah, but she seemed okay."

"But just sitting around with some girl that John's slept with. I felt awkward for her."

I wasn't sure why, but the idea of John having slept with Maura surprised me. "Really? They've slept together?"

Nick turned to me. "I assumed, I guess. They were together for a while, weren't they?"

"I have no idea. But I know that Lexie and John haven't, so I didn't think about it."

"Wait, Lexie and John haven't had sex?"

"No," I said. "Why did you think they had?"

"I don't know. I just figured... that was part of it."

"Yeah, I know, but not for them I guess." I turned the corner, the walk to the metro routine at this point. "I don't think I could do that. Be serious with someone without having slept with them." Nick raised his eyebrows at me. "Don't you think sexual chemistry is important?"

"No, I do. I just think it's good to be serious about someone before you take that step."

I felt myself blush. I didn't want him to get the wrong idea about me. "Right." I wasn't sure what else to say. We walked a block in silence.

"So have you ever been with someone and found out you had no sexual chemistry?" He didn't look at me when he asked, but looked up to check which street we were turning on. I got the feeling he was pretending, avoiding my eye line on purpose.

I thought for moment, surprised by the question. "Well... yeah, I guess I have. But I knew before that it wasn't really right. I just wanted to try to make it work."

"What was wrong?"

"He'd ask before he did anything. Like, 'Can I kiss you now?' I hate that." I looked at Nick. He was still avoiding my eyes.

"What else?"

"I don't know... it was kind of... passionless maybe? Everything just seemed so planned. Like he had a routine of what he was going to do and he just did it. It didn't translate well."

We started down the stairs to the metro. I could hear the rumble of the train underneath the escalator, and we picked up the pace down the stairs to make the last train.

"That doesn't sound good," he said. "But I know what you mean. You've got to mix it up."

I laughed. "Yeah, that's a good way to put it." On the platform in front of us, the train was just arriving. We stepped on board and walked to the middle of the car, holding onto a pole. "Have you heard Noelle talk about 'throw down'?"

Nick finally caught my eye. "No," he answered.

"It's the passion a guy has where, when he kisses you, you just want to throw everything down and have him, right there."

"Throw down. Huh." The metro groaned, swaying as we pulled away from the station and on to the next stop. "So what does a guy have to do to have 'throw down'?"

I couldn't believe where this conversation was going. I could feel butterflies in my stomach, nervous to be talking about this with Nick. I was nervous enough when I talked to him... but talking about sex?

I shook my head. "I don't know, I guess it depends." Suddenly, I felt incredibly shy. "I guess take charge? If the moment was right, and a guy wanted to kiss me, that he'd just do it."

I was sure he was going to see right through me, and see that what I really wanted, that I was asking him to take charge. The train shook as it slowed, then lurched to a sudden stop. I lost my footing, having stopped paying attention to being on a moving train and too much attention to Nick and his questions. His hand immediately darted to my hip in an effort to steady me and hold me up.

I stared at him as his hand lingered on my hip. His gaze was piercing and deep, as if he was trying to stare past my eyes and right into me. It was unnerving. The doors of the train opened.

"So what about you?" I asked, as Nick pulled his hand off me. "What are some of your turn-ons?"

He smiled a mischievous grin. The train sped off once more, and our conversation continued. Turn-ons and turn offs. Places we'd hooked up. Our favorite ways to be intimate. We held nothing back, talking about sex rather than having it. Along the metro stops, on our walk to the bus. On the 137, seated side by side, speaking quietly so other passengers didn't hear. There were more things we had in common than otherwise. I was surprised when Nick moved to get out of his seat, and looked outside to see we had made it to Urbanova. It was the fastest ride home I'd ever had.

My heart was pounding as we descended the steps of the bus. I stood awkwardly by the bus stop, waiting for some sign from Nick. Surely after all this we weren't just going to wave good night and see each other for midterms the next day.

"You're coming over, right?"

"Sure," I agreed, eager to keep our conversation going. I had no idea why it was supposedly so obvious that I was going over, but it was obvious that he wanted to keep talking, too. I followed him down the sidewalk and into the street.

We made our way up the cobblestoned sidewalk outside the cemetery and up his narrow street to Cozy House, our conversation lingering on places we'd hooked up. He opened the door for me, and walked straight into his bedroom. I followed, my heart pounding. I didn't know what to expect, but felt sure that something was about to happen.

I started at him as he recounted one of his favorite turn-ons, bustling around his room as if he was looking for something. I wanted to be the one to learn these things firsthand. I imagined myself walking over to him without another word and pulling him close to me, feeling his breath on my neck. His words floated above us and stayed in the room, making the air heavier with their pressure and the implications I was sure we were about to feel. He turned around quickly, and I knew he was going to grab me, hard, like I wanted him to. Instead, he reached out his arm, my laptop in his hand.

"Here you go."

I looked down at it, confused, as he reached it toward me, then back up at Nicholas.

"It's your laptop. I borrowed it to study, remember? For the Gender and Culture midterm?" His face was beginning to look puzzled. "Addie?"

I shook my head, as if shaking a nightmare out of my mind. "Right, thanks. I totally forgot."

"Why did you think I wanted you to come over?"

I looked at Nicholas. His eyes were as blue as ever, and I got lost in their oceanic depths, searching for an excuse. I came up empty-handed and continued to stare at him, my lips separating slightly to see if words might fall out of my mouth without effort. His light brown hair was pushed off his forehead, his freckles perfectly dotted across his nose and cheekbones. I couldn't take my eyes off of him and still, I had nothing to say. His face softened, his lips spread into a shy smile. He laughed a low, soft nervous laugh, and then went silent.

We stood there for a moment, staring. He took a small step toward me and I could smell his cologne. I reached my arm out to grab the laptop he offered me, and our hands grazed. We both paused.

"Good night, Nicholas."

He sighed. "Night, Adriana."

With that, I turned and left. It took all my strength to not look back to see if Nick wanted me to stay. But I knew it wasn't the time yet.

△

We were at Coffee and Cigars again, still booking hotels, on Thursday, the night our trip was to kick off. The boys' train was actually three separate trains: a 1 a.m. train from Prague to Bratislava, a seven-minute stopover at 4:30 a.m. to change trains to Vienna, then another switch in Vienna to Venice. By the time they finally arrived in Venice, they would have been traveling for over twelve hours. We finished finalizing all our plans just an hour before their train was to leave, and hastily decided where to meet the following day in Venice. With hurried good-byes, the boys rushed off to pick up their backpacks and catch their train. Celeste and Lexie walked back to their flat, and I went home to pack.

Once home, I pulled my backpack down off the top of my wardrobe. My laptop was open on my desk, bumping out Nelly Furtado. I danced around, relishing in an empty apartment and those wonderful moments right before a vacation. Sometimes those moments of anticipation can be better than the trip itself—the excitement of not knowing what's ahead, but knowing you will surrender yourself to it.

A breeze hushed through the window, blowing the curtain back across Emily's bed. I thumbed through my clothes, pulling out the essentials for the trip. Jeans, a few snug and colorful tees, my favorite pairs of black and brown flats. I decided to skip the blow dryer and straightener. Grabbed some pajamas. Wouldn't need anything fancy; we didn't have the budget for that.

Singing, I swayed my way over to my simple wood desk to turn down the volume a bit. As I adjusted the music, something caught the corner of my eye on the right side of my desk, just behind my laptop. A flame flickered in the orange candle I had been burning all month.

They were part of a set my brother had bought me for Christmas. "A Year of Wishes" the set had said. I remembered pulling the big bow off the box James had obviously had gift wrapped. Inside were twelve candles, each a different color, about six inches tall. On the front of each rectangular candle, was a silver plaque with a word engraved; each candle had a different word. *Fun, health, love, adventure, balance, joy, success, peace, comfort, longevity, luck,* and *wealth* were the wishes. At the start of each month, you were supposed to pick a candle for what you needed most that month, in part for a wish and in part to remind you of the power of positive thought. I had stuck with it, burning *balance* when I needed it most and *luck* before leaving for Prague. My mom had helped me choose a few to bring with me, to burn for what I may need most while I was gone. *Comfort. Joy. Adventure. Peace.*

I was in the routine of burning the candle for a little bit each evening, while I read or just got ready for bed. I didn't even remember lighting the candle tonight—I had picked *adventure* for the month of October—but the glow of the flame wasn't what had caught my eye. Just underneath and to the right of the wick, something silver was poking out of the candle. I picked up the candle and tilted it forward, wax dripping away from the shiny silver object. Quickly but carefully, I tried to push the mystery object free of the wax, burning my finger in the process. I sucked my wounded finger and fished out a pair of tweezers from my desk drawer. I grabbed a hold of the silver thing and pulled gently, breaking it free of the melted wax.

It was a small airplane, very hot from the candle's flame. What was this? How did it get there? Why was it there? I hadn't noticed any charms like this in the rest of my wishful candles, and I had burned nine so far.

The clock on my laptop read just after 1 a.m. The boys would be getting on their train right now. I reached out my phone to text Nicholas. *I know you probably can't text me back but I just wanted to say I hope you got on the train ok and you aren't cranky. Can't wait to see you in Venice.* His phone had been out of credits. I sat on my bed, clothes spread out on the bed all around me, turning the little airplane over between my fingers. My phone vibrated next to me, lighting up a purple T-shirt I had been deciding on packing. *We made it on the train, everyone is happy and comfortable with a cabin to ourselves. Feel honored, I'm spending my last credit on you. Good luck tomorrow.*

I looked down at the airplane again, running Nicholas' text through my head. The past week had been... different. Nicholas and I had become inseparable. Something had changed between Nicholas and me, although nothing had actually changed. Since his birthday, we'd spent all our time studying for midterms together and had dinner together every night, either with Lexie and John, Celeste and Charlie, or just the two of us. The night before, after a small EOO reception in Bara's office for some high-level executives coming to check on their newest program, Nick and I had spent the evening together. We had spent the day together after our Gender and Culture midterm, the previous night's sexually-charged conversation still fresh in my mind. We had walked through the Nový Smíchov mall, picking up some last-minute things for Italy, before making our way to the food court to grab some dinner and making our way home.

It was nothing. It was a night, like any other. A stop at the mall. Two friends sharing bad food court pizza. We'd made fun of each other to mask our feelings. He'd bet me I couldn't be nice to him for five solid minutes. I lost. I'd bet him he couldn't go twenty minutes only paying me compliments. It was a quiet twenty minutes, but he did it. He had reached his hand across the table and held mine, my eyes searching for the meaning of it all in his eyes. We had walked to the bus together and intentionally sat at different ends, him at the back and me at the front, and he called me from the back of the bus and we talked on the phone the whole ride home. Something had shifted. Our relationship was changing, and it was all building up to Italy. I couldn't see the next step in the story, but I knew there was a next step.

I squeezed the airplane between my thumb and index finger. I knew it was a sign. It had appeared out of my candle the night before our big trip to tell me my adventure was coming. I could tell, even before I left, that my life would never be the same after those ten days in Italy.

Δ

It was strange how normal it felt now to be waiting for the 137 at Na Knízecí. This was my routine now, and I no longer had to *think* about it as I walked toward the bus station. Like speaking in a foreign language, and one day, mid-sentence, you realize you aren't putting effort into it anymore. I felt truly at home, even around the bums sleeping on the benches and moms pulling their children's pants down so they could urinate in the flower beds.

I had just finished picking up a few things before I took the bus back home to pick up my backpack, grab the rest of my travel essentials, and head out to the airport to meet Celeste and Lexie. A calm excitement had taken over me as I ran my last errands before Italy. I wondered what the boys were doing in Venice for their first day. I thought of them eating pasta, ogling the Sophia Loren-esque women, and drinking Peroni. *What if my feelings about this trip are wrong?* I thought. It could be an epic disaster, Nick and I traveling together. If I couldn't get my feelings for him under control, with the romance of Italy around us... I didn't trust myself. I couldn't make a move and risk ruining the friendship we'd built the past few months, even if I was certain that he was holding feelings for me too. If he wanted something to happen, he would make a move and I would react in the moment. *One day at a time*, I reminded myself. *Just take it as it comes.*

The bus interrupted my thoughts, pulling up in front of me. I gathered my purse, lunch I had gotten to-go, and my Tesco bags and boarded, pushing against baby strollers and merry-widows. A woman's familiar voice came over the speakers, announcing our first stop. *Příští zastávka: Santoška.*

I held on to a plastic handle as the bus creaked and curved up the hill, and my cell phone jingled in my bag. I carefully rearranged my load to catch the call without dropping any bags or falling over. It was John.

"Hey! You guys make it okay?" I was surprised he was calling me.

"Yeah, the trip was... well, we'll tell you about it when you get here," Nicholas said on the other end of the line.

"Oh, hey. Hi." My breath caught in my throat. I tried not to give away that my heart was already beating faster than it was three seconds before. "Why are you calling me from John's phone?" I could hear Charlie's voice in the background, laughing about something.

"I wanted to call you but didn't have any krowns left," he explained. "Are you ready for the trip?"

"Yeah, I am just running some last errands before I head to the airport. Is that why you were calling me?"

"Well, you can't be trusted to these things by yourself." His voice was sarcastic.

"Oh, is that so? You know I traveled plenty before I met you, right?"

"Yes, but you're kind of a mess, Adriana. Are you all packed?"

"Yes, of course. And Lexie still has credits on her phones, so we'll get ahold of John or Charlie when we get into Venice."

"Okay. Be careful. You're sure you know where you're going?"

"Of course," I lied. "I just finished looking up how to get to the train station from the airport." It was a small issue, I hoped, that the train station was an hour away from the airport where we would be landing in Milan, and we had exactly one hour and fifteen minutes from when our plane was scheduled to land, until our train was scheduled to leave. We'd have to bust our asses to get our bags from the claim, then find the right bus that went to Milano Centrale station. Nicholas did not need to know this part, I told myself. *I can handle it.*

"Well then, don't drink too much on the plane, or the train. And see you when you get here." I could hear the life on the streets around him, and I couldn't wait another minute to be in Venice with him and everyone else—but mostly him.

"Yep. See you in Venice." My smile, stretched from ear to ear, could be heard in my voice in anticipation of the ten days to come. I was just sure of it.

17

October, Venice.

I bounced up the stairs of the metro from Dejvická, oblivious to the weight of the backpack I'd be carrying everywhere for the next ten days. Stepping past a purple-haired woman carrying a bowling bag, a feeling of total and complete independence came over me. I'd been alone in Prague for over two months now, but this was a different feeling. Italy would be my first trip out of my new country alone with my friends. The travel I'd done up until this point, though more than many people get to experience in a lifetime, was always coordinated by someone other than me. But this trip was different. Not only did the six of us plan this trip ourselves, but Celeste and Lexie were depending on me to get them to Venice. My very limited Italian was our best bet to find our way from the airport to the train station via bus, and onto the right train from there. I was exhilarated. I should have been nervous, but was far too excited to think straight.

I walked over to the bus stop bench and thought about sitting down. My backpack was strapped and buckled around my hips, with another buckle fastened between my shoulders above my breasts and collarbone. It was too complicated, and heavy, to take off and put back on if it wasn't absolutely necessary. The weather was just cool enough, the breeze crisp enough to not feel sweaty under the weight of my backpack. I stood next to the bench and waited. Our plan was for me to meet Celeste and Lexie at the end of the metro at the 119 bus stop, so the three of us could continue on to the airport together. Less than five minutes later, I heard the girls' giggles coming up the stairs from the metro station. Lexie was pulling a carry-on-sized roller suitcase behind her, banging up each stair loudly. It probably wasn't going to be the ideal bag for this trip, but it would be fine. We were all just making do with what we had on us.

"Hiiiiii," Lexie said breathlessly, grinning from ear to ear. I could hear the excitement in her voice. She yanked her suitcase up the last stair, and I saw Celeste trailing behind her. Out of the dark of the stairs, I could see the top of Celeste's head, her chestnut waves coming into view slowly as she clamored up the stairs as well.

"Hey, girl! Are you ready for this?" Celeste followed Lexie over to the bus stop bench and plopped herself down. Lexi took a bottle of water out of the side of her backpack, and drained about half of the contents.

"It's finally here. I'm so ready to be there. Have you heard from the guys?" I guessed that if anyone had heard, it would be Lexie.

"Yeah, they are barhopping."

"Barhopping? In Venice?"

Celeste rolled her eyes. "That's Charlie for you. You know he can't go half an hour without stopping into a bar."

Lexie cocked her head and gave her a tight-lipped smile. "It's fine, who cares what they are doing today? If Charlie just wants to go around to see if bars are really any different in Italy, then we'll do our own thing."

I nodded. I wasn't stoked about the idea of us all splitting up, but I certainly wasn't going to sit around in a bar for the majority of our trip, with or without Nicholas.

"Addie, that backpack is perfect. Where did you get it?" Celeste was checking out the straps on my bag, pulling at strings I hadn't even realized were there.

"I grabbed it a couple days ago at the Anděl mall. I only have my school backpack and the giant suitcase I brought all my stuff here in. Nothing for just a week. It's a little too big." I turned around to try and look at the backpack, and ended up turning in a circle like a dog chasing its tail.

"It's like the size of Charlie," Lexie said.

Celeste and I broke into laughter. "You're totally right," I replied. "I'm going to call this thing 'Charlie' now."

"So how are we meeting the guys? Do we even know?" I suddenly couldn't remember the plan.

"They are going to meet us at the train station," she replied.

I knew there was still a chance we wouldn't make the train, and shuddered to think what our backup plan would be, and if we would be able to communicate with the boys at all. Our only saving grace was that Celeste was the one who had booked our hotel in Venice, so she knew where we were staying. She'd booked it under Charlie's name, so they could check in before us, and we would meet them later. Worst-case scenario, we would meet up at the hotel at some point. We'd divvied up responsibilities for each city: John and Lexie booked Florence, Celeste and Charlie booked Venice, and Nick and I were in charge of Rome and Cinque Terre, since we were the only ones who had been to Italy before. We found a cute little spot in Rome, but Nick heard from a friend that when you got off the train in Riomaggiore, there were people who stood on the platform and offered rooms for the night, so we had booked nothing for that last stop. We were banking on that to be true.

The 119 bus pulled up, rattling to a stop at the covered bench we were standing in front of. Lexie and Celeste gathered their bags, and I climbed the steps and found us a spot to stand in the back of the bus. It was a twenty-minute ride to the airport, our trip delaying each time passengers pulled the string to signal our driver to stop. It was easy and uneventful enough to arrive to the airport, find our check in counter, and drop our bags. We joked about what the boys were probably up to, how many cigarette breaks Charlie had already taken, how many bars they'd stopped in so far. It wasn't until after we had started walking to our gate that I realized waiting for our bags at the Milano Orio al Serio airport would further delay our arrival at the bus station. *It will work out,* I told myself, thinking of the airplane charm I'd fished out of my candle the night before. It was going to be just fine. I couldn't explain it, but I could feel it.

My body moved easier, felt freer without the constraints of Charlie on my back. I made a mental note to not mention that around the boys, because the real-life Charlie would understandably take offense to being compared in height to a backpack. We cleared passport control and made our way to our gate, arriving just in time to board. *See?* I told myself. *No reason to worry.* On the plane, the three of us found our row of seats and settled in for the hour-and-a-half flight. I had the middle seat, sandwiched between the two people I was beginning to care about most in the world. I grabbed my phone and powered it down, vowing not to turn it back on until we returned to Prague ten days later. We got iPods out and spent the flight sharing headphones, trading stories, and daydreaming of the days ahead. I was the only one who had been before, on a very short trip, the only other time I was in Europe. The only thing I remembered, was walking with my roommates from the beach in Lido back to my hotel, and stopping for gelato three times on the way. I told them what I did remember, as Lexie flagged down a flight attendant to bring us mini bottles of wine.

It wasn't long before we were beginning our descent into Milan, and we started scheming how to get to the bus in as little time as possible. If our bags were delayed, we would miss the bus. If the bus was delayed, we would miss the train. There was zero room for error.

Another fact I'd chosen to keep to myself was that I'd failed the one Italian course I'd taken as a freshman. We were relying on my language skills. I always knew that I was good with languages. My family would be out somewhere, and pick up notes of a foreign language around us. "What language is that?" my mom would ask. I'd listen closely, not knowing exactly what they were saying, but be able to instantly tell from tones and sounds what they were speaking. The musical sounds of French. The harsh sounds of German. It was second nature to me. I'd also been able to decipher bits and pieces from Nanny, who spoke Italian occasionally as she cooked, and Pop, who spoke Italian exclusively when he cursed. They'd discuss grown-up topics in front of us kids in Italian, not wanting us to know which uncle was in financial trouble again, or who'd called off their wedding, or what happened to Joey-from-down-the-street's house in the fire that had started mysteriously. I remembered key phrases from my college class; *sinistra* was left and *destra* was right, and it was somewhat similar to French, which I'd taken four years of. How hard could it be?

Our plan was for Lexie and Celeste to grab our bags while I went to find the bus, and we would meet outside of baggage claim. Though we knew there was a bus that left from Orio al Serio to Milano Centrale Railway, we hadn't actually purchased tickets yet. My mission was to find all of this out and purchase our tickets. As our plane descended, we started gathering our things. There was no time to waste. I had no phone to use GPS, and little language skills. Once we disembarked, I darted down the halls, moving past Italians left and right.

"*Scusa, scusa, scusa,*" I repeated over and over as I pushed my way around slow-moving people in my path. I could feel adrenaline coursing through my veins. All around me, people walked with a purpose. To baggage claim. To reunite with loved ones. To their gate, departing for a new destination. I shoved my way through crowds until I was in the wide-open terminal. My eyes darted from one sign to the next, frantically looking for a familiar word or phrase. *Venezia* maybe? Or *autobus?* I wasn't sure exactly, but I knew once I saw it, I would know. Around me, I saw kiosks with signs above them. *Noleggio auto. Guida Turistica. Aiuto bagagli smarriti.* I recognized nothing. Stopping, I took a deep breath. It had to be here somewhere. Outside, taxis lined up, a queue formed at the taxi stand. A man stood in front, blowing a whistle and motioning to cars. Drivers leaned outside of their windows, yelling at one another, crude arm gestures flying. Further down from the taxi stand, I saw it. Busses were parked in a row, destination names illuminated over their front windows. I turned and walked toward them.

Within moments, I'd found the right bus kiosk, confirmed the next departure time for the central train station in my broken Italian, and purchased three tickets. I turned around and rushed back to baggage claim. Because it was a secure area, a large glass wall was put up between the passenger pick-up and where bags were dropped. I stood outside the doors, helpless, my eyes scanning for Celeste or Lexie. I had no watch and couldn't turn my phone on without incurring ungodly roaming charges from my prepaid phone. I had no idea how long my search had taken, but I knew from the timetable posted at the bus kiosk, that our bus would be pulling away from the curb in three minutes. I was beginning to panic.

A father with two young daughters pushed past me, one girl in each hand. Their brown curls were pulled into identical braided pigtails, each crying loudly. I surveyed the baggage claim area, scanning for my friends. They had to be there somewhere. Before long, I saw a mess of blonde hair bouncing up and down. I couldn't see what she was doing exactly, an elderly couple stood in the way. But once they cleared, I could see Lexie attempting to put Charlie the backpack on her shoulders. She hadn't unbuckled the straps from one another, and so each time she pulled the weight of the bag onto her shoulder, it would slide down, unable to stay perched up. Celeste was next to her, trying to figure out what the problem was with the straps.

"Just forget it!" I yelled to the glass barrier. "You don't need the straps!"

But I knew they couldn't hear me. The terminal was buzzing with people, reuniting and loudly sharing stories and greetings with one another. I could see Lexie laughing as she turned around, and immediately saw the reason Celeste was no use, was because she was laughing so hard she couldn't quite stand up straight. I had to get their attention somehow.

"HEY!" I screamed, waving my arms up ahead and jumping up and down. I knew I was being obnoxious, the stereotypical American, but I was out of options. "CELESTE! LEX! COME ON!" I was starting to get impatient. It was pretty funny, watching them struggle with the bag, but if they couldn't get it together in the next minute we'd have to find another way to get to Venice. Finally, Lexie turned around and spotted me. She broke out into a run to me, Celeste following close behind. I turned around, leaving her with my backpack, and started running toward the bus. I knew they would follow me. I slowed down as I reached automatic doors to exit the airport, and the girls caught up to me.

"WAIT!" Lexie cried, waving her arms. Her suitcase was bouncing over gaps in the sidewalk as she ran. "WAIT!"

The bus was still parked with its doors closed as we finally slowed to walk, realizing we would make it. The driver pulled the lever to open the doors and said something, scolding us in Italian while shaking his head and finger at us. We ignored him, but heaved our bags up the stairs and found empty seats in the middle of the bus before we sat down to catch our breath.

Although we would learn it was very rare in Italy, our bus left right on time. We pulled out of the station and headed toward the city, where we'd have to fight through traffic to make it to the train station. It was enough to let us sit and relax somewhat on the bus. It was no longer in our control whether or not we'd make the train, and we anxiously waited to see whether or not it would happen.

Δ

Our flight, bus, and train had taken us all afternoon and evening. As with the bus, we'd barely made our train in Milan, and the whole thing ended with us running yet again, to climb onto the train just as it pulled away from the station, after my poor Italian had us board the wrong train first. Once we'd found a cabin to ourselves, we all collapsed in exhaustion and laughter, thankful we were finally headed to Venice.

Almost four hours later, we descended the stairs of the Santa Lucia train station. It was so late, it was nearly Saturday morning. For a Friday evening, all was quiet. The soft glow of the street lamps was reflected in the water, giving everything a warm glow. Not a hundred yards from the bottom of the steps of the station, was the water, rippling and splashing softly against the walls of the canal. The sight of the water immediately took my breath away. I was in Venice. With my best friends. A wave of freedom, gratefulness, and excitement ripped through my veins.

The train station let us off right in the heart of Venice. A few more steps and we'd be underwater. There were no more trains to take, no more buses to track down. We had arrived. What we'd been waiting for, counting down to, was starting now.

Around us, people from our train were scattering. There was a short queue forming to board a water taxi, while others took off in either direction from the stairs. Not sure what to do next, I turned around to see my travel mates.

"Any sign of them?" Lexie asked. I shook my head. I wasn't sure where they were going to meet us, but everything inside the train station was closed. There was no way they'd been inside.

"Maybe we should just wait out here for a little bit?" Celeste offered. I looked around, but saw no one familiar.

"Lex, can you try your phone?" It was the only idea I had.

She fished her hands into her jeans pocket, and we waited as she powered her Nokia up. "No service," she said.

"Right..." I didn't know what was next. Where the hell were they? We exchanged confused glances, unsure of where to go next.

"We could wait here?"

"Or go to the hotel?"

"Or maybe see if there is a bar close by they were sidetracked by?"

No one idea was better or worse than the others. We took a quick inventory of what we should do, and decided though it might be wisest to stay at the train station steps, we were going to go ahead to our hotel.

Up ahead, just north of the grand stairs of the station, was the Ponte degli Scalzi that crossed the canal. We started walking. I couldn't help but feel annoyed that the guys had left us, in the middle of the night, in Venice. I was ready to see if my intuition was right about the change in my relationship with Nick, but that couldn't happen if I didn't see him. I was growing more annoyed with each step.

Before I could open my mouth to complain, I heard a familiar shriek of laughter. Lexie whipped her head around.

"I heard it too," she said to me.

"That was Nick!" My heart jumped inside my chest. Where could they be?

We kept walking toward the bridge, unsure of what else to do. After another few steps, we heard John bellow something we couldn't quite make out. Our guys were here, somewhere.

I started walking faster, passing Lexie, anxious to cross over. Finally, I reached the bridge, climbing one step after another. There were no street lights on the bridge, and with each step I walked further into darkness. After the first three steps, I could just make out a figure in front of me. Taller than me. Broad shoulders. He was climbing the steps opposite me. I could see two other shadows on the steps, just behind him.

"It wasn't my fault," I heard John saying. "You were supposed to take the bag."

"Why would I take the bag, I didn't buy the wine," Charlie argued.

Lexie rushed passed me, leaving her suitcase at the top of the stairs, running right into John. He grabbed her and lifted her up, spinning her around.

"We were going to greet you with wine, a bottle for each of you," John was saying a little too loudly, as usual. "But the bottles broke, so, sorry ladies, nothing to offer you."

I kept walking until I reached the dead center of the bridge, where Nick and I stood, face to face.

"You made it." His face slowly broke out into a grin. I wasn't sure when it had happened, but I could feel my mouth stretched out into a smile so wide, my cheeks were already hurting.

"We made it."

He pulled me in close and wrapped his arms around me. I closed my eyes and breathed him in. It was better than I thought it would be. Reuniting on top of a bridge in Venice, in the middle of the night. I felt calmer than I'd felt all day, no longer wondering how the trip would go. We were here, and it was all going to happen. Whatever that would be.

Δ

We couldn't afford much on our scraped-together budget. We decided we'd share beds when we needed to; we were more concerned with the location of our hostels than anything else, and were absolutely sure we could be sneaky enough to pull it off. In Venice, Celeste and Charlie reserved a room for four people in what they thought was a hostel. When the boys arrived to drop off their bags, they learned it was a bed and breakfast run by an elderly Italian couple. John had explained to us that they had two dogs, Snuffles and Carl. They were very *John* names that clearly John had given the dogs. There were two twin beds and a king-size bed to share between six of us. Charlie had a bed of his own, and Lexie and John were sharing the other twin, which left Nick, Celeste, and me with the king.

It was better than sharing a bed with Charlie and Nick, I'd told myself, and had hardly crawled into the middle before falling asleep. It was only for two nights; our train to Florence left on Sunday. None of us seemed to care about sharing beds, and we'd arrived so late our patrons weren't there—which was great, since we had snuck two extra people into the room.

The king bed faced a wall of floor-to-ceiling windows that opened up to a small courtyard. White lace curtains danced around the edges of the windows, stopping just above the bed John and Lexie were sharing. They were still asleep, John's legs splayed off the side of the twin bed. The sun was peeking out between the gaps of the lace, growing ragged with age.

It was a dog's barking that awoke me, a deep, low, growling bark, over and over. Whether it was Snuffles or Carl, I wasn't sure. I tried to gather my bearings. My pillow had fallen onto the floor. An arm that could only have belonged to Nicholas was draped around my waist. The heaviness of his arm told me he was still asleep. He was lying on his side facing me, his chin tucked down to his chest, hair pushed over his forehead. I'd never really looked at him while he was asleep. It felt like spying, intruding where I should not be. I gently turned my face to the left to see if Celeste was awake. To my surprise, she wasn't there. I thought momentarily about rolling over, stretching out as I hadn't been able to all night, but decided against giving up this closeness with Nick.

On the other side of the doorway from our bed, was Charlie. I was surprised to see him sitting up, legs stretched out, his nose stuck in a copy of Rick Steves' *Italy*. It wasn't like him to map out sights or plan out our day. In the bathroom, I could hear the water running. Celeste had grabbed the first shower. I knew if I wanted any hot water, I'd need to be next. I inched my way over to Celeste's side of the bed, letting Nick's arm slowly fall off my body. I was about to pick his arm up and lift it off me to make my getaway, when I was suddenly pulled back.

"Where do you think you're going?" Nick mumbled sleepily. I smiled to myself as I felt his warm body pressed against my back.

"Shower. Did I wake you?"

"Yes. You did."

I could have spent the day like this. But knowing we were going to be spending the day together exploring Venice made the prospect of getting up and leaving our bed behind just as lovely.

"How'd you sleep?" I asked.

I could feel him yawn, his breath warm on the back of my neck "You snore."

"I do not!"

"Yes, you absolutely do. And you talk in your sleep."

"Now I know you're lying." I turned around to face him. He moved his arm off my side, and we lay there facing each other, his blue eyes staring straight into mine. They were the only eyes I ever wanted to gaze into. I wanted to know everything they held. A string of earbuds was draped over his neck. I picked them up and held them in front of Nick.

"Guess I fell asleep listening to music," he said.

I smiled. "I do the same thing. I'm always making playlists of music to fall asleep to." I put the earbud in my ear, and taking my cue, Nick put the other earbud in his ear. It was strangely intimate to have this thing that was last imbedded inside his body now inside mine. I saw him fumbling around for the iPod the cord attached to, it's lifeline. Moments later, the music started. Soft at first, it wasn't something I'd heard before. What sounded like a Chinese-inspired melody began, backed by a strong drum.

"Incubus," he mouthed.

We lay there in silence, listening to the music, waiting for our friends to wake up around us.

Behind Nick, the bathroom door jolted open.

"Morning!" Celeste called cheerily. I quickly moved to shush her, but it was too late. Lexie and John started stirring.

"Snuffles! Carl!" John shouted. "Here, boys!"

We laughed. The dogs had finally stopped barking.

Lexie sat up, stretching her arms out wide. "You are impossible to sleep with," she glared at John.

"Me? Do you even see me over here? My legs aren't on the bed." John's face was fixed in pretend outrage. "You better get used to this, girl."

"So what's the plan?" Charlie piped up from the corner. "I've been trying to find some good bars for tonight..."

Celeste and I exchanged glances. Lexie couldn't help but laugh out loud.

"Well, let's get moving," John sat up.

I pulled the earbud out of my ear and jumped out of bed, grabbing my toiletry case from my backpack. I'd hastily tossed it into the corner between our bed and the bathroom last night, and now made my way to the bathroom before anyone else could claim it.

"Addie, I'm coming in to do my makeup," Celeste called through the door.

The girls and I shared the bathroom, rotating between sink and mirror and shower until we turned it over to the boys.

By the time we left our room, sneaking out one at a time to not alert anyone that there were six of us, it was nearing lunch. We decided we'd wander around the city for a while before stopping to eat, and skip breakfast for the day.

We wandered alongside the water. October was not peak tourist season in Venice, but still the sidewalks were crowded with people. Venetians and tourists alike filled the narrow walkways. The sky was gray and overcast, and a continuous drizzle fell gently from the sky, dampening my shirt and hair. I pulled the hood of my shirt up over my head, hoping to avoid too much frizz. When the rain grew more intense, we found a café and ducked inside for lunch, filling up on pasta and cheeses, passing around bottles of red wine that splashed onto the table. The sidewalks twisted and turned and we followed, caring little where they lead us. Venice wasn't very big, and it wasn't difficult at all to see all of the sights we wanted to in one day. The Bridge of Sighs. The Rialto Bridge. The Grand Canal. The Doge's Palace. We wandered past them all as we strolled the damp stone streets. It was easy, relaxed, and just what I had imagined it to be.

When we reached Saint Mark's Square, the rain had accumulated enough to flood it, as I'd read about and never seen. A dirty inch of water stood on the stones of the square. My cheap flats were drenched through, and for a moment I debated just taking them off and throwing them into my bag.

The square wasn't as full as I'd seen it before. It was summer the last time I'd come, the weather suffocatingly hot and the square packed with people, waiting in lines for everything. Lines to sit at a café, lines to get into the Basilica. Today, the cooler weather and rain seemed to encourage people to take cover. Toward the center of the square, a man in a yellow raincoat stood by a kiosk. Pigeons surrounded him, landing on his shoulders and arms, looking for food. One curious, gray bird was even perched on top of his head. People were stopping to purchase birdseed from him and feeding pigeons themselves.

By now, it was late afternoon, and Charlie was starting to pester us about finding a bar. It wasn't that he liked to drink—though he did, we all did—he was much more interested in local bartender culture. He found bartenders fascinating, and would oftentimes leave our table to sit at the bar alone and strike up a conversation with whoever was pouring drinks. He tended bar on the side back in Minnesota, and it wasn't something he was able to leave back in the States. We took turns reminding him that we were in Venice, and probably could not find the kind of bar that he wanted to spend hours in. We compromised on finding a patio, where we could sit outside and have some drinks.

We roamed the curvy paths once more, onto the first patio off the square where we could find reasonably cheap, house red wine. Carafes of wine rolled into dinner, which led to more wine. When we were through and the sun had set, we stumbled into the square, still partially flooded from the day's rain. Someone suggested we find a gondola to explore the city from its canals, and John tipped a gondolier to let all six of us bring another bottle of wine onto the boat.

Drunk on wine and liberation, on everything that was right in my life, I held on to Charlie's hand as he helped me down into the gondola. The six of us were a tight fit, and every inch of the boat was spoken for between our bags, our bottles of wine, and us. The boat rocked as our gondolier jumped onto the back and pushed off from the side of the makeshift dock, which in actuality was just sidewalk.

To my right, John and Lexie were holding hands, crammed together on a small seat. On the other side of the boat, Charlie was snapping photos, and Celeste let her arm drop down outside the boat, her fingers dipping into the dark waters below.

Our gondolier sang to us in Italian as he paddled down the canal. It was crowded and silly, and the boat shifted with our drunkenness and laughter. I couldn't remember ever having been happier.

18

October, Florence.

The budget-friendly route to Florence from Venice was a six-and-a-half-hour train ride with a stop in Bologna. As much fun as it was to explore Venice, I wasn't disappointed about spending most of the day on a train. The six of us were having a great time together, and it wasn't going to be a problem to spend hours crammed into a small train car. As a matter of fact, we were getting pretty good at it.

We bid farewell to Snuffles and Carl and headed to the train station, stopping on the way to load up on supplies. Fresh mozzarella and vine-ripe tomatoes, crusty bread spread with bright green pesto, prosciutto, and salami, usually only found at a deli back in the States, were wrapped up to go. John spotted a shop that sold wine, and we each picked up a different variety of red to be spread among paper cups later on, once on boarded. We were lucky enough to find a cabin to ourselves, and as the train pulled out of the station, Nick pulled a bottle opener out of his backpack. He cracked open the first bottle and filled each little cup about halfway full before passing them around.

We held up to toast to our time in Venice, staring out the windows to catch our last glimpse of the City of Canals.

John put his nose deep into his cup and animatedly took a deep breath, swirling it around. "It's a very good year for wine," he proclaimed, as we all drank. And drank, and drank, and drank.

I'd brought a deck of cards, and we made use of them with the bottles of wine, playing drinking games until our train finally reached Florence early in the evening.

John and Lexie had booked our accommodations in Florence, but as soon as we pulled the last of our bags from the train and stood in the station, we just kind of stood around.

"So... where do we go?" Charlie asked, lighting up a cigarette.

Lexie looked at John. "Uh..."

John shook his head. "You wrote it down, not me."

Lexie dropped her backpack and knelt, fishing around for the address. After a moment of us all exchanging nervous glances, she stood back up and handed Nick the address.

"Here, let me—"

"No." Lexie and I cut John, infamously bad at directions, off at the same time.

"We got it," I said.

We studied the map. It was too far to walk with our stuff, on the other side of the Arno.

"Can we take a bus?" Nick asked.

"I'm sure we can..." I trailed off. I realized that somehow, I was just put in charge of finding our way, but knew we had to get there somehow. I straightened my back and shook my head, emptying out the doubts I felt creeping in. "Let's go. I'll find us a bus."

I wasn't sure exactly how I would do this, but I knew in my broken Italian I could at least get partial directions to our hostel. We walked out of Santa Maria Novella station and out to the fleet of waiting buses and taxis.

"Looks like we could try the number six, or number eleven," Nick offered, still holding the map. "Can you check with one of the drivers?"

I nodded tersely. We found a driver leaning against the side of a number six bus, and I approached him, anxiously. Slowly, I asked if I could get to our address from his bus.

He pointed down the road with a "no," but I was unable to get the rest of what he said. I moved on to the next driver, smoking a cigarette in front of a number eleven bus. Again, I got a "no." Disheartened, I started to walk away, when I heard him say *trentasei, tesoro.* I didn't know tesoro, but I hurriedly looked for the number thirty-six bus, my friends following closely behind.

The thirty-six bus was loaded up and ready to close its doors, when I poked my head in and, for the third time, asked about the address of our hostel.

"*Si, si, vieni con me,*" he said jovially, and waved us on board.

I turned around, and let my friends board and find their spots, while I stood right behind the driver. He was a young man, with a mess of dark hair plastered to his head, his uniform too tight on his very overweight body. A crucifix was taped to his dashboard, and rosary beads hung from his rearview mirror. His brown eyes were warm and inviting, and he smiled at me knowingly. I was trying my hardest, and he knew. I was thankful for his courtesy.

The bus engine started up, and we backed out of the spot and pulled onto the busy roads of Florence. Scooters zipped around us, drivers yelling at our bus driver. Rather than ignoring them, he yelled back. I listened carefully as we approached each stop, making sure not to miss ours. After a while, I started to lose count of the stops. I glanced back at my friends, trying to convey that I had it under control. Inside, I doubted myself.

"*Questa è la vostra fermata.*" The bus driver looked back at me, and motioned for us to get off. I waved the rest of our group off the bus, and stopped to confirm with the driver where I should turn right and left. He motioned with his hand where I needed to go, then waved me off. "*Ciao, bella!*"

I climbed down the steps, following my friends, and led the way to our hostel.

We had once again fibbed on how many people were staying in the room. It was a larger hostel, not far from the Ponte Vecchio, and we didn't think we'd have any trouble getting six people in and out of a room booked for four. Florence was one of our longer stops, with three nights booked at the hostel. As soon as we got in the room, we looked around at each other, momentarily wondering how we would split up the four twin beds. There was no way Celeste and Charlie were sharing a bed, and we knew John and Lexie already assumed they'd share, which left Nick and me to share. A twin bed. For three nights.

Our bags found homes in different corners of the room. Two of the twin beds were against one wall, and at the foot of the beds after a narrow walkway were the other twin beds, placed end to end. Nick and I took the furthest bed after the walkway, and Charlie took the bed in front of ours. We decided we'd clean ourselves up and then wander out into the city for dinner. That wine had left us tired and hungry, and my head was starting to feel fuzzy.

Within half an hour, we had locked up our room and were walking out into the city. Our hostel wasn't far from the Ponte Vecchio on the south side of the Arno River, and we headed in that direction. We had no set destination in mind, but rather wandered until we found something that looked right to us. Tonight, that place was Piazza della Repubblica. Two of the four sides of the square, which was closed off to vehicles, were lined with restaurants. Tables and chairs were neatly organized like dominoes, all lined up in a row. Waiters, dressed in ill-fitting black jackets and bowties over button-up shirts with splatters of tomato sauce, approached us with menus, each inviting us into their restaurant. We pushed past them until we found a menu that looked good. In truth, they all looked about the same, but settled on one with a cheap pasta, plenty of wine, and a waiter that wasn't harassing people to come in.

We were led to a table right on the square. The evening was enchanting; October had so far proved to be the perfect time to visit. Tourists were scattered among locals; the days were just right for wandering cities without the smell of Europe in the summer. It was growing cooler outside, and I felt thankful I pulled jeans on when we had cleaned up for dinner. Celeste pulled a shawl out to wrap around her shoulders, and I saw Lexie zip up the North Face fleece she always had on her. Our view was uninterrupted, tourists and locals alike traipsed past our table. A waitress had just come by to take our drink orders and leave us with menus, when I heard it.

Was I hearing things? I immediately started turning my head around, trying to identify the source of the music. It couldn't be in my head. Nonetheless, I felt transported: I was no longer sitting at a table with my friends. I was in my own world, in a cloud.

Andrea Bocelli's unmistakable voice rang out across the square. *Quando sono solo e sogno all'orizzonte...* I pushed my chair back, and strolled into the square, searching. It was his favorite song. Pop would listen to it over and over again, until Nanny would holler at him to turn the damned song off. He had three great loves in his life: opera, birds, and his grandchildren. One day he'd come home with three parakeets: Caruso lived in the living room, Bocelli in the dining room, and Pavarotti right next to Pop's side of the bed. When Pop would put *Romanza* on for the hundredth time, he'd hold his arms out and pretend to conduct his bird singers. Sometimes Bird Bocelli would cooperate, chirping along with the song, to Pop's delight.

The music grew louder with each step into the center of the square, and I could feel myself on the verge of tears. I wasn't sure what I was looking for exactly, but still I walked, searching, until I reached the middle of the square.

Con te partirò, Bocelli bellowed. I collapsed onto a bench as the tears started to fall. It had only been eight months since he died. It all still felt so raw. I thought back to my interview with the NHL, the transit strike, and leaving Pop in the car alone. If I had known, I would have spoken to him more, or even just sat and listened to Bocelli with him, instead of running across the street to a shoe store.

I should have sat with him. I should have listened to Bocelli. And Pavarotti. And Caruso. I broke down in sobs. I missed him so much.

Two hands grabbed my shoulders. "Adriana?"

I snapped back to reality. I opened my eyes, remembering that I was sitting in the middle of Piazza della Repubblica, having just walked away from a dinner table of my friends with no explanation whatsoever, and was now crying.

Nick looked down at me with a mixture of confusion and concern. As soon as I saw his face, I fell into his arms. He wrapped them around me, running his hands up and down my back to soothe me. I felt so at home, safe. I didn't know if he would understand or think I was overreacting, but at that moment I didn't care. I just wanted to stay in his arms, nestled into his neck, where nothing bothered me.

He pulled away and tried again. "Are you okay? What's going on?" His voice was soft and genuinely concerned.

I wiped my eyes. "I'm sorry," I said, pausing to take a steadying breath. "This song... it was my grandfather's favorite..." My voice cracked. "I just miss him so much," I whispered, pushing more tears away from my cheeks.

"Oh gosh." He held me close again.

I took another deep breath, then another. I was feeling better. It was a bit of a ridiculous display of emotion, but there was nothing I could do about it now. I constantly felt myself pulled in an inexplicable way into my emotions, not always able to resist indulging myself. Nick loosened his grip on me again, but this time his hand found mine. He grabbed it, pulling me up from the bench.

"Come on," he said.

I followed, my hand in his. I looked back at our table, where our everyone else was sipping wine and falling back into conversation. Only my and Nick's chairs were empty, pushed back from the table.

In front of us was a charming—and remarkably out of place—carousel. I hadn't noticed it before this moment, which now seemed ridiculous. What was it doing here? Nick walked around to the operator and handed him some crumpled up euros. The man extended his hand and motioned for us to board the ride. Nick climbed up, turning around to make sure I made the big step as well.

"Are you serious?" I asked in disbelief.

"Why not?" He passed a horse, inspecting it, like a child deciding which one was best. This carousel was all horses; each fitted with a brown saddle adorned with gilded belts and headbands. Nick ran his eyes over a black horse and a creamy mocha-colored horse before finding two white horses side by side. He jokingly patted the saddle of the horse on the inside of the carousel before jumping on. I laughed and climbed on the horse next to him.

The carousel started up, slowly at first. Bocelli's voice had long quieted, and over the squeaks of the antediluvian ride was dingily recorded accordion music. The square rotated around us as our horses galloped in place, up and down, up and down, up and down. Our horses moved opposite one another, as I was lifted high, Nick's horse dipped down low. I gazed around the square dizzily at the lights, glowing and spinning around me. I took a deep breath, breathing it all in. The hurt and loss I had experienced. The beauty and adventure I was in the middle of. The unknown path I was walking down for the next seven days of our trip. I held it there, deep inside my lungs, then let it all go. The carousel kept turning around and around, bringing us back to right where we'd started before whisking us away once more.

Δ

243

We'd spent the afternoon gazing at sculptures, slowly making our way through the halls where the work of great artists stood. It was our last afternoon in Florence, and we were spent, feet raw and sore from walking more than we were already used to. The European lifestyle includes lots of walking; it is assumed that any particular destination can be arrived at with a combination of public transport and walking. We did a lot of walking. We'd crossed the Ponte Vecchio a few times each day, walked through the Uffizi, walked to the top of the Duomo, toured Palazzo Vecchio, and visited Santa Croce. It was much more sightseeing than we'd done in Venice, and we were all ready for some downtime.

"I gotta check my email," John said as we walked out of the Galleria dell'Accademia. This was rare from John, who was much less tied to laptops than the rest of us. But his ex-girlfriend Maura was studying in Florence, and he'd already floated the possibility of meeting up with her.

We walked into the grassy courtyard in front of the Galleria. I shrugged my shoulders in response. Lexie slowed her pace and hung behind the boys, falling into stride with me and Celeste.

"What is with this girl?" Lexie hissed.

"I'm sure it's nothing," Celeste comforted.

I chimed in. "You know John. He's friends with everyone. Don't worry about Maura."

We followed behind, making our way over the Arno once more, back toward our hostel. The sun was beginning to set, and over the hills on our side of the river, the sky was ripening, turning orange. I wondered how long it would stay like that, the color dripping like juices down onto the Arno below. The water was still and the sky reflected the color, like a mirror.

About two blocks before our hostel, Nick and Charlie took a turn. After a few blocks, we stood in front of windows with the words *Internet caffé* painted on the outside. John turned in, and we followed.

Inside, old Dell computers lined up against a wall on a long and narrow table, brown folding chairs scattered around each screen. The sign above the check-in desk explained, in Italian and English, that there was a flat fee to access a computer and then a charge for each ten-minute increment. Celeste, Charlie, and John each paid to access a computer, and I pulled up a chair next to Celeste. I had no interest in accessing the outside world. I'd promised myself before the trip that I would not use a cell phone or computer while we travel in Italy, and had no interest in the world outside the six of us.

I chatted with Celeste as she read through various emails, and shared what was going on with her family. I had the realization that Nanny's birthday was in a few days. I made a mental note to bring her something special. It would be her first birthday without Pop, and I hoped that everyone at home was remembering that.

After about ten minutes, Celeste and Charlie were both through. Nick and I went outside with them and waited. Charlie lit a cigarette and respectfully stepped into the street gutter, keeping the smoke as far away from us as he could while still joining in on our conversation. Celeste stood nearest to the café, wanting to keep her distance either from Charlie or the smoke. I wasn't sure. They were beginning to bicker here and there, mostly about politics. Though we didn't really bring them up; John and Lexie weren't politically inclined, and though Nick and I agreed with one another on most every issue, Charlie and Celeste were on opposite ends of the spectrum.

Nick and I tried to back out of the conversation, which had somehow drifted to the "war on drugs" and legalization of pot. I sighed impatiently, and Nick shook his head in exasperation. I stepped over to him to distance myself from the conversation.

The closeness I felt with Nick in Venice had grown with our last two nights in Florence. When we'd gotten back to our hostel after the carousel and dinner, and what was inevitably too many glasses of the house red, we had another night of sharing the bed. It was cramped in the best possible way. My sadness was still there, taking up room in our bed, and he tried to squeeze it out by holding me close. We'd started a routine of sharing an iPod before we went to sleep, Nick crafting a different playlist for us each night, our heads strung close together with the headphone cord. Our hands and limbs would become entwined naturally, as they had no place else to go but into one another. He'd hold my hand as we talked and joked, running his fingers up and down my arm. Sometimes they'd make their way down to the top of my jeans, daring to trespass just slightly, seeing how far those fingers could dip below the waistband before I'd stop him. I'd oscillate between shyly looking down at his hands, and boldly staring into his eyes, daring him into action. I could feel my lips throbbing for his. I didn't dare do it myself yet. Our relationship was a delicate balance that was nearing its tipping point, but I could feel that it wasn't time just yet.

Just as I was about to interrupt Celeste and Charlie's useless bickering, John and Lexie emerged.

"Who wants to dance?" John said, strutting around the sidewalk and pretending to grind up against Charlie.

Lexie widened her eyes. "So I guess we're going to meet Maura at a club tonight," she announced.

Apparently, Maura and John had caught each other online at the same time, and made plans to meet at some dance club. Back in Prague, after the night at the five-story club, we had all decided that wasn't our scene and had preferred instead to stick to pubs. We'd sit at long, beer-hall style tables and talk, getting to know one another with jokes and pints of pivo. Absolutely no part of me was interested in going to an Italian club, but I also didn't want to leave my friends and wander the city alone, or even worse, sit around at the hostel. I knew I would go, and from the beginning I had a bad attitude about it.

Hours later, we were queued up outside, music with incoherent lyrics blasting around us. Italian women lined up ahead of me. Most wore tight-fitting dresses, olive skin showing in carefully orchestrated patches, dark hair tied up or long and flowing. They chattered in Italian and moved around to the music. Men walking on the sidewalks outside the queue, or on the opposite side of the street, whistled and hollered. They were mostly ignored or shouted back at with extravagant hand gestures.

We hadn't exactly planned on going to a dance club, so Celeste, Lexie, and I stood around in our cleanest pairs of jeans. I'd dug up a black tank top that I thought was the most appropriate and slipped on my nicest flats, but still looked ridiculous in comparison to the women around us.

Ahead, Maura and her roommate, Diane, put our jeans to shame. I hadn't met Diane until today, but she definitely made herself stand out in a group. Defying physics, she'd pulled on a skin-tight red dress, adorned with rhinestones around the demure neckline and the hem of the skirt. Her black kitten heels also had rhinestones. Lexie was playing dutiful girlfriend and chatting up Maura alongside John. Maura was dressed somewhat more modestly in a miniskirt, and a loose-fitting blouse that billowed over her skirt. I looked down at my jeans once more and hoped there wasn't a splash of marinara sauce on them somewhere that I hadn't noticed yet.

I hadn't spoken to her yet, so I assumed it was the red dress, or perhaps the many rhinestones sparkling in the moonlight, that caught Nick's attention. He stood next to her in line, chatting about things I couldn't hear because I was blocking them out. He'd been able to dig up a button-up shirt, and looked right at home. I imagined him like this in LA, chatting up women in clubs and having just a drink with them, dangling the possibility of more only if they proved themselves worthy. Charlie was the only one as miserable as I was, and we stood together at the back of our group, complaining. He liked sitting at a bar. Getting up to dance was widely out of his comfort zone, and he instead chose to light up cigarette after cigarette. Tonight, I joined him, smoking two cigarettes before we even got into the club.

Once we cleared the bouncer, the music grew louder with each step. At the farthest wall was the bar, spanning the length of the building. In the middle was a dance floor, and surrounding that in a semi-circle were booths facing the dance floor. A few tables were in front of the booths, chairs scattered around them opposite the booths. At the front of our group was Maura, who walked over to a booth that was miraculously still unclaimed, Lexie and John close behind. My eyes fell on Nick, to see which chair he'd claim. As I looked over to him, Diane turned around and grabbed his hand, pulling him onto the dance floor. My annoyance with being at the club immediately tripled, and a knot grew in my stomach.

"I'm going to the bar," Charlie announced to no one in particular.

Celeste turned to me, mouth agape. "Whoa," she said, nodding to Nick and Diane.

I shook my head. "I'm with Charlie tonight."

"You want me to come?" she asked.

"I don't care." I was being short with her, but I didn't care. I pushed my way through the dance floor to the bar, scanning the barstools for Charlie. I glanced behind me to see Celeste had walked over to the table Maura had claimed. I was already counting the minutes until we could leave.

There were no empty stools at the bar, but I found Charlie standing right in the middle of the bar.

"Hey," I shouted above the music. "Mind if I hang with you?"

"Of course not," he yelled back. "What are you drinking?"

"Dirty martini," I said loudly. Charlie relayed my order to the bartender. My eyes darted back to the dance floor, looking for Nick. I hated myself, but couldn't help it. No matter how much I wanted to turn my eyes back to Charlie, they wouldn't obey.

"I didn't see this place in Rick Steves." Charlie pulled my attention back to him.

"Yeah, not quite the real city of Florence I was hoping to see."

"I even hate this shit back in Prague."

"Yeah. Me too."

He took a long swig of his Peroni. Behind him, the bartender put my drink on the counter. Charlie handed it to me.

I raised the glass to my lips and took a hurried drink. Still no sign of Nick. He was lost in the ocean of people dancing, the undertow having pulled him deeper into the center of the dance floor.

"Na zdraví," Charlie said, raising his beer glass.

"Oh right, yeah," I said, holding up my glass. I'd already downed a hasty few gulps of gin. "Sorry."

We stood in silence, focusing instead on our drinks. House music bumped loudly across the dance floor, reverberating across the bar. I ordered another martini, and when that was gone, Charlie ordered me another. We stood together at the bar, Charlie telling me about his relationship with his ex back home. I half-listened, my eyes bolting between the table where the rest of our group sat and the dance floor, where I was still hoping I'd spot Nick. He wasn't at the table, and if he wasn't on the dance floor that meant he'd left with Diane. The thought made me sick.

Somewhere near the bottom of my third martini, I spotted him. Nelly Furtado filled the club. *She's a maneater, make you work hard, make you spend hard.* He stood with his back toward the table, but still on the dance floor, dancing next to Diane. Every now and then she'd grab one of his hands or pull him closer to her. I couldn't look away. *Make you want all of her love.*

"You need to talk to him," Charlie said.

I spun my head around and glared at Charlie, at a loss for words. I wasn't expecting to have this conversation with him. "Yeah." It was all I could muster. Charlie was right. I moved to set my drink down and started to step backwards.

Wish you never ever met her at all. You wish you'd never ever met her at all. You wish you'd never ever met her at all. You wish you'd never ever met her at all.

Charlie grabbed my arm. "No, not now," he said. "When you're sober. When you're *both* sober."

I sat back down on my barstool. "Yeah, you're right." I sighed and dropped my head into my hands. "I don't even know where to start."

"Just be honest."

"And say what? 'Hey Nick, can I just talk to you about how we are basically best friends who aren't honest with each other?'"

"Tell him how you feel. How do you feel?"

I looked at Charlie. "Like I want to be with him. But I don't know how."

"How to be with him?"

"Well... yeah." I took another drink. "We're leaving in less than two months."

To my surprise, Charlie shook his head. "You don't have to have it all planned out. Just be honest and see what happens."

I knew he was right. Now that the seed of talking to Nick was planted in my mind, I felt as if I needed to do it now. But I knew that Charlie was right. No good would come of having that conversation while drunk.

Celeste walked up to Charlie and me. "I'm kind of done," she said, setting her cocktail glass on the bar.

"Thank God." I immediately got up and grabbed my purse.

"You guys need to settle up?" she asked me and Charlie.

"No, we're all good," he said. "Go ahead, Addie."

I followed Celeste and walked toward the exit. Outside, I could feel the air had cooled down considerably. Now I was happy I had worn jeans. Diane and Maura must have been freezing, though of course they'd never show it.

Leaving the dance club, I felt lighter, but my head immediately dizzied at being able to finally hear my thoughts. Nick, John, and Lexie were outside already, walking toward the bridge. I didn't see Maura or Diane. I gazed down the opposite end of the sidewalk and saw them walking in the other direction together, apparently going their own way. I breathed a sigh of relief. She was gone. All that remained was the mess with Nick. She'd been a night of gale-force winds, blowing over the house of sticks Nick and I had built. I felt rattled that though we had a solid foundation, there was really nothing keeping us together.

19

October, Rome.

I was ready to leave Florence behind and catch the train to Rome, to move on to the next thing. It had all been going just as I'd hoped it would, before the club, and I was ready to shake it off. Our trip was now halfway over.

Nick and I had found a little hotel in Rome where we could be honest about our occupancy, booking one room for four and the other room for two. I hadn't given much thought to who'd get the room for two, but by the time we got to Rome it was obvious.

We were less than a ten-minute walk from the Roma Termini station. Within minutes of leaving the station, we found the address. Double checking the instructions I'd written down, I rang the buzzer.

"*Ciao?*" a woman's voice answered.

"Hi, we're checking in," I replied.

"*Si, si,* come up the stairs please." A loud buzzing went off and vibrated through the doorknob, electronically unlocking it. I pushed it open and we walked up a narrow staircase to the second floor.

A short, plump woman opened the door we were headed toward before we'd even reached the second landing.

"*Benvenuto,* welcome to Giovy," she said, dramatically bowing and motioning for us to enter. Her frizzy hair was pulled back on the top, the bottom half cascading down past her shoulders. An apron was tired around her waist, faded with age, mirroring her face.

We walked past her and stepped into a long and narrow hallway. She quickly checked my passport, holding it at the front desk, as was customary. After the formalities were through, she pushed open a door to her left.

"This is the room for *due*," she said. Without discussion, John and Lexie walked through the door and set their bags down. It was a modest room, but for the first time there would be a bed for each one of us. It was hard to complain about that after the last five nights.

Leaving John and Lexie in their room, we followed our hostess down the hall. We passed three more doors and the kitchenette and breakfast room before she opened another door.

"And the room for *quattro*," she said.

We peeked our heads in. Immediately to the right was a bathroom, then a twin bed, a queen bed, and another twin bed underneath a large window. Two of us would be sharing a bed again.

"Umm, there are only three beds," I stated the obvious.

"*Si*, two in the big bed together. Sleeps *quattro*."

Charlie walked past me and placed his backpack on the farthest bed from the door, under the window. Nick was right behind him.

"Guess it's your lucky night, Adriana," he said, tossing his backpack onto the middle bed.

Celeste raised her eyebrows as she passed me and claimed the other twin. I wasn't disappointed about sharing a bed with Nick yet again, but I wasn't sure about us anymore. Though my feelings for him were the same, I no longer understood my place with him. Lexie had assured me that nothing happened with him and Diane—apparently she'd had her eyes on him the whole night—but still, Nick and I hadn't talked about it. For the first time since the beginning of our trip, when we'd gotten back to our hostel after the club, we hadn't said a word to one another or shared music, and even slept with our backs to each other. I felt a distance.

I put my backpack on the ground on the side closer to Charlie. No matter the emotional distance between us, there would be no physical distance. We were being pushed together.

Δ

We only had two nights in Rome, but we decided to take it much easier on ourselves than we had in Florence. There were things we'd wanted to see, but since Nick and I had both been before, we were able to weed out the things that weren't worth the time. After we cleaned ourselves up from the train, we settled on walking over to the Coliseum, then passing by the Pantheon before stopping at one of the many restaurants lining the surrounding piazzas. It was a long walk for us, but it was late enough in the afternoon that the midday sun was dying down. The streets bustled with life, and we laughed as we dodged ruthless drivers in oncoming traffic, and marveled at John's interest in the palm trees, which he'd claimed to never have seen before.

Darkness had long since fallen by the time we'd slurped the last of the pasta from our plates. A quick examination of the map showed we weren't far from the Trevi Fountain, I declared to everyone that we had to go throw coins in. John and Charlie had the idea to buy bottles of Prosecco to pop while we were there, and we popped in a liquor store off the Via delle Muratte, where we each pitched in for two bottles of champagne. Charlie swiped plastic cups from a gyro place next door.

The fountain was quiet, with only a few other tourists marveling at the tremendous work of art. The statue towered eighty feet over the pool below, water spewing down from layers of rock. Oceanus stood tall in the center, with statues flanking him on either side, and the Palazzo Poli behind. Water flowed from Tritons' shells and around Oceanus's chariot. We nearly had the place to ourselves, and easily found a place to sit on the surrounding carved stone benches facing the fountain. It was bigger than I'd remembered it being, and every now and then splashes of water spilled out and splattered onto the ground below.

I rummaged through my bag for some coins. "Does everyone have a few euro? Everyone needs two. In two separate coins."

My friends each dug through their pockets, swapping coins when necessary to make change.

"Okay." I continued, "So you're supposed to stand with your back to the fountain, make a wish, kiss the coin, and throw it into the fountain behind you." I stood with my back to the fountain and pretended to toss my coin over my shoulder and into the fountain below.

"What's the second coin for?" Celeste asked.

"The second one is for you to return to Rome."

"What if I don't want to come back to Rome?" Charlie said. I hoped he was joking.

"Like the statue on the bridge?" Lexie asked.

"Yeah," I answered.

Nick looked down the bench at her. "What statue?"

"There's some statue on the Charles Bridge you rub to return one day," she replied.

"And one you rub to make a wish," I chimed in.

"I didn't even know that was a thing," Nick said.

Charlie nodded in agreement, as did John.

"We'll all have to go together when we get back," Lexie said. She stood up, ready to toss in her coin. Then, grabbing one of my hands and one of Celeste's, she pulled us off the bench. "Let's throw our coins in together."

The three of us approached the fountain, coins in hand, and lined up with our back to the fountain. Droplets of water dotted the back of my T-shirt.

"Which should we do first?" Celeste asked.

"Let's do the wish first," Lexie said. She was holding her coin, rubbing it between her thumb and forefinger. I wondered what she'd wish for.

I gripped my coin tightly. What was I going to wish for? I'd been so eager to come to the fountain with my friends, that I hadn't considered my wish. Who seriously considers a wish? A wish on a star, on an eyelash, on a coin thrown into a fountain, on a statue rubbed on a bridge. What did it really signify? A statement to the universe: *this is what I want.* I want love. I want money. Happiness. Peace. I want something that isn't coming fast enough to me in this life. What was my life lacking? I thought of Nick for a moment, the ugliness with Mark I'd left behind, the mess of my family waiting for me back home. What did I need the most right now? *Clarity,* a voice inside answered. I'd been wandering for so long, stumbling along my life. I'd finally hit my stride in Prague, and felt like I was where I belonged for the first time. I wanted that feeling to continue. I wanted to feel at home in my own skin, and to really understand what that meant for me.

Together, the girls and I kissed our coins. I looked over at the guys. They were each watching, transfixed, as if anything more would happen when the coins hit water. Celeste, Lexie, and I glanced at each other and then let our arms fall to our sides before launching them up again, coins in hand, arms extending, fingers loosening around the coins, and letting them splash. Over the chatter of voices and the splattering of the fountain, it was impossible to hear our coins drop.

We turned our heads around nearly in unison, trying to see our coins hit the water. John lifted my camera, and then we tossed our next coins in, wishing to return to Rome.

John popped the champagne, the cork rolling underneath our feet, coming to a stop somewhere under the stone bench. The champagne was still cold and fizzed against the cheap and thin plastic as John poured. We toasted, to our time in Rome, to friendship, to

adventure and wanderlust, then sat on the bench and drank until both
bottles were empty.

Δ

I crawled into the middle of the bed, pulling the covers up to
my shoulders. I stretched out my arms and legs wide, each reaching for a
different corner of the bed. My body was tired from all the walking we'd
done, my feet throbbing and my back aching. Nick was still in the
bathroom getting ready for bed, so I had a few minutes to enjoy the big
bed to myself. The cheap, used mattress felt wonderful. My mind
drifted. It had been another perfect day. It felt like we were back on
track, Nick and me. That night in Florence had been a fluke, I told
myself. Our only full day in Rome had been spent mostly in Vatican
City. We'd finally allowed ourselves to sit and relax when we'd returned
and picked up dinner—loaves of bread, cheese, and sliced meat, along
with six bottles of red wine—and brought them to the Spanish Steps.
Nanny had told me to drink wine on the Spanish Steps at sunset the first
time I'd gone to Italy, and I'd missed that chance. It was the one thing I
really wanted to do in Rome. It was just how I'd imagined. We laughed
and ate, and drank every last drop of wine from all six bottles, and didn't
return to our bed and breakfast until well after midnight, a fact I didn't
think our benefactress had appreciated.

I let my body sink into the mattress, staring up at the ceiling. It
was dark in our room, besides a stream of faded, yellowed light from the
street lamps outside, that peeked through the threadbare curtains over
Charlie's bed. He was curled up facing the wall, snoring softly. I turned
my head toward the door to see if Celeste was sleeping. Her headphones
were on, covers pulled almost all the way over her head.

The bathroom door eased open, and Nick sat on the edge of
the bed, fumbling with something on the floor. I scooted back onto my

side of the bed, my legs parting the cool sheets. He rolled onto his back, and held an earbud out to me.

"Want to listen?"

I grabbed the earbud and put it in my ear closest to Nick and settled in, fluffing the pillow under my head.

"Good night," I whispered.

"Night," he replied, his face illuminated softly from the light of his iPod.

Music gradually made its way into my ear, Joshua Radin's voice quiet. I rolled onto my side with my back to Nick. *I should know who I am by now...* I closed my eyes. I inhaled and exhaled deeply. It was something I tried when I wasn't yet ready for sleep. I breathed like I was asleep, slow and steady breaths, calming my body and quieting my mind. *Your voice is the splinter inside me.* It always worked. *A warm December with you.* In. *But I don't have to make this mistake. And I don't have to stay this way.* Out. *If only I would wake...*

Next to me, Nick shifted his weight. I woke up slightly and tried to settle back into sleep. I closed my eyes again as a body moved up against mine, Nick's front to my back, holding me close. He placed his hand on my hip bone, running it slowly up and down my side. Goose bumps crept up my spine. A shiver in my neck, startling me awake. He moved softly, slowly tracing the line of my spine, from the small of my back up between my shoulder blades, then back down again. As if trying to feel every vertebra of my spine.

I opened my mouth slowly, happy he couldn't see my face. My eyes closed once more. His arm delicately moved under my ribcage and onto the soft part of my stomach, just over my belly button. He pulled me closer into him. I reached my hand over his and ran my fingers, softly, over his arm. Over the freckles I had tried to count, over the hand that had pulled me close to him so many nights ago in the five-story club. *I would give anything for that kiss again,* I thought. I imagined his impatient kiss, my silly excuse of the bathroom, and closed my eyes.

I woke up, music still flowing faintly into my ears. It was still dark out, and through my other ear I could hear the soft breathing of our roommates. Nick's arm had grown heavy over my side, and my arm was asleep. I rolled on to my back but didn't move any further. I didn't know if he was asleep or not, but I was petrified to come face to face with him, not ready for what might happen next. The shift in weight caused Nick to stir gently, rolling onto his back and then onto his side next to me once more. Again, his arm moved across my body, this time landing just below my belly button. I lay still. His fingers dipped below the top of my pajama bottoms and my breathing became shallow. I wanted him to feel more of me, to see the parts of myself I hadn't yet shown. Nervously confident, I rolled onto my side and came face to face with him.

Through the dark of our room I could just make out his open eyelids. He pulled his hand up and laid it on the side of my head, softly stroking my frizzy hair away from my face. I gazed at him and wondered if this was it, this middle of the night intimacy that had grown in the middle of our bed, in the middle of Rome, in the middle of our two friends asleep in beds beside us, wondered if this would be the time we would push it so far it would break. Nick untangled his hand from my hair and ran his fingertips down the side of my face. I closed my eyes and lifted my chin up, putting my hand behind his head and pulling gently at the base of the hair near to his scalp, and running my fingers through his hair.

Our playlist was still playing, and as one song faded into silence, I drifted off back to sleep.

Δ

Suddenly, I was awake. Before I even opened my eyes, I heard whispers in our room. I blinked open my eyes and noticed the curtains had been pulled open. Daylight poured in. The sounds of the city outside told me it was the beginning of a new day. Two people were arguing out in the street, their voices rising with each retort. Horns honked incessantly. Charlie's bed underneath the window was vacant, the covers pushed to the foot of the bed. His bag was gone. I rolled over onto my back to find I was alone in bed. Had I dreamed it?

I sat up to see Celeste walking out of the bathroom and over to her bed, rummaging through something in her bag.

"Morning, girl," I said to her, yawning. "What time is it?"

"It's seven thirty," she said, turning toward me. Her long, wavy hair was still damp as she pulled it back behind her head, low into a ponytail. "Aren't you coming?"

I considered the options: the warm, comfy bed and an hour or two of alone time, or heading out to see the Pantheon, which I had already seen a few years back and wasn't terribly interested in again. "You know, I think I'll stay. I'm so exhausted." I lay back down, pulling a pillow over my face. "I feel like I didn't get that much sleep."

"That's exactly what Nick said," she said suspiciously, her voice rising on the name *Nick.*

"What, that he's tired?" I asked groggily through the pillow.

"No, that he wasn't going. And yes, that he was tired."

I threw the pillow aside. "He said that? Where is he?"

"He went to talk to John, and they were going to grab some breakfast." Celeste pushed her pajamas into her suitcase and pressed it down hard with one hand, trying to zip it closed with the other. I groaned. I was thinking I could have just an hour or so at least to myself, to try and pull it together. And now that I'd decided to stay, he was staying too.

After a second try, Celeste was able to zip her suitcase. She pushed it onto the floor and up against the wall, then turned around and sat on the foot of my bed. "What's going on?"

I sat up and sighed. "I—last night—"

The door to our room opened, and voices from the doorway cut me off.

261

"Celeste, ready to rock?" John appeared in the hallway along with Nick. "Morning, Adriana." John nodded to me.

I managed a nod back at him before nervously glancing to Nick. He was still in his pajamas.   He looked back at me, studying me. I felt naked, and quite stupid for still being in bed while everyone else was dressed and walking around me.

"You aren't going to the Pantheon, lazy?" Nick said.

"No, I just heard you aren't going either. I'm so tired..." I faked a yawn, stretching my arms out and collapsing backward onto the bed.

"Me too. We'll head to the train station early and get tickets for everyone."

"Yes, that's a great idea," Celeste replied.

"Okay, we'll meet you two at the station. Celeste, want to grab your bag?" John motioned to Celeste's roller pushed up against the wall. "Charlie's dying for a cigarette. I told him to wait for us and he could have one on the walk."

Celeste turned around and raised her eyebrows at me. "See you two later..." she said, pulling the door close behind her.

Nick and I were alone.

"I hope you don't mind that I am staying," I said to him. He hadn't moved, but was still standing in the same spot near the doorway by the foot of our bed. He frowned and shook his head.

"Why would I mind? It's fine," he said. "I'm going to jump in the shower though. Unless you want to go first?"

"I... no, it's okay, I need to pack up. Go ahead," I said. My stomach was in knots. He seemed normal. But was that good, or was that bad? Shouldn't he have been acting differently? We had definitely crossed some lines last night. Friends don't put their hands underneath their friends' shirts while sleeping. Right?

"Okay. I'll be in here," he motioned toward the bathroom. I smiled and lay back down in bed, pretending to grab my cell phone from the nightstand until I heard the bathroom door click closed. As the shower water turned on, I jumped out of bed and quickly snuck out into the hallway, still in my pajamas.

"Hey!" I whisper-yelled. "Celeste!"

Her head whipped around. "What's up?"

"Come here. Now."

She trotted in my direction. "Are you coming?"

"Hey guys. Celeste will be just one sec," I called down the hall. Charlie sighed and rolled his eyes. His patience with what he called "girl stuff" was starting to wear thin.

"I could have had a cigarette..." I heard him mutter to John.

I grabbed Celeste's wrist tightly and pulled her into our room, shutting the door behind her. I looked her in the eyes, and took a deep, steadying breath.

"Something happened last night." I kept my voice down in a whisper.

"Something... like what?"

"With Nick."

She gasped, her eyes wide, her mouth stretching into a huge smile.

"Shhhh!"

Celeste dropped her voice to a whisper. "What happened? Did you kiss?"

"No, no, it was nothing like that..." I realized then that I couldn't even put into words what had happened last night. Had anything happened? Had it all been a dream? "We just... we didn't sleep much, and he kept tossing, and he had his hands on me..."

Celeste gave me the look, meaning *you-know-Charlie-and-I-were-in-the-room*.

"No, nothing like that. I can't explain it. But something happened, something—changed." I closed my eyes. What was I even trying to say? To ask? "I don't know. What do I do?"

She giggled, and pinched my stomach. "Just go jump in the shower with him."

I gasped, surprised at her forwardness. "I would *never!*"

She giggled again and shook her head, wide-eyed. "You guys... what are you going to do?"

Sighing, I turned around to look at the closed bathroom door. I could still hear the water running. "I really don't know. I won't throw myself at him, but... We'll see where it goes from here."

There was a soft knock at the door. "Celeste, are you ready?" Lexie was on the other side of the door. I reached behind Celeste and pulled it open. Lexie took one look at my face, at my guilty, nervous expression and dropped her voice. "What happened?"

"Will you guys go," I said, pushing Celeste out into the hall. "Tell her on your way," I instructed Celeste to Lexie. "We'll be fine here."

Lexie looped her arm through Celeste's, and the two started off down the hall, heads together whispering. I stood in the hallway and turned to look inside our bedroom. Gathering what little composure I had, I took a deep breath and went inside. Clothes were strewn around the floor. I started picking up T-shirts and flats in handfuls and shoving them inside Charlie. Once everything was inside, I realized I needed some clothes for today. I rooted around inside my bag for a clean pair of jeans, and pulled out a white tank top to go with it. We were just going to be sitting on the train all day.

I heard the water slow to a drip in the bathroom and the curtains open up. I quickly grabbed my pink bikini underwear and lime green bra with my clothes and makeup bag so I could run into the bathroom when he was finished. My stomach felt happily nauseous at the thought of being alone with Nick all morning, and I didn't want to do anything stupid. *Like jump into the shower with him uninvited,* I thought. The bathroom door opened and Nick emerged, clad in jeans and a snug navy blue T-shirt. I stared at him. He was the perfect specimen of a man. His broad shoulders may have looked big for his narrow waist, but his arms... his arms were the strongest and safest arms I'd ever been in. His wet hair was pushed to the side of his head, and he had an electric toothbrush sticking out of his mouth. I realized I hadn't moved or said anything since he opened the bathroom door.

"It all yours," he said over the hum of his toothbrush.

"Thanks," I replied, scooping my clothes up and walking toward the bathroom. I waited outside the door as he leaned back in and spit out his toothpaste, rinsing out his mouth. He turned to me.

"Minty fresh," he said. The corners of his mouth turned up ever so slightly into a flirty smile.

"Yeah, I can see." The words came out of my mouth quietly as I tried not to stare at his lips. I pushed past him, taking care not to bump into him on my way into the bathroom.

"Here," he said, stepping behind me. As he stepped backward, he placed his hand on the small of my back. "Let me get out of your way."

I froze, a shiver rushing up my spine. The smallest touch from him paralyzed me. I spun around and saw that, while he said he was moving, Nick was still right behind me, close. Almost too close. Almost.

My breath caught in my throat. I licked my lips, staring up at him, as he gazed at me. *This is it,* I thought. I waited, frozen to the spot. I couldn't move, for fear the moment would break, it would vanish, and he would be gone. Nick's hand made his way up to my hip. I felt my face flush. I was still gripping my clothes for the day in my chest, my pink bikinis right on top of the heap. His eyes were locked on mine, searching for something.

"The water should be hot for you," Nick said suddenly, blinking quickly and looking down, clearing his throat. Something had stopped him. He stepped out of the bathroom and pulled the door closed.

My knees felt weak. I sat down on the toilet seat lid, dropping my clothes to the floor. What had just happened? There had been so many times that he had gotten so close to me. I felt sure he knew he could have me at any moment, any of the many times our lips had been so close, they were his for the taking. All he had to do was pass those unpassable few inches, but he wouldn't do it. I was making him make the decision, and he was unable to do it. I would give him the signs and the signals, but it had to be *his* decision to act on it. I couldn't explain why, but I knew this. It wouldn't work if I forced him, if I made the first move and expected him to respond. What was holding him back?

I showered up, brushed my teeth, and pulled my curls into a pile on top of my head. I threw on a little bit of makeup. By the time I got back into the bedroom, I saw Nick tying up his backpack. Whatever had happened between us was gone. It had faded away, just as I knew it would.

"You ready to head to the train station?" I asked.

Δ

It was a few minutes before our train to La Spezia was scheduled to leave that Lexie, John, Celeste, and Charlie finally showed up. Nicholas and I had secured a cabin with six seats for us. The two of us were sitting across from one another in the seats closest to the window, talking about our shared love for the beach, when our cabin doors opened.

"Heyyy," Lexie said in her airy voice. "Look what we brought!" She held up her hands, each holding a bottle of wine.

Celeste filed into the cabin after Lexie, holding up two more bottles. "And John and Charlie each have two!" She laughed. "We won't be bored on this ride."

John and Charlie entered after Celeste, John also with a bag of sandwiches in his hand. "Well if we are going to drink this much, everyone grab a sandwich first." He laughed.

Outside us, the train's whistle blew, echoing through the station. The train shook, jerking forward.

"Whoa!" Charlie had been trying to throw his backpack above the seats when we moved, almost losing his balance. He grabbed Celeste's shoulder to keep from falling. "This is going to be quite a ride."

20

October, Cinque Terre.

Charlie had been right. By the time we arrived in Riomaggiore, it wasn't afternoon anymore. We'd passed five hours on the train, and all six bottles of wine were empty. Lexie and I had passed out for the last hour and a half, dizzy from wine and laughter. I'd woken up with my head in Nick's lap, him stroking my hair with his headphones on, gazing out at the sea.

Riomaggiore was the first of the of the villages of the Cinque Terre, and one we'd decided to pick for it's cheap accommodations. Nick had read online, and heard from friends, that the best thing to do was to not book a hotel online at all, but to take an offer from one of the few hoteliers that waited at the train station for disembarking tourists. This had made Charlie extremely nervous when he found out, but our gamble paid off when we found a man who could rent us three small cottages, each sleeping two, for €100 a night.

We followed our host out of the train station. I felt groggy from the wine and the nap, and found myself blinking my eyes over and over, adjusting to the sunlight. As my eyes adjusted and my mind began to clear, my mouth broke into a wide smile at the beauty before me. There was a small village straight out of a painting, stretched out in front of us and up the cliffs. Houses narrow but tall were stacked in the hillside, each painted different bright shades of pink, yellow, green, and blue. Some of the colors seemed muted, as if years of salty sea mist had faded them. Balconies dotted each window, all views facing the wide-open sea in front of us, shutters thrown open to the salty ocean air. A small, slanted dock served as a place for locals to tie up their wooden boats, most of which were as brightly colored as the houses above.

I had been to Cinque Terre only once before, but I did not remember stopping in Riomaggiore. I remembered the beaches, nothing more. But this small village was perfect. It was just what I wanted, what we needed after the week we'd spent traveling in bigger cities. No hustle and bustle, not even any cars. The perfect place to close out our trip.

There was only one road in front of us; a wide, paved sidewalk stretching up the hill and curving to the right. We continued behind our guide as the paved sidewalk slowly disappeared, making way to dirt. The path made a sharp tick, getting steeper and rockier as it curved up the hill, turning into what was a glorified hiking trail.

"Is this the way up?" Lexie asked, dragging her suitcase shakily behind her. It hit a rock and she stopped, yanking it harder to pull it over the jagged path.

"I guess so. It's not like there are any taxis." I waited for her to catch up to me, and checked out the path ahead.

Charlie and Nick were about twenty paces ahead of us, following our host closely. He was a big man, short but round, and at least sixty-five years old. His white hair was slicked back to cover the bald spot on the top of his head. Though he was clearly in the worst shape of any of us, he was making his way up the path, dodging the sticks and bushes, with much greater ease than the rest of us with our luggage.

We continued up the path for another ten minutes before finally coming to a wide clearing that turned into another wide, paved sidewalk. It was as if we had walked up to the third floor of the hillside, and we continued down the wide sidewalk, passing houses in the cliffside. After another few minutes, we came upon a break in the bushes of the hillside. There was a small garden on the right, and on the left, was nothing. The hill dropped off in front of us, leaving nothing to see but the open ocean.

He motioned for us to set our bags down and showed us inside the three small cottages that were clustered in the hillside together. Two were immediately to our right, with windows that opened to the water, and a small patio outside one of the cottages. The third was tucked behind the first two cottages, and had a bigger porch outside the front door.

I turned to Celeste and Lexie, our mouths agape at our home for the next three nights. Lexie squealed and squeezed Celeste's hand.

"Can you believe we get to stay here?" Lexie stared out at the water, eyes shining. "So who is staying where?" she asked, turning to face me and Celeste. "I want to stay with you two."

Celeste agreed. "Do we need three? Maybe we can share two?"

"I'll check this one," I volunteered, starting up the stairs of the nearest cottage. The stucco of the cottage was bright white, but the stairs were painted a coral color, faded away from years without touch-ups. Chipped terra cotta planters stood all along the patio walls, overflowing with wildflowers I did not recognize. I pushed open the door, the blue paint charmingly chipping off the wood all around the edges. I felt around for a light switch and found a button just a few inches past the door.

The cottage was small and simple. A kitchenette, all yellow, was on the left. An old yellow refrigerator from the fifties sat in the corner, with pale yellow Formica and linoleum to match. In the center of the kitchenette was a small, square table, with four mismatched chairs pushed in around it. A hand-painted blue vase stood in the middle of the table, contrasting perfectly with the yellow around it.

I walked to my right, through a small hallway and into a dark bedroom. Blue shutters were pulled tightly closed over the windows, and I walked past the queen-size bed to open them. There were no screens, and I leaned my head out to peek down to Celeste.

"This one has just one bed, but it's big enough for two," I called. "It's adorable." I turned back around to face the bedroom with the sunlight. The walls were all white, as was the linen comforter pulled over the bed. Three frilly pillows perched in front of the gold metal headboard. A small painting of wildflowers hung above the bed.

I walked out of the room to check out the bathroom, and found it immediately to the right. Green tile on the floor and walls matched the green tub. Whoever decorated this was really into one color per room. It suited the cottage.

I hopped down the stairs. "Oh, you guys, it's so charming. Just perfect. What are the other two like?"

Charlie, Celeste, and John were grouped in front of the cottage I was in.

"Well, there's only one cottage that has two beds," Charlie said.

"So whoever doesn't want to share a bed should stay there," John chimed. "I don't mind sharing a bed." He grinned at Lexie, reaching for her hand. "We can take the one in the back." So much for Lexie's idea of a girls' cabin.

"Nick and I will take the one with two beds," Charlie decided. That left Celeste and I to the cottage I had just inspected, and we hugged with delight. While I was excited to get some alone time with Celeste, a small part of me was disappointed. I had shared a bed with Nick our whole trip, and this meant that there would not be another night for us to share his headphones, cuddling together.

"I have an idea," Nick started. "Let's change our clothes and head down to the beach. We should make it in time for sunset."

Everyone enthusiastically agreed, and we decided we'd grab dinner after the sun was gone. Fifteen minutes later, we were carefully making our way down the path we had just climbed. Once we ventured down the hill, it was a short walk to the beach, just on the other side of where we had disembarked the train.

The sunlight had faded fast since we had arrived, and the evening was beginning to cool off. We found a spot in the sand for our shoes and bags, and walked down toward the shore of the Adriatic Sea.

All my life, I'd always felt a great connection with water. Our summer house had been just minutes away from the beach, and we passed each summer day on the cool, rocky sands of the Long Island Sound. We'd arrive in the morning, and within seconds of having sunblock clumsily smeared across our cheeks by our mothers, Charlotte, James, Kimberly, and I would be racing one another into the cold water. It would be hours before we'd emerge, skin wrinkly from the salt water, exhausted. Never in my life had I been to the beach without getting into the water, even if it were just my feet, no matter the season. My mom believed it was because I was an Aquarius, and maybe there was some truth to that. Whatever the reason, I felt more at home on a beach than anywhere else, and that evening was no exception.

I walked until the waves kissed my toes, returning again with each rush at the shore. Celeste and Lexie watched behind me. "Aren't you girls coming?" I asked. I walked further, the cold saltwater jumping up and wetting the legs of my cutoff shorts. Looking down at my feet, I decided to keep going until I couldn't see my toes anymore. It was only another foot farther before my red toenail polish was gone, deep beneath the water. The bottoms of my shorts were at the level of the water now.

"Are you crazy?" Lexie shouted to me. "It's freezing!"

"So? How often do you get this chance?" I called back to her. My legs were beginning to sting from the cold, so I decided it was time to move. I made my way through the water, feet sinking in the cool sand below.

By the time I made it back to where our shoes were, Celeste had already ripped off her shirt, and John's pants were off. We had all realized that, despite our plans in advance to come to the water, none of us had brought bathing suits. Everyone decided to swim in their underwear.

"I'm in," John said, smiling at me.

I slid down my cutoffs and pulled off my black tee, turning around to face the sea. The sun was moving quickly, and the temperature was dropping. The little hairs on my thighs stood on end as a breeze blew past me. I turned around to Charlie as John and Celeste ran down to meet Lexie and Nick, and the water's edge.

"Aren't you coming?" I asked Charlie.

"You guys go ahead," he replied. "I'll watch from the shore."

Down to the water I ran, my pink boy-short underwear and lime green bra bouncing with each step. Little rocks in the sand poked my feet, but I kept going, picking up speed until my feet carried me into the water. Eyes closed, I dived underneath. For a moment, all was silent. Water rushed past my ears, my body slow, cutting through the water like glass. I exhaled, water bubbling up from my nose to the surface. It was cool under the water, but not nearly as cold as I had expected it to be. I felt my hair rippling behind me, grazing my shoulder blades. I broke through the surface and looked out at the horizon in front of me, my feet planting down in the sand.

I'd come a long way from home. I'd made a gamble, and it had all paid off. I knew that now. Even if nothing happened with Nick. Even if I never saw these friends again after this semester. Especially if I never heard from Mark again, or if my parents didn't get back together, or if I didn't figure out what I wanted to do with my life. I had really gone out to Prague, not to meet other people, but to find out who I really was. For the first time in my life, I felt at peace, in that moment.

And I realized, as I heard my friends splashing in the water behind me, that I would have been okay if they didn't swim out to meet me. I was just fine all by myself. But I wasn't by myself. I had five best friends there with me, each one bringing something different into my life, making me more aware of different aspects of myself. I smiled to myself as the sun rose back home in the States, and I watched the sun dip below the Adriatic Sea, black as far as the eye could see.

Δ

It got cold quickly as we ran out of the water toward our towels. The sun had vanished and the stars were coming out, shining one by one above us. We had all brought changes of clothes to put on before we found a place for dinner. Celeste, Lexie, and I grabbed our clothes and towels and found a private place behind a rock formation to dry off and step out of our underwear. Pulling a sundress over my head, I thought how unbelievable it was to me that no one else had come down to the beach; the six of us had the whole place to ourselves since we'd come down to watch the sunset. I tugged on a sweater before the girls and I walked over to meet the boys, on the other side of the beach near the stairs.

"Anyone up for seafood?" Nick asked. "We passed a place on our way down to the beach that said it was open kind of late."

Starving, everyone agreed. Within half an hour we were sipping wine on the patio of the restaurant Nick had found, at the only occupied of the eight tables in the restaurant. We each ordered a different kind of seafood and passed plates around, sampling everything the sea had to offer. I devoured linguine alla vongole, savoring every last clam and garlic clove. No matter how long we could stay in Italy, I would never tire of Italian food or wine. It was in my blood.

The night was black and the village was silent when we exited the restaurant. "What time is it?" Lexie wondered, snuggling up to John in the cool air.

Nick pulled back the sleeve of his sweatshirt and checked his watch. "Only ten."

A sigh was heard across the sidewalk. "So I'm guessing there are no bars around here?" Charlie asked, putting a cigarette in his mouth. Celeste looked at me, rolling her eyes.

"Nope. But we could stop in that store and pick up some booze," John said, pointing down the sidewalk to a small bodega with its lights on. "Bring it back up to our rooms."

We walked to the bodega and each picked up a beer of our choice, mostly Peroni, though Charlie was far from satisfied.

"I thought there would be some nightlife here—like a beach resort," he complained to no one in particular.

"Charlie, we've been out every night. It's okay if we have a relaxing evening," I said, putting my hand on his shoulder. "We can find a bar tomorrow night in another one of the towns."

"So what now?" Celeste asked.

I looked to Nick, who had been standing next to me. He was walking away from the group, back toward the water.

"Is he going back to the beach?" I asked.

Charlie shrugged, taking another puff of his cigarette.

Nick continued past the restaurant and toward the stairs that led to the beach. I watched with curiosity as he turned away from the stairs, instead stepping over the railing and onto the rocks below.

"Nick!" I yelled, walking over to him. "What are you doing?"

The rocks were big, some pointy and others flat, and stretched probably just less than a hundred yards into the ocean. They were surrounded by the sea, seaweed and barnacles stuck on the sides of the bigger rocks. He kept walking, jumping from rock to rock.

"Are they sturdy?" I called after him.

"It's fine! They are huge rocks, come out here!"

Not one to shy away from the ocean, I stashed my beer bottle in my bag and grabbed hold of the fence, first throwing my right leg over, then my left. The rocks were bigger than they looked, but Nick was right, they were also flatter. I jumped with ease from rock to rock, looking ahead to Nick. He was nearly at the end, at a grouping of rocks together that looked like one giant boulder.

I turned around to call to the girls. "Guys, bring the drinks out here!" I called.

Celeste appeared over the fence, with John right after her, helping Lexie over. Charlie brought up the rear. My bag bumped against my side as I held my arms out wide, steadying my foot on each rock before leaping to the next. I was terrified that I'd fall, but what was the worst that could happen? I reminded myself. I'd get wet. I could swim. I laughed and leapt again, this time springing over a rock and landing two rocks away. I found my footing once more and kept moving, rock after rock, chasing after Nick. The ocean air felt cool, damp against my face in the dark. I couldn't see much, but could hear the water lapping against the sides of the rocks I jumped over again and again.

At the end of the line, Nick was sitting down, looking up at the stars. I noticed the boulder he was sitting on was slightly slanted but flat, definitely big enough for two. He looked up at me a few rocks away. "Come here, I found a spot for you," he said, motioning next to him.

I smiled and sailed over the last rock, landing shakily next to him. I gave out a little scream and he jumped up, grabbing my wrist and my hip to help steady me.

"Thanks," I said, slightly embarrassed. In the dark, he couldn't see my face flush from his touch.

Around us, our friends scattered and settled onto rocks. Everyone sat and gazed up at the stars, some lying flat on their backs. I heard the crack and hiss of beer bottles being opened. I lay back on the rock, the back of my neck hitting Nick's arm.

"Oh, sorry," I said, thinking I'd hurt him. I wasn't expecting to feel him so close to me.

"It's fine. I wanted it there," he said, smiling to me. I beamed back at him as he rolled his eyes up to stargaze. "What a beautiful place."

I sighed, settling in to his arms. "It's hard to believe that a place like this exists all the time. Does that make sense?" The stars were so much brighter here, away from the city lights. My mind traveled back to Budapest, when I had lain back in Nick's arms just like this on our hotel roof, as he showed me Orion and told me about LA. I had wanted to kiss him so desperately that night. *Not much has changed,* I thought to myself.

"Yeah. You can see the stars so much better out here," Nick replied.

"It reminds me of that night in Budapest, remember? On the hotel roof?"

"Of course I do. That was a great night."

"It really was. It seems like forever ago already, but it was just last month."

Nick turned to face me, pulling his arm out from under me and propping himself up on it. "You seem like a different person from that night."

I rolled my face toward his and scoffed. "Really? I think *you* seem different."

"I guess we've just gotten to know each other better." He reached behind him and grabbed his beer bottle. "You were so... I don't know. Now I just feel like I know you."

"You didn't feel like you knew me before?"

"Well, no. But I didn't really know you. It had only been a few weeks. It's different now."

I reached for my beer and took a long, slow sip. "It's definitely different now," I said softly, turning my head toward him. Everything was different in Italy. It had been just like I imagined; a new level with Nick, but at the same time we had not yet abandoned the bounds of our friendship. "That night, on the roof... I really thought..." I couldn't finish the sentence. I didn't want to bring up the kiss we hadn't had, the kiss that clouded my every thought of him, that seemed always like the elephant in the room. "I just knew we'd get to know each other better," I finished.

"It's funny. That night, the night at the five-story club... You seemed like a completely different person that night, too."

I giggled, thinking of that night. The night we started out, this strange friendship. "Yeah, that was a long time ago," I agreed. "I didn't know you at all then."

"And if you'd known me then, like you know me now, would you still have kissed me?" Nick's face turned toward me once more. His eyes were challenging, daring me to answer.

I sidestepped the question. "I didn't kiss you. You kissed me."

"Oh, my God, no, absolutely not, I did not!" Nick exclaimed.

"Yes, yes, you showed me down to the bathroom, and then you had me up against that wall—"

"Lies, all lies, that was you!"

I collapsed into giggles. "It was not!"

Nick shook his head at me. "You know it was you."

"Nope." I turned over and buried my face in his chest. His arms wrapped around me, holding me there.

"I like cuddling with you," he said softly into my hair.

I closed my eyes and smelled him, the mixture of his cologne and the salt water around us consuming me.

"I'm not usually a cuddler, but with you... I don't know, it just feels good," he said.

"I like it too. It's nice to have someone to sleep next to sometimes."

We both gazed up at the stars. There were millions, as if someone had wiped glitter all over a black sheet above us. *These are the moments I came out here for*, I thought. It was so much more than I ever thought it would be.

"So are you going to find another guy next semester?"

I lifted my chin and looked up at Nick, who was pulling his head up and staring at me. I had no idea what he was talking about. Clearly this wasn't a normal friendship. But we hadn't yet crossed that line. We could still claim we were friends, even though my heart would scream otherwise. If I had him in my life, even just to share an iPod with once in a while, I could manage. But the thought of spending the next semester, the next few months in Prague without Nick was too heavy.

"Absolutely not," I responded. I knew I'd never share this bond with anyone else. It wasn't a bond with him as much as it was myself. He was teaching me things about myself. Opening doors. Showing me who I was, encouraging me to be the person I knew I could be. The person I wanted to be, but never truly felt free enough to be, before now.

He settled his head back down, looking back up at the stars. "Good."

"Do you see Orion now?" I asked, scooting off his chest and laying my head back on the rock next to his.

"Let's see..." His hand grabbed mine and pulled it up, toward the sky. He pulled my index finger up and pointed to a bunch of stars in the corner of the night sky. "This should be it."

I gazed up at the constellation as Nick brought our arms back down. Our hands stayed together, fingers intertwined, and laid our arms between us. My heart skipped a beat and my breath quickened. Holding hands with Nick was a rarity, but something that I had found made me feel more connected to him than anything. I kept my eyes on Orion, nervous about what would happen if I dared to look at him. For something I wanted more than anything else, it terrified me more than I could admit.

Just then, a bright light streaked across the sky. It was bigger than any shooting star I'd ever seen, like a small ball of fire had been thrown across all the glitter.

I gasped loudly and pushed myself up to sit. "Oh, my God!"

Nick jumped up. "Holy fuck! Did you see that?"

I stood up, pointing at the sky. "Yes, I saw it! Jesus, I saw it! What was that?"

Celeste panicked. "What happened?" John and Lexie were looking at us too, as was Charlie, who set down his beer.

"Is everything okay?" Charlie called over from his rock.

"Yeah, it was just... what was that?" I looked at Nick, searching for an explanation. It was too big to be a shooting star.

"I don't know. It must have been a shooting star, but it was huge!" He looked at John and Lexie. "You guys didn't see it?"

John shrugged. "No, we didn't see anything," he said.

Lexie shook her head.

"Oh, my God, you guys scared me! I thought it was a bomb," Celeste said, putting her hand over her heart.

"Why would it be a bomb?" Charlie asked.

"I don't know, I just—I heard them yell, and I thought something was wrong," Celeste said. "I didn't see anything."

I looked at Nick. "How did no one else see that?"

He laughed in disbelief and shook his head. "I have no idea."

Down on our rock, I noticed we had both kicked over our beers. Around us, John and Lexie were getting up, and Charlie was already hopping over to a rock closer to the shore.

"You okay, Celeste?" John called over. Celeste jumped off her rock to walk back with Lexie and John.

"I really can't believe no one saw that," I said to Nick.

"It must have been meant just for us." He grinned at me, and I saw the twinkle of the stars in his blue eyes. "I hope you made a wish."

"I just did." I slid my hand into his, and we made our way back to the shore, leaving the ocean behind us.

21

October, Cinque Terre.

Perhaps the most wonderful thing about Cinque Terre was that there wasn't anything to see. There was a hiking trail, the Via dell'Amore, that stretched from Riomaggiore up through the four other villages, ending at northernmost Monterosso al Mare. If you didn't want to hike, there was also a train that wound through the cliffs, along the waterside, that stopped in each of the five villages. But besides walking around each sleepy village, or passing time on the beach, there was no form of entertainment in Cinque Terre. No historical sights. No cathedrals. No museums. And, perhaps best of all, no bars; only small cafés and restaurants filled the sidewalks.

We slept in late, all of us tired from the nonstop travel we'd been putting our bodies through the last week. It felt unseasonably warm for late October, and we decided over the meat and bread our gracious host had brought by, that we would spend the day at the beach. Nick consulted his guidebook and suggested we head up to Monterosso for the best resort-like beaches. I made sure to wear underwear that could pass for a bikini, and we made our way up to the village.

It was sunny but not too hot; ideal for sitting outside and drinking in the sand. I guzzled water from my water bottle and looked around at the little town around us. It looked exactly the same as it did yesterday, just as sleepy as I had hoped it would stay. In the daylight, I noticed another sidewalk I had missed last night, leading back to a small cluster of restaurants. I pointed it out to Lexie as somewhere we should check out for dinner that night, and we headed off to find the Via dell'Amore.

While we'd read that some of the trail was tougher to climb than others, the path from Riomaggiore to Manarola was tame. The sidewalk was carved out of the side of the cliffs, with nothing between us and the water below a thin metal fence. We wound in and out of the hillside, never leaving sight of the water. The sky mirrored the same bright blue as the water, looking like an ocean-colored canvas stretched around the cliffs. The sky seemed to fade right into ocean, the blue hues hardly shifting. The day heated up quickly, and not long after we'd started the walk, we were ready to jump into the water. We decided rather than hiking for the next few hours, we'd take the train straight to Monterosso for the beach.

Monterosso was bigger than Riomaggiore or Manarola, and had lots more tourists—though still far fewer than we had expected. The narrow, winding roads were filled with souvenir shops and cafés. Postcards and little Italian flags stood on stands outside the stores, doors thrown open to catch the cool breeze coming off the ocean. Clotheslines were strung from window to window above the slim walkways, and old men stood outside their stores, gossiping and smoking.

By the time we got to Monterosso, we were ready to eat again. Lexie had the idea to grab some sandwiches and bring them down to the beach, along with the wine we'd picked up. We split up to find our individual lunches and wandered into the cafés of our choosing. I found a slice of spinach pizza that caught my eye, then headed down to the sand where we'd planned to meet back up. The beach was much bigger than in Riomaggiore, stretching half a mile across underneath the cliffs above. We had snagged a few beach towels from our cottages, and Lexie had found a blanket on her couch that served as our beach blanket for the day.

Celeste opened the first bottle of wine, passing around little plastic cups for everyone. We each made small holes in the sand for cups as we snacked on our lunch. The tide was low, leaving us plenty of space to play with. Celeste grabbed her cup and said she was going for a stroll down the beach, while Charlie announced he was going to go find a bar for us to check out later. I unrolled my beach towel onto the sand next to Nick, who was next to John and Lexie. They were already lost in their own world, laughing and filling John's hat with sand. I shimmied off my cuffed-up jeans and took off my white T-shirt, leaving just my boy shorts and bra. I lay on my back, my towel already warm from the sand beneath and the sun overhead.

This Monterosso beach was the antithesis of the beach I'd grown up on. The bright teal water was nearly translucent, making it easy to spot rocks and fish below the surface. The sand was soft; water shoes definitely were not needed (or worn) around here. Every so often, a boat would drift across the horizon, far enough to not disturb the sound of the crashing waves near our feet. The beach was quiet so late in the season, but the sun was still warm on our skin.

I sat up and pushed my feet into the sand in front of my towel. My polished toes slowly disappeared under the grains. I reached my hands over my feet, feeling the warmth of the sand spread over my fingers. It hadn't been that long since I was at the summer house and our beach back home, where the water was murky, rocks cut the bottoms of our feet, and we often dodged jellyfish in the water. But it seemed so far away to me at the moment. It was almost strange to wrap my mind around the fact that these two beaches both existed at the same moment, as different as they were. It was hard for me to remember that home existed at all. It wasn't a place I felt ready to occupy, mentally or physically. Whatever was happening to me, out here, away from it all... it wasn't done yet. I wasn't done yet.

Small grains of sand hit my back. I whipped my head around to see what was going on.

"Are you still with us?" Nick asked playfully. He peered over the top of his sunglasses. "You've been staring at the water for like twenty minutes."

I shook my head, trying to physically clear the thoughts from my mind. I shifted my weight and turned around, my back to the water, to face Nick. "Yeah, just spacing out. Thinking of the beach back home."

"Let's put this wine to good use," Nick said to no one in particular.

"King's Cup!" Lexie called out, then immediately stood to pick out another cup and fish out a deck of cards from her backpack. The rest of the afternoon collapsed into drinking and cards, as the sun made its way from high in the afternoon sky to low near the water. We sipped wine and laughed, removed from reality as ever.

Δ

Celeste and Charlie bickered the entire hike back to our hotel from the train. This time, it was President Clinton and the impeachment. They'd spent the entire evening after the beach quarreling. It was clear that after eight days of traveling, they were reaching their limits. The four of us had tried to keep the peace and make jokes, but we were all ready for a break. John and Lexie had made their way well ahead of them, neither one being too political or wanting to get involved. Nick and I held back, preferring to laugh with each other instead of getting caught up in Charlie's bad mood and frustration of another night with no bar.

As we got to the top of our hill, we started saying our good nights. John and Lexie headed back toward their cottage, holding hands. Even in the dark, Lexie's hair shimmered, and you could see the smile stretching over John's face at the sound of her laugh. Charlie had finally had enough of Celeste, and had marched off in the direction of the cabin he was sharing with Nick. But Nick and I, bringing up the rear, didn't quite know where to go.

"Want to see our place?" I asked him. Celeste was already angrily marching up the stairs. We would not be alone there, but I wasn't ready to part with him yet.

"Don't you have a roommate tonight?" He smiled at me mischievously.

"Well yeah, but I just thought you could stop in for a moment. I didn't invite you to stay over."

Nick laughed, poking me in the side. "That's true, I guess." I laughed and pushed his arm away from my side. He kept at it, and his pokes turned into tickling me as he wrapped his arms around me. I laughed, trying to kick him away.

"Cut it out!" I shrieked. My arms flailed, and finally Nick pulled away. I heard the bathroom door close behind Celeste, leaving Nick and I alone in the cottage kitchen.

"Well..." Nick's voice trailed off as he stood in front of me. We weren't touching anymore. He lifted himself up and sat on the narrow Formica kitchen counter, cracked and peeling away from the wall in places.

"Well..." I repeated. Looking at him, I realized how close this all was to ending. We only had two more nights in Italy before returning to Prague. I wasn't ready to give this up. Our relationship had been building to something, but exactly what it had been building to, had not yet made itself clear. I wanted him, to be near him. I wanted to be in bed with him again, to be close to him, to share his headphones. It wasn't about sex. *If I could just have that much*, I thought. *I'll give it one last shot.* I took a deep breath and moved closer to Nick, standing between his knees.

"You know, I kind of miss sleeping with you," I tested the waters, looking up at Nick's face to gauge his reaction.

His eyes darted up to meet mine, bluer than ever. He raised his eyebrows. "Really?"

"Well, I just really like the music," I added. Inching forward, I put my hands on his knees. I moved all my emotion into my eyes, gazing into his. My heart, my desire for him, the flutters my stomach did every time he touched my knee or grabbed my hand. With my eyes, I told him he could have me, all of me, if he'd only say so.

Without breaking my gaze, he replied softly. "We could try out my small bed."

I nodded my head and smiled up at him. "Okay. I'll get my pajamas."

He jumped off the counter, landing next to me. He grabbed my hand with both of his, giving it a squeeze. "Go get changed and come over when you're ready." And he walked past me and out the door into the night.

I smiled and jumped up and down in the dark kitchen, then moved my celebration into the bedroom.

"Celeste, Celeste, Celeste, I'm going over to stay with Nick tonight." I could hardly get the words out, I was already so nervous.

Celeste was sitting in bed. She looked up from her journal. "Are you really?"

"Yeah, I just... yeah. I've got to get changed." I grabbed my pajama pants and tank top from the top of my backpack. "It's the last chance I'm giving him." I didn't believe the words as they were coming out of my mouth, but something inside me knew we were reaching our breaking point.

"Good. I'm glad. Ohmygosh, I'm nervous for you! Well... I'll see you in the morning?" She was holding her breath for me. "Hey, why don't we get up early, and us three can go grab a cappuccino down at that café. We haven't had any girls' time."

"Yes! Definitely." I shimmied my jeans off and fluffed my curls. "I'll meet you back here at eight?" I ran out to brush my teeth.

Celeste followed me. "Are you guys going to... I mean, did he say..."

I spit into the sink. "I don't know. For all I know, nothing will happen, again. We'll just listen to music and fall asleep. But you know, that's okay. I just want to be near him. I... I think...I think I'm..." I stuttered, my voice shaking. I couldn't say the words.

She stepped forward and hugged me. "I know, Addie. I know."

I nodded. "Thank you." I was so grateful for her for not making me say what I didn't want to say out loud, what I didn't want to admit to myself. *It's just an infatuation,* my mind repeated, over and over. *It's not a big deal.*

I repeated this, over and over in my mind, as I walked over to Nick's cabin. I knocked on the door, taking a deep breath to steady my nerves. It didn't work.

The door opened. Nick was shirtless, in the same plaid pajama pants I'd come to recognize. "Come on in," he invited.

I stepped inside. Their cabin was different, much smaller than ours. The kitchenette was to the right, outfitted with a mini-fridge and a two-burner stove. Directly in front of us and to the left was a small, round table. Fresh yellow flowers brightened up the plain wood table, and matched the yellow floral drapes across the windows perfectly. Behind the table, was the entrance to a bedroom.

"Is that where Charlie is?" I asked Nick. It was quiet inside, still.

"Yeah, the bathroom is in there too. Do you need to go?"

The door was to the bedroom was pulled shut.

"No, I'm fine," I said.

To the right of the room behind the kitchen, was a small twin bed, turned down for the evening. Nick's bag was haphazardly shoved underneath it, clothes spilling out from the overstuffed backpack. I stared at the bed. Pale yellow sheets dotted with flowers stretched across the mattress, with a red floral comforter thrown over it. It was quaint, the perfect uncomplicated cottage you'd expect to have wood shutters thrown wide open to the ocean, as they were now.

"Are you ready?" Nick moved toward the bed, switching the lights off on the way. "I made us a new playlist. I think you'll really like it."

"I always like them," I remarked. "You pick the best songs to sleep to."

Nick smiled and climbed into the bed, scooting his back all the way against the wall, leaving room for me. It was going to be a narrow fit tonight, just like in Florence. I stood in front of the bed, waiting for him to get settled. After a few moments, I climbed in with my back to Nick, and as much space between us as I could afford.

"You comfortable?" Nick asked. I peeked over my shoulder at him and nodded. I was as comfortable as I was going to be. He handed me an earbud from his iPod, and moments later, the soft music flowed into my ear.

The bed was slanting toward the middle, and every few minutes, I slid further away from the edge and closer to Nick. I could feel the heat off his body growing closer and closer on my spine, until he gave in. He pulled my body close against his, further yet into the middle of the bed. His arm came around my waist, taking ahold of my hand laying in front of my chest. My heart pounding, I took a deep breath. *It's no different from any other night we had spent crowded into a twin bed,* I told myself. My eyes closed, I focused on the music. My body relaxed and I felt the tension and nerves ease away with each passing breath. This was where I wanted to be. It was all I wanted. I could hear Nick's deep breaths behind me, his music softly flowing into my ear.

One song passed, then another. Slowly, my leg was falling asleep. I needed to roll over. I gently flattened onto my back, then rolled onto my right side. I expected Nick to back up further toward the wall, but he didn't move. Assuming he had fallen asleep, I was surprised to find his eyes were open, fixed on me, as I landed my face just inches from his. He didn't scoot back, and following his lead, I didn't either.

We could have been mirror images of one another: our knees touching, our hips facing each other's just inches away.

My heart picked up again, promising to burst out of my chest. I was certain he could hear it from where he was, even with headphones on. My heart knew this time was different. I could feel his breath on my lips, hot and heavy. The room was dark around us, but his eyes still seemed bright. The song we had been listening to faded away.

I chewed on my lip, my breath shallow. I was determined not to move. I was three inches from his face—if he wanted to kiss me, this was his moment. I stayed as still as I could, trying to focus on the music. Nick clicked to put on the next song, and the cord to the headphones moved, landing on my lips. Without saying a word, he moved his face forward and softly bit the cord to move it away from my face. Our lips touched ever so slightly; mist on early spring flowers, the foamy edge of the ocean on the furthest line of sand, the flick of a fresh sheet on top of a mattress. Still, I didn't dare move.

As a new song spilled into my ear, Nick moved his face toward mine, until I felt his lips once more. The kiss was slow and soft, but deliberate. He pulled away and looked at me, gauging my reaction. I exhaled, my mind, my body begging for another kiss. I didn't take my eyes off of him.

His arm reached around the small of my back, pulling me hard against his body. His lips found mine, aggressively this time. I kissed him back, hard, with all the passion I'd been holding in all week, all month, all semester since we'd gotten to know one another. I didn't just want him, I *needed* him.

Before I could register what was happening, Nick pulled his head back. "I know how you feel about me." The words gushed out of him and hung in the air, begging a response. I didn't want to give one.

I considered the obvious for a moment. I was lying in bed kissing him, clearly I had feelings for him. But I knew that wasn't what he meant. He knew, or thought he knew, I'd been hiding feelings for him. I tried to think of something to say, but all I could manage was, "What?"

He sat up, leaning against the wall, his legs drawing toward his chest, and pulled his earbud out of his ear. "I know you were mad when I went out with that Czech girl. And I know you got upset when I asked for John's friend's phone number at the bar in Florence. You don't deserve—you deserve someone better, someone who can give you what you want, because that isn't me. I can't give you everything you want. I don't want to hurt you, please don't think that's why I just kissed you and now I'm saying this..."

I listened to his words as my heart sank into my stomach. What was he saying? I hadn't asked him for any commitment, I had only kissed him back. I had waited for him to do it, knew he had to be the one to make the move. But it didn't seem to matter to him now. "I don't know, or at least I didn't know..." I tried to interrupt, before my voice trailed off. I didn't know where I was going.

But he was still talking. "...and I just can't start a relationship. We don't know what's going to happen, we aren't here long. Sometimes I feel so close to you. I feel like I can't have only known you for two months, because you get me. And I know that if I wanted to be in a relationship, I could do that with you. But I didn't come out here to be in a relationship. I wanted to explore, to learn, to be free... and I thought I was doing that, not getting entangled with you, until the night before we left for Italy. Mason was so drunk and I was walking him home, and he told me I was a selfish ass for how I was treating you, that it was obvious that you had real feelings for me, and I was just fucking around with you, leading you on. And I thought about it..."

As Nick continued to talk, I realized he wasn't talking to me. He was talking to himself, out loud, to me. He was reasoning with himself, a conversation between head and heart. Or, more likely, head and body. As much as he wanted to continue what we had just started, his brain wasn't letting him, until he talked this out with me. *It takes a real man to bring this up now,* I thought to myself. A million things had rushed into my mind after his lips first brushed against mine, but I didn't want to stop. I didn't want to think. For once, I wanted to not think about Nicholas. I just wanted to *feel* him.

Inside, my head, heart, and body were saying different things. My body wanted to shut him up with my lips, to run my hands down his strong arms and down his chest, to do whatever I could to make him unable to speak. My head was listening to him. *Listen to what he's saying,* my brain urged. *He's saying he can't do this. Don't press him.*

But of all the conversations going on at that moment, the only one I cared about was my heart. I felt something here, a real connection with Nicholas. I was ready to take my chances with whatever would happen. And despite what his lips were saying, I knew this wasn't a one-night thing for him. He cared about me, he'd admitted it. And he wanted me, that much was obvious. He continued to reconcile his conflicting desires out loud to me as I stared at him. Finally, I pressed my hand gently but firmly against his chest.

"Stop," I said softly. "It's okay. I don't know that I want a relationship either. Mark and I broke up not that long ago, and it's not like I came out here looking for someone. You know I didn't." I looked into his eyes. He was searching for the words I'd say next. "We can just take it as it comes."

He laid back down and kissed me again, stroking my hair with one hand and pulling my hips closer to him with the other. "Italy could just be our time together, we'll see what happens when we get back to Prague," he said.

"Just tell me this isn't purely physical," I said, pulling my lips away from his for a moment.

"No, no, of course not." He breathed as he kissed my cheeks and neck. "I love our friendship. That's what's taken me so long, knowing how complicated this could all get." He was looking at me now, and I could see in his eyes that he was being honest. Nick was genuinely conflicted, and I understood how he felt. Every ounce of my heart and body wanted to be with him, but my brain knew better. There was no way we'd have a future past December fifteenth, when our semester ended. It was a terminal case.

I ran my hand up and down his arm. I loved his arms. They were just the right size. His shoulders, broad for his height, made me feel safe. I thought back to a few weeks ago, staring at Nick's arm as I counted the freckles. I'd wanted to know everything about him. Was this my chance? I moved my face closer to his again and pressed my lips into his. We were done talking for the night. Our hands fumbled, mouths moving quickly and eagerly, with everything we'd been holding back for weeks.

Δ

I woke to the sound of crashing waves. I knew before I opened my eyes it was morning.

Nick's arms were still around me. I wasn't used to sleeping so close to someone, but since we'd shared a twin bed last night there wasn't anywhere else for our bodies to be other than fitting into one another, my back to his chest. Feeling me move, he pulled me closer to him.

"Don't go," he breathed, rubbing his face into my hair.

I hesitated a moment before pushing myself out of his arms. "I should go before Charlie gets up. I don't want him to feel weird."

I sat on the bed and looked around the floor for my pajama pants. I found them crumpled up in a pile, right underneath Nick's.

"No, you're right." Nick said, yawning. He pushed the upper half of his body up, watching me pull my pants on. "Last night..." he started. His hair was messy from sleep, the light, floral sheets bunched around his waist.

"Yeah," I interrupted. We looked at each other for a moment. I wasn't sure of where he was going with that thought. I felt my face flush, and looked at the floor. I pretended to search for my shoes, even though I knew I had walked over barefoot, sand dirtying my feet. I couldn't stand to hold his gaze. I wasn't sure I wanted him to finish his thought. Was he already having second thoughts?

It was still quiet. "Okay, well I guess I'll see you later." I stood awkwardly facing his bed, inching toward the front door.

He nodded sleepily. "Yeah, of course."

I held my hand up in a strange sort of half-wave, and turned around, pulling the door open. Instantly the little bungalow was filled with sunshine, the smell of salt and the sounds of the water below.

I walked back to my room with Celeste, my head buzzing. Had last night really happened? I felt so relieved our kiss happened the way it did, and very relieved we'd stopped short of having sex. We weren't drunk; there would be no blaming it on booze and bad decision making, and no rushing into anything. He must have meant what he said, and everything he'd done. I was still impressed that he'd stopped anything from happening before we'd talked, but I also wasn't sure what would happen next. It didn't matter. I was content to just be, here, in Italy, with my best friends—one of whom was Nick. I stopped walking and looked around. I saw the bungalows we'd rented, paint chipping away from the sea salt in the air. I listened to the birds and the waves. I saw the bright pink and red bougainvillea blooms, tumbling down the side of the stone wall that separated our patio from the steep hill that led to the town below. I wanted to be present, in this moment, in this space. That was something my time abroad was teaching me, and I was trying to be open to that lesson.

Inside, I walked right into the bedroom and plopped down on the bed. The windows were open slightly, blowing the floral curtain around gently. I heard the water in the bathroom shut off. Moments later, Celeste appeared in the doorway.

"Hi! You're back!" She sat on the bed, wrapped in a towel. Her hair hung wet past her shoulders. "So? What happened? Tell me everything!"

I smiled at her. "I'll tell you and Lexie when we get to the coffee shop."

She rolled her eyes. "Ugh, I hate that you're making me wait."

"I'll only be a minute, just let me take a shower," I said, grabbing a towel and heading into the bathroom.

Less than twenty minutes later, the three of us girls were slowly descending the hill. We found the only sleepy café that was open, and snagged a table outside in the sun. After ordering a round of lattes and chocolate croissants, Celeste immediately rounded on me.

"Okay, time's up, spill."

I took a deep breath and looked at them. They looked nearly as excited as I was to see what would happen last night. "We kissed."

They both squealed. "I knew it!" Lexie said. "And...?"

I was blushing. "Just some other stuff..." I shook my head. "I wasn't sure how much I should tell. "He's so passionate. It was..." I looked down at my latte. I wasn't sure I had the words. I could feel the girls looking at me.

"We didn't have sex," I clarified.

Celeste nodded. "Good for you."

"Really?" I asked.

"Yeah, I mean... do you even know what's going to happen?"

"No. I don't know what any of this means."

"You know he's into you," Lexie said. "He's told me, and I've told you, and it's obvious. No one acts like that to someone else if they aren't interested."

"Yeah, but interested doesn't mean that much," I argued. "After last night, it's just so complicated."

"What's complicated about this?" Lexie looked at me. "You like each other. You're in Italy. You'll be in Prague together for another six weeks. Can't you just enjoy it?"

"No, of course we can. I mean, I can. I don't know about him. It's just that... I think I'm falling for him."

The girls looked at each other. "We know," Celeste said. She reached her hand out and put it on top of mine. "It's okay."

I looked at Lexie. "What about you and John? Are you just going to enjoy Prague, and then figure it out later?"

Lexie smiled. "I don't think so. We're already talking about seeing each other next semester when we are back in the States."

I knew that would be the case. They were unmistakably in love with each other. We knew they were taking things slow, and it made sense for them.

"I can't imagine not seeing Nick," I uttered. "Not listening to music with him, not talking to him, or joking with him. I want to be with him so badly, and I don't know if I can take that not happening."

"Maybe he's feeling that way too. You don't know," Celeste argued. Always the optimist.

I shook my head. "I don't know. He stopped things last night before they got too far so we could talk. And he mentioned that he didn't want to be in a relationship, so forget that. Even though this *is* a relationship, just a really fucking weird one."

A silence fell on the table as our croissants arrived, steaming from the oven. All of a sudden, I lost my appetite. The only thing I wanted was Nick. I wasn't sure what was going to happen, and for all I knew the clock would run out on our time together after we left Italy the next day. I wasn't sure I was ready for that to happen.

I hastily changed the subject, and we talked about going back up to the beach in Monterosso, enjoying our last day in Italy. After we finished our breakfast, we hiked back to our rooms to get our towels and makeshift bathing suits. Lexie went to go tell John our plan, and we ran into Charlie outside, smoking. He said it sounded good to him, and agreed he and Nick would get their things ready and meet us back outside in ten minutes.

Inside our bungalow, I nervously changed into something to wear to the beach. My stomach was in a knot. I couldn't wait to see Nick. I threw my unruly waves into a ponytail and grabbed my bag for the beach, heading outside into the warm sun.

It was already heating up outside. I was the last one to join the group. My eyes immediately sought out Nick's.

"Morning," he said to me with a sly grin. I could feel my entire face light up.

"Hi."

The rest of the group was discussing if we should pick up wine or beer to bring to the beach.

"You look pretty tired," Nick said to me jokingly. "Didn't get much sleep last night?"

I kicked his foot playfully. "Not much."

The group started walking down the hill, and Nick put his arm around me. We followed, together. Once we got to the beach, we laid our towels down in the sand and split up. Charlie immediately declared he was sick of the beach and went to find a bar. Celeste decided she was going to go for a walk, and John and Lexie headed toward the water. My lack of sleep was starting to catch up with me, and the warm sand felt like the perfect place to rest. I laid down on my towel, and looked over at Nick, who was shaking sand off of his.

"What are you going to do?"

"I want to go in the water, but I think I'm going to sleep a little first," I replied.

"Good, I was hoping you'd say that." He let his towel fall next to mine, and lay close next to me. "I sleep so well with you." His arm wrapped around my belly, and once again he pulled me close to him. Within moments, I was asleep in Nick's arms once again.

It was over an hour before we were both up, and everyone was back at the towels. Charlie was annoyed at not having found a bar, but we tried to lift his spirits by playing another drinking game. John had forgotten the cards, so we opted for shoulders—one of his favorites. Another afternoon passed in a haze of wine and sun and sand. We laughed hard and drank heartily, stopping only to pick up sandwiches from a stand to eat on our towels.

The sun started to dip and the beach began to empty, but we stayed. It was our last night in Italy, and none of us were quite ready to let it go. The boys skipped rocks over the waves into the darkening sea. Celeste, Lexie, and I polished off the bottles of wine and watched. We reminisced about our favorite moments of our trip, the ones we swore we'd remember forever. Floating down the canals of Venice in a gondola. Nearly missing the train in Milan. Sipping prosecco around the Trevi Fountain in Rome. John's nightly "journal entries" he did out loud over wine, recapping the day to us all through jokes. Once the sun was gone for the night, and the moon had taken its place over the water, we packed up our towels and took the last train back to Riomaggiore, bidding Monterosso farewell.

Δ

I lingered outside my bungalow, waiting for Nick to walk past. It was our last night in Italy, and I was hoping for one last night with Nick to end the trip.

"I would kill for another beach day," he said, finally catching up to me. "It all went by so quickly."

I nodded. "Totally. I'm not sure I'm ready to go back to Prague... but it's pretty fantastic that we are going back there. It's not like we're going home," I said. It was always a bit of a surreal feeling to go home. To Prague.

"Yeah. Back to school, back to semi-reality."

I looked up at him, catching his eye. "Well, reality doesn't have to start tonight. Want company in your room again?"

He cleared his throat. "Uhh, I... I think I need to catch up on some sleep tonight," he said. "It's not you—I mean, no offense, I just..."

I tried to keep my face from visibly falling. Was he being honest with me? He had said he wanted to see where this would lead for the rest of our time here, and that was ending in the morning. "Yeah, okay." I shifted my weight uncomfortably. "I shouldn't leave Celeste alone another night." I wasn't offended—instead, I felt nervous. I wasn't sure what reality I would be going back to in Prague. This closeness we'd had, Nick and I... it was probably over. The product of wine and romantic Italy. We hugged good night, and I watched him walk over to his bungalow, hoping he'd turn around.

He didn't.

22

October, Prague.

Just as we had arrived in Italy separately, our departures were scattered throughout the day. The boys were leaving in the morning, first to Zurich, then connecting to Prague from there. They wouldn't arrive back until the day after the girls and I arrived home. Our flight didn't leave Milan until much later that evening.

I'd opened the windows in our room as wide as they could be, sunshine and sea air pouring in. It was the last time I'd smell this salty air for months. Prague had been in a gorgeous phase of fall when we'd left, yellow and red leaves crunching under our feet to class, but I wasn't sure what we'd go back to. I had a feeling this would be the last strong sunshine I'd see until spring.

It wasn't as difficult to pack as I'd thought it would be. Celeste was an early riser and I'd gotten up with her, took a shower, and got my backpack in order. We hadn't done any shopping in Italy, and except for a rosary I'd pick up for Nanny from the Vatican, I was going home with exactly what I'd brought with me. I started at the contents of my backpack on the bed. Everything was upside down, strewn about, messy. I felt the same way inside.

I was uneasy about our return to Prague. What did this mean for Nick and me? These past ten days in Italy had been a sort of vacation from the relationship we had in Prague. We'd let loose. Cuddled on the beach. Held hands on the train. There was nothing to hide among John,

Charlie, Celeste, and Lexie. Would a return to Prague mean a return to our old relationship? I wasn't sure I was ready for that, and knew there was no way I could pretend these last ten days hadn't happened, or that they hadn't meant anything to me.

Footsteps reminded me I was supposed to be packing, and I picked up a pair of jeans and immediately started folding. Out the window, I saw a blonde head of hair bouncing up our steps. Lexie pushed open our front door and appeared in the bedroom moments later.

"Morning!" she called out with energy, her voice wispy as ever.

I strained a smile. "Morning."

She plopped onto the bed next to my mountain of clothes. "Where's Celeste?"

"She's rinsing off in the shower, she's already packed," I said.

"Well, we are ready to go whenever. John's just grabbing his bag now."

"Have you seen Charlie or Nick?" I asked, trying to sound nonchalant.

Lexie raised her eyebrows. "You haven't seen Nick today?"

I fumbled with the same pair of jeans I had been holding since she walked in. "I stayed here last night. He said he wanted to get some sleep." I shook my head. "I don't know if he was blowing me off..." I shook the jeans out. Why could I not remember how to fold jeans right now?

"He spent how many nights with you? I'm sure he didn't mean anything by it. Maybe he needs to sort things out," Lexie offered.

Across the hallway, the bathroom door opened. Celeste came out, dressed.

"I am so not ready to go back." She shook her head. "You know it's probably going to be freezing?" Celeste started shoving her toiletries in her bag.

I looked over at Lexie. "Are you packed?"

She nodded. "Yeah. Let's meet outside in ten." She bounced away to grab her things.

I hurriedly shoved the rest of my things in my bag and went outside to take in the view of the water until the last possible moment. I was also hoping I'd catch a glimpse of Nick, and say a proper good-bye. Until I saw him the next day in Prague, of course. I knew I was being silly, but I couldn't help myself. It felt like I needed to say a good-bye to Italy-Nick, feeling certain that back in Prague I'd meet closed-book-Nick. I wasn't ready for that one.

But when the door to his bungalow opened, it was Charlie who stepped out. He locked the door behind him, and walked over to the flower pot where we had been instructed to leave the keys.

"Morning, Addic," he said. "Ready to head back?"

"Eh, I guess," I said. "Where's Nick?"

Charlie was already fishing around his pocket for a cigarette. "He went down already to reserve our seats on the train. These damn Eurail passes are such a pain." He shook his head as he lifted the lighter to his mouth, cupping his hand around the flame. "Shoulda just flown like you girls."

My heart sank. How could he have left without saying good-bye? It was a few minutes before I realized I had been blankly staring at Charlie without talking, and his cigarette was almost gone. He threw it on the floor and stepped on it, turning to walk down to the train.

Before he reached the trail, Charlie turned around to me. "Don't worry about it, Addie. You deserve someone who... you deserve exactly what you want. Don't worry about it."

And with that he started down the mountain.

Δ

The doors opened automatically for us, the harsh cold of the Czech air hitting us hard. When we had left for Italy, the warmer days of fall had also gone. The breeze couldn't hold back; winter was coming. The sun was gone and the cold evening stretched before us. It had been a long day of traveling and there was no more to say. Moments had been hashed over, kisses analyzed, inside jokes securing their place in our memories for years to come. Celeste, Lexie, and I walked to the bus in silence, me shrugging my backpack off. It landed on the concrete with a thud, right next to the bench at the bus stop. Between the bus, the metro, switching lines, and the bus again, it would be at least an hour before I'd be back at my apartment.

Lexie and Celeste talked about what to make for dinner for most of our first bus ride. I tuned them out, gazing out the window. I was already missing the taste of fresh pesto. No one would pour me a glass of house red when I got home. There was no homemade pasta waiting. There were many things to love about Prague, but the food was not one of them. It was always a faintly surreal feeling, coming back to Prague after being away. After a vacation, there's something about familiarity—your own bed, a home cooked meal, even an alarm clock in the morning—that is comforting. I did not know what I was going back to. An IKEA bed that had been mine for just two months now. A kitchen I would never cook in. And a friendship that had been potentially forever fucked up in Italy.

When the three of us parted ways at Můstek, I was ready for some alone time. I put my headphones on, looking for something comforting to listen to. I wished I'd had any of the songs Nick had put on one of our nightly playlists, but I didn't. Almost all of them I'd never heard of before, except for one Coldplay song. I had a few of their albums. As I scrolled down my iPod, looking through the album names, I figured one of the albums must have the Coldplay song. I started playing each song, one by one, remembering each of our nights together. The towel between us in Venice. Afternoon naps in Florence. The uncomfortable feeling and awkward silence that joined us in bed after the dance club. Our night together in Riomaggiore, Charlie in the next room.

If I was being honest, I knew it was going to happen. I knew, when I left for Italy, that I was leaving for something more than just a ten-day vacation. Those ten days had changed me. I'd been to Italy before, we'd left Prague before. But not like this. There was something about the sheer independence of it all, the six of us going where we felt and eating where we wanted. No itinerary. No plans. Not so much as a phone call in ten days. We had been off the grid, in the world, living it. In it. I had lived the moments I had come out here to live.

It was kind of an amazing thing, this semester. It had all happened so spontaneously, with no planning. It had come from a place of unhappiness and restlessness, and here I was. Meeting people who were changing me. Living with a level of independence I'd never felt before. I could feel the confidence in myself, in my own decisions growing each day. Though I had no idea what to expect in this semester away, it was turning out to be better than I had ever dreamed it would be.

The metro lurched to a stop at Anděl. I grabbed my backpack from between my legs and threw it onto my shoulders. I stood still on the escalator as it climbed up to street level. Just five bus stops, and then I'd be home. I was exhausted, ready to throw down my backpack for good and not share a bed with anyone. I had no clue if Emily or Alex were home—they'd be back from their trip to Spain by now—but I hoped not. I needed some time to be alone and process everything. I was starting to feel the emotion of the last ten days bubbling up.

I found a seat on the bus right by the door. It was a Monday night, and late enough that I could throw my backpack on the seat next to me guilt-free. Coldplay was still coming through my headphones. I let my head fall softly onto the window next to me and closed my eyes. The bus started with a rumble, and off we went, heading toward the seemingly endless series of twists and turns I could never understand how the bus fit through. At this late hour, the bus skipped the first stop, and then the second.

And then, I heard it. The song I'd been looking for, but had forgotten about until it started playing. I did have the Coldplay song Nicholas had put on our playlist. I turned it up, as loud as my ears could stand it, as the 137 approached my stop. I pulled the cord and rushed out the door, stumbling to the bus bench and tossing my backpack. I stared up at the sky as the words filled my ears. *Come on, oh my star is fading. And I see no chance of release.* Stars lit up the street around me. I was alone. There were no pedestrians, no friends, no ex-boyfriends, no parents. Just me, sitting on a bench at a bus stop in Prague Five. I had come all this way for this. I understood it now. I needed this space from everyone else to just be. To live. To experience. To breathe.

I thought back to something Nick had told me when we were in Florence, wandering through the Accademia. We'd stopped at Michelangelo's sculpture of David, as everyone does. "Did you know Michelangelo didn't think of himself as an artist?" Nick had whispered to me. "He felt he was more of a liberator. The figures themselves lived within the stone, and he just was the one to chisel the rock away to set them free." I felt as if this time had been my way of chiseling the rock away to free myself. I had felt it, months before, when I made the decision to come to Prague: that something was breaking in me. Perhaps it hadn't been a breaking, so much as an urge to break *out* that I had sensed and could now recognize. More rock chiseled away with each week here, and I knew that I wouldn't be free at the end of December when everyone else went home. It would take more work than that.

In that moment, I didn't care what happened with Nicholas. I understood that what I'd needed was to meet him and see that people like him existed in the world. That love wasn't something you settled for, something you compromised yourself to have. I could truly just be myself with someone else. I didn't have to be the person I had been expected to be. I needed to meet people like John, and learn not to take myself too seriously. My heart needed to know people like Celeste, who never gave up hoping, for anything, and who always had room in her heart for forgiveness. I needed to meet people like Lexie, people who were always cheery, who saw the best in everyone. *And I know, I'm dead on the surface, but I am screaming underneath. And I'm pushing you down, and all around, oh it's no cause for concern.* Tears fell down my cheeks as I looked up at the sky. I understood why I had left.

I also understood that the same Adriana would never return.

Δ

It was a regular day of class, which meant I only had one. Tuesdays was anthropology, one of my two classes with Nick. But when I showed up to class and took my normal seat, there was no Nicholas. I had assumed he'd be back by now, but wasn't sure what time his train arrived. Our midterm exams were handed back, and I was surprised to see I had actually passed mine with a B. Grades were the last thing from my mind, and as long as I was passing my classes, I wasn't concerned. Our professor pulled out a computer and centered it in the room, then walked to the front of the class and pulled down the projector screen. Today we'd be screening a documentary. We wouldn't be taking a break, but could leave as soon as the film was through.

I glanced at Nicholas's empty seat to my right. I was trying not to spend every moment thinking about him, but it wasn't working. The prospect of seeing him was the only reason I'd really been able to get to class that morning. I did not know what to expect, and wondered if we would go back to how things were before Italy. We had been close, of course, but not truthful about our feelings for each other. Just a few days prior, I had wanted it to be all or nothing, but after my moment of honesty with myself last night at the bus stop, I decided whatever it was would be fine. What could possibly happen after this semester, anyway? *At least we'd always have Italy,* I thought to myself.

After the documentary was over, I gathered my laptop and headed toward the EOO office to check my email for the first time since before we'd left for Italy.

Bara was seated at her desk, glasses pulled high over her nose. She peeked over her computer. "Adriana, hello, how was your holiday?"

"Hi, Bara! It was... wow, it was great, thank you. I'm sure you enjoyed a break from all of us for the week." I knew that Bara couldn't travel herself, having to stay close to the EOO office in case any of us needed her during break.

"Yes, it was quiet here for a change." She went back to typing, then stopped suddenly. "Also, when you can, you will tell me which apartment you want for next semester?"

I hadn't even started thinking about next semester. "I get to pick?"

"Yes, you and Mason pick. You do not pick your roommates but you pick your apartment." She looked at her computer screen again as I started daydreaming about which apartment I'd pick. Definitely not the one I was in. "Uh, your friends, they are back. They were just telling me about your journey," she said with a smile. I cocked my head to the side.

"Celeste and Lexie?" I asked.

Just then, I heard John's booming voice, yelling something in a thick German accent, apparently mimicking a train conductor. I walked into the next room and saw John and Nick sitting at the two desktop computers, talking across the room to Stephanie and Noelle and a tall, lanky guy holding Stephanie's hand.

"Hey, when did you make it back?" I tried to look at John, but my eyes could only stop on Nick.

"Hey, oh, you didn't hear the story?" John asked loudly.

Nicholas looked up from the computer, noticing me for the first time. He smiled at me and our eyes locked. John pressed on with his story of their train ride.

"So we were headed back to Prague through Zurich, which is like, of course, why wouldn't you go through Zurich from Italy, and this guy, he must've been like six foot..."

A grin spread across my face, eyes still on Nicholas. He smiled back, and I giggled. I couldn't help it. I walked over to the table to set my laptop up, knowing all was going to be right in our world.

"...and finally, we got something to eat, but there was only one vending machine, and we each ate, like, a cracker." John was still going with his story. Noelle was laughing at him. It was impossible not to laugh at him, the manner in which he spoke and told his stories. Telling stories was his thing. "So I'm starving. Anyone want to go get something to eat? Zanzi?" John stood up and logged off the computer.

"I really have to get caught up on emails, you know, tell my parents I'm still alive over here," I said. Noelle was collecting her bags to go with John.

"Yeah, I'll come," Nicholas said. He slid on his coat and pulled a beanie on, raising his eyebrows to me. "Talk later?"

"Of course," I said.

Stephanie threw me a look. I realized the guy holding her hand must have been her boyfriend. He had been planning on coming out for break, and apparently, she hadn't told him not to come like she'd wanted to. He pulled a guide book out and started to point something out to her that they should go see, and I looked away, opening my laptop.

I had thirty-six emails to read after deleting junk messages. My parents had both emailed me, a few times. A few from friends. Responding to emails, and sharing photos and highlights from the trip took a few hours, and by the time I was ready to get up and stretch my legs, I noticed Bara switching the lamp off on her desk. I peered out the window behind me and realized the sky had darkened. I packed up my laptop and grabbed my jacket, and walked out with Bara as she locked up the office for the night. Figuring everyone was probably still at

Zanzibar, I headed next door. I stopped by the bar to grab a drink, and said a quick hello to Charlie, who was chatting up one of the bartenders. John, Lexie, and Nick were sitting at our regular booth in the back, and I slid in next to Nick.

As usual, Lexie was mid-laugh, and John was animatedly telling a story, this one about the time he and the guys got stuck in Duisburg, Germany, on their way home from Amsterdam. My eyes immediately searched out Nick's. He smiled at me and grabbed my hand under the table. My heart settled, and the nerves I'd held since arriving back from Italy calmed. It was all going to be okay.

We spent the rest of the evening with pivo, laughing and talking as we always did, like nothing and everything had changed. After a few more rounds, I checked my phone and saw it was midnight.

"I'm gonna call it a night," I said, gathering up my bag. "I'm so wiped from all the travel."

Across the table, Lexie nodded. "Yeah, I'm about ready to go, too."

"Your place or mine tonight?" John asked, signaling to the bar for the check. I smiled. They were already in that place, and I loved it about them.

"Do you want me to go with you?" Nick asked me.

I shrugged, scooting out of our booth. "If you're ready to go, then yeah."

He slid out past me, moving me out of the way, his hands on my hips. "Let me go grab Charlie," he said.

I walked outside with Lexie and John into the cold night. Above us, the sky was dark with clouds. I wondered when we would start seeing snow here. Knowing the trams and bus schedule wouldn't line up and get me home in less than an hour, I decided to splurge for a cab. A minute later, the door to Zanzi opened behind me.

"I'm going to stay with Charlie a bit longer, he's not ready yet," Nick said, walking over to me.

"Okay." I nodded. "I just called a cab, it's fine."

John and Lexie were standing on the sidewalk next to me, also waiting for their cab. This time of night it was hard to get anywhere out of Malá Strana in under an hour.

"Hey guys. Night," Charlie called, peeking his head out of the door as well.

I waved, and started walking toward the corner, when Nick unexpectedly grabbed my hand. In one quick movement, he pulled me until my body was up against his and kissed me. I sunk into him immediately and kissed him back, before breaking away.

Sudden as it was, what shocked me most was that we'd never kissed in front of our friends. They knew about us, of course, but couldn't help reacting nonetheless.

"Yes!" John bellowed, and punched the air. Lexie whistled loudly, and Charlie slapped Nick's back as he blushed, stepping away from me.

It was perfect timing when the cab pulled up in front of the bar, and I hastily slid into the backseat.

"Text me when you get home," Nick said as he pushed my taxi door closed, and the taxi pulled away.

It was all I could do to stay awake on the drive back. I started thinking about the week ahead, going back to classes. It was such an easier transition, coming back to Prague from Italy. It wasn't quite like going back to the real world. It was our little fantasy bubble, this ancient city, our playground.

I'd finally pulled off my jeans and brushed my teeth when my phone buzzed on my desk. A text from Nick. *Did you make it home?* I smiled. *Just getting into bed,* I texted back. I walked into my bedroom. A new message from Nick popped up. *Haven't stopped thinking about you yet.*

I couldn't help but blush, alone in the dark of my room. I held my phone in my hand, unsure what to respond with. If he only knew that

I never, ever stopped thinking of him. Of what he had brought into my life, of what would happen now that we were more than friends. Of what would happen when we had to leave. And I drifted off to sleep, phone in hand, still thinking of Nicholas.

23

November, Prague.

Winter had arrived nearly overnight. The few weeks between our trip to Budapest and when we left for Italy, was apparently all of the fall that we would get in Prague. It snowed, gently but consistently, as soon as November arrived. Classes were once again in session, our last session before finals next month. Finals, and then the semester would be over: we would be going home. I'd worked it out with my parents that I would go home for Christmas, and then return before New Year's with my cousin Charlotte and her boyfriend. Spring semester didn't begin until the first weekend in February, so I'd have lots of time to kill. Mason would be here too, and Bara was going to make sure we could be in our apartments before the new students arrived. I was going to be moving into the Bazaar Apartment, where Celeste and Lexie lived now, and Mason was going to be very close to me at the Garden Apartment. We'd have each other for company.

Though I could feel the end nearing as we reached our second to last month in Prague, there was still so much more to go. Bara had planned another trip for us in the middle of November. We were taking another overnight train, this time to Krakow. It was going to be less fun, and more educational. She'd made arrangements for tours of Auschwitz and Birkenau, which none of us were necessarily looking forward to. Nothing about it screamed *fun weekend trip,* but I knew it wasn't something to be missed, and committed to going along with Lexie,

Charlie, and John. Both Celeste and Nicholas had visitors coming out that weekend and would be staying behind. Celeste was going to take a trip to Paris with her old college roommate, and Nick's mother was coming.

I was very curious about Nick's mom. I wanted to meet her, but knew we weren't in a place to introduce each other to parents. He had told us about her before, when talking about our families from time to time, and what I knew about her was that she was German and he loved her fiercely.

Nicholas and I still seemed to be teetering on the edge of something. After the night outside of Zanzibar, we hadn't kissed again, and I was beginning to wonder if there was something about being openly together that was holding Nick back. I wasn't looking forward to a weekend away from him, but knew it was going to be good for me. I packed up my weekend bag once again, shoving in as many scarves, hats, and gloves as it could hold, and lacing up my big winter boots. November in Poland. I shivered at the thought, and begrudgingly made my way to the bus stop. My roommates had gone to grab dinner before our train, but I had waited till the last possible minute to pack and planned to meet them at the station.

The leaves that once had dotted the sky and sidewalks red, orange, yellow, and gold were now dead and matted with snow. I stepped over them, crossing the street to the bus stop. Up ahead, I saw another person waiting for the bus.

"Hey," Nicholas said.

"What are you doing here?"

"I came to see you off."

I walked right into his arms. "Thank you."

"You're going to have a good time."

"Visiting concentration camps in the snow? Not likely."

He nodded. "Yeah, true."

I pulled away from his arms and we sat on the bench. "You can stay at my place this weekend if you want."

"Really?" I knew Nick wasn't looking forward to staying at Cozy alone, and it was further from the bus stop than my flat. The thought of him staying in my bed while I was gone was strangely comforting. "That would be kind of nice. I'm dying to get out of Cozy. Maybe I'll do that."

In the distance, I could hear the rumble of the 137 making its way up the hill from Farkáň. We both stood up from the bench and I turned to face Nick.

"Well..." I said, my voice trailing.

He kissed me on the forehead. "I'll miss you," he said shyly.

"I'll miss you too. But you'll have your mom here, you'll be busy."

The bus pulled over to the stop and groaned as the doors opened.

"Have fun," I said.

He held his hand up and waved as I climbed up the stairs, the doors closing noisily behind me.

Δ

It was 6 a.m. on Monday when our overnight train arrived from Krakow. Prague was still dark, just as we'd left it. The bitter cold and sadness we'd seen in Krakow had deflated everyone's moods, and we were all ready to climb into the comfort of our own flats. Alex and Emily both had classes, but I knew I would be able to go back home and sleep. I was so grateful for that.

Krakow had been a good distraction from Prague, and Nick. It was a heavy trip, and made for a lot of introspection. John, Charlie, Lexie, and I had enjoyed long talks over beer and Polish sausage, sharing pierogi and talking about the sadness we all felt, what we wanted in our lives and what made us happy. The four of us had shared a sleeper cabin on the way back and I'd stared at Lexie as she gazed out the window as we pulled into the now-familiar Hlavníi Nádražíí. I'd wondered if it was the last time we'd return to Prague as our home.

Alex, Emily, and I sleepily said our good-byes to the group and took the escalator down to the yellow line metro, heading toward Anděl. Alex and Emily found seats between locals on their way to work, and rested their heads on one another's shoulders, drifting off to sleep. I leaned my head against a pole and tried to stay awake enough to hear the name of each station called out over the loudspeaker.

As we left the metro behind and boarded the 137, I let my mind daydream. How perfect it would be if Nick really had stayed at my place while I was gone? Maybe he'd even still be sleeping in my bed now, and I could slide into bed right next to him and we could sleep there, together, like we had all those mornings in Italy. I missed that. There were no excuses for us to share beds at night anymore. I'd thought of him so much while I was in Poland, but something told me that the space had been good, necessary even.

We left the bus, and walked through the chilly morning air to our building in silence. As we made our way up the stairs and to our apartment door, Emily claimed the shower first. I didn't care, knowing I was going to go straight back to sleep.

I pushed the door open to my room, and instantly saw something was different. There were books and mugs around my bed, and a pair of pants crumpled up on the floor next to it. My face spread into a huge grin as I saw Nick, starting to stir in my bed with the noises now filling the apartment.

I gave him a warm smile as I set my backpack on the floor.

"I just missed you," he said.

I kicked my shoes off and climbed into bed with him, the weight and seriousness of the last few days melting away.

Δ

My descent into love with Nicholas came naturally, as if it were something we should have been doing the entire time. Every waking minute we could spare was spent together, whether it was just us or with Lexie, John, Celeste, and Charlie. We were inseparable, usually doing absolutely nothing together. We'd ditch class and ride the bus up the winding hill to spend afternoons huddled together on the couch. We'd watch old DVDs of *Friends* if it was really cold out, which it often was, or simply made cups of tea and lay in my small bed and talk. It was the simplest time together, and one I felt we needed after months of a complicated friendship. I wasn't sure exactly what had changed with Nick, but since I'd found him in my bed after returning from Poland, we'd been inseparable. Whether he wanted a relationship anymore or not, we were undoubtedly in one.

One evening, over the usual rounds of beer at Zanzibar, Nick turned to me. "Let's ditch class tomorrow," he said, with a devilish grin on his face.

"Really?" I asked. I was usually the bad influence, pulling him out the door of class if we arrived before our professor, or begging him on the tram to let us go to something *fun*, that we weren't really there just to *study*, that we had so many more important things to do than learn about *whatever*. Sometimes I'd win, but usually he dutifully pulled me to class.

"Yeah, we'll make a day of it. Something really fun. We'll spend the whole day together."

I smiled, and leaned in to kiss him.

We planned to meet for breakfast at Bohemia, and would make plans after. We each only had one class on Wednesdays, so I didn't feel too guilty for missing. Nick and I had done a lot of things together so far, things that normal couples don't do in the first month of dating, but one thing we hadn't done is go on an actual date. The prospect of an entire day-long date thrilled me.

317

It was a crisp November day, and I pulled a beanie out of my backpack as I walked to the bus stop. It was cool and cloudy, gloomy, even. But I felt anything but. I sat down on the cold metal bench, thankful for the partitions blocking the wind. Posters were plastered on the plastic walls, advertising things I couldn't understand. *Omezenou dobu, nabízejí se v naší úzké-out podnikání prodej! Support Lesbiens v koncertní večer, jen jeden víkend! Jen 100 vstupenek zůstává!* Occasionally there were signs for bands I knew, or clubs I'd visited, or movies I'd heard of. They were always peeling up at the corners, victims of obvious vandalism at the hand of a teenager in the neighborhood with a permanent marker. Even if it was a poster I'd never seen before, they always looked like they had been posted years ago.

"Hey," I called, seeing Nick round the corner toward the bus stop. I wasn't sure what our plan was for the day, but knew he could ask me to wait with him in a dentist's office all day and I would happily agree.

He greeted me with a kiss, his lips lingering longer than I'd normally let them at a bus stop. "Hey," he smiled at me. "Bohemia?"

I nodded, and within minutes our bus groaned down the hill. It was nearly lunchtime by the time we finally grabbed a booth by the window and sat down with our breakfasts.

"So what do you want to do?" Nick said between bites of his bagel. "Want to go see a movie? *The Illusionist* is out."

"No," I replied, taking a sip of my coffee. "I'm not really in a movie kind of mood. Want to go walk through Old Town?"

"Eh, it's a little too cold to just wander around outside. Hey, I have an idea. Want to check out that tea shop over by Můstek?"

I nodded. "That sounds perfect." The idea of staying warm in a tea shop, sipping tea with no agenda or distractions, sounded just like what I wanted to do.

We finished up our bagels and walked outside, jogging across the street, as the cold November wind blew against us. It had gotten bitterly cold in the hour we'd been inside the bagel shop, and I was beginning to wonder about what winter would be like here, in just a few short weeks, before we were to head home. I knew we still had a month left, but each day it started to feel closer and closer.

"...but I still feel like I'm closest to my younger sister. It's just always been that way, despite the whole 'twin' thing." Nick was talking about his family, and I quickly realized I'd completely stopped listening to him and dazed off.

Nick noticed that I hadn't said anything. "What's up?"

"What?" I was jolted back to Earth, back to the city, back to the cold streets of Prague Five.

"What were you thinking about?" Nick looked at me quizzically as we stepped up onto the tram toward Můstek.

"Oh, nothing." I shook my head, looking down at my feet. "Just about how we are going to be leaving soon. I've made such good friends here, and..."

The bell of the tram jingled, and we paused. A cold burst of air ripped through the car as the doors opened. We sat in silence. I realized Nick hadn't said anything.

"What?" I asked gingerly.

He turned to look me dead in the eye. "It's just that... sometimes I think you aren't honest with me."

I felt confused. Had I missed something? I felt lost, disoriented, like I wasn't really a part of this conversation at all.

"What are you talking about? How am I not honest with you?" I objected. I didn't even know what else to say.

"I just... I don't think you're honest about what you want from me. I don't think you just want to be friends." Finally, it came out. The subject we were, apparently, really talking about. I didn't even know it.

I simply stared. Who was this guy? Of course I just didn't want to be his friend. But what were my options? We couldn't stay together, since we only had one month left to live on the same continent, but we couldn't keep our hands off each other to maintain a friendship. Why was he bringing it up, and why right now? What sort of self-respecting guy wants to have an open and honest conversation about where his casual relationship is going? I had no answer to give him.

I weighed my options. "Okay, fair enough." If he was going to say he didn't think I was being honest, then fine, he could think that. But that didn't mean I had to tell him the truth. Apparently, I didn't have the great poker face I thought I had, but that didn't mean I had to show him my whole hand. I just had to hold my cards a bit closer to my chest, that was all.

The tram rounded a corner, and I felt Nick's body weight shift toward me. "So do you want to tell me the truth then?"

"Can we not talk about this?" I asked. What could I possibly say to him? I could tell him how I really felt. That I couldn't stop thinking about him, even when I was alone, that he had kissed me in ways I knew that no one would ever be able to kiss me again after we left each other, that he was even in my dreams, that I had already begun to miss him, even though we were still spending every day together. But what good would that do? Or, I could lie. I could tell him I did want to be just friends, that I like this friends-with-benefits thing we had going on. But the problem was, he clearly wasn't buying it, having already told me he didn't think I was being honest.

I moved my leg away from Nick's, quietly. I was determined not touch him, to let him feel my growing anxiety. I couldn't let myself get closer to him now that I could see where this was going.

But where was it going? Nick hadn't said he knew I wanted more from him, he didn't suggest that we should stop now before things got too intense, to the point of no return (which we had not yet come to, at least physically). I searched my short-term memory for the exact words he had used. All he had said was that he felt I wasn't being honest, which meant that maybe he really did want honesty from me. Perhaps it wouldn't be such a bad conversation to have, after all.

The tram leaned again, and my body eased softly toward Nick. I closed my eyes and inhaled deeply, smelling his cologne mixed with his natural, sweet smell before readjusting myself.

"Okay, I lied. I don't want to just be your friend," I blurted out.

His blue eyes flashed at me, and his lips quivered as if he weren't sure if he should smile or say something.

"But I don't want to be your fuckbuddy either," I said.

"Whoa, can you please not say 'fuckbuddy' on the tram like that?"

"Well, what do you want me to say? First you accuse me of lying, and now you don't want to hear the truth? I can't just shut up about it. I don't want to be your friend, I don't want to backtrack." I lowered my voice. "But I don't want to continue on like this, just being friends with benefits. But we also can't be any more than that. Don't you see the problem?"

He stared at me, seemingly content with my vomit of words and emotion all over him in this very public conversation.

"Besides," I continued. "It's not like you've been entirely honest with me. One week you're telling me you don't want a relationship, the next week I'm getting home from Krakow and we haven't left each other's side. This is a two-way street." I held my breath, waiting for him to respond.

Instead, Nick wrapped his arm entirely around me, his hand gripping my shoulder and pulling me into his chest. We looked at each other, his blues burning into my greens. And as the tram rocked and swayed the last block to Můstek, Nick kissed my forehead.

"Okay," he half-whispered in my ear. "I don't know what to say. I just didn't think I'd miss you so much."

We never spoke of it again. And I knew we didn't need to.

24

November, Prague.

Thanksgiving, of course, is not celebrated in the Czech Republic. The uniquely American holiday meant that we did not have Thanksgiving off from classes, but it felt odd to ignore it.

They didn't sell turkeys in Prague. Pilgrims, Native Americans, turkeys, pumpkin pies, afternoon naps, Macy's Day Parade, football games... We knew we wouldn't have a traditional American Thanksgiving. But this year more than any other, we all had very specific things to be thankful for.

The Bazaar girls were to host; the rest of our places were nearly inhospitable. Everyone was in charge of a different menu item. But, as we all found out relatively quickly, Thanksgiving items were not available outside of the States. Not only could no one find a turkey anywhere in Prague, but there had also been no boxed stuffing, no cranberry sauce, no canned pumpkin, and no sweet potatoes or yams. We definitely needed to improvise.

Some of us emailed family members at home and asked for immediate care packages; my Mom sent over canned pumpkin and mix for corn muffins (my offerings for the holiday), Nicholas's mother mailed boxes of stuffing, and we decided to strike the cranberries (they were there merely for tradition anyway; by a simple poll we found out no one actually ate cranberry sauce) and made a chicken instead of turkey. We could all do with regular mashed-by-hand potatoes. We could really splurge on our favorites—we would even purchase some fancy wine for the occasion. Nicholas insisted on the Beaujelais Nouveau. Because we still had classes, we picked the weekend before Thanksgiving to host our Fakesgiving.

We'd all picked one thing to contribute to our makeshift Thanksgiving dinner, and, against my wishes, Nicholas suggested that we head to the Tesco, because it was the only store that had even a few international food items. I hated Tesco. It was by far the worst place I had visited in all of Eastern Europe, and that includes some extremely questionable beer halls and herna non-stops. It was always crowded with people who seemed extremely harried and upset about things; I usually assumed everyone inside was extremely upset that they had to be shopping at Tesco just like I was. Everyone was rude and pushy, and the people inside seemed to hate me more than words could explain for not speaking Czech. Once I had made the mistake of getting into a line, with lots of people behind me, where it was cash only and I had not seen the sign. The clerk merely shook her head furiously when I handed over my Visa; the Tesco shoppers in line behind me shouted various things in Czech (which sounds a lot like Russian—mean and angry—when shouted) and it was all I could do to not run out of the store crying. I had always hated shopping in large bargain stores like that, the panicky feeling of the masses of people, overcoming the thrill of getting a good deal.

But off to Tesco we went. Once we stepped off the 12 tram at Národni třida, and fought our way through the crowds of people getting on or off the public transport, I grabbed Nicholas by his arm and pulled him to the side.

"Okay Nick, do you have all the krowns you need?" I asked very seriously.

"They take cards here," he said, somewhat confused.

"Yes, in some lanes. But sometimes you get into a lane where they don't take cards and you won't know it until it's too late," I warned.

"Well, I think we'll be fine," he laughed, kissed me on the forehead, and grabbed my hand to pull me inside. As we pushed against the crowds fighting to get inside the seven-floor mega store, I could feel the small round spot on my forehead, where he kissed me, grow cold from his saliva hitting the freezing air. We took the stairs past the first level of drugstore items and down to the grocery level, which for reasons I'll never understand, was in the basement.

"Don't let go of my hand," I whispered feverishly into his ear. He reached for a red plastic basket, moving the one on top that had some sort of mysterious, brown sticky substance, and heading all the way to the left as we braved the aisles.

"Okay, first up... sugar. These girls don't fucking have sugar in their apartment? Does it have to be brown sugar for their pies? What is 'sugar' in Czech anyway?" Nicholas seemed a bit exasperated that he was now in charge of the shopping list, since the crowds and pressures of Tesco had rendered me helpless.

"*Cukr*," I replied, barely audible over the people pushing and shoving and speaking so loudly in the same aisle as us.

"Okay, cukr, cukr, cukr. Here's some. Okay, let's see if we can find frozen pie crusts. Czechs eat pie, don't they?" he asked.

But I wasn't listening. I was looking at the woman next to me. Heavyset with bright reddish-purple hair, she was picking up every single bottle of pickled herring she could find, which for some reason was in the same aisle as our cukr. She grabbed one glass bottle and held it up to the light, apparently examining the contents inside for God knows what. And then I watched in horror as she didn't even bother to see if anyone was watching her before she opened the top of the bottle, the safety and air-tight seal button making a faint *pop* sound that was audible to me, a few feet away. She put her head down and immersed her nose in the glass jar, inhaling deeply. Apparently, whatever she smelled wasn't good enough for her ever-so-high standards of pickled, room-temperature, wet, jellied fish. She replaced the jar on the shelf and grabbed another jar down, repeating the process. I couldn't take my eyes off of her.

"Adriana!" Nicholas shouted. "Come on!" He yanked my arm hard, leading me to the frozen food section.

There were many things I had never seen before, and many things I had never seen *frozen* before, but we searched for pie crusts. We found them and fought our way through the crowds, obtaining nearly everything else on our list plus a few shitty bottles of Moravian wine to drink, after we had gotten through the good stuff and our taste buds didn't know the difference. We made our way to the register, Nicholas still holding my hand tightly. There were two people in front of us, being arguably normal, waiting for their turn to pay, and finally be free of this seventh circle of hell. Nicholas unloaded our items onto the mini-conveyor belt and flipped through a Czech magazine in front of me, finally dropping my hand while I people watched-around us. *I suppose it's not that bad here*, I thought. *People are just grocery shopping. Everyone has to eat, right?* And then a man came up right behind me.

He was pushing a cart filled with items. At first glance, nothing made this man stand out from any other person shopping. But I was not one to dismiss someone with one glance, and studied him carefully as he started unloading groceries onto the conveyor belt. The short, stumpy, bald old man unloaded a raw chicken wrapped loosely in plastic onto the belt and reached down to grab more items. Another raw chicken was placed onto the belt. Then another. And another. And another. This man's shopping cart was absolutely full of raw chickens. Panic started appearing inside me like goosebumps, one small bump at a time until my body was nearly shaking.

I poked Nicholas. No response. I poked again, harder.

"What's up?" he said jauntily. I said nothing, just pointed to Serial Killer Raw Chicken Man behind me. He shrugged. "So?"

"So?" I whisper-hissed. "He could be a serial killer!"

"Why would buying strangely large amounts of chicken make him a serial killer?" Nicholas looked at me confused, a wry smile appearing on his face.

"I don't know but it's weird and creepy! What the fuck does he need all of those chickens for? I don't know! Maybe he as some sort of weird fetish!" My face was absolutely panic-stricken.

"Adriana, it's weird, I'll give you that. But it isn't creepy and he isn't a murderer."

I was not convinced. I edged closer to Nicholas while the murderer continued to unload chickens onto the conveyor belt. After a strangely long amount of time, he finally realized I was staring at him. The man looked up at me with tired, gray eyes, and met my horrified gaze. We started at each other for a while before he mumbled something in Czech and reached into his cart for the rest of the chickens.

I fucking hated Tesco.

The sun was bright on Fakesgiving morning. There was much to be done and not a whole lot of time; I was in charge of the pumpkin pies, but with only one oven we had to time the baking just right. I got dressed in my holiday best that I had packed, and met up with Nicholas.

The afternoon and Fakesgiving preparations went off without a hitch. John mashed the potatoes, Noelle stuffed the chicken, Nicholas mixed the stuffing, and I baked the pies. We all had wine while we cooked, and John and Nicholas sat in the living room watching my Friends DVDs, while us girls set the table and talked. I had never really been a part of Thanksgiving before; I had always been young enough to get away with just showing up at Mom's, and if I was with Dad in New York, I didn't need to cook. I really enjoyed not only being a part of putting together the Fakesgiving meal, but also preparing such a crucial piece as dessert.

We all sat down around the table and served the potatoes, chicken, and stuffing. Other than one potluck dinner early in the semester, we hadn't really had a good home-cooked meal throughout the entire semester. We passed the bottles of wine around the table, everyone filling their glass to the top.

"At my family's Thanksgiving, we always do the thing where we all go around and say something we are thankful for," I suggested. Everyone nodded and joyfully agreed.

"Oh, I love that idea!" Lexie said from the other end of the table. "Addie, you should start."

"Okay, well that's easy. I am thankful for this semester. I'm thankful for everyone at this table." Although I hadn't thought that I would, I choked up. The words began to get caught in my throat, and my eyes filled with tears at the thought of the words leaving my lips. "I am thankful that I have met every single person here, that you were all brought into my life for different reasons, that these past few months I have shared the happiest moments of my life with you. I'm am very thankful today, for the best Thanksgiving—whether it's fake or not—that I have ever had." As soon as I had said it all, I realized it was true. While of course I knew how happy I had been over the past few months, and how much everyone had meant to me, saying the words out loud gave them a profound meaning. My heart began to sink. *This will be the only holiday I ever get to spend with Nicholas, our first and our last.* It truly was the best Thanksgiving I could ever have imagined.

Celeste and Lexie got teary and choked up as well, Noelle let out a small "awwwwwwwww" from the other end of the table. Nicholas grabbed my hand underneath the table and squeezed it. I wondered if he had heard my thoughts about our only holiday together, if it had been so loud inside my heart, that his heart heard it as well.

One after another, everyone shared their thoughts of thankfulness, and then we dove in to our meal, sharing our first and last holiday together.

25

November, Vienna.

My phone buzzed on my desk. I ran from the kitchen, grabbing it just in time.

"Yeah?"

"Did you make it back yet?" Nick asked.

"Yep, I'm upstairs now. How'd it go?"

I could hear him smile. "Come see for yourself."

I threw the phone down on my bed and made my way over to the sliding glass door of my balcony. I felt the cold air in my lungs first, as I slid the door open and stepped outside.

"Oh, my gosh, it's heeeeeere!" I squealed down to the street.

Nick had pulled up outside the apartment building, a small, emerald green sedan pulled over on the side of the road. He stood outside the driver's side, door still ajar. "I just drove. Here. From Old Town. Can you believe that? I haven't driven a car in months."

I smiled down at him. "Did it feel strange?" I called down to him. Something about the city, the cobblestoned streets and the medieval cathedrals, didn't seem conducive to driving. It was a dichotomy, the strangest marriage of old and new: cars on bridges that once held horse-drawn carriages. There was too much beauty to be distracted by to drive through Prague. And with the strange street signs that were meaningless to us as English speakers, I imagined there would be a lot of guesswork in the traffic laws.

Nick stepped onto the doorframe of the car and leaned over the roof, spreading his arms, giving the machine a huge hug. "It was amazing." His head popped back up as he looked at me. "Do you have your shit packed yet? Let's go."

I wasn't sure whose idea it had been to take a road trip, but the idea had snowballed quickly. It was our last European hoorah, before we came back to Prague for the last wind-down, of packing and finals. A long weekend was enough travel time, and after looking at rental cars for a few days, we quickly came up with an itinerary: southwest to Vienna, then cross into Slovakia for a night's stop in Bratislava, and head back to Prague. If we had time, we figured we could stop in Brno. The car gave us too much freedom, we realized, after months of sticking to train schedules. Celeste had a cousin visiting from the States, and Charlie wasn't interested in the road trip. But as we planned in the EOO office, Noelle managed to invite herself along with Nick, John, Lexie, and me. Noelle broke some of the couple's tension, despite the fact that the four of us were most definitely split into couples. With Noelle along, the weekend wouldn't feel like a long double date. Our plan was to drive to Lexie and Noelle's flat, where John was also waiting, and leave from there.

It was only five hours to Vienna from Prague. Nick offered to drive the first shift and John rode shotgun. John had dug up a CD for us to listen to and was taking his role as DJ very seriously. We were crammed in the back, and I squeezed in the middle between Lexie and Noelle. I felt like I had a front row view to the winding streets of Old Town.

There was no internet on our phones, no GPS or Google Maps. Whoever was in front acted as navigator, holding the map and plotting out which highway we were to get on. Though he was doing a fine job selecting nineties pop for us to listen to, John was famously bad with a map. After our third turn around Wenceslas Square, it was getting less funny and our patience was starting to wane.

"Okay, now make a right up here after the Albert," John said, pointing out the window.

"Doesn't that just take us back to Wenceslas Square?" Noelle piped up.

I turned to Lexie and raised my eyebrows.

"Okay, that's it," she said. She reached over into the front seat and grabbed the map out of John's hands. She spread it out and Noelle quickly turned to inspect where we needed to go.

With a couple more twists and wrong turns, it was another hour before we finally left Prague. Once we were out of the city, the route seemed much more straightforward. John turned the music up loud, and we sang and laughed until we got to the Austrian border.

Noelle had invited herself along with us, because an exchange student that had stayed with her family, lived in Vienna. They'd stayed in contact over the years, and she wanted to pay him a visit. Noelle had arranged for him to meet us upon our arrival in Vienna, and he'd show us a few of his favorite pubs.

We had booked a hotel at the last minute. The holidays were a peak time to visit Vienna, and prices were sky-high by our cheap college-budget standards. We'd finally selected an Ibis Hotel that was centrally located, had parking included (an extreme rarity in European hotels), and found a room that had two full-size beds. The five of us were splitting it, but as far as the hotel knew, there were only two people in the room. Each couple would share a bed, and we figured we'd create a makeshift bed for Noelle.

It was after ten o'clock when Nick finally pulled the car into the parking garage underneath the hotel. John and Lexie went up with their bags to check into the hotel, saying they'd text one of us after with the room number to meet them.

I stretched out in the backseat, leaving one door open to let my legs hang out. Noelle was walking laps to move her legs. After a few minutes, Nick walked around to the open door.

"Scoot over," he said, pushing my legs toward the back.

I sucked my belly in, flattening my body as much as I could, making room for him in the backseat. He lay down next to me on his side, facing me, his elbow on the seat to prop up his head.

"I still can't believe we drove here," I laughed. It felt strange to be in a car, in a parking garage. It all felt so normal, except for being in Austria.

"I'm a pretty fantastic driver, wouldn't you say?"

I nodded. "If you say so."

"What does that mean?" His mouth opened with faux outrage.

"You drive like you're from LA." I smiled. I knew it would get to him.

He tickled me, his fingers sticking between my ribs. "How would you know anything about how people from LA drive?"

My legs curled up to my chest as a reflex, and I laughed until tears started to fill my eyes.

"Do you think you guys could cool it for like five minutes?" Noelle said sharply from outside the car.

"What's your deal?" I called to her.

Nick rolled his eyes to me.

"You and Nick, and John and Lex. I'm surrounded by couples."

I could tell by the tone of her voice she was vying for attention.

"Well, you knew who was going on the trip when you signed up," Nick reminded her.

"I'm going to go on a walk," she said huffily.

"In a parking garage?" I looked at her as she walked away.

Nick and I lay back down in the back of the car, holding hands, kissing, and talking about Thanksgivings we'd had with our families. It felt strange to think that back home, at this time, our families were just waking up to put turkeys in the oven, as we lay in the back of a car in a parking garage.

About fifteen minutes later, Nick's phone buzzed with the room number from John. We called for Noelle to come back to the car, which she did, grumpily. We grabbed our bags from the trunk of the car and headed up to the room.

The hotel room was small, but comfortable. John and Lexie had claimed the bed closest to the door. Nick and I threw our bags on the other bed closer to the window. Under the windows overlooking the street was a nice padded window seat, nearly the length of a twin-size bed and just a hair narrower. We found some extra pillows and blankets in the closet, and within minutes Noelle had a bed of her own.

We took turns using the bathroom and cleaning ourselves up before Noelle announced that her friend, Hans, was coming to meet us outside our hotel in fifteen minutes. Hats and scarves were thrown on, and we all went down to meet Hans and have him show us the nearest bar. He was waiting for us outside, and as soon as Noelle introduced him to us, her attitude improved.

Hans was at least a foot taller than Noelle, and towered over John, the tallest among us. He had dirty blond hair and a football player's build, and spoke with a very strong accent. Hans and Noelle walked in front of our group, and the rest of us followed. His gait was swift, and every so often, Noelle broke to into a slow jog to keep up with him leading the way.

The pub he led us to was just four blocks over from our hotel. We'd all underestimated the cold, and my brown corduroy jacket wasn't cutting it. I pulled my scarf tighter around my neck, and reached into my pockets to find my gloves. Next to me, Nick was blowing on his hands to keep them warm. He looked at me with rosy cheeks, and held his arm out for me to come walk next to him. His body heat didn't help much, but I didn't give it up. We walked the last two blocks huddled close together, taking in the sights. Around us, the city was adorned with lights. Snowflake lights hung over the streets, stretched between buildings. The smell of cinnamon and roasted nuts permeated the air, though we were nowhere near the famed Christmas market.

We followed Hans into the pub, and inside it was warm and inviting. A fireplace burned bright in the middle of the pub, the warmth radiating out from the flames in all directions. Hans waved to a bartender who pointed to a table near the windows, where we could people-watch. The glass was speckled with frost on the outside, and dotted with condensation from the humidity inside.

The bartender walked over to our table and jovially greeted Hans, who stood up and gave the man a hug. They conversed in German for a moment, before Hans introduced Noelle. She shook the bartender's hand, and turned around to introduce us all before Hans cut her off in German. He motioned to the table and the bartender shook his head rapidly, then turned around and walked off.

"He will bring us some beer and eat," Hans announced to us.

We looked at each other quizzically.

"He brings the best eat," he explained again.

We all pulled out barstools and sat down, nodding our thanks. A few minutes later, the stout bartender came back to our table with a tray of steins, overflowing with beer, forming a puddle on the tray beneath them. As was traditional, the beer was served just a bit colder than room temperature, and in heavy, thick glass mugs.

"*Na zdraví!*" Lexie, John, Noelle, Nick, and I put our glasses together in the middle of the table.

"This is Czech way?" Hans asked, holding his glass out.

"First you clink the top of the mug, then the bottom," I explained.

Beer splashed onto the table as we pushed the tops, then bottoms of our mugs together.

"Then tap it on the table, like this," Lexie continued, as we all hit the table with the bottoms of our mugs.

"Then drink!" John finished, as we all lifted our mugs to our lips.

Hans laughed, a big, booming, laugh.

"Yes, this!" he exclaimed, and then insisted we do it again.

Again and again we smashed our mugs together, each *Na zdraví!* louder than the one before. We were already on our third round before the food that Hans had ordered for us arrived. Heaping plates of spaetzle, pork schnitzel, and fried potatoes were set on the table, along with seasonal roasted vegetables. We dug in, starved from our journey, not having eaten since we were back in Prague. Hans stayed with us through dinner and then excused himself to go meet some friends in another corner of the pub.

We were among the last of the bar-goers to leave after one in the morning as we slowly walked back to our hotel. By the time we finally ventured outside, the cold was a welcome relief from the stuffiness of the pub. The walk back took much longer, with John having Lexie ride on his back, stopping frequently to adjust her. When we finally arrived back at our hotel room, no one cared that we were sharing a small room with even smaller beds. It was a warm and comfortable place to sleep, and sleep we did as soon as our heads hit the pillows.

Δ

It was just after five, but dark had descended upon the city. The cold reached over the necks of our sweaters, under the tops of our hats, into the fingers of our gloves. It was visible in little crystals of ice that sat on lamp posts, fences, and statues we passed as we quickly made our way toward Rathausplatz. Noelle insisted on stopping in every Starbucks we passed—there were none in Prague—"just to warm up," she'd reiterate before standing in line again, ordering her favorite sugary coffee in a mix of poorly pronounced German and English.

We spent the day wandering the city without too much of a plan, as usual, making our way past the State Opera House and silently through Saint Stephen's Cathedral. After a stop for lunch and beer, we visited Schoenbrunn Palace, lingering at the little Christmas market outside. Among Europe's Christmas markets, Vienna had the best reputation by far. A dozen were set up, scattered throughout the city, the little wooden shops lit up with lights and gifts and local foods, begging to be sampled. The whole city smelled of sweet roasted nuts, and warm cups were handed out to gloved passersby as Christmas music filled the streets. At night, the crowned jewel of Christmas markets was at Rathausplatz, and we were not going to miss the lighted spectacle, no matter the temperature. I could hear Lexie and John laughing behind us, lagging as John would stop to make Lexie laugh in any way he could.

It was my first visit to a Christmas market, and I was enchanted with the idea. Anticipation filled each step on the sidewalk. Christmas was my favorite time of the year. My family had what I was certain were the best Christmas traditions of any family, anywhere, and I looked forward to them with more joy each year.

With my grandparents on each side split between two states, for as long as I could remember we had switched off Christmases. One with my mom's parents in Colorado, the next with my dad's parents in New York. It was always a wonderful time, but the magic that filled Nanny and Pop's home in December was something I couldn't describe and I hated to miss. Plastic holly came out by the trash bag full, the same pre-decorated tree set up in the same corner of the apartment, with decades-old glass candy canes hung and gold ribbon strung abundantly. The same tree skirt wrapped around the base, with red felt that caught every rogue piece of glitter from the ornaments above, and a white fur trim. It was wonderfully familiar. Though it was all the same every single year, it was never boring.

Christmas Eve was always held at my great-grandmother's home, downstairs from Nanny and Pop's apartment. Her home filled with all of the people alive because of her—her three daughters, who had all married (which included Nanny and Pop); her grandchildren (eight of them); and their children. The total number of people for our "family dinner" was around thirty, the number growing each year when new babies joined the family. Close family friends who had nowhere else to go also came, usually my godmother's friends who were given the honorary titles of *Aunt* and *Uncle*.

Old Roman Catholic tradition had dictated no meat on Christmas Eve, so we celebrated the Feast of the Seven Fishes. The women of the family would fill the kitchen, ran by my godmother, who shouted instructions to aunts and grandmothers who made use of the kitchens upstairs and in the basement. Wine bottles would make their way into the kitchen only to be returned empty, and as cooking neared its end, songs and laughter could be heard from anywhere in the home.

After we all would sit down to eat, crammed in every corner of the apartment where a person could fit, it was time for presents. Despite the number of us, Uncle Franco made a show of handing out presents one by one. He'd don his Santa hat and stand in front of the tree with a tambourine, Charlotte by his side as his elf. She'd hand him a gift, and Uncle Franco would shout it out. "Jack!" He'd shake his hand and toss the present to Dad, as family would clap and cheer.

The gifts would be placed at each person's feet, everyone accumulating their own little pile of Christmas presents. Only when the last gift had been handed out, did we open them, all at once. The tearing of wrapping paper was all that would be heard, followed by *ooohs* and *ahhhs* and squeals of joy. People would step over one another to hug one another, kissing on the cheek. Great-grandchildren would bring toys into the hallway to share, parents looking everywhere for batteries.

It was the energy of the house that I loved the most. The bustling of people with plates. The front door opening every few minutes, more uncles and aunts and cousins pouring in with packages stacked up high in their arms. You wouldn't be able to move in the apartment without bumping into someone else. Someone who cared about you, who wanted to kiss you and hear about school. My father's contagious laughter could be heard from any of the apartments. The basement was always the gathering place for those of us who needed a drink—the tequila bottle always stashed in the same place.

When the mayhem had died down and the last of the wrapping paper had been shoved into a trash bag, coffee was brewed. Plates of sugary, colorful cookies would be set out along with Panettone, saucers of cream sloshing over the sides on their way to the table. As everyone had settled down, at the table and on the couches, children on parents laps or playing together on the floor, my uncle—Charlotte and Kim's dad—would read a poem. Every year it was a spoof on *'Twas the Night Before Christmas*, written about the various goings on in our family from that year. One year, it included how my godmother was dating a guy in Pittsburgh and had toyed with the idea of spending Christmas with him in Pennsylvania, leaving all of us to fend for ourselves in the kitchen. The goings-on of each year, written in rhyme, each line eliciting more laughter than the one before.

After the last cookie crumbs had been picked off the plates, coats would be found. Gloves would come out and hats straightened. Carpools would be configured to Midnight Mass, the younger children staying at the house with Pop, the only adult excused from Mass. James and I would sleep in Nanny and Pop's bed, while my cousins retreated to their own homes. Once I was in college, I was allowed to attend Mass with the adults, and James, Kimberly, Charlotte, and I always sat in our own pew. We'd get the giggles during the service sometimes, and others we'd hold hands and get teary, overcome with the emotion of the *Ave Maria*.

I still felt the emotion of the holidays far more than any other time of year, every feeling magnified at Christmas. The joy of family, the pain of my parents being apart, all so big inside my heart it felt as if it would burst. This Christmas would be no different. Our first Christmas without Pop, but the first with my parents together once again. James had emailed me a few days before, reporting that Mom was flying out to New York with us to spend Christmas there. I wanted to look forward to it all so badly, but all I could feel was a knot in my gut as I looked toward the end of the semester. It was too much for me to think about Christmas without Nicholas, knowing we would have said our good-byes by then.

Ahead of us, the Christmas market came into view. We had walked right into a real-life snow globe. At least a hundred wooden shops were assembled, rooftops covered in snow. Austrians and visitors alike filled the walkways between shops, lingering at shopping stalls, enjoying the Christmas music coming from a band I could not yet see. The windows of the church up ahead had been converted into an advent calendar, each window alight with the number of days until Christmas. Bright white lights on blue backgrounds showed us there was less than twenty days to go. Round white lights were strung above us and around each wooden shop, giving everything a warm glow. A Christmas tree to rival Rockefeller Center's stood in the middle of it all, every branch glimmering with lights. I noticed there weren't any ornaments on the tree, yet the lights were all it needed with the festive Christmas scene around it.

We walked past a nativity scene reenactment, hay swishing underneath our boots. Somehow, Noelle had already found a giant gingerbread Christmas cookie and was happily munching on it ahead of us. Up ahead, I saw a stand with CDs laid across the front, and I stopped to browse. I didn't recognize most of the names, but out of the corner of my eye, I saw Frank Sinatra's familiar face.

"Look!" I exclaimed, picking it up and spinning around to show Nick. "Christmas music for the ride home," I said, reaching for my wallet. The price tag said ten euro. I handed the merchant a twenty and waited for my change.

John and Lexie had nearly disappeared into the crowd, Lexie pulling John toward a booth across the way that housed nesting dolls.

Nick had pulled his turtleneck sweater up over his mouth and nose, so just his eyes were visible.

"What are you doing?" I laughed.

"It's fucking cold!" I could almost hear Nick's teeth chattering.

"How am I supposed to kiss you like that?" I smiled up at him.

Nick pulled his turtleneck back down below his chin. His gloved hand reached up below my chin, tilting it toward his face. His lips were cold, his breath hot. "All you had to do was ask." He grinned at me mischievously. His hand dipped back down again, searching for mine.

Through the rows we wandered, passing some stalls, pausing to linger at others. One stand sold hand-poured beeswax candles, in varying shapes. Each shape had a different scent. Pine, lavender, honey, rose... We stopped and smelled them all before making our way to the next stand. The scent of freshly baked pretzels and spices of mulled wine greeted us. Another stand boasted hand-carved ornaments depicting different Christmas characters. Nick picked out a gold necklace for his one of his sisters, and I found a beer stein for James. For at least an hour, we ambled through the snowy walkways, laughing and admiring the local crafts.

"I'm frozen," Lexie called across the walkway to us. She and John had reappeared just a few shops down.

"You guys want to grab something to eat?" John asked.

My stomach had been growling for a while now. "Yes, please!"

Noelle pulled out her map. "There's a pub not far from here that Hans recommended," she said, and lead the way.

Snow crunched under our feet for a few blocks before we arrived at the pub a few blocks down. A small, wooden sign hung above the door and candles flickered in the window. It looked like a locals-only spot, and as we opened the door, we were greeted by a fire burning in the back corner. We grabbed the table nearest to the welcoming fire and sat, savoring the heat. We spent the next few hours eating, drinking, and sharing Christmas memories.

It was late when we crammed back into our hotel room. We took turns in the bathroom, pulling on pajamas and washing the day off our faces. After everyone was finished, I pulled my laptop out.

"A little Sinatra, anyone?" I waved the CD I had purchased from the Christmas market earlier in the evening.

"Yeah, I could go for some carols," John said. Noelle and Nick agreed, and I loaded the disc into my laptop and laid it on the floor between the two twin beds. Nick hit the lights as Sinatra began crooning.

I'm dreaming of a white Christmas...

John and Lexie settled into their bed, John singing along with Sinatra. Noelle was laying on her couch bed, reading the paperback she'd brought along for the trip. I sat on the floor in front of my laptop. It was the first Christmas carol I'd heard all year. Mom had always started the season off with The Carpenters, the gold standard of Christmas carols, but this year was going to be a little different. Sinatra's voice instantly made me feel at home and melancholy, all at once.

"Are you coming up here?" I felt Nick's hand on the back of my head, stroking my hair. I felt warmth spread through my shoulders as his hand made its way to the back of my neck, rubbing it softly.

I climbed up into the bed with him.

Sinatra made his way through the Christmas carols, one fading into the next, the album apparently a recording of a one-time radio special. About halfway through "O Little Town of Bethlehem," Noelle's light clicked off.

My mind wandered. How could it already be Christmastime? Didn't I just arrive in Prague? It seemed like just a week or two ago I was on the Charles Bridge with Mom and Dad, watching them make their wish to return to Prague. I drifted back to everything that had happened since then. That kiss at the five-story club. Budapest and the stars. Nick's epic birthday party. Meeting the guys on the bridge in Venice. My steamy night with Nick in Rome. Coming home from Poland to what I never thought I'd find. It was happening so much faster than I ever thought it would. I was learning more about myself with each new experience. What would happen to me, inside of me, when our adventure was over? It was now less than a month until we all started to fly home, one by one. When each one of my new friends left, they would take a piece of me home with them, replacing it with a piece of themselves. I closed my eyes, not ready to think about leaving. Especially not what it meant for me and Nick.

"*Merry Christmas*," Sinatra's voice cracked over my laptop speaker as the last carol ended.

"Merry Christmas, Frank," I whispered. But it sounded much louder than a whisper. Noelle, John, Lexie, and Nick had all said the same thing at the same moment, and laughter echoed through the room immediately. Smiling, I rolled onto my side, turning into Nick. He kissed my forehead and pulled the covers up.

"Merry Christmas, Addie," he said before closing his eyes.

"Merry Christmas, Nick," I replied softly, kissing his cheek.

I continued to stare at him. His light brown hair fell over his forehead. It needed to be cut, he kept saying, but I liked it long. His eyes fluttered as he fell into sleep. I couldn't close my eyes. The freckles that dotted his nose and cheeks were staring at me. I didn't have enough time. I hadn't counted them all. I didn't know what his favorite Christmas memory was, or what his favorite gift of all time had been. I hadn't heard his favorite Christmas carol or heard about when he stopped believing in Santa. *All I want for Christmas*, I thought, unable to finish the thought. My eyes filled with tears. I was nowhere near ready to be done with this semester, this adventure, this relationship that was just beginning to bloom. I was falling for him, fast, unable to stop myself. It was in the way he grabbed my hand when we ran across the street. The way he told me what he was thinking, all of the time. It was in the impatience of his kisses. The way he seemingly knew everything, from soccer players to Austrian history. The way none of my ideas were stupid, and what I had to say was always important to him. He was the most interesting person I had ever met, and it just wasn't enough time. We had hardly scratched the surface.

The hum of my laptop silenced as the battery died. Noelle was softly snoring from her makeshift bed. Soft whispers were coming from Lexie and John's bed next to mine and Nick's. I matched my breathing to Nick's to quiet my mind and let sleep wash over me.

26

November, Bratislava.

It was 10 a.m. by the time we were up and out of our hotel. John headed to check out, keeping up the appearance of just two occupants in the room, while Nick went to get the car.

Noelle, Lexie, and I once again stopped at Starbucks at Noelle's insistence. Snow had fallen overnight, making Vienna look like even more of a winter wonderland. The snow crunched under our feet as we walked down the block. It magnified the sun overhead, making it beautifully bright outside. It made me think of Colorado.

Inside, the coffee shop was bustling. Noelle stood in the back of the line and pointed over to a corner table and chairs, and Lexie and I walked over to save them.

I sunk back into an overstuffed chair, letting my head lean back against the headrest.

"Bratislava," I sighed.

Lexie fell into the chair next to me. "Yep. I really have no idea what to expect. I don't know anything about it."

I shook my head. "Me neither. The only thing I know, is that Nick and I will have a room alone—" I stopped. The moment we booked the hotel, I knew what was coming. There were only two rooms—one with one big bed for two, one with one big bed for two and a twin bed for another. It had been easy to sidestep the issue in Vienna where all five of us crammed into one room. But the moment Nick volunteered us for the solo room, it was inevitable. From the corner of my eye, I saw Noelle waving her hands, trying to get our attention. "Just coffee," I called to her.

Lexie's head had whipped in my direction. "What do you mean?"

"I mean, a night alone, in a hotel..."

Her jaw dropped. "You guys haven't had sex?" Her voice dropped to a whisper at the last word.

I shook my head. "No. There was one night we almost... but no, not yet."

Nick and I had only spent one night alone since Italy. Though we were very openly together around other people, we were careful not to cross any lines physically when we were alone. In all our lazy afternoons in my apartment, all the nights after bars we'd gone home on the bus together, all the time we'd spent kissing on the metro and missing our stops, we had stopped short of having sex. It was a very conscious decision by us not to take that step.

There had been one night after an evening spent laughing for hours in a smoky pub, sharing too many pints of pilsner. We'd gone home to Cozy house together, stumbling into Nick's room in the dark, falling onto his bed in laughter. Clothes had come off piece by piece, without discussing the consequences. It wasn't until everything had been shed between us, and he was on top of me, that we saw it in each other's eyes. *I'm not ready,* I'd said. *I don't want it to be like this,* he'd agreed. And we'd reached for his iPod, with its familiar playlists, and held each other in the twin bed until we drifted off to sleep. The next morning we were hungover, shy, but grateful. It hadn't been right. But now, with the night to ourselves in Bratislava, it finally felt like it could be right. Nick and I hadn't talked about it, but I felt good about it—if he wanted to.

Noelle had finished paying and was waiting for the coffees. I turned back to Lexie. "What's the big deal? I mean, it's not like you and John have."

"I just figured you had."

I looked down. "I'm just worried. I already don't know how I'm going to handle our good-bye. It's just going to make it worse." I exhaled, running my hands through my hair. "But if he starts making a move..." I blushed. There was no way I'd be able to say no.

Noelle started over to us, coffees in hand, and a few minutes later, Nick and John pulled up outside of the coffee shop. We loaded up the car once more, heading to our next destination. My eyes lingered on Nick, studying the way he shut the door with his hip, the way his fingers felt on mine as he grabbed his coffee from me. I stood, stalled on the sidewalk. Would tonight be the night? I couldn't imagine it not happening, but now that I was starting to let my mind wander, I felt nervous and sick.

"Addie! Coming?" Nick was holding the door open to the backseat, everyone already inside waiting for me.

I laughed and jumped into the backseat next to Noelle, Nick sliding in next to me. I felt hyperaware of his touch, and continued to stare at him anxiously.

"You ready for the next stop?" he asked, putting his hand on my thigh and squeezing gently. I put my hand on top of his and smiled, and we started out of Vienna.

There was something so distinctly familiar and comforting about packing our things up in a car and driving off. It was strangely freeing. Though train travel was my favorite, it was somewhat limiting. There was no stopping when you wanted, pulling over to take a photo, or explore something that caught your interest out of the window. First we stopped in Melk, a small town housing a monastery between the Slovakian and Austrian borders. Nick had visited there with his German grandparents when he was little, and when we unfolded the map to chart our way to Bratislava, he insisted we stop.

Later, we stopped to see the sun set. We grabbed cheap beer from a convenience store and sat on the hood of the car, and on the ground in front of it, toasting to the beauty in the world we'd made ourselves go out and see. It was a perfect day on the road.

By the time we arrived in Bratislava, we decided to check in to our hotel and set our bags down, then head right out for dinner. Bratislava was a smaller city than any of us had thought, and we quickly stumbled on a restaurant off the city's main square, Hlavné Námestie. I spent the evening pushing food around my plate, and nervously drinking my beer too quickly. I couldn't keep my eyes off Nick, who kept fidgeting with my foot under the table. Each time his foot found mine, I'd nervously grab my drink. As the last beer glass was cleared from our table, Noelle ordered a piece of honey cake. I couldn't take it anymore.

"I'm sorry guys, I'm just wiped," I said, throwing Nick a look. I stood up from the table and threw some euros down. "I'm going to walk back to our hotel."

"I'll walk you back," Nick stood up quickly, his chair falling onto the floor behind him. I saw our friends exchange glances as we grabbed our jackets and left the pub, without picking up the chair.

We left the warmth of the pub behind, hurriedly, and rushed out into the piercing cold. He immediately grabbed my hand, and we walked in silence back to our hotel. Inside, he closed the door softly behind him. I'd already drawn the shades and pulled the curtains closed, and was standing in the middle of the room, so nervous my hand shook. I unbuttoned my jacket and kicked my flats off without sitting down.

Nick walked toward me, slowly. Without speaking a word, he put his hand behind my neck and pulled my face toward his. Our lips met. I closed my eyes to our Bratislava hotel room, nothing else mattering but the feel of his hands and that he never stopped touching me. Between kisses, he tried to whisper something.

"It's okay if you're not—"

"I am, I am," I said, feverishly breathing my consent. "I just can't wait anymore."

"You don't have to," he whispered back, heading for the button at the top of my jeans.

We moved to the bed, clothes falling onto the floor. I was surprised at how nervous I was, how timid I felt. I wanted him and was ready for this next step, and felt confident it would only bring us closer. Still, my hands trembled and my voice shook as Nicholas pulled my shirt over my head and fumbled with the clasp on my bra. I took a deep, steadying breath. Whatever was going to happen with us, I was ready for it. Whether this was the culmination of every interaction we'd had since meeting on the sidewalk outside of my apartment in August, or this was the beginning of my biggest heartbreak, was yet to be seen. This wasn't something that was happening to me, but something I was fully participating in. For the first time, I tried to be assertive, helping Nicholas find that last part of me I'd kept hidden, and showing him exactly what I wanted. If we couldn't have the honest conversation we had been sidestepping around for weeks, we could be honest with our bodies.

And everything we'd been holding back, in those weeks leading up to Italy, and then the weeks leading up to where we were now, we left there, on the bed, in Bratislava.

Δ

After popping in a bakery for rolls and Nutella, it was time to make our way back to Prague. We threw our bags in the trunk, John and Lexie laughing about whose bag was heaviest (Noelle's). They piled into the backseat, leaving Nicholas and me at the hood of the car. His sandy hair moved in the breeze, his evergreen jacket unzipped. Throwing me a smile and taking a sip of his coffee, he threw me the keys.

"Want to drive?"

I pretended to look honored. "Finally! I thought you'd never ask." I opened the driver's side door and slid in, shedding my coat and hat and stuffing them on top of the middle console. Nicholas opened the map and helped me navigate out of the city, and before long, I was the only one awake, driving on the open Slovakian road ahead of us.

I felt at peace with where Nicholas and I had finally brought our relationship. For the first time ever, I didn't worry about what he was thinking, or how what had happened in Bratislava would change our relationship. It didn't matter anymore. It had happened, we had waited as long as we possibly could, and now it was time to enjoy what was left. And what was left was nineteen days. It was almost over, the sands in our hourglass numbered.

For the first time, I started to seriously think about what would happen when I boarded my plane to New York in less than a month. What could possibly be arranged between us, one in LA, one in Prague? Nicholas had never committed to anyone before, and my last commitment had been a disaster. What did I feel for him, truly? I got like this sometimes, met a guy I couldn't take my eyes off of, or one that interested me, or just presented a decent challenge. And I'd pursue him and let him pursue me, until we reached this very point I had now reached with Nicholas, after which I would inevitably lose interest. This thought had been in the back of my brain for a while, a cautionary signal of what I'd done to screw things up in relationships past. Was I even ready to be in another relationship after what had just happened with Mark?

But was this a relationship? *We'll see how things go for the rest of our trip*, Nick had told me. Had I not agreed to those terms in Riomaggiore, lying in his twin bed, our fingers entwined, his hand stroking my hair as it laid across the pillow? I knew, with the few weeks that stretched ahead of me, I didn't have any other options but to take them as they came. To pressure him into boundaries, especially a long-distance relationship with no opportunities to see each other, would turn him off immediately. I needed to accept the fact that we had just three more weeks together—most likely, nothing more. To push for something beyond that would risk the three weeks we still had.

I promised myself to not hold anything back, but also not to turn this into something it wasn't: a serious relationship. My heart ached and my eyes burned with tears as I considered the inevitable good-bye scene we'd share, but my mind was made up.

What was more than the impending breakup of Nicholas and me, was that my time with these wonderful people would be over. I thought about each one of my new friends in my mind, wondering if any of them could possibly fathom the effect they had had on me, in varying ways, these past few months. Celeste's big heart, her ability to never take herself too seriously; John's humor and big personality, but his candidness when the moment called for it; Lexie's infectious laugh and big smile and the way she trusted everyone, all the time, without question; how different Charlie was from me yet how much he could really make me think about the differences between our worlds; Nick's ability to make someone feel like they were the only person in the world, the way he spoke so easily about any topic and could always teach you something. That nagging voice inside of me had finally been quieted, and I no longer had any doubts about where I was going.

Almost as if he knew I was thinking about him, Nicholas reached his arm out and put it behind my neck, his thumb gently rubbing the back of my head. He turned his head around to face the backseat. Lexie had fallen asleep on John's shoulder, who had then fallen asleep with his head on the window. Noelle had her headphones on and was writing something with intensity in a notebook. John stirred, and noticed Nick looking at him.

He yawned. "I could really go for a pivo."

"Absolutely," Nicholas agreed. "We aren't far from Brno, let's stop before we get back to the city."

We stopped for a quick bite to eat and some beer. As we walked around, looking for a beer hall to duck in, to get out of the biting air and threatening sky, my mind abandoned the beauty of the evening and wandered to the first time we had passed through Brno back in September. It wasn't nearly as cold, but beautiful all the same. I had roomed with Celeste. John and Nicholas had drunk absinth, and Lexie and I tried to teach Charlie how to dance. Soon after, we'd made it to Budapest, to our amazing room on the top floor of the hotel and the night we spent on the roof. I remembered Lexie and John huddled under a blanket, Nick and I staring up at the sky. He had shown me the stars, had pointed out Orion to me and told me how it made him miss home, he had held my hand for the first time and it was one of the happiest moments in my life.

After we washed our potato latkes and sausage down with Budvar, we got back into the car. I had grown tired of driving and asked Nick to take the last leg. As we headed toward the highway, snow began to gently beat against the windshield. Big, fat, thick white flakes, the kind that make you understand how each and every individual snowflake could be different. Maybe we were all like those snowflakes, each one of us in the same place at the same time, bringing something a little different to the table, but with the same desire that drove us all to Prague.

As Nick drove us toward Prague, we all fell silent. Perhaps we all knew what we were driving back to. The beginning of the end.

I wished that I could find a clock, any clock, and grab the hands. I'd bend them and twist them, I'd make them stop and do whatever I had to do to pause my life where it was. I had come to know Prague as my own, my home—something I had never found before. I wasn't ready to go. I had known these feelings were coming since September, since I had signed up for the next semester, purely to prolong having to go home. I hadn't anticipated the relationships I had since built, hadn't seen it all coming and I didn't know what to do with these feelings now. But it didn't matter... I had nineteen days to figure it out.

27

December, Prague.

It was sometime after Bratislava, after the nervous and softly spoken *I love yous*, now routinely whispered across pillow cases, that we really became *us*. It's the simplest of gestures that end up marking a new phase, a turning point. The minutes we spent together turned into lost afternoons, weekends spent wandering around the city. Soon we were getting ready to say our last good-byes. A knot had begun to form in my stomach, pulling tighter each day.

The week after we returned from Vienna was like any other. Winter was in full swing, with overcast days, the sun dipping low in the sky by late afternoon, and bitterly cold nights. We made the most of them, knowing our days were numbered. After a day trip out of the city to visit the spa town Karlovy Vary—of which I'd learned about on my initial flight to Prague, courtesy of Queen Latifah—we'd thrown a surprise twenty-first birthday party for John at my apartment. All of the EOO kids were there, knowing it was our last hoorah together, a group sleepover on the floor of our massive living room.

The days picked up steam, and nothing was slow anymore. It was our last week in Prague. Our last week *together* in Prague... After my less-than-two-week trip to the States, I would be back, before the beginning of the new year. It seemed incredibly insensitive of our professors to give us finals. Besides packing and visiting our favorite places for the last times, there were exams to study for—for those who hadn't yet completely given up on school during this lost semester. The last week became hectic as we tied up loose ends, picking up souvenirs for family members back home, becoming nostalgic for the city we were to leave, even before we'd left. I was grateful to only be leaving for ten days for the Christmas holiday, but knew coming back to Prague without Celeste and Lexie, without Nick, would break my heart. Other than not being at home, I couldn't think of anything I was excited about for the next semester. I felt unfinished, incomplete, not ready to say my good-byes, but also not ready to go home. I was an emotional wreck, but one who finally no longer felt lost. I'd found myself in Prague, and knew I was making the right decision to stay, whether this affected my chances of staying with Nicholas or not.

In between taking finals and packing, Nick and I decided to steal off for one last afternoon together. There was a tea shop we had both been wanting to try; we had walked in there once only to be hushed and pushed out of the way by the waitress, eager to close for the night. Although it was right off of Wenceslas Square, it was removed far enough from the street to feel hidden, forgotten almost, if it hadn't been for the tables of people inside, sitting on the floor, sipping tea and speaking in hushed tones as if to keep secrets from the owner.

After the bell sounded for class to end out, people hung back, trying to figure out their next move. Nick wordlessly grabbed his notebook, slid it into his backpack and walked over to me, grabbing my hand. It was warm from his essay writing during our class, and I grasped it without a word. He led me out the door of the classroom and down the windy stairs of our school. Once we opened the front door and the cold, fresh Czech December air stunned our faces, we broke into a jog, never letting go of our hands. We jogged all the way to our tram stop, where Nick jumped up every other stair onto the last door of the 22 tram and I followed. We stood in the back, neither of us daring to break our silence, as the tram curved up the hill to Malostranská. When the decrepit tram finally lurched to a stop, I jumped off first, pulling Nick behind me, never for a second thinking that he might let go. He didn't. He didn't let go as we ran all the way down the steep escalator stairs to the green metro, where we were heading to Můstek to our tea date. It was the perfect silent transition to the beginning of our good-bye.

It wasn't shocking, the transition from the freezing, snowy air to inside the warm, humid, and dark atmosphere of the tea shop. It was like being embraced slowly, and as the front of my body welcomed the change, the back of my body said good-bye to the cold, darkening sky. Nick, used to the culture here, walked up to the first available waitress and asked her to please seat us. She led us to a large round table on a platform where we were instructed to leave our shoes at the bottom on the floor. I removed mine first, putting the snowy boots inside a cubby of their own. Nick followed, slipping the heel out of each boot, slowly shaking his foot until each shoe came off and placed them next to mine.

We climbed two or three steps up a timeworn ladder, padded with colorful cloths, and around to the other side of the table that looked out over the room. I slid around the pillows on the floor over to the back of the table, facing out. Nick sat right next to me. She left menus for us to view and we looked them over, reading the names of teas out loud. They had suggested moments for when to drink each tea. *Good for contemplating life. Should be sipped while considering a big decision. Not to be drank during the summer months. Enjoy when under stress.* I flipped through the pages, trying to find a tea to drink before saying good-bye to your love. There were none.

Nick settled on a green tea, and I chose a jasmine. We stacked the menus neatly on the table and faced one another. It was likely going to be our last, our only, date ever. We were down to just five days left. Some of us had started packing, others, like me, were waiting until the last minute. I only had to pack for a week in a smaller bag; the rest of my things I was just throwing in a big suitcase and bringing over to Celeste and Lexie's apartment, what would be my new apartment. I thought I'd just shove everything in, yank the zipper closed and spring for a cab to drop it all off.

"Have you started packing yet?" I asked him.

"No."

I shook my head. "Nick, the end is coming. Whether you pack or not."

"I have time. Your plane leaves before mine, I'll pack after you go."

My mouth dropped open. "You can't be serious."

He rubbed my legs, crossed underneath me. "Don't worry so much, Addie." His hand found mine, and he squeezed it.

And that was the last we spoke of it. There were no mentions of good-byes, or where we would do them, or what would happen after we boarded those planes. Instead, we talked about flight arrangements home, about Christmas plans and traditions. I told him about my plans to be in New York for a week, before coming back with Charlotte. James had emailed me just that morning, saying Mom had booked our flights to New York for the holiday. It was surreal to me. The first Christmas without Pop, would be Mom's first Christmas back with Dad in New York. I thought of all the things that had changed in my life since I first came out to Prague. I thought of the people I'd met and the growth I'd experienced. I felt as if the person who would be flying home was not the person who had come out here. And for that, I was thankful.

Δ

My phone buzzed on my desk. As it rattled against the wood, I stared up at the ceiling, unable to reach my arm out of the warm comfort of my bed to answer. I couldn't believe this day had already arrived, and the thought of what I had to face filled me with dread. I wasn't ready to say good-bye. I had no idea how I could face Nick today.

My phone went silent. I pulled the covers over my head, wishing it were last month. *Just one more month*, I silently willed. *Then I'll be ready.* I closed my eyes tightly, concentrating, as if I could pull the covers down, and it would again be November. I threw the covers off my face, and cool air from our poorly heated apartment hit my face. My phone was vibrating again. I picked it up.

"Hiii, love! I know it's early, but we are meeting at Bohemia, because, you know... Want to come?" Lexie's voice was upbeat and breathy. I needed this dose of positivity today. I wanted to enjoy it all, and not sulk all day.

I tried to sound like I hadn't just woken up. "Of course. I'll be there."

Hanging up the phone, I rolled over to face Emily. Her bed was empty. The digital clock on my phone's face showed just after eight.

"Hellooooo?" I called out to my apartment. Silence. I kicked my covers off and wandered into Alex's room, which was also empty. Where was everyone?

Clothes were everywhere. Literally. Determining we didn't have enough space in our bedroom, Emily had dumped out her wardrobe in the living room to pack up there. Alex's clothes and coats were strewn around the kitchen table, the counters littered with toiletries she had yet to pack. I had been up 'til nearly three in the morning packing, despite the fact that I was coming back. Everything had been sorted into piles of what I needed to bring with me, what could be moved to the Bazaar apartment, and what I didn't need in the first place and would be brought to the States for good.

I grabbed some leggings and a sweater from the top of the pile that was my suitcase, tied my hair into a topknot, and pulled my boots on. After I skipped down the steps of my unwelcoming apartment building, I stopped just short of the building's doorway. *It's all going to be okay.* Taking a steadying breath, I pushed the door open to meet Nick at the bus stop, like I had countless mornings before.

It was a rare sunny day, despite the cold. I felt the sun on the top of my head, while the tip of my nose simultaneously froze. I closed the door and turned around, walking out from under the spider nest Nick had killed. I walked past the doorway John and I had sat in for hours one of our first nights here, when he first talked about his feelings for Lexie. I passed the place where Nick had parked the rental car, hugging the top of it, before our road trip. I crossed the street and looked across to the neighborhood bar, where I'd passed so many late nights with Mason, Charlie, and Nick. I passed the bench where tall Mason had sat next to a little old Czech lady, and she smiled for a picture with him. All these memories flew through my mind before I finally got to the bus awning where Nick sat, waiting for me.

"I've been waiting for you, you took so damn long," he said, getting up and walking over to me.

"Really? Did you miss a bus?"

"Yeah, three." He was standing right in front of me now, our toes nearly touching. He wrapped his arms around the small of my back and pulled me close to him, kissing me softly. I kept my eyes closed for a moment after he pulled away.

"Hi," I whispered to him.

"Hey." He grabbed my hand, and we stood staring at one another.

"Did you really miss three busses?"

He smiled. "No. Besides, I told Charlie I'd wait for him too. I wanted to get out of the place. Mason's in a mood."

Just then, Charlie rounded the corner and waved at us, puffing away at his cigarette, and we heard the bus chugging up the street. We hopped on, and our final day began.

After breakfast, Celeste, John, Lexie, Charlie, Nicholas, and I spent the afternoon wandering around the Christmas village in Old Town Square and through the winding streets of Staré Město. It felt as if we were all leaving on a trip, now that Prague felt like home, rather than all leaving for home after a trip to Prague. I held Nick's hand tighter than usual, laughed more than I normally would have at John's jokes, and exchanged parting gifts with Celeste and Lexie (we'd all framed our favorite photos of the three of us). The day ended as almost all days had, sipping pivo at our regular table in the back of Zanzibar.

Outside, the sky was black. Streetlights lit the street up, as they did every night, revealing a fairytale city out of a storybook. As we had so many nights before, we walked toward the river—this time to get one last view of the castle, of our city all lit up at night. Lexie and John took the lead, John's arm wrapped tightly around her, her blonde hair shining in the moonlight. As we headed down Mostecká, I recalled how foreign the cobblestones once felt under my feet. I had forgotten what it was like to walk on smooth pavement. I could hear Celeste laughing behind me, and I turned around to see her and Charlie walking arm in arm. I flashed back to our last days in Italy, when they were at each other's throats over politics. I laughed to myself.

Without talking about our destination, we had reached the gate at the Malá Strana side of the Charles Bridge. The statues stood tall as ever, lightly dusted with snow. I hadn't even noticed that flakes had begun to fall, but I looked up, tiny dots falling from the heavens, as if someone was shaking confectioner's sugar on us. Lights from the street lamps glimmered between each statue, and at the other end of the bridge, the city in front of us glowed. Spires stretched up into the sky. I could recognize this skyline anywhere.

Though it wasn't too late, the bridge was completely deserted. Vendors had packed up for the day and tourists were rare this time of year; those that were here gravitated toward the Christmas stalls in Old Town Square. Locals tucked inside pubs and beer halls, drinking and singing around fireplaces. It was just the six of us.

We all split off. John and Lexie were kissing at the feet of Saint John, while Celeste took pictures of Kampa Island on the other side of the bridge. Charlie was taking pictures of everything, today being the day he finally got his camera out. Nick was leaning over the side of the bridge, staring down at the rushing Vltava below. I watched my friends, these people who had become like family to me. The weight of our time together was beginning to press on me more heavily, rocks being shoved into a backpack. I didn't know if I was strong enough to face our good-byes, to carry it all.

I walked over to Nick and stood next to him in silence. He turned to face me. His eyes were bright with cold, and his cheeks flushed red. We looked at each other. There were no words that could change anything, and to recognize the moment would be to break it.

Celeste started venturing further down the bridge, and Nick grabbed my hand. We walked behind her as she went to catch up to John and Lexie. As we caught up to them, I realized where they were standing. My breath caught in my throat, my pulse quickening.

Above them towered Saint John of Nepomuk. Just as he was when I first saw him, his head was cocked to the side, mouth agape, eyes seemingly searching out some lost truth far beyond the light of the stars. A few inches above his crown was a halo adorned with stars, and heavy in his arms was a cross. He still looked as if he was exhausted from carrying the weight of the world. Beneath him lay three different panels depicting his time in the military and his death, when he was thrown from this very spot on the bridge. The two shiny spots on either side of the state, one on the left panel and one on the right, were still as shiny as when I first saw them. I felt lightheaded, and my eyes filled with tears at the realization.

"Wow, look at this statue," Celeste remarked, leaning her head back to observe his full height. "Why are these spots so shiny here?"

John and Lexie were already rubbing them. "It's so smooth..." Lexie's voice trailed off.

"I came here with my parents my very first day in Prague. There's a legend that if you touch the spot here, where Saint John is being thrown from the bridge, you make a wish. If you rub the spot on the left, where the dog is, you're supposed to return to Prague someday."

Nick smiled, and wrapped his arms around my stomach. "Just like Rome," he said. "Well, we all need to touch it."

John and Lexie went first. Having already rubbed Saint John, they leaned together over to the dog to ensure their return to Prague.

"If you lick it," John said, starting a joke. "What does that do?" Lexie hit him and remarked how gross he was.

Celeste and Charlie went next, Celeste touching the dog first and Charlie, Saint John. They paused for a moment before switching. Charlie patted the dog lightly, then moved away to light a cigarette, the tip slowly turning orange in the dark. Celeste made her way over to Saint John slowly, her eyes sparkling. She put her hand over Saint John, her fingers stretching out over the scene, and bowed her head as if in prayer. We all stayed silent while Celeste made her one true wish. I wondered what it was. She looked so sincere in her wishing that I almost considered making my wish to ensure hers came true, whatever it was. But I knew in the end, what my wish would be.

Celeste lifted her head and looked over at Nick and me. It was our turn.

Could it really have been four months since I was here with my parents, telling them I wasn't ready to make my wish? I remembered it so vividly. Four months really isn't long at all, but I felt like I was someone else when I last was here, not the person who is standing here now.

Once more, just as on that summer's day with my family, I felt the hand of fate again. I had been waiting for this moment. I had known it then, when I couldn't raise my arm to touch the statue, I just didn't know exactly what I was waiting for. But here it was. The people I had been meant to share this with, and the person whose hand was supposed to guide me to Saint John.

"Let's do it together," he suggested. I nodded my head at him, tears already sliding down my cheeks.

I slowly removed my gloves. Nick's left hand gripped my right, and he moved them slowly to Saint John. "Make it a good wish," he whispered to me. "Make it count."

My eyes were locked on his when the cold metal met my fingertips. I was surprised how smooth the statue was; despite being outside for hundreds of years, it felt like it had just been carved out and sanded. I looked at my fingers, my short, uneven nails up against the glittering gold Saint John. He was sent to his death here, but his face didn't look desolate. Instead, he's calm, his eyes closed and his arms crossed, as if falling into the deep, dark water below was his destiny.

I closed my eyes and thought of my wish. I knew what I wanted, but couldn't find the words. I was in love with Nicholas. More in love with him than I knew you could be with a person. But what did I want? There was no answer. I decided to give it up to fate. *I wish for Nicholas and me to be together*, I wished, *whatever that might mean, and wherever that might be*. I knew I could be happy if we were together, somehow. What that would look like, I couldn't wrap my head around, but I knew that somewhere out there was an answer.

I opened my eyes to see Nick staring right at me. His eyes were shining and bright, and he smiled as he wiped away a tear from my cheek. Did he know what I wished for? He squeezed my hand, and we moved it over to the dog, rubbing it gently together. Now we would have to return to Prague. I let the tears fall, and as we finished, our friends walked over to us. Nick grabbed my hand, and we walked slowly behind our friends, over the bridge once more.

Acknowledgements

For now and forever, thank you to Philip, my love for always believing in me, encouraging me, and supporting me. Without you, I would have had no story to tell. Thank you for pushing me to tell it.

Thank you forever to my parents for your encouragement, even when it must have been impossible. As a parent, I understand now how hard that must have been.

Alexander Weinstein, I'm forever grateful to you for giving me the push I so desperately needed, at the time I needed it most. Without you, this book would have died, half written, in my desk drawer. Matthew Gavin Frank, thank you for not laughing me off of that picnic bench in the backyard. A shout out to my peers at the Martha's Vineyard Institute of Creative Writing for their invaluable feedback and nurturing community.

Jean-Pierre, thank you for being my first reader and champion when I felt totally clueless. To my book club, thank you for your motivation and feedback and support; specifically Sarah Humphreys Weeg — the Michaelangelo reference is for you, to Carly Billings for taking this so seriously, to Jessica Hardin-Kremheller for living this story alongside me on so many different levels, to Dana Watt for letting me tell the world how wonderful you are, and to Julia Behringer because someday this story will be yours, and you will look back at it with fondness. This, I promise you.

I could never forget the help that Brandon Whalen provided me when I was struggling. Annie Montgomery, you brought this book to life with your beautiful translation of my vision. Also, Angie Wade, I couldn't have done this without your guidance. Thank you.

Thank you to all the women who tell stories, for helping me feel as if my story deserves to be told. Yours does too, and I can't wait to read it.

About the Author

Alaina Scarano-Isbouts is a nonfiction freelance writer. She holds a degree from the University of Colorado and has studied language, literature, and culture at the Anglo-American college in Prague. Her work has been published in *Litro* and *Holl & Lane*. She is a recovering vegetarian, compulsive spaghetti-eater, and a hockey fanatic (don't try to tell her that anyone was a better goaltender than Patrick Roy). You can usually find her and her husband at an airport. When she isn't traveling, you can find her at home, snuggling her two boys or binge watching *The Americans*. This is her first novel.

Text on the cover was hand lettered by Annie Montgomery. Author name is set in Amatic. The primary font is Baskerville, with chapter numbers set in Poiret One.

Sections within chapters are separated by a white up-pointing triangle, or the Greek letter Delta. It is used to symbolize change.

65863737R00231

Made in the USA
San Bernardino, CA
06 January 2018